The Pathfinder
by
Robert Brooke
ISBN: 978-1-914933-13-4

Published By: -

i2i PUBLISHING

i2i Publishing. Manchester.

www.i2ipublishing.co.uk

Acknowledgments

Ms Stephanie Parkyn for her excellent, professional proofreading and constructive critique. Her comments taught me some valuable writing lessons.

Mr Shaun Rogers for his constant help, encouragement and friendship throughout the journey.

Mr Edward Goldsmith for his timely input right towards the end, picking up on a couple of small, but important, inaccuracies which I was able to correct. After a life-long friendship with my family, I am happy to overlook his obvious antipathy towards the Oxford comma.

My mother, Mrs Ailsa Brooke, my sister, Ms Fiona Brooke and my daughters, Ms Laura and Christine Mills for their continued love and encouragement.

Lastly, my wonderful wife Patricia for her endless support, love and enthusiastic acceptance of the adage that "When all else fails, it's time for a glass of champagne."

Glossary of terms

ATA (Air Transport Auxiliary) An RAF branch established for shipping newly constructed aircraft to their assigned squadrons. They frequently used female pilots, many of whom served for the duration of the war and became respected, highly experienced flyers in their own right.

AVM (Air Vice-Marshal) A senior Air Force rank, equivalent to the army rank of Major-General or the naval rank of Rear Admiral.

Bounced Unexpectedly attacked, usually from above with the attacker using the sun to blind his opponent.

Circus RAF nickname for a short bombing raid over coastal occupied France, supported by fighters.

Erk RAF nickname for general ground staff, usually of lower rank.

Heavies Heavy, four-engined bombers.

Immelmann Also called the 'Immelmann Turn' or a 'roll off the top', named after a German WW1 pilot Lt Max Immelmann. It was a half loop with a half roll, allowing a pilot to gain height and reverse direction in one manoeuvre.

LMF (Lack of Moral Fibre) At a time when the condition of Post-Traumatic Stress Disorder (PTSD) was little understood, servicemen who were so afflicted were often viewed as shirkers or even worse, cowards. They were referred to as having a 'Lack of Moral Fibre'. To add to the awful effects of the condition, sufferers all too often were court-martialled and imprisoned. In the worst of instances, they might even be shot by Firing Squads, although this extreme punishment was more typical of WW1 than WW2.

OTU (Operational Training Unit) A facility for the advanced training of pilots.

Rhubarb RAF nickname for a fighter sweep over occupied France. Intended to draw up German fighters for combat.

R/T (Radio/Telephone) The main form of air to air/air to ground communications was by VHF radio.

Scramble RAF nickname for the command to get a squadron airborne urgently.

Prologue

May 1941

The aircraftman deftly finished fastening the last of the parachute harness buckles. Then he stepped back, patted the pilot on the shoulder and jumped from the rear of the wing down to the ground. Two other aircraftsmen stood by, ready to pull away the chocks wedging the Spitfire's wheels. As soon as they were both in position, the pilot was given the 'thumbs up' signal to go ahead and start the engine.

Pilot Officer Peter Garland had been running through his pre-flight checks prior to this point. Now he confirmed the brakes were on, a half-inch of throttle, four pumps of the fuel primer, then pressed the starter button and flipped the magnetos to 'on'. The great Rolls Royce Merlin engine ahead of him slowly turned over several times, then came raucously to life. Flames began erupting from the exhaust openings, their glow showing clearly in the strengthening dawn light. The large accumulator, essentially a huge battery which provides electricity for the aircraft's start-up, was disconnected and wheeled away. The individual, discordant firings of each cylinder quickly settled and blended into one continuous, deafening roar as the Spitfire began to buck and vibrate, as though it were alive. The chocks were pulled away whilst Peter waited as three other Spitfires taxied past him. Then, releasing the brakes and gently opening the throttle slightly further, he took his place as the 'Tail End Charlie' of Red Section.

The four Spitfires rolled into a line astern formation as they taxied toward the start of the long grass runway. Then, following the leader, they each took it in turn to straighten up, open the throttle fully and propel themselves forward, accelerating with irresistible urgency until each of them had lifted free of the earth. As soon as they were airborne, the pilots retracted their landing gear and began to climb.

Peter adjusted the pitch of the propellers and eased back on the throttle. Now that it was in its element, the Spitfire settled into its beautiful, familiar rhythm; the harshness of its manner on the ground, instantly transformed into smoothness and tractable grace. The four pilots in his section arranged themselves into their combat formation with well-practiced smoothness. Peter, settled into his usual spot as the leftmost aircraft; he liked this position. He was the most experienced pilot in the flight, even though he wasn't the leader. From, here he could keep an eye on the entire formation off to his right. If they ran into trouble, they could immediately break into two units of two. A leader and one wingman, a flexible and effective fighting unit.

Red Section was now on its way to visit France. Their task was to provide cover for a short, sharp bomber attack on a German airfield near the town of St Omer near the Picardy coast, south-east of Calais. These types of attacks had been nicknamed 'Circuses' and the pilots were coming to hate them. In the air fighting over England, if a pilot was shot down and survived uninjured, he could often be back in the air that same day. For those who survived being shot down over France however, it usually meant having to sit out the war in a German POW camp. This was becoming the fate of far too many experienced pilots but, despite the increasing voices of complaint coming from the Squadrons, the tactic showed no sign of ending.

Peter's flight was soon joined by two others. The full complement of twelve operational aircraft of 371 Squadron was now in position and climbing to eighteen thousand feet, or as it was called by the pilots, Angels 18. They would be in position to cover a raid of Blenheim bombers that were to be the main attacking force. 371 Squadron would be poised to dive onto any German fighters, rising to engage the bomber formation flying some six thousand feet below them. There was very little radio traffic between the individual aircraft. They all knew their roles and followed the commands sent from their sector HQ.

They finally reached full operational altitude halfway between the English and French coasts. Once at full height, they throttled back and waited for the bomber formation to appear below them. They didn't have to wait for long.

The Blenheim bomber was, by no means an old design; however, such was the pace of aircraft development that it was already obsolete. Relatively slow and poorly armed, it needed all the protection that the RAF Fighter Command could provide.

Peter looked down at the small squadron of twelve Blenheim's. In their formation, they seemed to lumber through the sky over a mile below. The formation now began its ponderous journey, almost directly east across the Channel. The voice of Squadron Leader Hugh Trehearn, crackling and distorted, came through on the VHF radio.

"Enemy coast ahead. Sharp eyes everyone."

The formation crossed the coast south of Calais, and immediately turned right to launch their attack from the north-west. The distance from Calais to the target was only about twenty-five miles. Less than ten minutes flying time; but it was also the most dangerous period of the mission.

Peter's flight was on the far left, the most inland side of the formation. They had the best view of the air approaches that any intercepting Luftwaffe fighters would be likely to take. Sure enough, several voices erupted in his earphones at almost the same moment. Incoming aircraft had been spotted to the left, climbing fast. The voice of the leader of Red Section, Flight Lieutenant Mark Charters, cut though the babble.

"Pipe down the lot of you and maintain R/T procedure, I can see 'em. Hold position everyone, can you see them Blue Leader?"

Squadron Leader Trehearn was leading Blue Section today.

"Yes, Red Leader, I can see 'em. I can make out nine or ten bandits, keep an eye out for others."

There was a few moments of quiet as all eyes scanned the skies to see if there were any other German fighters rising to meet them. Then a new voice joined in.

"Green Leader here, Blue Leader. There is a second bandit squadron approaching from over the Channel."

Trehearn strained his eyes but couldn't see anything.

"Are you positive Green Leader?"

"Yes, Blue Leader. They've gone behind clouds now, but a definite sighting."

"Very good Green Leader," replied Trehearn.

"Alright everyone, hold position. The bombing run will commence shortly, let's let our guests get closer first. On my mark, prepare to attack."

Peter felt the adrenaline begin to rush through his body. Excitement and apprehension seemed to heighten every sense and nerve. A few seconds later, another voice came through, "Bombers have opened their bomb bay doors!"

The Blenheims were commencing their attack.

Barely a few moments later, Trehearn's voice came over the R/T.

"Okay everyone, Green Section stay high and keep scanning to your right. Red and Blue Sections, attacking now!"

The Blenheims were beginning their bombing run, they had no option but to hold their line. The German squadron of ME 109s approaching from the left were now less than a mile away, closing on the bombers at over three hundred miles per hour. Bare seconds had become crucial. The Spitfires were now falling on the 109s at nearly four hundred miles per hour. The German pilots could see them coming down and some began to break from their formation to take evasive action. Others stayed on their attacking line as they neared the firing range on the bombers.

Squadron Leader Trehearn had the front position. He aimed his aircraft at the leading 109, aiming just ahead of it, he opened fire. The 109 flew into the stream of bullets and was raked along its full length. It rolled onto its back, almost in slow motion and began to dive away at full power towards the ground twelve thousand feet below. The pilot had been killed instantly by a direct hit from Trehearn's guns.

Peter Garland had focused on another 109 positioned further to his rear. The 109 pilot was still chancing his luck, continuing with the attack. Peter's tactics echoed those of Trehearn and he had similar fortune. The two second burst he fired found a concentration on the forward fuselage of the 109. The bullet-shattered engine seized immediately and erupted into flames. Peter had the barest glimpse of the pilot opening his canopy as he rolled the stricken aircraft onto its back, about to bail out. His high-speed attacking dive from above took him right through the enemy formation. He gently eased the Spitfire out of its power dive, feeling the press of gravity pin him hard against the seat. He began his climb back towards the wheeling, milling aircraft, now nearly two thousand feet above him. He saw a parachute descending in the distance, to his right. A brief hope that it was his 109 kill.

Back into the fray, he noticed black puffs of smoke appearing in the air around the bombers. They were almost directly over the Saint Omer airfield and the German anti-aircraft guns; known as Flak by the RAF, were finding their range. He was still over a thousand feet below the dogfight when he saw a Blenheim suddenly erupt in flames from the left engine. It was off to his left and he could clearly see a 109 on its tail as it weaved and dodged the bullets firing from the Blenheim's upper turret. The bomber's gunner was fighting for his life as he tried to keep the nimble German fighter from being able to get a killing burst onto the now crippled aircraft. Peter had opened the Spitfire's throttle to full power as he desperately tried to close the distance. If he could get there in time, the German pilot would almost certainly not be expecting an attack from below. He had a chance if the bomber could only hold out for a few more seconds. The German pilot had switched his attack now, he was trying to take out the gunner. That would then allow him a couple of additional seconds to adjust and complete the destruction of the aircraft itself.

It proved a fatal error. Those few vital seconds allowed Peter to close to within three hundred yards and open fire. The 109 had steadied itself, ready to deliver the killing burst into the damaged British bomber. Just as he was beginning to apply pressure on his firing button, his aircraft received a massive, shattering jolt from below. The exposed belly of the 109 had little effective armour, it took the full brunt of a four second burst from the eight Browning machine guns in the wings of Peter's Spitfire. The Messerschmitt almost seemed to stop dead in mid-air. Peter's burst had destroyed the aircraft's engine and killed the pilot outright. The 109 just rolled to the side and fell away in a cork-screw motion as it fell back to earth, almost directly above the German aerodrome.

Mere moments later, he felt the great satisfaction of seeing the Blenheim, in turn, release its payload of five hundred-pound bombs directly over its target. Once freed of its load, the bomber immediately turned right, heading towards the safety of home over a hundred miles to the west. Smoke and flames were still streaming from its port engine, but the starboard seemed okay. If they could get the fire under control, they should be able to make it home.

Peter quickly turned his attention back towards the dogfight. To his amazement, the sky was now completely empty. He couldn't see another aeroplane anywhere. He checked his altimeter; he was now back to over twelve thousand feet - good. Next, his compass - this showed he was flying nearly directly east. He had become disoriented in the last attack; he was now too far inland of the air battle. Continuing to climb, he turned a hundred and eighty degrees and scanned the sky ahead for anything that looked like an aircraft. There was nothing at all, the sky remained obstinately empty. Peter held his course, now flying due west. The sun was behind him and he was alone in enemy skies. He realised the danger he was in. He continued to climb and make occasional small course changes.

A fighter pilot's rule was never to fly straight and level for more than thirty seconds whilst in the combat zone. He counted off the seconds in his head, as soon as he reached thirty, he made a slight course change to the right. Almost immediately, his aircraft was rocked by a stream of bullets as they smashed into his left wing. He had been 'bounced' by a German fighter that was diving on him out of the sun. If he'd delayed his turn by even another second, he would have been dead.

The 109 flashed past him at well over three hundred and fifty miles per hour and Peter instinctively turned to follow it, seizing his chance to take the attacking initiative. His Spitfire still seemed to respond normally to his touch, nothing vital appeared to have been damaged. The German pilot was good, clearly very experienced, he tried every manoeuvre he knew to shake Peter off. For his part, Peter could never get him in his sights long enough to open fire. Peter was good also, he'd been flying since he was seventeen, back in his native New Zealand. He quickly realised the ability of his foe, he had to stay on the attack. The Luftwaffe pilot would have him in a moment if he broke off his pursuit. The German soon realised that he too wasn't taking on a novice. This guy knew how to fly. Their deadly aerial game had brought them close to a dense cloud bank. The 109 seized the opportunity to choose discretion over valour and headed for it at full throttle. Peter breathed an inward sigh of relief. He knew he was well matched and was looking for an opportunity himself to end the engagement. He checked his compass again and turned back towards England. His fuel reserves were now very low, he had no more time to spare over occupied France.

He took to a cloud bank himself and flew on the compass for the next several minutes. When he broke free of the clouds, there, far below, was the gratifying sight of the English Channel. Its grey waters letting him know that enemy airspace was now some distance behind him. Peter looked around again, in the never-ending scanning of the skies that is the habit of every fighter pilot. There was nothing to see, he seemed alone in the vastness of the sky.

He took to the R/T, "Red Four calling Red Leader, do you read me? Over."

To his immense relief, Mark Charters voice answered almost immediately.

"Reading you Red Four. Where are you? Over."

"Red Four answering. Over the Channel, Red Leader, I got two, and then wound up inland with a 109 on my tail. Over."

"Red Leader here. Are you okay? Can you make it home? Over."

Peter checked his fuel gauge again.

"Red Four answering, I'm critically low on fuel Red Leader. I should be okay to make the coast and get to Hawkinge. I shall have to put down there. Over."

Hawkinge was one of the south coast aerodromes that had been right on the front line of the air battles over Britain only five months earlier. It was now the air-field closest to Peter's current position.

"Red Leader here, very good Red Four, do you have any damage? Over."

"Red Four answering, I took some damage to the inner left wing. All seems to be okay. All controls are answering normally. Over."

"Red Leader here, check your undercarriage before you land. Over."

"Thank you, Red Leader. I should be fine. Red Four out."

Radio conversations between pilots were monitored at the Sector Control. RAF Hawkinge was promptly alerted to expect a damaged Spitfire to be arriving shortly. By the time Peter had arrived overhead, several emergency vehicles had been deployed. All he had to do now was to put his aircraft back onto the ground. He pulled the large quadrant lever to his right hand side fully back, lowering the undercarriage. He could feel the airflow over the wings change and become louder as the drag of the wheels affected the trim. A light illuminated on his control panel to advise the undercarriage had deployed successfully. He had enough remaining fuel to make a circuit of the airfield and to get the 'All-Clear' from the ground that his wheels had deployed properly. He could see the 'thumbs up' signal from the ground and he flew off to make his approach. He then lowered the landing flaps and reset the propeller pitch, a perfect approach.

The moment the wheels touched the grass landing field, the Spitfire kicked viciously to the left and flung itself briefly back into the air. It hit the ground again at nearly forty-five degrees to the direction of the runway and grabbed again on the left side. This spun it even further to the left. The extreme lateral pressure on the undercarriage then saw the right-hand wheel strut tear away completely. The right-hand side then collapsed as the aeroplane continued to slide along the runway sideways. It was still travelling at over sixty miles per hour when the tip of the right wing dug into the ground, becoming a fulcrum. The stricken aircraft then pivoted, flipping upside down, then skidded on for another thirty yards before finally stopping.

Peter's harness had kept his torso secured in place, but his arms and legs were at the mercy of inertia as the Spitfire was wrenched and tossed around like a child's toy. After it finally settled, his whole right side felt as though it was buzzing, and his mind was quickly going foggy. The last thing he heard was the sound of the bell on the ambulance as it approached. Then everything went black.

Chapter 1

"Well then! I'm so glad you've finally decided to wake up and join us."

Flight Lieutenant Mark Charters had flown from the squadron's base at RAF Redhill, down to Hawkinge as soon as he heard of Peter's crash landing. Once there, he left instruction that he be notified as soon as Peter had regained consciousness. Mark pulled up a chair beside him as he lay on his back, gazing up at the ceiling. Peter turned his head slightly towards him and managed a weak smile, moving his neck hurt.

"What the hell happened?" he asked. "I thought I had everything under control. I can't believe I stuffed it up so badly."

Mark leaned forward, speaking in his laconic, public-school drawl.

"Well, it seems that for once, you didn't old chap. What you couldn't have known, was that one of the bullets that went through your left wing, ruptured the tyre. It didn't damage anything else. Clean as a whistle, straight through. The chaps on the ground couldn't tell either when you did your fly-over. It all looked fine until you tried landing on it. In the end it seems, you were bloody lucky."

"You call this lucky?" said Peter, nodding gingerly towards the plaster and bandages that seemed to swathe most of his right side. "No one's actually told me yet what I've gone and done to myself. Am I going to be able to fly again?"

"I can't see any reason why not," replied Mark. "I can give you a bit of a run-down on the damage if you like?"

Peter nodded slightly.

"Well," continued Mark, rubbing his hands. "Apart from writing off one perfectly good Spitfire, which we may have to deduct from your wages, you have also managed to break your right leg just above the ankle. Dislocate your right knee, do some fairly spectacular bruising and soft tissue damage to your entire right leg and lower torso. Break both bones in your right forearm, give yourself a dose of whiplash and knock yourself out cold for nearly half a day. Apart from all that, you're pretty much unscathed!"

Peter lay there for a moment, taking it all in. "So, nothing too drastic then?"

Mark laughed. "Nothing that's likely to be permanent at least. You'll be off flying for at least a couple of months I would think. You've got some serious healing to do. Anyway, an ambulance will be ferrying you back up to Redhill tomorrow, so we'll be able to keep an eye on you."

Peter let that news sink in, it wasn't all bad. As much as he loved flying, the crash had shaken him badly. He had been through a relentless combat schedule since the beginning of August the previous year. Some down time might be a good thing.

371 Squadron had been based at RAF Redhill, south of London. They had been part of the front line throughout the long months of the Battle of Britain. Each pilot in the squadron had flown many hundreds of hours of desperate combat. After it became obvious that Hitler was not going to invade, the nature of the air war changed. The Luftwaffe ceased most of its daylight attacks and concentrated on night bombing, with London being the main target. For the frontline day fighter squadrons, it was a time to rebuild and finally get some rest. They were still on standby and were often called on, but they also began to experience the luxury of occasionally having several days at a time in between 'Scrambles'. The squadron had changed much over the summer and autumn of 1940. Peter, Mark and the Squadron Leader, Hugh Trehearn were among the very few pilots remaining, who had been there from the beginning. Peter had been a Sergeant Pilot then. Even though he joined the RAF as a qualified pilot, he was not a university graduate. Nor had

he been through the usual RAF flight training programmes, thus, he was not offered a commission. Mark, however, was freshly out of flight training, via the RAF Volunteer Reserve programme. He joined the squadron as a Pilot Officer, the lowest commissioned rank. He was still very inexperienced as a pilot and had to learn the deadly skills of aerial combat the hard way. He had been shot down twice but had somehow avoided serious injury. He proved himself to be a steady learner, and after he finally secured his first kill in combat, he quickly matured, and grew in both confidence and skill. His promotions when they came, were well earned.

Peter, however, had been the star, he had learned to fly in his native New Zealand while still only seventeen. His family lived in Hastings in the North Island, and their house was within walking distance of a small airfield. Peter would see the little biplanes flying over his home every day. He would often go and spend time talking to the pilots. His enthusiasm and desperation to learn endeared him to one pilot in particular, who had flown in the Great War. After getting permission from his parents, Peter arranged that, in return for his assisting in the maintenance of the aeroplane and doing odd jobs around the hangar, he would be given lessons. The aeroplane was an old Avro 504, a well proven and extremely stable aircraft for a novice pilot. Peter took to flying like a duck to water, even if the war had not intervened, it was clear his future lay in the air.

But the war did come. For Peter, there was never a moment's doubt that he would travel to England and enlist in the RAF. He was now nearly twenty-two and had hundreds of flying hours logged. His family helped pay his passage and the Air Force had no qualms about accepting him. He did not care that he was not being offered a commission, an active fighting role was all that mattered. He had quickly adapted to the faster, more modern aircraft and revelled in the environment that the RAF offered. Surrounded by young men of his own age, all as excited as he was about flying, all pushing each other to excel, he soon felt as though he had been born for this time. It was announced that he was being given his squadron posting; it was to be 371 in Redhill. They had just been equipped with Spitfire Mk1s and thus Peter was sent to familiarise himself with the RAF's new thoroughbred.

It was love at first sight for him, the aeroplane flew as beautifully as it looked. Soon enough, he had grown so accustomed to it that it seemed to fit like a favourite set of clothes. He didn't fly it, he wore it, like a perfectly tailored suit, four miles up in the sky.

Peter and Mark joined the squadron at the same time, in early August 1940. Hugh Trehearn was still a Flight Lieutenant then, and Peter and Mark were assigned as his wingmen. The two of them found an instant bond. Polar opposites in their personalities, Mark was the true *bon vivant* against Peter's quieter, more introverted outlook. Their contrasts complimented each other though and they quickly became inseparable friends. They had barely unpacked their kits when the Germans launched their plan to destroy the RAF as a prelude to invasion. The Battle of Britain had begun.

Initially, Peter excelled as much as Mark struggled. He had three confirmed kills to his credit before Mark could even lay claim to have damaged one. Mark had been shot down for the first time after only four days of operation, whereas Peter had never even received as much as a single bullet hole. Mark's frustration was growing at his lack of success. By now, he and Peter were extremely close, but he was growing increasingly jealous of the way his friend's skills were developing. Then, on the 5th September, he was shot down a second time. This time, he was slightly injured, he had sprained an ankle when he landed awkwardly under parachute. He was taken off Ops for a week; the enforced rest did the trick. From the moment he was back in the air, he seemed a different pilot. He handled the

Spitfire more assuredly and had become more decisive. On his second sortie, he found a Dornier bomber filling his gunsights and gave it a long, four second burst. The German aircraft began to break apart in mid-air before his eyes. No parachutes appeared as it began to fall away towards the ground, many thousands of feet below. Mark felt no elation at the time, he simply resumed scanning the skies for other targets. After that, his confidence blossomed and he soon received his first promotion, becoming a Flying Officer.

In the meantime, Peter had notched up his fifth kill. He was now officially an Ace. Shortly afterwards, Hugh Trehearn took him aside, with a broad smile on his face, he told Peter that he had just been awarded the Distinguished Flying Medal (the DFM) after his achievements so far in the air war. Peter had never even thought about medals and official recognition. He was too focused on the day-to-day struggle to survive and do his job. Nevertheless, once it sunk in, he was secretly thrilled.

At the end of October, Mark experienced the same elation, as he too, became an Ace. The nervous, defensive flying of his early days was now well past him. Like Peter, he was now an accomplished flier and an expert killer. His recognition came in the awarding of the Distinguished Flying Cross (the DFC). Only officers could be awarded this medal, with the news of his 'gong' came an additional reward. He was to be promoted again, this time to Flight Lieutenant. For his part, Hugh Trehearn was promoted to Squadron Leader after the previous incumbent failed to return from a mission over the Channel. No trace of him was ever found.

While those around him who were commissioned officers made their way up the promotional ladder, Peter still remained a Sergeant Pilot. Whilst at first he had been happy just to be part given an active role as a fighter pilot, he was now growing discontent at the procession of less experienced officers, with lesser achievements being promoted whilst he still languished as an NCO. Although, some had been given the recognition, the RAF still seemed generally unwilling to promote NCO pilots to commissioned status. This time though, Peter had a very vocal ally in his new Squadron Leader. Hugh Trehearn began to insist that Peter be promoted. He was too good a pilot and too strong a leader to not be commissioned. Eventually, the RAF buckled and in mid-November, Peter became a Pilot Officer. The decision was helped by his becoming a double Ace two weeks earlier, ten kills confirmed.

His satisfaction at the promotion was added to with the news that he was also to be awarded the DFC. At last, he was receiving the recognition he felt he had earned. Now he knew, he could progress on his merits.

***

"So, it looks like you're going to be stuck in bed here for at least a couple of weeks before they start to get you up and about," said Mark. "It could be worse you know. I've checked out a few of the nurses here, some seriously lovely crumpet!"

Peter tried to smile; it wasn't a very convincing effort. He was settled into a bed at the small base hospital adjacent to the airfield back at RAF Redhill. He had been dosed up well on pain killers during the drive back from Hawkinge, so he didn't remember much of the previous twenty-four hours. At least now, he was close to his squadron and his friends.

"You know what," he said, trying to wear his pain and discomfort lightly. "Someone should send a message through to Jerry and let that bastard know that he can claim me as a kill."

Mark laughed. "Don't worry old chap. If he got a single bullet within fifty yards of you, he'll have already claimed it. All those Luftwaffe bastards do."

Mark now sat up straight and looked serious. "I do have one thing to tell you though, you know how you called in that you got two kills on that last sortie?"

Peter nodded.

"Well, both of them have been confirmed. You had thirteen before that, you are now officially a triple Ace my old mate, congratulations!"

Peter hadn't even thought about his current score, it was a lot to take in, fifteen German aircraft shot down. For the first time, reality jarred his conscience as they were actual men that he may well have killed. That last one was certainly so. He had a sudden, unexpected pang of remorse, an emotion he'd never encountered before as a fighter pilot. Now, as he lay in pain in a hospital bed, it suddenly meant something to him. To do his job well, he had to be good at killing German pilots. It was a sobering thought to realise that he was indeed. That stark reality was something that he had always been able to overlook. There was too much flying, too much fighting to be done to allow such matters as morality or ethics to intrude. Besides, the other fellow was shooting back, each was doing their job, it was a fair fight. To the winner went the prize of staying alive to fly again another day. The aircraft plummeting to earth in flames could just as easily have been his. That thought dragged Peter out of this unsettling moment of introspection.

"It'll mean another gong, you know," continued Mark. "DSO this time no doubt. You'll have the full set. Not a bad effort at all, for an ignorant colonial. There'll probably be a front page article about your exploits in whatever passes for a newspaper in your heathen part of the world."

This time, Peter managed a laugh, he immediately regretted it as his whole right-hand side screamed back in agony.

"Bloody hell! Sorry, old chap!" said Mark when he saw the look of pain on Peter's face. "I promise, that's the last time I shall try and cheer you up! Ungrateful, damned bugger you are."

This time Peter went with a smile, the pain was quickly settling down again.

Peter asked, "Did everyone else get back alright? It looked like the bombers were taking some hits."

"Yes, they lost two, a few others got back heavily damaged. The C/O got a call from his opposite at the Blenheim Squadron. He wanted to pass on a personal note of thanks to you for getting one of them out of trouble. That was your second kill, I take it?"

"Yeah," said Peter. "I was trying to regain height after my initial dive, the Jerry wasn't paying attention to what was below him. I got him just in time, I think. He must have been about to give that bomber a blast."

"That's what the bomber crew said, those that were left," said Mark. "The Jerry had made a right old mess of the upper gunner. Apparently, they had to hose him out of the turret, can't have been a pretty sight."

Peter lay there contemplating that thought. "No, not at all," he said quietly.

"Anyway," said Mark, "I shall leave you to rest up in peace. Try not to hog all the nurses, leave one or two for the rest of us!"

Peter smiled as Mark stood up, turned and left the room. He lay back, gazing up at the ceiling, thinking of nothing in particular, disjointed thoughts just flashing by. This meandering trail of random thoughts was broken several minutes later when a nurse came in, brandishing a thermometer.

"I need to take your temperature. I shall just pop this under your tongue for a minute."

Peter opened his mouth and the nurse inserted the thermometer.

"How are you feeling?" she asked.

Peter just looked at her with the thermometer sticking out of one side of his mouth. The nurse realised what she had said and started to laugh.

"I certainly can pick my moments, can't I?"

After a minute, she removed the thermometer and Peter was able to speak. "In answer to your question, I feel just bloody awful, thanks!"

"Yes, I suppose you must," replied the nurse. "Are you in any pain at the moment? I can fetch you some pain killers if you need some?"

"Thanks very much," said Peter. "I think I do need some."

"Okay, I'll be right back."

As she left the room, Peter couldn't help but agree with Mark's observation. She was indeed very pretty. She was back momentarily with a glass of water and two pills. She helped Peter into a more upright position so that he could manage the drink better.

"Now these are quite strong you know," she said. "They will certainly manage the pain, but they're likely to put you asleep for a while. Do you need to use the bedpan first?"

"The what?" asked Peter, after swallowing the pills.

"Don't you know? It's for relieving yourself while you're unable to get out of bed."

Peter looked aghast. "I know that, but how can I possibly manage it while I'm all trussed up like a turkey at Christmas?"

"You just lie back and think of England. I do the real hard work," she said with a devilish grin.

"Oh, my Lord!" said Peter. "Isn't there some other way?"

"Of course, there is, silly!" the nurse said. "I'll just go and get the Matron; she would be delighted to take over. I can assure you; she will make it an experience you shall never forget!"

Peter turned pale, and the nurse burst into laughter.

"So, shall I go and fetch her, or shall you bow to the inevitable?"

Peter let out a long sigh. "It appears that I don't have much choice, do I?"

"None at all!" replied the nurse in a merry voice. "As I said, just lie back and think of England. It'll all be over before you know it."

"Oh, believe me," said Peter resignedly, "I'll know it! Normally, I would expect to at least know your name, I mean, if we're going to get so intimate and all..."

"If you behave yourself like a good boy and don't go spraying things around the room, I may consider telling you what it is. But you must do your business first."

Peter looked at her. "You're enjoying this, aren't you?"

She gave him her best look of affronted innocence.

"That would be highly unprofessional of me now, wouldn't it? I assure you, it's a lot less glamorous than you think. Now come on, it has to be done!"

Peter surrendered and became the compliant patient as the nurse set about the process. After she had cleaned him up and helped position him as comfortably as he could be made, she placed the now full bedpan on a trolley, and made a motion towards the door.

"You said that you'd tell me your name?" said Peter in indignation.

"I said, I would tell you my name if you were a good boy!" replied the nurse.

"Well, wasn't I?" asked Peter.

"Yes, I suppose you were," she said as she opened the door.

She turned and smiled back at him. "It's Anne."

She left the room and closed the door behind her. "Anne" thought Peter as the mist of sleep began to settle over him, the pills were beginning to work.

Chapter 2

Being bedridden was a new and thoroughly unpleasant experience. Peter had always been highly self-reliant, but now he had become totally dependent on others to help him perform even the most basic of human functions. Having both a broken arm and a broken ankle was his main impediment. He was completely unable to walk unaided or manipulate a pair of crutches. After nine days, he was becoming impatient and irritable.

"It's your own silly, damn fault you know!" said Mark, who was on one of his regular visitors. "A bloody monkey could have landed that Spit better than you did. The lads have all voted that we send you back to Flight School."

"Ha, bloody ha!" replied Peter. "Mate, this is just driving me barmy! And there's still bloody weeks of this before I'll be up and about. Plus, I'm itching like blazes inside these plaster casts, I just know I'm going to go mad."

"Now, now old man," said Mark affecting an air of seriousness. "Enough of that talk, you do realise that half the men in the Squadron would give their eye teeth to be where you are. Unfettered access to the beautiful nurse Anne Galloway. Plus, all the others as well, there is some serious crumpet tucked away in this hospital! You should count yourself a lucky man. If you don't have a permanent lady friend nailed down by the time they let you out, we're going to post you out of here and give you to Coastal Command. You can spend your days convoy spotting; it'll be all you're good for!"

Peter couldn't help himself, he had to laugh. "At least you're right about that. But, let me tell you, it's bloody hard to strike up a pleasant conversation with a nurse when she's wiping your bum and washing your willy! I'd like to see how you manage it!"

"My God, how you bloody colonials over complicate things," laughed Mark. "I shall have to leave that particular quandary in the care of your naturally incisive antipodean intellect to solve. Don't take too long though, that Anne is a real looker and I didn't come over here just to spend my time catching up with a grumpy bugger like you, you know! She may just end up learning that there are other willies worth washing around here, if you don't hurry up."

"Excuse me!" exclaimed an outraged Anne, who had chosen that precise moment to enter the room as she performed her rounds.

Mark leapt to his feet, knocking over his chair and blushing furiously. "I'm most frightfully sorry Nurse." He quickly turned back to Peter. "Well, old man, I must be getting along. Huns to shoot down, you know what it's like, see you soon."

Mark smiled meekly at Anne and hurried for the door. Anne casually walked over towards the window and watched as Mark hurriedly walked away from the small hospital, a look of cold fury on her face.

Peter lay silently in his bed, trying to prepare himself for the tirade that was surely about to be unleashed upon him. Anne turned away from the window and looked down at Peter as he lay there, desperately trying to cover himself as best he could with the sheet, the only form of defence he had. Anne felt her anger evaporate in an instant. She stood there for a moment gazing at Peter, and then burst into almost uncontrollable laughter. A second later, Peter saw the humour and joined in, immediately regretting it as his damaged body responded painfully to the convulsions. Anne saw him suddenly wince in pain and reacted by laughing even harder. Only for a brief moment, though, she quickly recovered her composure. She knew Peter well enough now, to realise that he was unlikely to have been the one who had initiated so disrespectful a conversation, as the one she had just walked in on. Even so, she was secretly glad that his laughter had caused him a moment of discomfort. It might teach him a lesson about good manners!

"Now," she said, "I trust that you and your dubious colleagues might have learned a thing or two about civility and respect, particularly when discussing me and my dubious colleagues!?"

Peter smiled guiltily but also with relief, clearly Anne had seen the humour in the situation.

"I strongly suspect he shall be a tad more circumspect in future, when visiting," he replied.

Anne stood there, arms crossed and looking intently at him, Peter took the hint.

"As indeed, shall I. I do apologise Anne."

Anne stood there with an inscrutable look on her face. "Thank you," she said grudgingly. "In future, you may just have to be left to wash your own willy! For the life of me, I can't fathom the huge fuss you men make over such a tiny thing."

"Hey what!" exclaimed a mortified Peter. Anne's façade cracked and she laughed again.

***

Frustration began to give way to optimism over the course of the following weeks. Peter felt the pain in his right-side easing, and some mobility returning.

"Alright, let's give it a try, shall we?"

Anne stood several feet away from Peter as she encouraged him to attempt to stand up for the first time since the accident. Peter pushed himself up into a sitting position using his left arm. There was still some pain in his right side, but it was far from unbearable now. He tolerated it without complaint. He wiggled his bottom towards the side of the bed and swung his left leg over. The feel of the floor beneath his bare foot immediately invigorated him, he was returning to the real world. He tried to move his right leg around, but the weight of the plaster cast and the weakness in the damaged leg soon stopped him.

"Would you like some help to lift that leg down?" asked Anne.

"If you don't mind," replied Peter with a weak grin. "It doesn't seem to want to budge on its own."

Anne came over and gently lifted the immobilised leg by the heel and slowly swung it round, clear of the bed. Peter positioned himself right on the bed's edge and nodded to Anne, who eased the leg down onto the floor. Peter slowly positioned his weight onto his good left leg and stood up for the first time in nearly three weeks.

"Okay, what the heck do I do now?" he asked with some trepidation.

Anne smiled encouragingly at him and said, "Just try holding you weight on your good leg and see if you can maybe swing the right leg a bit. Don't try and walk, just see if you can get a bit of front and back swing."

Peter, in furious concentration, centred his weight on the good leg and tried as Anne instructed. He managed to get some swing to the front happening almost immediately, but the weight of the cast quickly unbalanced him and he began to fall forward. Anne promptly stepped towards him and caught him before he fell too far. She continued to press forward and helped him return to an upright position, carrying his own weight again. Peter was acutely conscious of Anne having her arms around him and realised he was in no hurry to have her step back again. After a moment, she released her hold on him and took a step back. Peter was watching her closely and noticed that her complexion was quite flushed. He allowed himself to entertain the thought that she might have found the closeness of the contact with him exciting as well. Then it struck him that it was probably just the physical effort of catching and supporting him that caused her redness. For her part, Anne gave nothing away.

"Now let's try that again, shall we?" she said. Less smiling, more professional this time.

This became the routine, three times a day. There were other nurses on duty, but it always seemed to be Anne who attended to Peter during the daytime. The exercise was helping, he began to practice moving his broken right arm. Soon he was able to hold pens and cutlery again. Next, the sling went and although the plaster cast was still an impediment, he found he could now manage a pair of crutches for short distances. He was healing well.

Nearly five weeks had now passed since the crash and Peter's increasing mobility had taken the edge off his frustration. He could hobble about on crutches for short distances and get himself into a wheelchair if he needed to go further. It was Saturday, the early summer weather had enticed him out into sun with a book. He had heard the squadron take off from the airfield earlier and he wanted to be outside to see them return. He could only assume it was another sortie over the French coast. No one had been to tell him; for the time being he was out of the loop. However, these were his friends and he felt a deep pull to be on hand when they returned, even if only to see them fly in overhead and count the returning kites. He was feeling a sense of helplessness that he never experienced when in the air with the rest of the squadron. It was an uncomfortable new sensation. This must be what it's like for the families left at home, sitting and waiting, worrying, helpless.

He was losing himself in his book when a familiar voice caught his attention.

"I see you've managed to get yourself out here all on your own today. Aren't you the clever boy!"

Peter looked up smiling. "Well, hello Anne, what brings you into work on your day off?"

"Well, I was actually feeling at a loose end, I only have a small flat and at times it feels rather restricting, I suppose. I was wondering if you might care for a bit of company."

Peter was delighted but surprised, nonetheless.

"I might have thought you'd have been pleased to see the back of me for two days, I seem to take up most of your time when you're on duty. Come to think of it, this is the first time I've ever seen you in civvies, but if you're offering, I would love some company."

Anne smiled; Peter couldn't help but notice how different she looked today. She was wearing her blonde hair down instead of the usual severe looking bun style she had it in whilst on duty. She was wearing a gaily coloured, floral pinafore dress; Peter noticed how beautifully tailored it was. He realised she must have bought it before the war began. She was also wearing discrete, but carefully applied makeup. Something else she couldn't have done whilst on duty. His initial surprise at seeing her quickly wore off. He was now looking at her in wonder, she was attractive enough when she was at work, but today she was looking quite stunning. He found himself hunting for words, almost at a complete loss for something to say.

"Look at you!" he finally said. "You look absolutely radiant, and I'm sitting here in my staggeringly ugly pyjamas and a rather unkempt dressing gown. I hardly think my appearance is doing you any justice whatsoever."

Anne laughed. "I am happy to overlook the social shortcomings of your current attire. I was just thinking that I've spent so much time with you lately and I really know very little about you. You don't talk much about your home, or where you're from, you know. I was hoping you might be happy to tell me more."

As she spoke, she went around behind Peter's wheelchair and began to push him over towards a small outdoor table and chair in the gardens behind the hospital. She set Peter's wheelchair at the table and took a chair for herself.

"There's not really all that much to tell actually. Hawke's Bay is mostly farming, I'm from a town called Hastings. About the most exciting thing that ever happens there are earthquakes, we had a monster one about ten years ago. Destroyed most of the town, it's all been rebuilt since then, but it was a truly extraordinary thing to go through."

"Nothing like that in England I'm afraid," replied Anne. "We have to resort to more mundane forms of entertainment."

"Such as?" asked Peter.

"Well, I always loved riding, we've had horses for as long as I can remember."

"I wouldn't call that mundane," said Peter. "I used to ride a lot too, before the flying bug bit me. I'm afraid my life has been revolving around flying ever since I was in my mid-teens. I guess I must have become a rather boring chap now that I think about it. Ever since I've been in England, the RAF, the war, well… it's been that and virtually nothing else really. I do try and write to my parents as much as I can, I'm their only child, you see. They were very supportive of me coming over to England and joining up, but I know they worry a lot."

Anne sat looking intently at him. "What does your family do in New Zealand?" she asked. "Are they farmers?"

"No, not at all. It's a farming region, but dad is actually a doctor."

"Really!" exclaimed Anne, suddenly brightening. "So is mine! He practices in London."

"What an extraordinary coincidence," he replied. "I'm not sure a small practice in Hastings is in quite the same league as a shingle in Harley Street though."

"Oh, daddy's practice isn't in Harley Street, he's in St John's Wood."

"So, even better than Harley Street," said Peter with a teasing smile.

"Well… yes, you're right, it is!" laughed Anne. "None of the pompous pretensions that go with a Harley Street practice, he loves it there. Close to home, he walks to the rooms each day."

"What about your mother?" asked Peter.

Anne's face suddenly clouded over. "Mummy died four years ago. She developed meningitis and went very fast, barely two days after complaining of feeling sick. Gone, just like that!"

Peter looked horrified, "Oh Anne, I'm so sorry, I had no idea."

He reached out and took her hand, gently squeezing it. He was looking deeply into her eyes as she took a breath and composed herself.

"It's alright, it's long enough ago now that I've grown accustomed to her absence. It hit daddy much harder, he's a doctor and couldn't do a thing to help her. He nearly walked away from the practice."

"Is your father alright now?"

"He's okay now, it took him a while, but he's got a wonderful circle of friends and they have helped him so much. He's quieter now than he used to be and much more focused on his work, but he's found a new balance and seems to have a purpose about him that I don't really remember from when I was young. He's even been talking about joining up and being a part of the Medical Corps, he's only just turned fifty."

"So, what made you become a nurse?" asked Peter.

"I decided before mummy died, I thought about studying medicine but in truth, I was never that good as a scholar," she smiled shyly. "I didn't want a boring office type of job and nursing seemed a good choice. There were times when I thought I'd made a huge blunder by choosing it, but now I'm glad I did."

"So am I," said Peter.

He and Anne locked eyes, he wanted desperately to kiss her and he could sense she felt the same. The two of them began slowly leaning towards each other. After a few moments, Anne stood up suddenly.

"I can't Peter, not here. It could cost me my job, I shouldn't have come here, I don't know what I was thinking."

Peter tried struggling to his feet despite the impediment of the cast.

"It's alright Anne, I'm sorry if I embarrassed you, I just got caught up in the moment."

"So did I," she replied. "I'd best take you back to where you were sitting, I'm sorry Peter, I can't let this happen."

She broke her gaze and motioned for Peter to settle himself back into the wheelchair. The electricity between them was suddenly released by the sound of a Merlin engine faintly in the distance. The squadron was returning. Anne wheeled Peter back to his spot in the garden. The Spitfires were now circling the airfield and beginning to take their turn in landing. Peter counted them in. Twelve aircraft made uneventful landings, three flights of four Spitfires, everyone home safely. Peter looked up at Anne as she stood alongside him, she smiled down.

"I'll have to let you get back to your bed on your own."

Peter smiled, not happily, but with understanding. "I understand. Will I see you on Monday?"

Anne looked at him without any sign of real emotion. "Of course," she said flatly. "I'll see you then, thanks for your company. Goodbye Peter."

She turned and walked back along the outside of the small hospital building towards the front entrance. She didn't look back. Peter sat there in his wheelchair, confused emotions coursing through him. What had just happened? One moment, she had seemed so close to him and then, it was as though a light switch had flicked and she had turned off completely. He stayed motionless in his wheelchair for some time, struggling to make sense of things. Eventually, he shook himself out of his reverie and turned the wheelchair back towards the hospital door. He needed to lie down.

***

"Dull as dishwater old chap!" drawled Mark. "We stayed high, thinking we might entice a few of the buggers up for a bit of a scrap. Not a bloody sausage!"

He had called in to visit Peter after the debriefing following their Rhubarb sortie over the French coast.

"They must have known that I wasn't there," added Peter. "Figured you lot weren't worth getting out of their beds for. Without me, the rest of you are hardly a fitting challenge for them, you must admit."

"Well now, look who's getting all full of himself!" said a bemused Mark. "It's more likely that there was a holiday back in Germany. Hitler's mother's underpants', wedding anniversary or something like that. Whatever, it was a complete no-show, just a waste of bloody petrol."

"Ah well, at least there are no letters to have to write," reasoned Peter.

"I guess that's true, about the only positive thing I can think of," Mark agreed. "Anyway, are there any updates on how things are going with the lovely nurse Anne? She does seem to have taken a special interest in you."

Peter sighed, "She came by this morning, even though she was off duty. We had a very nice chat for a while and then she just sort of upped and left. She said she could lose her job."

Mark's eyebrows raised. "How very interesting! Just keep on being your charming rustic self, old chap. All is not lost."

"There are times when I wish I could understand how your deranged Pommy mind works, Mark," said Peter, looking quizzically at his friend. "She's got me completely baffled."

"All will be well, you simple-minded colonial. Just wait and see. Anyway, I must be going, C/O is off the base so I'm acting for the weekend. Good to see you looking so much better, you'll be back with us in no time."

"Thanks for dropping in, see you later," replied Peter.

Mark smiled, patted Peter on the shoulder and left the room, closing the door behind him. Peter remained on his own, sitting propped up in his bed, and contemplating the ebb and flow of the most emotionally confusing morning he could remember. Ever since he had discovered flying in his teens, it had been his obsession. He had had a couple of girlfriends, but they had always wanted more attention than he was able to give them. Relationships had come a poor second to flying, something was happening here that he didn't understand. The all-consuming bond he had shared with the joy of flight was now being tugged at and strained in unexpected ways. He was thinking about Anne more than he had ever thought about any woman before. His mind was no longer entirely filled with thoughts about flying, about getting back into the air. Another human being had found the crack in his consciousness and he had allowed them to squeeze their way in. It was an alien, disconcerting feeling.

Chapter 3

Anne breezed into Peter's room at the start of her shift on the Monday morning.

"Good morning, Flight Lieutenant, I do hope you had a restful weekend."

Peter looked at her quizzically. "Flight Lieutenant? Aren't we getting a tad forgetful?"

Anne blushed. "Oh dear! Haven't you been told yet? I'm sorry to have spilled the beans."

Peter took an involuntary deep breath and exhaled slowly, promotion to Flight Lieutenant was a jump of two ranks.

"Crikey!" was all he could say.

Anne couldn't help but laugh. "Well I must say, you certainly have a talent for erudition."

Peter smiled too, "It's just a wee bit unexpected, that's all, they're jumping me up two ranks."

Anne continued to chuckle. "I guess someone thought it mightn't look too good, to have a highly decorated, triple Ace serving as a mere Pilot Officer. It might make all the others wonder what they needed to do to get ahead in life."

This time, Peter laughed. "I guess that's right, I might become the figure-head for a workers revolt!"

The two of them were both chuckling at the thought when a knock sounded through the door. It promptly opened and a small party of senior officers came into the room. They were followed by the Matron of the hospital, and a few of the other nurses. Peter immediately recognised his own immediate commanders in Mark and the Squadron Leader Hugh Trehearn. It took a couple of seconds before he recognised the third officer as being Air Vice-Marshal Trafford Leigh-Mallory, commander of 11 Group, the strategic department to which Peter's squadron was attached to. Peter tried to sit upright as best he could, as Anne retreated towards the back of the room.

"Please, please, stay as you were, my boy," said Leigh-Mallory jovially. "Sorry to catch you unawares, but I wanted to be the one to inform you first."

Peter and Anne exchanged quick, surreptitious glances.

"Word of your achievements has got around, young man," continued Leigh-Mallory. "It is my pleasure to advise you that you are to be promoted immediately to the rank of Flight Lieutenant and also, to be awarded the Distinguished Service Order. Please allow me to be the first to congratulate you."

The Air Vice-Marshal approached Peter's bed and held out his hand. Even though his forearm was still encased in plaster, at this moment it wasn't in a sling and Peter was able to take Leigh-Mallory's hand in return and shake it. Peter couldn't help himself, though naturally self-effacing, he beamed with pride.

Hugh Trehearn stepped forward and handed a small presentation box to Leigh-Mallory. The Air Vice-Marshal opened the box and drew out the medal from within. He bent down over Peter and pinned the clasp to his pyjama top, then stood erect to attention and saluted. He was immediately joined by Hugh Trehearn and Mark. Peter returned the salute as best he could from his semi-recumbent position and looked around at everyone in the room. In particular, he noted Anne, she seemed as delighted in the moment as he felt himself.

The formalities finished, Hugh and Mark stepped forward to join Leigh-Mallory in congratulating Peter. The time of a senior officer is valuable, Leigh-Mallory soon had to call an end to the gathering and bid his farewell to Peter and the nursing staff. Mark and Hugh promised Peter that they would come back later, and the room suddenly emptied. Except for Anne.

She walked over to the door and closed it. Then she returned and sat on the edge of Peter's bed, something she had never done before. She and Peter were unable to take their eyes off each other. Their first kiss was tentative, as if seeking physical confirmation of what they both knew in their hearts. Their second kiss though was pure passion, It unlocked the longing they had both been trying to keep under control. To Peter it seemed more seismic than emotional, it felt to him like an eternity before they drew apart. Neither spoke for a few moments, finally, Anne broke the silence.

"If you say 'crikey' right now, I shall run away and go back to daddy!"

Peter smiled. "Now you've got me worried that I might have been about to!"

Anne leaned forward and they kissed again, not as long but very tenderly. Anne finally stood up and smiled down at him.

"You need a shave you know and that medal was sticking into me, the rest was rather nice though."

"In my defence," replied Peter, "you did catch me somewhat unprepared and I don't normally wear medals in bed!"

Anne smiled warmly. "I guess that's true, also, I suppose I did rather throw myself at you."

"Did you?" asked Peter. "I thought it was my animal magnetism that drew you over."

"Of course, that must have been it," chuckled Anne. "But you must please try and keep it under control for the time being. This truly isn't allowed, nurses and patients; it really could cost me my job and I do love nursing."

Peter nodded understandingly. "I know you do; you're just going to have to make sure you get me better as soon as possible then."

"Believe me, I'll be doing my best! But for now, I do have other work to do believe it or not, I shall see you later. Bye."

Peter couldn't take his eyes of her as she left the room. After she had gone, he gathered his thoughts and settled himself back into his bed and thought back on the events of the previous half hour. Just two days earlier, she had left him feeling confused and alone. Now this! He couldn't recall a time when he had felt so completely happy, even his first flight was a different kind of emotion. This was overwhelming, Anne clearly felt the same way towards him as he felt for her. The thought was intoxicating. That she was there to watch as he was presented with his promotion and the DSO made the moment complete. He unpinned the medal from his pyjama top, he held it up and examined it closely. He'd seen others with the ribbon on their tunics and knew that it was highly prized. Now it was his to wear as well.

***

"Your promotion is only a part of the news, old chap," said Mark. He had returned later in the afternoon to spend time with Peter privately.

"Now the AVM was rather concerned that if you were to become a Flight Lieutenant like me, then you might somehow get it into your head that you were suddenly my social equal."

Peter erupted into laughter.

"So, in order to immediately erase any such nonsensical notions from your naïve, antipodean skull, he has, in his infinite wisdom seen fit to elevate me to the rank of Squadron Leader, effective next Monday."

"That's wonderful!" exclaimed Peter. "Congratulations, sincerely, I really mean it, well done!"

"Many thanks old boy, I must admit I'm a tad nervous about it but if old Trehearn can do it, I guess I can too."

Peter suddenly realised the implications of Mark's promotion.

"That's a thought, what's going to happen here? Are you going to be posted? Will you get a new squadron of your own?"

"As a matter of fact, it's not me who's being posted, Trehearn has also been booted upstairs. He's being made a Wing Commander; I'll be taking over here."

"Wow!" said Peter, trying hard to process all this news. "Will he be staying on base or going somewhere else?" Mark paused for a moment before answering.

"Well, in fact, he's leaving Fighter Command altogether, he's moving over to Bomber Command."

Peter's jaw fell in shock. "What?! Has he suddenly developed a death wish?"

"Apparently not," replied Mark. "It seems he's been seduced by a new aircraft coming online. Technically, it's a light bomber, but from all reports it's potentially quite a multi-role beast, it's called the Mosquito, a De Havilland job. I had a look over one myself last week. It's rather a good-looking kite, I must say, sort of like a twin-engine version of the Spit, in terms of being a looker. Apparently, it's supposed to be faster than a Spit and can almost handle like one. The only worry I can think of is that it's made out of wood."

"Wood!!" exclaimed Peter. "You're having me on!"

"No, I assure you, it's completely true," replied Mark. "I don't think I like the idea that if the kite gets banged up, they'll send for a Cabinet Maker rather than a mechanic, but the boffins seem to think it'll be fine."

Mark paused for a moment and poured himself a glass of water from the jug on the table alongside Peter's bed.

"Anyway, it's Hugh's future not mine. One engine is quite enough for me," continued Mark. "On another, far more important matter, how are things progressing between you and the lovely nurse, Anne?"

Peter's eyebrows raised, had they been too obvious this morning when everyone was in the room? He tried to remain calm and off-hand, even though he was desperate to tell someone. He knew that, for Anne's sake he couldn't.

"Oh, things are okay, I guess. She seemed much happier today, we were having a nice chat before your little entourage interrupted us."

"I see," said Mark with a sly grin. "I couldn't help but notice she stayed behind and closed the door after everyone had left. By the way, you still have a small bit of lipstick on your upper lip."

Peter looked aghast and rubbed frantically at his mouth.

Now it was Mark who burst into laughter. "I knew it! I knew it! You really do need to pay attention old chap. She wasn't even wearing lipstick! They never do when they're on duty. That was the easiest fish I've ever landed!"

Peter looked desperate. "Please Mark, don't breathe a word, it'll get her in serious trouble if anyone finds out. They're strictly forbidden from… getting close to patients."

"Don't worry old bean, discretion is my middle name, it'll just be our little secret. At least I won't have to get you posted to Coastal Command now, I really wasn't looking forward to having to do that. But I am impressed, the quiet, shy Colonial gets the best-looking girl on the base. Wonders will never cease! Did you tell her you owned a sheep farm back home or something?"

"Not at all!" said Peter. "It turns out, our fathers are both doctors so we had quite a bit in common to talk about."

"Well, I suspect that talking is all you're going to be able to do really, until they let you out of here. They may have to start putting Bromide in your tea for a few weeks. Have they said how much longer you'll be kept in?"

"Four weeks, at least," said Peter with a sigh. "I can't really get about the base with both a leg and an arm in plaster. I'm pretty good at managing most things now, but there are still lots of times when I'm as useless as a mewling infant."

Mark smiled and stood up, he needed to get back on duty. "Hang in there, old bean, tempus fugit and all that. At least, you're both close together, even if you can only look and not touch. That's better than nothing and fear not, I'll stay 'mum'."

Peter smiled in relief. "Thanks for dropping in Mark, I'm actually quite glad you know now. I needed someone I could tell."

Mark left with a cheery smile. "That's what C/Os are for!"

***

If Anne's tenure in her nursing position meant that she and Peter had to maintain required standards of decorum, then the two of them rose to the challenge. She continued to tend to him as she always had and gave nothing away whenever there were other nurses or the Matron present. What had changed was the conversation between them. It was easy and comfortable now as they both probed each other's pasts, rejoicing in their new understanding.

Three days after Peter's medal presentation, the Base's consulting doctor came in to visit whilst Anne was putting Peter through his leg movement exercises.

Dr Gavin Hennessy was middle aged and had served in the previous war. He had the gentle, unhurried manner of a well-practiced country physician about him. Although now a civilian he lived nearby and had reached out to the Air Force to offer his services at the Base Hospital. They were quick to accept the offer.

"Well, my lad, I want to cut away some of the cast on your leg. The dislocated knee-cap should be well mended by now and it's time it received some gentle exercise."

"You beauty, Sir!" replied Peter with obvious enthusiasm.

The doctor smiled at Peter's lapse in protocol.

"It means you'll find it easier to get about and it will be much more comfortable. You'll no doubt get some aches and moments of pain as it settles in again, but if you follow the nurse's instructions, you should be well on the way."

Peter asked the question which was burning inside him. "How much longer before the casts can come off completely Doctor?"

The doctor checked the chart at the end of Peter's bed.

"Well, it's over five weeks since the accident and everything seems to be mending nicely. We will see how you go with increased activity now that the knee is free. We may have you out of here within the next fortnight, how does that sound?"

It was music to Peter's ears; he beamed a delighted smile at Anne who looked just as pleased.

"All right then Doctor, let's get started then, shall we?"

Half an hour later, Peter's right knee now pale and hairless, was once again free from the rigid confines of the plaster cast. The doctor instructed Anne on the particular exercises he wanted Peter to practise over the next few days. They both paid careful attention, neither of them wanted anything to happen that might hold up Peter's recuperation. Once he was happy that everything was understood, the doctor prepared to leave the room.

"May I have a few moments of your time nurse, outside?"

"Of course, Doctor," replied Anne, who followed him out of the room closing the door behind her.

"Just make sure he doesn't over-do things will you," said the doctor smiling. "These fit, young chaps think they are indestructible. Just keep him on the regime I have set out for at least for five days. That should have the knee settling in again, we don't want any setbacks."

"Don't worry Doctor," said Anne earnestly, "I'll keep him under control."

"I've not the slightest doubt of that," said the doctor with a knowing smile. "Soon he'll be out of here, and all yours!"

Anne looked stunned. "But how?... I never… we never…" she stammered.

The doctor put his arm around her shoulders and said warmly. "I haven't seen two young people so totally and obviously besotted with each other in a long time. Do not worry my dear, I am well aware that you are approaching all this with complete propriety. Your professionalism has been exemplary."

"Has it been that obvious?" asked Anne quietly. "Do you think anyone else might suspect?"

"It's quite all right my dear, nobody else suspects anything; they are all completely convinced!"

Anne looked horrified. "Everyone?" she blurted out.

"Everyone," said the Matron who heard the last part of the conversation as she emerged from her office.

Anne looked as though she might burst into tears.

The Matron hugged her closely. "It's quite alright my dear. We all know you are trying your very hardest to behave with decorum and respect for our hospital standards. You have nothing to be worried about, let me assure you. You are a much loved and respected member of our team here Anne, but we all have eyes!"

"What should I do?" asked Anne. "Should someone else take over his care?"

"Not at all my dear," said the Matron reassuringly. "Continue as you have been, it would be cruel of me to separate you now. It is not long before he will be fit to be released anyway. In truth, we are all quite delighted for you, he really does seem a particularly nice young man."

Anne was steadily recovering her composure after the emotional shock of a minute earlier.

"He is. He's quite different from the others in the Squadron. Much quieter. Not a show-off, like most of them."

"I completely agree with you there. But now, young lady, I am sure you have other tasks requiring your attention. Let us get back on duty, shall we?" said the Matron, affecting her stern voice, but still with a gentle twinkle in her eye.

"Certainly, Matron," replied Anne with smile of gratitude and relief. "I just need to finish in Peter's room first, I shan't be long."

She quickly slipped back into the room as the Matron and the doctor smiled conspiratorially to each other and left together, talking happily.

"Is everything alright?" asked Peter as Anne closed the door behind her.

"Everything is wonderful!" said Anne. "I do believe I may even have permission to do something."

Peter looked at her quizzically. "That sounds intriguing, permission to do what?"

Anne did not say another word, she simply crossed the room to his bed and kissed him.

***

Peter sat, quietly flexing his right arm now that it was finally free of the cast that had encased it for the last seven weeks. Apart from looking extremely pale it showed little residual sign of having been subjected to the violent trauma of the plane crash. Whilst he contemplated his arm, the doctor and Anne were working at cutting away the plaster from around his right lower leg, ankle and foot. His knee felt completely normal now, and soon he could put the ankle to the test. Best of all was the thought that he would be walking out of here in about an hour's time and returning to life as a fighter pilot again, but this time, he would have another priority to consider. He would have Anne in his life.

He looked at her as whilst she was preoccupied helping the doctor cut away at the cast. Would having a girlfriend affect his flying? Would it take the edge of his ability in combat? Would he worry about getting home to Anne instead of focusing completely on the hunt? He knew other pilots had wives and girlfriends; they were fine in the air. Many had been killed or severely injured, some had been horrifically burned. How would Anne cope if something like that happened to him?

Having another person to worry about was a new sensation. Being in hospital, he had been able to avoid these thoughts, but now he was getting out and they were coming at him in a rush. The doctor stood up, interrupting Peter's reverie. He was holding the remains of the now removed plaster cast.

"Well young man, you know what comes next."

Anne looked up at him. "Would you like us to support you?"

"No thanks," replied Peter. "I'd like to give this a try on my own first."

Peter stood up from his chair and initially taking his weight on his left leg, gradually began to shift it over to his right. It felt fine, completely normal, he did not really know what to expect, whether it would ache or make creaking noises, it did neither. He allowed his weight to balance normally on both legs.

"How does it feel?" asked the doctor.

"It feels good, no pain at all," said Peter beginning to relax.

"Don't expect miracles immediately," said the doctor. "You will have lost a bit of muscle bulk and tone while it was in the cast. It'll be weaker than before. Just do short walks for a few days and drink plenty of water. You may experience a few cramps."

Anne spoke up. "Alright then, let's try a few steps, shall we?"

Peter tensed himself as he prepared to take the first step. Anne had moved a few yards back and beckoned Peter to walk to her. With great concentration, he swung his leg forward. It was a complete anti-climax. He walked over to Anne without the slightest problem.

"Well, that was strangely disappointing," said the doctor. "I had hoped for something a little more melodramatic."

"I was half expecting something like that myself!" replied a relieved Peter. "Let me try a few more steps."

He walked slowly over to the window beside his bed and looked out. It was a beautiful day outside.

"I must say, I can't believe how normal it feels. I didn't know what to expect, but it certainly wasn't this."

"You appear to have healed remarkably well, young man," said the doctor. "I must say, it's something I've come to expect from you chaps from the Colonies. I've treated quite a few of you now. Chaps from Australia, New Zealand, South Africa, Canada… I don't know what they feed you, but you certainly seem to have better constitutions than we have here in England. You just seem to heal better and faster than most of our young men."

"Whatever it is, right now I'm very grateful for it," said Peter. "So, does that mean that I'm allowed to go now? Am I ready to be discharged?"

"Well, I don't see any reason why not, but don't go too far. Stay on the base for the next few days, and don't try doing anything silly like running just yet. Try going for short walks several times a day. Build it up over three of four days. Come back in if you have any problems."

Peter and Anne looked at each other. Soon their waiting would be over.

"Anyway, young Peter," continued the doctor. "Your uniform has been sent over from your room, so you may once again present yourself to the world as an officer and a gentleman. Or, at least, an officer!"

Peter and Anne both laughed. Peter held out his hand to Dr Hennessy.

"Thank you so much Doctor. I'm truly grateful for everything you've done."

Dr Hennessy laughed. "And that, young sir, is the reason we become doctors. We only have to do about ten percent of the work, and yet we get ninety percent of the credit. I suspect we can thank the ministrations of the nursing staff here and perhaps one in particular, for the fullness of your recovery. Don't you agree?"

Peter smiled at Anne. "You may well have a point doctor.'

"I rather suspect I do! Well, I shall be on my way, I hope we encounter each other again in the near future and under slightly more convivial circumstances. Good day to you both."

"Goodbye Doctor," said Peter. "Thanks, once again.'

Dr Hennessy smiled at them both and left the room. Peter turned back to Anne.

"Well then, good nurse, it appears I am now a free man at liberty to do whatever I may choose, provided the Air Force deems it permissible."

"And what do you think these choices might be, oh good Officer of the Kings Air Force?" replied Anne with suitable solemnity.

"I'm not entirely sure, do you think we may be able to discuss some possibilities over dinner tonight, unless you have something else planned, of course?"

Anne pretended to think carefully for a few moments. "As it turns out, my card is completely free tonight. I do believe dinner sounds wonderful."

Peter felt a glow of radiant happiness spread through him as he drew her close and they kissed tenderly.

Chapter 4

August 1941

The entire squadron, pilots and ground crew were standing out in the high summer sunshine. All eyes turned skyward, watching as the first nine of their new Spitfires circled the airfield, putting on a show before they landed. A further nine were scheduled to arrive the following day. At last, the squadron would be back to full strength. 371 Squadron was surrendering their well-worn Mk1 Spitfires and were now taking delivery of the latest MkV type. Faster, more powerful engines with better armour to protect the pilots, but above all they were better armed. Equipped with 20mm cannon as well as machine guns, these were potent weapons of war.

Every pilot in the squadron was angling to be among the first to get one into the air. The men began to crowd in front of the Dispersal Hut as the first of the new aircraft taxied to a halt a short distance away. As soon as the propellers had stopped turning, the pilots and ground crew moved in close to give the new Spitfires a closer examination. Apart from the barrels of the cannon protruding from the wings, they looked no different to their old Mk1s. They did, however, look brand new. Their old kites were just about worn out.

Mark put his hand on Peter's shoulder.

"Well, old chum, you've been out of hospital for two weeks now. How do feel about getting back in the air?"

"It's about time I did, I don't think I'm going to get any more recuperated than I already am."

Peter had been champing at the bit to be flying again. Apart from the voyage from New Zealand, this was the longest he'd been on the ground in over five years.

"Good O!" exclaimed Mark, slapping Peter on the back. "Once we get these refuelled, we might get the squadron up for some familiarisation exercises. They might look the same, but these are supposed to handle quite differently from the Mk1s."

"So I've heard," replied Peter. "I'm dead keen to give one a go, which one will be mine?"

"You might as well have the one over there with the 'P' marking. Just think 'P for Peter', that way, you won't forget which one's yours."

Peter chuckled at the jibe, but he wasted no time in taking up Mark's suggestion, immediately heading over to his new kite. The female ATA pilot who had flown it in was walking in the opposite direction, towards the Dispersal Hut.

"What's she like? Is there anything I should know?" asked Peter as they approached.

"She's an absolute darling!" replied the pilot. "This is a lovely Mark; you'll fall in love her in no time. More power, better rate of climb and more responsive on the controls that your old ones."

"So I've heard," said Peter. "This one is supposed to be mine now." Peter nodded towards the Spitfire from which she had just emerged. "You must have flown quite a few to be able to compare the Marks like that?"

"I've flown well over a hundred different Spits by now I guess," came the reply.

Peter was impressed. "Wow! That's incredible, this will be only the fourth different Spitfire I've ever flown. I'm delighted to meet you, my name's Peter Garland by the way," he held out his hand.

She took it and they shook warmly. "Ah, I've heard of you, Triple ace now I believe. I'm delighted to meet you too, my name's Mary Ellis."

The two of them bade each other farewell and Peter strolled over to have a closer look at his new kite. It was so similar to the old one, but it looked and smelled new. After lunch, it would be taking him back into the air.

***

Peter was effusing to Anne about the new aeroplane over dinner that evening.

"It's like the old one, but just… better, it does everything just that little bit faster and with the new cannon! Well! That will certainly give us a real edge when we meet up with some Jerry again."

At the mention of his going into battle again, Anne seemed to lose some of her glow. A slight shadow had fallen across her features. "I guess that's likely to be happening soon, I take it?"

Peter was so engrossed in his talking that he hadn't noticed the change in Anne's mood.

"Quite soon, I would think, we've been stood down for a week now waiting for the new kites. Group won't want us getting rusty, I've had a much longer lay-off than the other chaps and I'm perfectly fit now. They'll no doubt think it's time I started earning my pay again."

Anne looked like she was about to burst into tears.

Finally, Peter noticed her distress. "What on earth is the matter? Are you alright?" He felt sudden concern and instant remorse at the thought that he might have said something to upset her so.

Anne took her handkerchief out of her bag and dabbed at her eyes. "I'll be fine, I just haven't had to think of you going back up there. I've had you all to myself and now you're going back into the war. What will I do if something happens to you?"

Peter tried to sound as positive as he could. "I've got pretty good at looking after myself my darling. These new planes are even better for that. I have no intention of letting any damn Luftwaffe joker get me. I've got far too much to live for now."

Anne managed a weak smile again. "You've told me several times that it's as much luck as it is skill. Maybe you've just been lucky so far?"

Peter nodded. "That's true, but I do my best to make my own luck. Look Anne, I can't promise you anything, I can only do my job the best I can and stay alive. I have you to come back to now, that's a powerful reason to stay intact."

Anne looked intently at him and dabbed at her eyes again. "I know and I also know that I'm just one of many thousands of women who are feeling the same thing right now. Until you came along, I wasn't one of them and now I am. It's a shock, It's a very helpless feeling. All I can do is wait and worry."

Peter began to understand. "I think I get it now, you're quite right, it is a helpless feeling. I felt a touch of it that day out in the garden in the wheelchair, the day you visited. I was waiting for the lads to return from a circus over France. I couldn't do a thing to help because I couldn't be with them. It was such a relief when they all came back. I remember Mark telling me what a disappointing, uneventful sortie it was. I didn't say anything, but I was grateful that it had been."

Hearing Peter speak thoughts that so closely echoed her own fears was a deep relief to Anne. He truly understood what she was thinking. She felt her emotions begin to settle and a new strength beginning to rise.

She reached across the table and took his hands. "I do believe I have fallen very much in love with you Mister Flight Lieutenant."

Peter smiled contentedly. "You do realise that I was about to say something remarkably similar, Miss Registered Nurse."

***

As soon as he had finished switching his Spitfire's engine off, Mark lowered the small cockpit side hatch and climbed down to the ground. He desperately wanted to take a swing at something or anything. He stomped back to the Dispersal Hut and waited for the other pilots to arrive. By the time the last few approached he had started to cool down.

"Well, let me start by saying 'well spotted' to Flying Officer Fraser."

A young, red-haired Scottish pilot fresh from Glasgow, felt a rush of pride.

"If he hadn't spotted those other bastards high up," continued Mark, "we would have been well and truly bounced this time. As it is, we've just learned a valuable lesson at no cost. They've clearly thought out a clever new game to try and tempt us in. Anyway lads, head over to debriefing."

He waved the squadron away. Peter stayed back. He wanted a word with Mark alone.

"Fraser's got eyes like a hawk, I was checking the sun and didn't see a bloody thing."

"Me neither," replied Mark in an uncharacteristically surly tone. "Do you realise that I almost flew the whole squadron into an ambush. They would have had us cold, the bastards!"

Peter didn't respond at first, Mark was taking this personally and Peter didn't want to add to his guilt.

"Look Skipper, if it weren't us, it would have been some other squadron on some other rhubarb. It's like you said, we've just learned a valuable lesson at no cost. If this is to be their new tactic, we should try and think up a way of turning it around on them. Anyway, we both need to get over to the debriefing, come on."

Mark exhaled deeply and nodded. "You're right, It's just a bit of a blow to the old ego, that's all."

Mark smiled again and slapped Peter on the back. The two of them started to walk over to the main administration building to join the rest of the squadron.

***

That night, Peter told Anne about the events of the day, she was his guest in the Officer's Mess.

"It was all looking very uneventful for most of the trip, we weren't that far away from giving up and heading back home. Then one of the lads spotted a small flight of MEs some way inland. Only about three of four of 'em. We all checked high to look in the sun for others and there were none so, Mark gave us the order to attack."

Anne was listening intently; she was glad that Peter always told her what really happened on the sorties. He didn't try to shield her from reality.

"Anyway, we were all on the new heading and about to go into our attack dive, when Jamie Fraser calls out that we were about to get bounced ourselves. There was a whole squadron of MEs really high, maybe thirty thousand feet, but they weren't in the sun where we would have expected them. They had obviously flown right out to sea, over the Channel. They were coming at us from a completely new direction. They came so close to catching us cold."

"Do you mind if I pull rank and join you?" asked Mark who had just appeared at their table.

"We would be delighted!" smiled Anne. She had long since forgiven Mark for his indiscretion in the hospital.

"I see that our resident Antipodean is telling you about our little escapade today. Not my finest hour I'm afraid." Mark was clearly still ruminating on their close escape.

"Stop worrying about it Skip," said Peter. "No harm was done and we'll never let them spring that one on us again."

Mark looked intently at Peter for a second before breaking his gaze. "You're absolutely right of course. I might call a meeting of all the pilots in the morning. We'll talk about today and see if we can't come up with some ideas about how to muck up Jerry's new game."

The moment of positivity seemed to recharge Mark. He turned to Anne with a conspiratorial look. "My dear child, I feel there is something that I must tell you about our mutual colonial friend here!"

Anne and Peter both leaned forward in intrigued anticipation.

Mark continued, "We have three distinct classifications for the various types of pilots here in the RAF. It's obviously of crucial importance that you understand where young Peter here, fits into the great scheme of things. We can't have you surrendering you chances for social advancement by mixing with the wrong type now, can we?"

"This'll be good!" said Peter, fighting to keep a straight face.

"Please do continue, good Sir," said Anne primly. "Clearly, if I'm about to make a tragic error, I should be forewarned."

"My sentiments exactly, dear child," Mark was warming to his theme. "Now, as I was saying, here in the RAF, we have three classes of fellows who are allowed to sit in those rather expensive machines out there. The first, are those chaps who joined up years ago when the Air Force was just a glorified Flying Club. Those chaps are known as pilots, desperately trying to be gentlemen. The next group to which I rather proudly belong are the newer bods who joined up when the war was starting. We are referred to as gentlemen desperately trying to be pilots."

Anne and Peter both guffawed in laughter.

"OK then, let's hear it. Where do I fit in?" asked Peter, still laughing.

"Well then," continued Mark, a look of triumph spreading across his face, "as we all know, you came up through the noncommissioned ranks, a tragic social faux pas." He turned to Anne, "Peter's lot are referred to as neither, desperately trying to be both!"

The laughter from their table caught the attention of everyone else in the Mess. Mark had managed to put his earlier concerns to one side and quickly became his old self again. He began looking around the Mess. It was time to make a show of congratulating the young Flying Officer whose sharp eyes had helped avert a disaster earlier in the day. He quickly spotted Fraser sitting at a table with some friends and stood up.

"Is Flying Officer Fraser with us tonight?" he announced in a loud voice.

"Aye Sir," said Fraser from across the room, hurriedly getting to his feet.

"Well please come hither, my young Hibernian. In recognition of your efforts earlier today, the bar is going to shout you a beer which you, being the responsible young officer that you are, shall drink in one go!"

Fraser nervously made his way over to his Squadron Leader, who was now standing theatrically by the bar, waiting while a pint of Brown Ale was pulled. Fraser was not yet out of his teens and no one expected him to be able to down the large glass all at once. To the collective amazement of everyone in the room however, he downed it like a well-seasoned drinker and slammed the empty glass on the bar, wiping his mouth with the back of his hand. Mark and everyone else in the room applauded enthusiastically.

Fraser looked up at Mark. "Thank you, Sir. Oh, and by the way, I support Rangers. I hate Hibs."

Mark looked nonplussed for a moment. "Oh that! I meant Hibernian in the sense that you are Scottish… Oh bugger it! Go back and join your friends and well done today, young lad!"

Fraser was grinning broadly as he returned to his table.

***

Another week passed by; August had slipped into September. 371 Squadron had flown three more operations over coastal and near inland France since their close call. Not once had they seen a small flight of enemy aircraft such as the small decoy group they had encountered that day. Either the Germans were aware that their tactic had been exposed or they were refusing to come up and engage. Most curious of all, was an empty airfield where, only a month before, German activity was like a beehive. The squadron flew over it unmolested, unchallenged and disappointed.

Air Vice-Marshal Leigh-Mallory was once again visiting the Station.

"We're planning on pulling the pin on these rhubarb operations. It looks very much as though the Germans have pulled quite a few of their squadrons out of coastal France and redeployed them to support the invasion of Russia or sent them to North Africa."

He was addressing a full meeting of the squadron.

"Continuing these operations seems like it will cost us more than we're ever likely to achieve. So, our role is about to change. Bomber Command are now bringing some new, heavier aircraft on line and we'll no doubt find ourselves becoming more involved in escort operations from here on. There is now a larger strategy coming into play gentlemen. The RAF is going on the offensive. There will now be much greater coordination between Fighter and Bomber Commands. What I can promise you, is that the Germans will most certainly start sending up their fighters now. If you've been missing some action, you're about to start getting it again. Do you have any questions?"

Mark spoke up. "When are these operations likely to get underway Sir?"

"Soon Squadron Leader, certainly before the end of the month."

Mark continued, "Are we off operations then in the interim or shall we continue as we are in the meantime?"

Leigh-Mallory looked thoughtful for a moment before he replied. "Continue on as you have been for the moment. There are still German squadrons over there and we don't want to alert them to any pending changes at our end."

He looked around the room. "Well, if there are no further questions, I won't detain you any longer. Thank you, gentlemen."

Mark and the other senior officers stayed behind with Leigh-Mallory, but Peter and the rest of the squadron filed out of the meeting, all of them deep in thought. The air war was about to change again.

Soon they would lose the ability to roam freely and fight on their own terms. Soon, they would be tied more closely to the bombers they had to protect. Combat initiative would no longer be theirs. The risks were growing.

***

The squadron turned towards France once more and climbed to its assigned height of twenty-two thousand feet. They wanted the German radar to see them clearly.

Peter hadn't added to his total since his accident. Neither had Mark. It wasn't through want of trying; the Luftwaffe had been very cagey over the last few months. Other squadrons had seen plenty of fighting, but the sector of the French coast that fell within the scope of 371 Squadron had seem to be unexpectedly quiet.

The squadron crossed the French coast south of Le Touquet, turned right and continued flying south. They had only been a few minutes in French air space when the sharp eyes of Flying Officer Fraser spotted rising aircraft in the distance.

"Bandits at 9 o'clock. Looks like twenty plus."

All eyes turned to their left and examined the sky.

"I see them," replied Mark. "Same height as us. They got up fast."

Another voice on the R/T. "They've seen us, they're turning towards us."

Mark's voice was calm. "Alright everyone. Turning left now. Keep with your wingmen. Let's take them head on."

The two flights of aircraft were approached at a combined speed of over seven hundred miles per hour. Each had bare fractions of a second to select a target and fire. Neither side scored any damaging hits in the first pass. Both squadrons wheeled around in the high altitude, lines of condensation trailing from their wingtips, marking their courses through the cold, thin air. Both formations began to break up as they all turned hard to try and gain an advantage before the enemy did.

A voice over the R/T crackled. "They don't look like MEs."

Another voice. "Christ, they're faster than 109s."

Soon, the voices of all pilots became a cacophony of sound in each other's earphones.

The Germans were flying a new type of fighter. Faster with a better rate of turn.

Peter found one in his sights for an instant and fired his guns but the German quickly made a fast, climbing turn to his right and escaped undamaged.

"My God, these things can turn!" shouted Peter down the R/T.

Peter caught a flash of light off to his right. A Spitfire had exploded in flames.

He suddenly found himself in clear air again and pulled hard at the control column to make a quick, vertical turn.

The fight had quickly spread itself over a seemingly vast stretch of sky as individual dogfights drew the combatants off in different, unplottable directions.

Peter instinctively checked his mirror again. His eyes widened as he saw a dark shape closing in on him. He waited a second until he was sure the enemy pilot was about to shoot and then threw the Spitfire into a violent, diving turn to his left. He felt his aircraft shudder as several bullet holes appeared in his right wing.

He kept the turn going, spiralling the Spitfire in a tight turning corkscrew. A desperate manoeuvre. The German couldn't stay with him and broke off the attack.

Peter opened the throttle fully and climbed back towards the whirling, spiralling mass of aircraft above him. He watched as another Spitfire, trailing heavy, black smoke began to fall away from the fight. No parachute emerged.

Two other Spitfires had managed to disengage and were heading back towards the coast at full throttle.

Peter reached combat height again. Once again, he experienced the sensation of being in a sky devoid of all other aircraft, even though his earphones were full of the voices of his comrades.

A sudden flash of reflected sunlight caught his attention over to his left and slightly below.

A German was glued to the tail of a Spitfire that was trying desperately to shake him off. Peter could see that this German was a better pilot than the one that engaged him only moments earlier.

He turned towards the duel, still with the throttle wide open. He caught a quick flash of the Spitfire's markings. It was Mark.

Peter was still over a thousand yards away from them, but he opened fire, nonetheless. None of his shots came close.

The German aircraft suddenly steadied for an instant as its pilot got a good bead on Mark's Spitfire.

He fired a long burst which caught Mark across the left wing and raked the entire forward cowling. The stricken Spitfire rolled to the right and began to pour billowing smoke from the engine. The German broke off the pursuit and turned away to the right, not noticing Peter who was closing behind him.

This time, Peter ignored the German, he sped on towards Mark's aircraft.

"Leader! Can you hear me Leader?"

Mark was fighting to regain some control of his mortally damaged aeroplane.

Initially, he appeared to have things under control. "I'm okay. I'm going to bail out."

An instant later, everything changed. He cried out into the R/T. "Shit, I'm on fire!"

The Spitfire's petrol tank was immediately in front of the cockpit. It was meant to be self-sealing but had taken so much damage it had begun spilling fuel regardless.

Peter had brought his aircraft alongside Mark's as he fought for control. Peter could see Mark in the cockpit, desperately trying to open the canopy as the flames began to engulf the cabin.

Mark began to scream in agony and horror as he realised what was happening to him.

He was no longer trying to open the cockpit. Panic had robbed him of the rational thought to get out.

Peter could see him frantically trying to beat at the flames with his gloved hands.

There was nothing he could do except call out Mark's name in impotent, tortured frustration as he watched his best friend being consumed by the furnace that his Spitfire's cockpit had become.

Suddenly, Marks terrified screaming was silenced as his R/T failed. The flames had burned through the cable.

Peter could still see him flailing at the flames in futile, agonising despair as his aircraft went into a steepening dive, falling away, trailing a dense plume of smoke.

Peter never took his eyes away from the awful sight of his best friend's ruined aircraft, falling downwards towards the French farm lots far below, made golden brown by the warmth of the high summer.

***

The ground staff guessed that something was wrong when Peter didn't emerge from his Spitfire after he had shut the engine down. They hurriedly climbed onto the wing and slid open the canopy, thinking that he might have been wounded. A quick check showed no sign of apparent injury.

"Are you alright Sir?" asked a corporal with obvious concern.

At the sound of another voice, Peter finally started to become aware of his surroundings.

"Can you help me out please?" he asked politely.

The corporal undid the buckle securing Peter's harness and helped lift him until he was standing upright again. Peter felt completely disconnected from the activity going on around him as, with help, he stumbled numbly out of the cockpit and down to the ground. He stood, looking at the people gathering around him, not taking in any of it. The corporal and a fitter each took one of his arms and helped lead him over to the Dispersal hut nearby. They guided him inside and sat him in one of the old, tattered armchairs that furnished the room.

"Can I get you a cuppa tea Sir?" asked the corporal.

Peter didn't respond at all. Thankfully, shortly afterwards, to the corporal's great relief a medical orderly entered the room and asked if the Flight Lieutenant had been hurt.

"I don't know what's the matter wiv 'im, he won't say a bleedin' word," said the mystified corporal.

The orderly knelt down in front of Peter and looked into his eyes.

"Can you hear me Sir?"

"Yes," replied Peter. "Of course I can hear you."

He didn't make eye contact with the orderly. His voice sounded flat and emotionless.

"Have you been wounded Sir?" asked the orderly.

"No, I don't think so. You need to look after the Squadron Leader. I think he's been burned."

The orderly and the corporal looked at each other.

"The Squadron Leader hasn't come back yet, Sir. Do you know what happened to him?" asked the orderly.

There was a long pause before Peter spoke again.

"He caught fire!" was all that he could say, his voice breaking as the words came out. Intuitively, the orderly guessed what might have happened.

"Don't worry Sir, I'm going to get you something that might help you sleep. I'll be back in a tick."

He went over to the telephone and rang through to the hospital. Then he went out to the ambulance and brought back a glass bottle of sedative pills.

***

The Matron may have run a tight hospital, but she was also a woman of deep compassion. When she was told of the circumstances of Peter's readmission, she immediately took Anne off duty and allowed her to remain with him. It was obvious that he had suffered a deep emotional trauma. He had just watched as his best friend had been incinerated alive. Mark's had been one of four Spitfires that hadn't returned. The other pilots reported seeing only a single parachute. None of them could report a success against the new German aircraft. It had been a terrible day for the squadron.

Anne watched intently as Peter's eyes fluttered and opened. He just lay there, staring ahead, focused on nothing in particular.

"I'm right here, my darling" she said softly.

Peter turned his head towards her and slowly half smiled.

"I'm sorry if I gave you a fright."

Anne leaned forward and took his hand, squeezing it more tightly than she realised.

"That's quite alright! How are you feeling? Are you able to talk about what happened?"

The words rushed out; Peter's face clouded over again. At first, he said nothing, but after a minute, he slowly shook his head. Anne smiled slightly and gently nodded.

"I understand, it's too soon. You do know that I'll be here for you when need to talk about it, don't you?"

He looked back towards Anne again and nodded slightly. "Of course I do," he said softly. "I'm so sorry for this, I don't want to be useless..."

Anne laughed gently. "You're not being useless, that's the last thing anyone could ever say about you. You just might need a little time to come to terms with what you saw, that's all."

Peter shook his head forlornly, he opened his mouth as if to speak, but nothing could come out. Anne laid his hand back across his chest and sat back. Peter simply continued to stare at nothing for a minute and then closed his eyes again.

"Would you like to be left alone for a little while, my darling?" asked Anne quietly.

After a moment, Peter nodded slowly. She reached over and briefly squeezed his hand once, then slowly rose from her chair and crossed over to the door. She looked back at this quiet man she had fallen in love with and felt powerless. He was clearly in a very dark place and she didn't know how to lead him out of it.

***

With four aircraft missing, its Squadron Leader dead, his most obvious successor in hospital under sedation, 371 Squadron was immediately stood down for forty-eight hours while new leadership was drafted. The Base Commander at RAF Redhill was Group Captain Allan Hawthorne. He called a meeting the day following the fateful sortie, after he'd had the chance to read through the pilot's debriefing comments.

"Well gentlemen, it certainly looks as though the Luftwaffe have gained a march on us this time. Did anyone get a good look at this new fighter? Does it appear to be a further development of the 109?"

One of the pilots spoke up. "No Sir. It's quite different. It looks completely new. It looks quite square at the front, as though it has a radial engine."

"Aye Sir," chimed in F/O Fraser. "And it has a sliding canopy, I definitely saw that."

Another pilot spoke. "It's certainly faster than our Mk Vs Sir, and they easily out-turned us."

"So then," said Hawthorne, "it does sound completely new. I'll get this information on to Group. They will need to get this around all the squadrons quickly. If the Germans get these new fighters in large numbers, it could change things dramatically."

He paused for a moment and looked over the assembled pilots. "On the subject of Flight Lieutenant Garland, did anyone else see what happened to the Squadron Leader? Garland seems profoundly traumatised by the experience."

Another officer, Flight Lieutenant Allen spoke up. "We all heard it over the R/T Sir. It sounded like the Squadron Leader's Spit went up in flames before he could bail out. Mr Garland must have been flying close by him at that time. He was yelling his name over and over again; he must have seen him burn."

There was silence in the room after Allen stopped speaking. The Group Captain hung his head for a moment as he thought. He decided he owed it to the assembled pilots to speak with unaccustomed candour.

"The two of them were very close, they had both been with the squadron since shortly after Dunkirk. Been through a lot together. I think seeing your best friend incinerated right before your eyes would test the strength of any man. There, but for the Grace of God, go all of us gentlemen."

Hawthorne had known both Mark and Peter well. 371 Squadron had been stationed at RAF Redhill for well over a year. The events of the previous day had left him just as shaken as the pilots themselves. He regathered his thoughts and his demeanour.

"There is going to be some reorganising of the squadron. There will be a couple of promotions, all of them well earned I assure you. It's likely the new C/O will come from outside the squadron. A decision will be made today and he should be here tomorrow or the day after at the latest. Thank you for your time gentlemen, you are dismissed."

After the last of the pilots had filed out of the room, Hawthorne walked over to the window and watched as they broke into small groups and talked amongst themselves as they walked back to their various stations. He had seen other pilots who had reached the point of breakdown. Some had been able to recover after time away from flight duty, but others seemed to be permanently scarred. He could only hope for Peter that he would be one of the lucky ones. Thankfully, the decision as to what to do with him in the meantime was not his to make. That would be a difficult call awaiting the new Squadron Leader, whom ever he might prove to be.

Chapter 5

The Morris saloon, wearing its official Royal Air Force blue livery, drove onto the grounds of RAF Heston in the county of Middlesex, in the full light of a bright, late morning, autumn day. Peter opened the passenger's side, rear door and slowly emerged from the vehicle. He went to the rear of the car, opened the boot and took out his kitbag and valise. Closing the boot-lid he knocked on it to let the driver know he was finished. The car slowly pulled away, its tyres crunching on the gravel as it set off on its next assignment. Peter looked around, taking in the sights of his new, unexpected posting. Slinging his kitbag over his left shoulder, he let himself into the entrance of the Administration building and went up to the Duty Sergeant.

"Flight Lieutenant Peter Garland reporting, Sergeant. I'm here as a new flight instructor."

The sergeant saluted him without standing up and checked his paperwork to see if Peter was expected.

"This says here that you're not due to start until tomorrow? The C/O's off the base at the moment Sir, but I can get an Erk to help you with your bags and show you to your quarters if you wish?"

"Thanks, that would be most appreciated. I hope there's no problem with me getting here a day early?"

"Not at all Sir. When the C/O gets back, I'll let him know you've arrived. However, that's not likely to be until this evening. In the meantime, I'm sure we can find someone to show you around after you've settled in."

Peter nodded his thanks, the sergeant got up from his desk and left the room. He returned shortly after with a flight cadet to help show Peter to his room.

"Good morning, Sir," said the cadet, saluting. "My name is Campbell, please let me show you to your quarters."

"Thanks, I'm Flight Lieutenant Garland, I take it you'll be one of my students?"

"Possibly Sir, there are quite a few trainee pilots here. It would be an honour to learn under you Sir."

Peter noticed that the cadet was staring at the medal ribbons above his left coat pocket.

"Well then Mr Campbell, I hope I don't disappoint you. Now, if you'll be so kind as to show me to my quarters, I should be most grateful."

Campbell led him out of the Administration building and on a surprisingly long walk to the Officers' Quarters. Peter couldn't help but smile as he noticed how far they were from the airfield itself. This was an arrangement common to many Air Force bases. It seemed the RAF loved nothing more than making their officers walk a lot if they needed to get to their aircraft. The airfield had served as a commercial aviation centre before the war and had well established facilities. Peter's quarters were small but comfortable and he needed little time to unpack and settle himself in. Campbell had offered to show him around the base but Peter had declined. He wanted to lie down for a while.

Once he was finally in the solitude of his room, he took off his jacket and tie and removed his shoes. He lay down on the bed and exhaled deeply. He tried closing out the present and let his mind wander, whilst simply lying on his back and gazing up at the ceiling. The memories of the last two weeks filled his head with a labyrinth of conflicting emotions. Was it only a fortnight? So much had happened…

***

Anne had been closely monitoring Peter's progress over the three days since Mark had been killed. He had slept a lot at first, thanks largely to the sedative pills he had been prescribed. The forced hours of recumbence had certainly helped. He seemed to be treading the path that would lead him back to his old self. He had become noticeably quieter and he had lost that happy spark that she had so loved, but that was to be expected surely. That was the nature of grief. She was certain that with time and love, it would come back. Last night had been his first night without any sleeping pills. Two nights was enough, he had been told, it was time to see how he would manage without them.

"Good morning Flight Lieutenant. How are we feeling today?" she asked breezily as she entered his room.

Peter looked up and smiled. "All the better for seeing you, good nurse!"

Anne felt a wave of relief wash over her. This was the cheeriest she had seen him since before that terrible mission.

"Did you sleep alright Peter? How did you go with no pills?" she asked with concerned interest.

"I didn't sleep that well. I drifted off several times but never seemed to get more than an hour or so sleep each time. I found myself lying there, back in the cockpit, watching Mark…" he couldn't finish the sentence.

Anne sat on the edge of the bed next to him and reached for his hand, grasping it tightly.

"The memory just keeps coming back. It won't leave me alone. I don't know how to stop it."

Anne looked at him intently. His initial good cheer at seeing her was fast fading back into the deep gloom that now held such a grip on him. She thought carefully before she spoke again.

"The new Squadron Leader arrived yesterday. He called in, but you were sleeping at the time, so he didn't stay. How would you feel about getting out of here, having a wash and a shave, and going back to the station to meet him? He seems a very decent man."

"Are you trying to get me out of here? I guess everyone in the hospital must be fed up with the sight of me by now."

Anne chuckled in relief; he had seemed to pick up again at the thought of getting out of the ward.

"Well then! That's decided, I'll have your uniform brought in and you can go and clean yourself up Mister!"

She stood up, kissed him lightly on the forehead and left the room, feeling more positive than she had in the last two days.

Peter sat up and swung his legs over the side of the bed. The thought of getting back into squadron life didn't fill him with the excitement that it usually did, but knew he had to. His body felt completely leaden as he walked over to the bathroom. Moving his legs seemed to require a level of mental effort that surprised him. Even his mind seemed dull-witted and sluggish. He washed his face and shaved automatically. The feel of the water however, seemed to help pick him up. The simple routine of his morning shave felt like a return to something close to normal. By the time Anne had returned with his uniform, he had finished in the bathroom and was sitting again on the edge of the bed, waiting for her.

***

The new Squadron Leader had arrived to replace Mark the morning before. Tony Harcourt had been the senior Flight Lieutenant of a Hurricane squadron based near Norwich. He had been hoping that he might be given a promotion to Squadron Leader of his own unit at some point, but was delighted instead to be offered the move down to Kent, to take over a Spitfire outfit that had just lost its C/O. He had called a meeting of all flight officers and station NCOs to introduce himself, the only absentee had been Peter.

He was unsure what to make of Peter's emotional condition when he was told about it. He had never had first-hand experience of a pilot breaking down under sudden stress before. He had settled himself into the C/O's office and was beginning to familiarise himself with the personnel files of his pilots when there came a knock at his door.

"Come in!" he called out in a loud voice. Group Captain Hawthorne came in with a wry smile on his face.

"No need to shout around here Squadron Leader. You'll find out soon enough that the walls are very thin in this building."

"My apologies Sir," said Harcourt, hurriedly lurching to his feet and spilling the contents of a file on the floor in the process.

"I'm dreadfully sorry Sir," he blurted out with obvious embarrassment.

Hawthorne was unable to suppress a smile. "Please relax Squadron Leader. I'm sorry if I startled you. I've always felt very much at ease coming into this office. Perhaps, I should get into the habit of ringing ahead for a while at least, that is, unless you enjoy filing?"

Harcourt looked down at the paper strewn across the floor near his feet and looked back up at Hawthorne. His mouth moved silently in wordless agitation for a few seconds before he suddenly burst out in laughter.

"I'm so sorry Sir. I didn't realise how nervous I was, this has all been very sudden."

Hawthorne joined him in the laughter. "That's quite alright Squadron Leader. I'm aware of your record with your previous squadron. I have no doubt you'll do very well here. I really just wanted to say hello and to see if there was anything you might need from me to help you settle in?"

"Thank you very much Group Captain, as a matter of fact, I do have a couple of questions I'd like to ask, if you don't mind. Would you like to have a seat?"

They both sat down on either side of the large desk that dominated the room. Once seated, Harcourt briefly disappeared as he bent forward to pick up the leaves of paper from the dropped file. Reappearing and gathering his composure, he carefully rearranged the file and passed it over to Hawthorne. It was the file on Flight Lieutenant Peter Garland.

"Ah, I was thinking Peter might be your first question. What would you like to know?" said Hawthorne.

"Well Sir, I've been reading his record, It's extraordinary! The man is a triple Ace, DSO, DFC, DFM. Possibly the most competent and experienced pilot in the squadron and now this? I just don't understand."

Hawthorne thought for a few moments before speaking. "It's been a shock to all of us in fact, I know Peter well, he's a first-class chap. He's all those things you said and a lot more beside."

"So how could he just break down like this then?" asked Harcourt.

"I'm afraid that psychiatric analysis is not my forte Squadron Lead… when we're alone, do you mind if I just call you Tony? I love the Air Force, but our rank titles are so bloody long!"

Harcourt smiled warmly. "I'd be delighted Sir, thank you. As I was saying, I'm not a qualified expert, but I've been able to watch Peter for more than a year now. Like many pilots, he's seen extraordinary service in that time, with hardly any respite. A few days leave here or there, but constant operations virtually all that time. He's seen close friends be killed or badly injured, like we all have. He himself was badly injured only three or four months ago. It took time for that to heal sufficiently and then straight back into combat operations."

There was a knock at the door, a WAAF popped her head around the door and asked if either officer would like some tea. Both Hawthorne and Harcourt accepted gratefully and after she left, Hawthorne resumed.

"Peter and your predecessor here, Mark Charters were very close. They'd been all through the Battle of Britain together, through all these pointless cross channel beat-ups and bomber escort trips."

Hawthorne took a sip of his tea. "He was flying right alongside Mark, soon after his Spit was shot up by that new Jerry fighter. He saw it all as Mark's plane suddenly burst into flames inside the cockpit. He just had to sit there and watch as his best friend was incinerated alive. After he landed, he just went into his shell completely, a nervous breakdown you might call it. That was just two days ago. The doctors have kept him pretty well drugged up since then, but I believe they're going to stop the medication tonight."

"So, we don't know how he's going to be then?" asked Harcourt.

"He's a strong lad is Peter. My gut instinct is that he'll be alright, but, as I've said, I'm no expert. At least, his girlfriend is a nurse in the hospital, she's a wonderful girl and a first-class nurse. I'm sure having her nearby will be a powerful help to him."

Harcourt thought for a few moments before replying. "I might take myself over to the hospital and introduce myself. Certainly, I'd like to speak to the doctor who's treating him. It's important that I find out if he's able to resume duties soon."

Hawthorne leaned forward, noting his words with interest. "Really? Is there something I'm not aware of here?"

Harcourt nodded in reply. "Yes Sir. When I was offered the role here, I was advised that the squadron has been earmarked for overseas transfer, either to Malta or to North

Africa. Both are desperate for more squadrons of fighters, particularly Malta from all reports."

Hawthorne sat back in his chair. "I see your point, you would certainly need your most experienced Flight Lieutenant to be on his game with a posting like that. Have you been told how long you have before the posting?"

"No Sir, nothing specific as yet. I've just been advised to have the aircraft well-serviced, ensure all equipment and spares are in stock and properly stowed, and to expect further orders at any time."

Hawthorne smiled slightly and got to his feet. "Well, it certainly looks as though you've been given precious little time to get to on top of things here. I can assure you that you have some excellent NCOs and junior officers to work with. Almost all of the ground crew were here through the air fighting last year. I have no doubt they'll be of tremendous assistance to you."

"Thank you, Sir," said Harcourt, getting to his feet as well. "I think I might go over to the hospital now and see if I can meet Flight Lieutenant Garland. No time like the present."

Hawthorne nodded in agreement. "Unless you have other arrangements, I'd like it if you chose to join some of the other senior officers and myself for dinner tonight in the Officers' Mess. It would be an excellent chance to get to know the Ops team here at Redhill, they're a good bunch."

"I'd be delighted Sir. Thank you very much. What time?"

"Any time, sixish on would be fine," replied Hawthorne. "See you then."

They both saluted and Hawthorne showed himself out of Harcourt's office. Harcourt stood at his desk in deep thought for several moments before straightening his uniform and walking towards the hatstand near the door and retrieving his cap. He left the building and started the walk over towards the hospital.

***

Peter entered the administration building and went to see the senior WAAF in the officers' typing pool.

"Good morning, Mr Garland!" she exclaimed with surprise. "It's wonderful to see you again."

"Thanks Gwen," replied Peter. "I was hoping to see the new C/O if he's in."

"He's over in the hangars at the moment Sir, I can ring and let him know you're here if you'd like?"

"That's alright. Thanks Gwen. I might walk over there instead. It's nice to be outside again. Thanks."

"It's so good to see you up and about again Sir," she replied with a smile. Although, in his naivety Peter had been unaware of the fact, he had become a favourite amongst the single women on the base.

He entered through the huge portal of the hangar doors and noticed a group of men towards the rear of the building. They were apparently inspecting the stores and maintenance equipment. He could see that one of them was unfamiliar to him and wearing an officer's cap, so he made his way over.

As he crossed the expanse of the hangar, an aircraftman recognised him and called out, "Good morning, Mr Garland."

Peter smiled and waved in reply. The sound of Peter's name being called out immediately caught the attention of Squadron Leader Harcourt, who turned and looked towards this person, silhouetted against the outdoor light beyond the hangar, as he approached.

"Good morning Sir, Flight Lieutenant Garland reporting," said Peter, saluting as he came to attention in front of his new C/O.

"It's good to meet you at last Flight Lieutenant. I'm Squadron Leader Harcourt. I tried calling in on you yesterday but the sleeping pills still had you well accounted for it seemed."

"Yes Sir, I was told you came by. I do apologise. I must admit, I do feel rather foolish with all that's happened recently."

"Not at all! We'll have none of that talk, you're certainly looking fine right now."

Looking over his shoulder at the others he had been with, he held up his hand to Peter in a 'halt' gesture.

"Will you please excuse me for just a moment?" he said to him.

Harcourt returned his attention towards the group of aircraftsmen and spoke briefly to the senior NCO.

"You'll have to excuse me for short while 'Flight', I need to give Mr Garland a briefing to bring him up to date with things."

"Of course Sir" replied the Flight Sergeant, "plenty here to keep us occupied in the meantime."

Harcourt indicated for Peter to join him as he started to walk back towards the entrance of the hangar.

"Tell me Peter, how are you feeling? Are you ready to go back on Operations?"

Peter didn't say anything at first, a response which was not lost on Harcourt.

"I'm not actually sure Sir. Last night was my first night off the pills. In truth, I can't say I slept very well."

"Well, that may be simply because you'd had so much sleep over the previous days. Perhaps you just weren't tired enough."

"Perhaps Sir, I hadn't thought of that."

Peter knew that wasn't the reason he hadn't slept, but also knew this was not the time to speak of the constant nightmares that had plagued him.

"How would you feel about going up for a test flight now? We could kit you up and have you off the ground in half an hour."

Harcourt was deliberately pushing for a response, he needed to know what he was dealing with. He didn't have the luxury of time to allow a psychologically compromised officer a lengthy emotional convalescence.

Peter felt he had no choice but to respond positively. "Yes Sir, I'd like that."

"Excellent!" said Harcourt with enthusiasm. "I'll come up with you. I don't have too many hours on Spits yet, so it'll do me good as well."

"What were you on before, Sir?" asked Peter with genuine curiosity.

"Hurricanes mostly. Up in 12 Group, outside Norwich." He walked over to the window and looked out over the dozen or so Spitfires parked outside the Dispersal Hut.

"Nice aeroplane the Hurricane, but I'm beginning to see why you chaps seem to love your Spitfires so much."

Peter smiled. "Yes Sir. They're a handful for a novice, especially in landing, but once you've got the feel for them…" He didn't need to finish the sentence. Harcourt led them into the Dispersal Hut and they pulled flying overalls on over their uniforms. They each logged their flights and signed out their aircraft. Peter's Spitfire was fully prepared and waiting for him in its usual position, fifty yards from the Dispersal Hut.

The ground crews had given both aircraft a quick check to ensure they were fully fuelled and ready to go. Peter settled himself into the cockpit and fastened the buckles on his parachute harness. This wasn't an operational sortie, so there was no hurry and he did it himself.

He went through the familiar checks and preparations that were a part of every pilot's routine before starting the engine. It was a process he had done hundreds of times before, but this time it felt as alien as it did automatic. It was as though his body was completing the movements, but his mind was a detached, slightly confused onlooker.

The deafening roar of the mighty engine coming to life cut through this strange reverie and drew his attention back into focus. The ground crews cleared away the chocks from his and Harcourt's aircraft. He looked over towards Harcourt's Spitfire and saw the Squadron Leader signalling him to take off first. He released the brakes and felt the beautiful aeroplane start to roll forward, eager to gain speed and leave the earth behind. Peter turned it onto the runway and closed the canopy.

Almost immediately, the normal smells of the Spitfire seemed to become infinitely more intense. He felt a powerful claustrophobic impulse grip and almost overwhelm him. He fought hard for several seconds to regain his self-control and breathe normally again, but he could feel his heart still racing. He had no choice though, he had to push through with this. He opened the throttle and felt the tremendous surge of acceleration as the Spitfire sped down the runway and took to the sky.

Once airborne he felt himself begin to settle, and his breathing became more regular. Perhaps he was going to be alright after all.

"Red Leader calling Red Two. Can you read me?" Harcourt's voice came through on the R/T.

"Yes, Red Leader, Red Two answering."

"Okay Red Two. Let's go up to Angels 12 and try a few aerobatics, shall we? We have the sky to ourselves."

"Okay Red Leader. Anything in particular?"

"Red Two. Show me what you've got," came the reply.

Once they reached twelve thousand feet, Peter led the way with a series of rolls, loops and Immelmann turns. Very quickly, their simple aerobatics turned in to a mock dogfight, each trying to get onto the tail of the other.

Once again, Peter found himself revelling in the pure joy of flying the finest aircraft ever built. After ten minutes of playing aerial games, Peter heard Harcourt call him on the R/T.

"OK Red Two. Beautiful flying Peter. That's enough for now, let's head home."

Peter felt himself relax for the first time in days and slowly turned his aircraft on a heading back towards the airfield. Momentarily lost in his thoughts, he didn't notice as Harcourt brought his Spitfire alongside his own. Peter caught the movement to his right out of his peripheral vision and looked over towards Harcourt's Spitfire. It was in exactly the same relative position as Mark's had been only three days earlier.

The unexpected sight of the Spitfire suddenly triggered an uncontrollable cascade of images in Peter's mind. In his mind, the aircraft was now engulfed in flames and once again Mark's voice was screaming in agony and terror through the headphones.

Peter desperately slid back the cockpit's canopy and started frantically screaming Mark's name into the R/T. Gavin Harcourt looked on in horrified shock at this extraordinary and frightening change in the man he had been flying alongside. He could do nothing except call out to Peter, but he was beyond hearing anyone at this moment.

Peter was looking straight at him, but it was clearly a different aeroplane, in a horrifically different circumstance that he was seeing. Harcourt eased his Spitfire away and behind Peter's in the hope that his absence might let Peter regain some control. After a minute, it did. Peter gradually became aware that the airspace alongside him was now empty and he went quiet on the R/T.

After a minute, a shaken Harcourt spoke again. "Red Leader calling. Are you okay Red Two?"

A few seconds later, a weak voice came back with the reply. "I think so Red Leader. I'm sorry…"

"Okay Red Two. We'll talk about it later. Are you okay to get us back to Redhill? We've strayed way off course and I don't know the landmarks around here yet."

"I'm okay now Red Leader. Follow me."

***

The flight controllers on the ground at RAF Redhill had heard Peter's breakdown, in all its agony, coming through the static over the R/T transmission.

They had alerted the fire tenders and an ambulance to be on hand as the two Spitfires approached to make their landing. In the event, the landings were unremarkable; Peter had regained his composure adequately enough to lead Harcourt back to Redhill and bring the aircraft in safely. He had left the canopy open for the remainder of the flight. The cockpit had become stiflingly claustrophobic for him with it closed. He taxied the Spitfire towards the Dispersal Hut and Harcourt drew up alongside, looking intently in Peter's direction.

No sooner had he drawn to a standstill and shut down the engine, than an aircraftman had leapt onto the left wing and was opening the cockpit's side hatch. Peter was oblivious to his presence for few moments as he fought to control his emotions and thoughts. The depth of his reaction had shocked himself as much as it had his new C/O. The power in the imagery of Mark's burning Spitfire had completely overwhelmed him. It didn't seem to be a mere chimaera, it felt as real as if he were living the moment again. Sitting in the now silent cockpit, he started shaking at the thought of the experience.

He was drawn out of this dark introspection, by the aircraftsman shaking him by the shoulder. Harcourt had jumped out of his aircraft and came running over to Peter's. He climbed up onto the other wing just as Peter was clearing his head of his demons.

He almost shouted at Peter. "What the hell happened up there? Are you okay now?" his voice a confused mixture of anger and concern.

Peter wearily pulled his leather flying helmet and goggles off and buried his face in his hands. He broke down into uncontrollable tears, sobbing seemingly from the very depths of his soul. Both the aircraftman and Harcourt stood upright from their hunched positions, leaning over Peter. This was a situation neither of them were familiar with nor knew how to manage. Harcourt looked sadly at Peter and turned to the ambulance men that now were waiting just behind the rear of the wing. He had no choice but to turn Peter over to them.

***

Dr Hennessy had finished reviewing the notes on Peter's chart but continued looking at the page, giving himself time to think before lifting his head and addressing the patient.

"Well my lad," he finally uttered, "the medical profession is just beginning to devote more serious study to conditions like this. Psychiatry is far from my area of speciality. I've done some reading over the last few days, since you were first admitted after what happened to Squadron Leader Charters."

He hung the clipboard with the notes back onto the end of Peter's bed and came around beside him, pulling up a chair and sitting down.

Peter looked forlorn, lying back in a hospital bed for the third time in short succession.

Dr Hennessy continued, "From my reading, I think I can offer you some quite positive news. You are far from being the first person ever to succumb to this type of condition. It seems that being an active participant in war tends to place you in circumstances of extremely high stress and continuous risk. I'm sure that's of no surprise to you whatsoever."

He broke the moment with a smile.

"We all seem to have different ways of dealing with the stress. For some, it never seems to have any real effect on them, they just carry on as though the war was a normal part of their existence. For others, it can have the quite opposite effect."

He adjusted his glasses and leaned closer to Peter.

"I've also read over your service file Peter, the more I look at the last two years of your life, the less surprised I am to see this happen."

Peter looked at him with renewed interest. "What do you mean?"

Dr Hennessy's eyebrows raised as he paused for a moment and clarified his thoughts.

"Well, you've left your home and family and travelled, quite literally, half-way around the world. You've joined the RAF and learned the gentle art of killing other young men in fast aeroplanes. You've now had well over a year of unrelenting, deadly action. You've seen friends die; you've killed men yourself."

Peter motioned to speak but Dr Hennessy put up his hand to stop him. "Don't try and tell me that it's just your job, something like that is never just a job and don't tell me it doesn't affect you, because I know that it does. Part of the reason you're here now is because it does."

Peter lay back, and Hennessy's own posture relaxed again. "Most recently, you've just been through a traumatic physical experience with your own crash, which must have had some kind of emotional effect on you. Last of all, you've just experienced the utter horror of a ring-side seat – if you'll forgive the expression – to the ghastly death of a man who I believe was your closest friend here."

He paused for a moment again to regather his thoughts. Peter lay back, staring up at the ceiling, deep in thought himself after hearing Dr Hennessy's words.

"Peter, as I've said, this isn't my area, so I'm going to recommend that the Air Force involve a psychiatrist in your case. I do believe that you will come through all of this, it will simply take time."

"How much time?" asked Peter, suddenly becoming anxious and agitated at the thought of being referred to a psychiatrist. "Are they going to send me to the loony bin? Will I be discharged from the Air Force?"

His mind was racing away in a cascade of negativity. Dr Hennessy leaned forward and put his hand on Peter's forearm, trying to calm him.

"I can't tell you how long, I'll need to leave that to the specialist, but I very much doubt that you'll be sent to a psychiatric institution or that you'll be discharged from the service. Your record is that of an elite flyer, you're a valuable commodity young man! The Air Force will not want to lose you."

Peter relaxed slightly, though he was clearly still tense and nervous.

After a minute, Dr Hennessy stood up. "Well Peter, I have to leave you now in the tender care of the nursing staff here. I do believe that you should have no problems in that regard!"

He raised his eyebrows and gave Peter a knowing smile.

"I am obliged to have a meeting with the new Squadron Leader and let him know my recommendations. Do you have any problems with my doing that?"

Peter shook his head. "No, please be my guest. Let them know how hopeless I've turned out to be."

Hennessy frowned. "Enough of that please! Or else I'll start instructing Nurse Galloway to give you large doses of Ipecac syrup three times a day."

Peter managed a weak smile.

"That's better," said Dr Hennessy. "Now, I want you to rest, and to try and think more positive thoughts. I have no doubt at all that you're going to be fine, it just might take a little while."

He left the room and made his way up to the administration building to speak to Squadron Leader Harcourt before he went back to his own practice.

***

Anne had seen Dr Hennessy leave the hospital and begin his walk towards the airfield. She quickly went into Peter's room to see how he was. Peter looked up at her as she stood beside his bed, and let out a long, weary sigh. She sat down on the edge of his bed and cupped the side of his face in her hand. Peter managed a smile of sorts as she gazed at him.

"Well, the good doctor seems to think that I need to be handed over to a 'Shrink'. God knows what'll happen then, they might put me up as an LMF case and shove me in prison."

Anne was shocked at the darkness of his thoughts.

"Lack of Moral Fibre? You? I don't know how you could even think such a thing! Anyone looking at your record can see that isn't true!"

Peter sighed again. "That's pretty much what Hennessy said. I just… I just…"

He put his hand over his eyes and despite his best efforts, began to sob deeply, his body convulsing as the tears tore at him. Anne leaned down and put her arms around him, holding him tightly for several minutes until he was able to regain some control over his fragile emotions again. When she released him and sat up again, she was shocked to realise that she had been crying as well. Peter saw the tears on her face and managed the first real smile Anne had seen from him in days.

"What a fine pair we are, look at us!" he said.

Anne grasped his hands and fixed her gaze on him intently. "Don't you ever forget that we are a fine pair! You are not in this alone, don't you ever forget that! I'm seeing qualities in you now that just make me love you more. If it takes the two of us to get you through this, then that's the way it's going to be!"

The two of them remained, almost frozen in that moment, for several long seconds. Finally, Peter sat up and the two of them hugged each other powerfully, almost desperately. Anne was the one who broke the embrace. She released him and reached for his hands.

"You are going to be fine, that's all you need to know. Now, I must get about my duties; you're not the only patient in here you know. Why, anyone might think I'm showing you some sort of favouritism!"

She stood up and stepped back from the bed, straightening her uniform and her hair.

"How do I look, not too dishevelled?"

Peter couldn't help but smile. "You look exactly like the angel you are."

Anne almost felt another tear well up again, this was the most positive she had seen him in days. She realised that the powerful release of emotion he experienced a few minutes earlier had actually done him a world of good. Peter seemed to be thinking the same thing.

"Wow! I remember my Mum telling me years ago that sometimes, a good cry was the best medicine, maybe she was right."

Anne smiled again. "Well, she was the wife of a doctor, she must have picked up a few hints along the way."

Peter was still smiling when Anne left the room. Once outside, she leaned against the wall of the corridor and exhaled slowly. Her minutes with Peter had eventually proved to be positive, but emotionally taxing none the less.

***

"It's good to see you up and about Peter," said Squadron Leader Harcourt.

He had come down to the hospital to have what he knew was going to be a difficult conversation with Peter. He was surprised to see Peter in uniform and sitting out in the sun at the same table where he had chatted with Anne several months before. Harcourt had sat and listened to Dr Hennessy's briefing the previous day and had finally made his decision as to what must be done with his senior Flight Lieutenant.

"Good morning, Sir," replied Peter, "would like to join me for a cup of tea?"

"Thank you, Peter, I will if you don't mind."

He sat down across the table and proceeded to pour himself a cup from the tea service that sat in between the two of them. Taking his first sip, he put the cup down onto its saucer and leaned forward.

"Peter, I have some news, I'd rather you hear it from me than second hand. I'm sure it'll be all over the station before too long."

Peter gazed intently at Harcourt, both interested and concerned.

"Peter, the squadron is being posted overseas, we are to be leaving within a week. We haven't been told exactly where just yet but it'll be somewhere in the Med, that will mean either Malta or North Africa."

Peter continued to hold his gaze, not speaking, but he knew what was coming next. Harcourt braced himself for his next words.

"Peter, you won't be coming with us. Clearly, you're in no condition to be on Ops yet, and we can't take you along as a passenger."

Peter picked up his teacup and took a sip.

"Well then, what will happen to me?" he asked in an even voice, trying hard not to betray the desperate anxiety that he was feeling. Harcourt took another sip of tea himself; he was hoping that the next piece of news would be well received.

"Peter, I had a long discussion with Dr Hennessy yesterday afternoon. He feels very positive about your prospects and recovery from... whatever this condition is that you're experiencing. I'm sorry I put it like that, I'm new to this myself."

Peter nodded understandingly.

"Anyway," continued Harcourt, "the doctor believes that with suitable specialist help, you'll be able to resume flying duties in due course. He actually paints a very promising picture of your recovery."

"So, has a decision been reached about me?" asked Peter, a quiver of nervousness showing in his voice.

"Well, there are a couple of options; the first is that we take you off flight duties altogether and send you to work with a psychiatrist until he thinks you're OK to go back to an operational squadron. No one can know how long that might be. It could keep you out of an aircraft for a long time. There is a second possibility however, which I suspect might appeal to you more."

Harcourt left this point hanging whilst he sipped more of his tea. Peter continued to stare intently at him as he awaited Harcourt's next words.

"The other option is a posting to an Operational Training Unit as a flight instructor. There will be a psychiatrist available for you to have regular consultations with, and I thought that being able to keep flying might be good for you also."

Peter sat back in surprise at this unexpected consideration.

"You have a wealth of experience that would be invaluable to pass onto the flight cadets and their training aircraft might prove less intimidating than a Spitfire. At least, until you're ready to get back into one. How does that sound to you?"

Peter felt as though an enormous weight had been lifted from his shoulders. He wasn't being grounded; he would still be able to fly!

"Sir… I would welcome that as a choice. That's the most important thing for me, being able to return to duty. If this is the best way to get there, then I would gratefully accept that option."

"I thought that might be your response, I'm delighted to hear you sound so positive about it. It sounds very much as though Dr Hennessy's opinion of you is entirely correct. I must admit, I didn't have you pegged as a shirker either."

Peter was taken somewhat aback at the thought that there were some who might have been thinking of him in those terms. The accusation of 'Lack of Moral Fibre' was perhaps the most serious allegation a serviceman could face. It was viewed as nothing less than a euphemism for cowardice. Peter was being spared that particular stigma.

He gathered his thoughts and spoke, "What happens now Sir? When do things start to happen?"

Harcourt put down his teacup. "Well, there's an OTU not too far from here, at RAF Heston. I've already taken the liberty of speaking to Group Captain Hawthorne about it and he's making arrangements for you to go over there. They seem quite keen to have you join them in fact. Before you go there though, I should let you know that you're being given a ten day leave pass. Dr Hennessy convinced the Group Captain and me that some time away from an Air Force environment might also prove highly beneficial to your recovery."

Peter looked shocked. "Ten days leave? But I don't know anyone outside the Air Force that I could stay with! I've got no idea where I could go."

Harcourt was fighting the impulse to smile. "We're not complete fools you know. We're well aware of what a menace you would be to yourself and to England if you were let loose alone. That is why someone else has just been informed that she is now on ten days leave also."

Harcourt motioned for Peter to turn around and look over his shoulder. Anne was standing in the doorway of the hospital looking at the two of them, her face beaming in a radiant smile.

***

Peter's kit had been packed and left for him to collect in the front office of the administration building. His delight at the thought of spending time with Anne on leave had been quickly tempered with the reality that he would be saying goodbye to his friends and comrades from 371 Squadron.

The grimly hazardous nature of their posting meant that it would be quite probable he would never see many of them again. He made his way around the airfield and called into all the hangars, looking for the ground crews who always kept the aircraft flying, but never seemed to be given the recognition their tireless efforts deserved.

Peter was determined that he would not leave without shaking the hand of every member of the ground staff that he knew. They, in turn, were delighted that he had made the effort and were all deeply sad to see him leave the squadron. He was the last of the old Battle of Britain flight crew left. His leaving the squadron was a melancholy moment for everyone. After he had finished his rounds, he went over to the Officers' Mess to say farewell to his fellow pilots.

Group Captain Hawthorne was there along with the officer contingent of 371 Squadron and many from the other squadrons that also shared RAF Redhill. Peter only allowed himself a single beer, he was still on medications and was walking an emotional tightrope. He couldn't afford to have his tenuous self-control slip. The Mess was rapidly developing into a raucous party atmosphere so Peter quietly made his way over to Group Captain Hawthorne to say his farewell.

"Thank you for everything you've done for me Sir. It's been a privilege to have served with you."

"The privilege has been mine Peter. All the very best to you, especially with Anne! Don't let me hear that you've let that girl get away now."

Peter smiled warmly. "Don't worry Sir. I'm not that sick."

"Excellent, now you get yourself right. Don't expect it to happen instantly, it may take a while, just listen to the doctors. Away with you now, Godspeed to you Peter."

Peter shook his hand one last time and quietly slipped out of the Mess. He returned to the administration building one last time and collected his kitbag and suitcase. There was an Air Force car waiting for him, then he would go and collect Anne from her room where she had been doing her own packing. After that, it would deliver them to the station to catch the first available train up to London. The two of them were going to stay with Anne's father, Alistair for the first few days whilst they planned their leave. For the next, brief window of time, they could forget about the war and learn how to be together and in love.

Chapter 6

November 1941

"How did she feel Sir? A bit different to a Spit?"

"Absolutely delightful!" replied Peter. "What a beautiful little kite she is."

He had just climbed out of the open cockpit of one of the De Havilland Tiger Moths that filled the role of basic trainer at the Operational Training School.

"Must have reminded you of your early training, did it Sir?"

The aircraftman was unexpectedly chatty as Peter was occupied with removing his flight helmet, goggles and gauntlets. He didn't mind as the flight in the simple biplane had left him feeling refreshed and invigorated, and he realised the man was just 'feeling him out', trying to get some idea of what the new officer was like.

"Actually, it's the first time I've ever flown one," he replied. "I did all my early flight training on an Avro 504. This is a lot more fun than that was."

"Really Sir? All the lads were saying that you were flying it like you were born in it."

Peter turned smiling towards the aircraftman. "I'm sorry, I don't know your name?"

"My name is Jones, Sir, Leading Aircraftman Ian Jones," the man replied.

Peter extended his hand and they shook, Jones seemed taken aback by the gesture.

"Excuse me Sir, but we don't get many officers who shake hands with us."

Peter laughed. "I guess I haven't quite got used to being an officer and a gentleman. I came up through the ranks myself. I much prefer a bit of informality if I can get away with it."

Jones smiled himself. "Just to let you know Sir, most of the senior officers here do like to keep things rather formal. I think it's because of all the cadets in training, they want them to understand the correct order of things."

Peter tapped the side of his nose. "Thanks for the 'heads up'. I'll try to be as military as possible if the 'Brass' are around."

He and Jones saluted in affable farewell and Peter made his way across the tarmac to the main building where he was due to commence the day tutoring his assigned group of cadets.

It now was his third day at RAF Heston and his second day on duty as an instructor.

The first day was spent familiarising himself with the two main advanced training aircraft he would be using, the Harvard and the Anson. It was the moment he had been most apprehensive about, his first flight since his mid-air breakdown with Harcourt, a fortnight earlier.

Fortunately, the Harvard turned out to be such a different aircraft to the Spitfire that the memories which might have triggered a response from him, never surfaced. The Anson was different again. He could feel himself relaxing as his familiarity with the new aircraft grew. He took that positivity into his first appointment with the psychiatrist, later in the afternoon.

Peter had no idea what to expect as he was ushered into the consulting room. His constant dwelling on the thought had built up a heightened sense of anxiety at the notion of going into psychiatric care. In the end, it proved to be a profound anti-climax. The psychiatrist introduced himself as Dr Markham. He didn't have horns or a forked tail and seemed very content just to sit with Peter and talk.

He led him around to the trauma of Mark's death and the ceaseless stress of the preceding year. Towards the end of the session, he steered Peter towards discussing the positive things in his life. They spoke of Anne and the short break they had just had together. Of how Peter had bonded so quickly with Anne's father Alistair, a man very much like his own father in so many ways. They spoke of Peter's love of flying and how it made him feel when he first learned. In the end, Peter found himself looking forward to their future sessions. He had experienced some good days recently. His first full day at RAF Heston had proven to be another one.

***

May 1942

1942 had begun with the growing realisation of what the war meant – now that the USA was in the thick of it. The Japanese attack on Pearl Harbor had instantly changed the complexion of the struggle in Europe as well. To the people of Great Britain, they now knew they were no longer alone. Thoughts could now embrace ambitions that extended beyond merely holding out. For many, they could now dare to dream of victory. The tide hadn't turned yet, but the ebb was fast slowing. Soon enough, the flow would commence.

***

Dr Markham sat back in his chair and paused briefly to look over his notes. "It's nearly six months that you've been here Peter. I have my own thoughts on how you've progressed. I should like to hear how you are feeling about things. Do you feel that these sessions have been worthwhile?"

Peter exhaled and collected his thoughts. "Well, I guess they must have been. I just feel like myself really. I don't know how else to put it. It's been a while since I've felt that I don't have control of myself. In fact, last night I was thinking about Mark a lot. I wasn't thinking about how he died. Just about the fun we had. I missed his company. I'm not sure I'll ever have a better friend."

Dr Markham looked at Peter for a while before replying. "You may not realise it, but that is the statement of a very well-adjusted man. I think your progress has been remarkable. Over my years of practice, I've seen many men with severe battlefield stress. Both from this war, and many still suffering from what they went through in the last one."

He paused to adjust his glasses. "I've learned that some men never seem to be able to return from the depths of their torment. I have also seen many examples of men who, with the right environment and the right support, come back remarkably well. I am very confident that you are in that category Flight Lieutenant. I propose that whilst I should like to see you on a monthly basis for the time being, I intend to sign you off as being fully fit for service again. How does that sound to you?"

Peter's eyes widened. Even though he had come to welcome his meetings with Dr Markham and was well aware of how much better he felt about himself, he was still deeply conscious of the stigma that attached to being in psychiatric care.

"Thank you Doctor! That's wonderful! Does this mean I can go back to an operational squadron?"

His question took Dr Markham completely by surprise.

"I presume so. I have nothing to do with that side of things. I should like you to remain close by for a while at least though. I think it's important that I am able to see you monthly for at least the next three months or so. You've done very well Peter, but don't let's get too ambitious just yet."

"So, you think I should stay here as an instructor for a while yet? It isn't what I joined the RAF to do."

Markham took off his glasses and leaned forward.

"Peter, as you know, I have regular meetings with Wing Commander Leveret here to keep him updated on your progress. If I may risk breaching a confidence with him, he regards you as perhaps the best flying instructor he's ever had here. It's not just your ability as a pilot, which you seem to have a remarkable ability to pass on to your protégés, it's also your combat experience. Those cadets that train under you, leave here better prepared to face the reality of air fighting than those of any other instructor, so I've been told."

Peter sat back, amazed to hear these words.

"I had no idea. I just teach them with what I think they need to know if they are to survive and succeed."

Dr Markham nodded in agreement, putting his glasses back on.

"My point exactly. Don't underestimate the contribution you are making here. There are men here right now who will survive this war because of the quality of the instruction you are providing them. If it is your wish to return to an operational squadron, I would certainly never recommend against it, but I do suggest you take a little more time to think it through. Your presence here is highly valued."

Peter's shoulders slightly slumped as he sat back in his seat.

"Do you know Doctor; I've never even stopped to give that a thought. I must admit that I've viewed my time here as a sort of penance for my failures before. I had promised myself that I would go back into an operational squadron as soon as I was given the OK."

Markham leaned forward in his chair. "My recommendation, purely personal, is that you think about it for a while first. That's all. I'm a civilian. I can't give you orders, just advice."

Peter smiled warmly. "Your advice has always served me extremely well so far Doctor. Perhaps I might give myself some time to think things through first."

Dr Markham stood up, indicating that the consultation was over. Peter stood also.

"Well Peter, I shall expect to see you in a month's time. I hope you feel proud of yourself. You should. I flatter myself that I may also take some small credit for helping you get to this point."

Peter gave him a huge grin. "Do you realise that I was terrified the first time I came in here? I had no idea what to expect."

Doctor Markham laughed loudly. "I get that all the time. Everybody seems to think that we can read people's minds or control them with ungodly mind tricks. Psychiatry is just a new branch of medicine. That's all. We're just trying to find ways of helping people who have emotional, not physical ailments. It's rather fascinating actually. I can assure you, we get just as great a thrill when a patient of ours recovers, as any other doctor does."

"Well," said Peter, "this particular patient feels very much in your debt. Thank you for everything, Doctor."

They shook hands warmly, and Peter saw himself out.

***

He had never needed a car before. His whole life in England had been contained within the confines of different RAF bases. If he had ever needed to travel by car, it was in the company of some of his friends, many of whom owned their own vehicles and could give him a lift.

But now, things had changed. His posting at RAF Heston was about forty miles from where Anne continued to work at RAF Redhill, and the distance between them was maddening. He had now been at Heston for over a year, and in order for him and Anne to see one and other, they each had to catch separate trains into London. It had finally proved too inconvenient and wasteful of their limited free time.

He never set out to live frugally, but as most of his needs were met by living on base, Peter had managed to save most of his pay. It was time to spend some of that on what was to be the first car he would ever own. That car turned out to be a beautiful Alvis 'Firefly' saloon. Although it was nearly eight years old, it was in perfect condition. Peter loved the look of it and the quality of the engineering.

"Better than a Bentley!" he was told by the man at the garage where it was up for sale. The deal was soon done and Peter drove back to the airfield, happily crunching gears and occasionally wandering over the road as he endeavoured to master the skills of driving - something considerably more complex than his father's old and very basic Austin.

That evening he rang Anne.

"Do you think you might be available for dinner on Saturday at The Plough?" he asked.

"So, you've gone ahead and done it then? You bought the car?" replied Anne excitedly.

"I certainly did, and I insist that you be my first passenger. Some of the lads here are a bit put out because I won't let them ride in it until you have. So you see, you really have no choice. My life may depend on it!"

Anne laughed, the lilt of her happiness carrying down the phone line to Peter.

"Well, since you put it so romantically, what choice do I have, but to accept?"

"Wonderful!" replied Peter enthusiastically. "What time do you get off?"

"I'm supposed to be on until 5, but it's been rather quiet ever since 371 shipped out. I'm sure Matron will let me finish an hour or two early."

The mention of his old squadron caught Peter's breath for a moment. He had missed seeing them leave and had heard nothing of them in the meantime. He didn't even know where their final posting had been. He quickly regathered his thoughts.

"I certainly hope she does, will you be able to ring me tomorrow and let me know? I have the whole weekend off so I can come over and be there to meet you at the end of your shift."

"I shall, I must go now, duty calls. Good night my Darling," said Anne tenderly.

"Good night, sweetheart. See you soon," replied Peter.

After he hung up the phone, he reached into his trouser pocket and took out the small box which contained the second major purchase he had made recently. He flipped up the lid and looked down at the contents. He had every hope of making Saturday evening a very special one indeed.

***

Anne had found the Matron more than happy to allow her to finish her Saturday shift early. She had surprised Anne still further by suggesting she finish at 1pm instead of the 3 o'clock that she had asked for. Anne had no idea that Peter had already rung the Matron and told her of what he had planned for their evening. The Matron was more than delighted to be able to play her part. Peter had left Heston earlier than he needed to and found himself with some spare time once he arrived back at Redhill. He made his way up to the administration building and asked if Group Captain Hawthorne might be available.

Hawthorne immediately asked for him to be sent through to his office.

"Peter my boy! How wonderful to see you," Hawthorne was genuinely delighted to see him again. "How are you? You're looking well again. I'm hearing very impressive accounts of how fine an instructor you've become."

"Thank you, Sir, it's good to see you again too. I hope you don't mind my dropping in like this?"

"Not at all Peter. I'm not really supposed to be here today anyway, but I just wanted to tidy up some paperwork. Was there something in particular you wanted to see me about?"

"Well... yes Sir. I was just wanting to know about 371 really. I have heard nothing since I left here. I don't even know where they were posted to."

"Ahh! I see," said Hawthorne thoughtfully. "Well if I was in your position, I should be deeply curious too. I guess it's probably safe to let you know that they were posted to North Africa. They got there in time to have an important role in providing air support during the breakout from El Alamein. I suspect at this moment, they're all heavily sun-tanned and living it up in Cairo."

Peter smiled. "Have you heard what casualties they've had Sir?"

"I haven't heard anything for many months really. I know they lost three between leaving the Aircraft Carrier and when they landed to refuel in Malta, but everyone else made it from there to Alex safely."

Peter looked concerned at the news.

"No one you would have known Peter, replacements that joined the squadron after that first encounter with the Focke-Wulfs. Like all junior pilots, they got given the worst of the available planes. Impossible to know what really happened, they just never arrived in Malta."

Peter nodded quietly. "Thanks for letting me know Sir. Obviously, I'll keep it all to myself."

"I know you will. Anyway Peter, tell me, how are you feeling about things now? Do you ever have any thoughts about getting back into an operational squadron again?"

Peter smiled. "All the time Sir. I do appreciate the value of what I'm doing at the moment, but there are other good instructors now. I think I have more to offer than just instructing."

"I thought you might say something like that. I was having a chat with an old friend a few days ago. Would you mind if I was to mention your name to him? I think he might be keen to give you a call."

Peter was slightly taken aback by this cryptic offer. Still, he was intrigued enough to want to know more.

"By all means Sir, I'm fascinated now."

"Excellent, you should be! Anyway, I have to bid you farewell I'm afraid Peter. I have a wife waiting at home who has my afternoon minutely planned. Gardening, I believe!" he rolled his eyes.

Peter laughed and then said in a slightly conspiratorial manner, "I have to let you know Sir, that I have plans for this evening that might see me in a similar circumstance before too long."

Hawthorne's eyes lit up. "Really? Well my goodness! What will you do if she says no?"

Peter looked horrified. "Oh hell! I hadn't thought of that!"

Hawthorne laughed again. "Don't worry Peter, she won't. I was just having a little fun at your expense. My very best wishes to you both. I do hope I might swing an invitation to the nuptials?"

"Of course Sir. Actually, I was hoping you might be the one to give me away!"

Several people in the corridor outside of Hawthorne's office stopped and gawped at the sound of raucous laughter coming from the room. It was not a sound they were used to hearing in wartime.

***

Peter had planned to propose to Anne at dinner in the evening. However, circumstances got in the way.

Anne's early finish gave them some time to kill before going to the old pub called The Plough, which was only a few miles from the airfield.

It was such a lovely mid-autumn day that they decided to go and relax by Earlswood Lake, a popular local picnic spot. They lay down on the grass under a shady tree near the water and Anne snuggled into Peter happily.

"What on earth is that?" she asked as she bumped against a hard, angular lump in his pocket.

Peter had forgotten to take the ring box out of his pocket and secrete it in his bags.

"Oh… it's nothing!" he said in a painfully awkward attempt at being offhand.

Anne grasped the moment. "Come on! What is it? I'm going to tickle you until you tell me!"

She started to tickle him enthusiastically up the sides of his chest and under his arms.

"Come on, tell me!" she was giggling like a schoolgirl as she teased him.

Peter laughed, squirmed and grew redder with embarrassment as Anne was pinning him down.

"All right then, if you are so determined to upset my plans for tonight."

Peter reached into his trouser pocket and brought out the little jewellery box and held it up to Anne who was now sitting firmly on his chest. Slowly, she slid off him and knelt, sitting back on her heels, by his side. She opened the lid and promptly burst into howling tears.

"Oh yes! Yes! Yes!" she wailed through a torrent of tears and threw herself on top of him, kissing him fiercely.

After several minutes, Anne had regained her composure, sat up and tried the ring on. She held her hand out at arm's length taking in the sight of the ring on her finger.

"It's a perfect fit, how did you know?"

"I had help; your dad measured one of your other rings for me," said Peter.

"So, my father knew?" said Anne with a grin. "Anyone else?"

"Well... I did call Matron and tell her," said Peter blushing.

"Peter!" said Anne in astonishment. "So that was why she let me off so early today! I had no idea you could be so cunning, anyone else?"

"Well... most of the chaps at Heston know. Also, I did let it slip to Group Captain Hawthorne. He gives us his best wishes by the way, and also the people at the Pub tonight. They've got a bottle of champagne chilling for us."

"So what you're really telling me is that half of southern England knows! The only one who didn't know was me!" said Anne in happy umbrage.

"Well, I did want to do it right. That does take a bit of planning you know and then I mucked it up by forgetting to put the ring back in my bag before I saw you."

Anne smiled contentedly again and lay back down beside him.

"You do realise that you haven't actually proposed to me yet. I don't recall hearing the proper words from you," she said with a grin.

"That's because I couldn't get a word in edgeways! Also, you were crying so much, I wasn't sure if I was proposing to you or to Niagara Falls."

Anne rolled onto her back laughing uproariously.

After a minute she said, "Yes, you might be right there. It wasn't quite the dignified reaction that I had planned and rehearsed in my mind several thousand times. The emotion slightly got the better of me."

"You can say that again! However, since you insist..." Peter lifted himself up and steadied himself on one knee and took both of her hands in his.

"Anne Galloway, you would make me the happiest man alive if you would consent to become my wife. Would you like to live out your days with this mere colonial who loves you with all of his heart?"

Anne smiled impishly. "I seem to recall that I've already said 'yes'. I certainly see no reason to change my mind now, not after all the trouble you've gone to!"

"The most gracious acceptance that I could ever have hoped for," said Peter with a happy smile.

Chapter 7

April 1943

"You're coming along well enough Ian," said Peter as he and the cadet pilot he was tutoring walked away from the Anson. "You just need to develop some more finesse in the way you handle it, especially on landings. You're still a bit ham fisted. It'll come; it's just flying hours that you need."

His cadet, Ian Anderson was looking distressed.

"I've logged over thirty hours now Sir. I should be doing better."

Peter chuckled. "Don't be too hard on yourself Ian, those thirty hours are on four different types. You haven't had long enough on any one type to really get a feel for it. When it all comes together, you'll be a damn good pilot with solid skills on single engines as well as multis. Now, go and get changed and head over to the Mess for some lunch, it's been a full morning."

"Yes Sir," said the young cadet, saluting and leaving Peter standing on the tarmac.

His attention was promptly drawn to a WAAF who was hurrying towards him.

"Excuse me Flight Lieutenant!" her voice carried across the diminishing distance.

"Good morning Helen. What's up?"

"Sorry to bother you, but there's a Group Captain in the office who's wanting to see you."

"Really!" exclaimed Peter in some surprise. "Did he say what it's about?"

"No Sir, he's not really said much at all."

"I wonder what's up? Did he tell you his name?"

"I believe his name is Group Captain Trehearn, Sir," he replied.

"Trehearn!" exclaimed Peter in even greater surprise. "Shortish chap with a waxed moustache?"

"That's him Sir. You must know him."

"He was my old C/O at 371. I haven't seen him in ages, I wonder what brings him down here?" Peter turned to the WAAF with a beaming smile. "Well then Helen, lead on. It won't do to keep the Group Captain waiting now, will it!?"

As soon as they came through the front door, Trehearn stood up from the lumpy, uncomfortable chair that was one of several so afflicted, placed in the foyer. The two former colleagues were obviously both delighted to be in each other's company again.

"How good to see you again Peter. You're looking excellent. Married life is clearly agreeing with you!" said Trehearn.

"It's been nearly six months now Sir. We're almost like a boring old married couple these days. You're looking well too Sir. What on earth brings you down to our neck of the woods?"

Trehearn's face took on a more serious look.

"I was wondering if I might have a few minutes of your time Peter. There's something I'd rather like to discuss with you."

Peter suddenly guessed what might be coming.

"Yes, indeed Sir. If you like, we could chat on the way over to the Officers' Mess and then over lunch."

"Excellent idea!" Replied Trehearn. "Would you care to lead the way?"

"If you don't mind giving me five minutes Sir, I just need to change out of my flight suit. They're a bit more formal in the Mess here with so many cadets around."

"Of course Peter, I'll wait."

Once they were clear of the office and out in the open air, Trehearn broached his subject.

"Some months ago, I was chatting with an old friend at Redhill. He mentioned to me that you might be interested in returning to an active operational role."

Peter smiled. "I do seem to recall saying something to that effect to Group Captain Hawthorne shortly before I got married Sir. He told me that he knew someone who might be interested in getting in touch with me. I had no idea that it was you he was thinking about. It seems so obvious now that you're here."

"Indeed. Now I'm sure you recall that I left 371 to go into Bomber Command. I was rather keen to get into one of the Mosquito squadrons that were just coming online back then."

"Yes Sir. I remember that well," said Peter.

They arrived at the Mess and found themselves a quiet table, after ordering sandwiches and a beer each. Trehearn picked up from where he finished earlier.

"Well, one thing has subsequently led to another and I am now a Group Captain in the PFF."

"PFF Sir?" asked Peter quizzically.

They paused briefly as their meals arrived. Then Trehearn continued. "PFF, the Pathfinder Force, Peter. A new idea, championed by one of your antipodean cousins in fact, an Australian chap by the name of Bennett. We've been operational for a good few months now. Quite a bit of resistance at first from those above. It took a while to get the senior staff behind the idea, but the results are now starting to become too positive for them to ignore."

Peter was listening avidly. "I've heard the name Pathfinders being spoken about the place, most of us have now. You go out ahead of the main bomber force. Identify and mark the targets with flares and incendiaries, is that right?"

Trehearn nodded, "That, and quite a bit besides!"

Peter continued, "I thought they were flying heavies? Stirlings and Lancasters."

"We do but we also have several squadrons of Mossies, there's quite a range of functions we're undertaking now. Bombing raids in their own right, meteorological reconnaissance flights, photo recon. Quite a varied set of operations really."

Peter was amazed at what he was hearing. "It sounds like this PFF is becoming an entirely separate department within the Air Force itself," he said, hoping he wasn't sounding too ignorant.

Trehearn nodded in agreement. "Still technically a part of Bomber Command, but it's taking on a life of its own. It's continuing to grow, hence my being here today." Trehearn stared closely at Peter. "Well, my lad? Are you interested?"

Peter exhaled slowly; his heart was pounding.

"I am indeed Sir, but I have to admit, I'm not too keen on the idea of flying heavies."

Trehearn laughed, "That's not a problem, you won't be, I have you marked for Mossies. Have you ever flown one, by the way?"

"No Sir. Though I have racked up my hours on twin engines now. What are they like to fly?"

Trehearn broke into a broad smile. "Tremendous fun, I remember how much you loved your Spitfire. You'll come to feel the same way about the Mosquito, they're a real pilot's aeroplane."

Peter swallowed hard; he knew he'd have some serious explaining to do to Anne. They had never talked about it, but inside he knew that she thought his days of combat flying were over. He could only guess at how she would take the news of him returning to operational flying.

"What do I have to do from here Sir?" he asked.

"I can't conscript you Peter; you need to volunteer."

"What is the process Sir? Do I need to write a letter to someone? Or is there a form I need to fill in?"

Trehearn smiled broadly. "There is a form to fill in, and to submit. Fortunately, for you I happen to have one with me."

He reached into the inner breast pocket of his uniform coat and withdrew an envelope. He held it teasingly for a moment before he handed it to Peter. Peter opened the envelope and withdrew the folded form. He opened it out and read it over.

"You've already filled it in for me! It appears that all I have to do is sign it."

"I've even brought a pen!" said Trehearn, unscrewing the cap off a fountain pen.

Peter sat still for a moment, deep in conflicted thought.

"Sir, my intention is to sign and submit this form to you and soon. But would you mind if I had the chance to talk it through with Anne first, please? I would feel better signing it after she knows. I don't think it would be fair to her otherwise."

"War is never fair Peter, but I do understand. That's fine of course. What will you do if she says no?"

It was Peter's turn to smile. "She won't, she might not like it, but she understands that I'm a Serviceman and that I have to do what is required of me. I just would like her to know that the final decision was made with her, not in spite of her."

Trehearn sat in contemplative silence for several seconds.

"I believe that if I were married, I would feel exactly the same way. When will you be seeing her next?" asked Trehearn.

"Saturday Sir. I'm planning to drive over to Redhill and spend the weekend with her. I'll send this off on Monday."

"Very well then Peter, may I have the envelope back please?"

Peter passed it to him and Trehearn proceeded to write his own name and address details on it, then he handed it back.

"There you go. When it's all signed, just mail it from here and I should get it a day or two later at the most. Things might start happening fairly quickly after that."

Peter put the folded-up form back in the envelope and slid it into the inside pocket of his tunic jacket.

"One more thing Sir, where would I be based? Where would I be posted to?" asked Peter.

"I intend for you to join one of my squadrons up in Cambridgeshire, Peter," replied Trehearn. "Excellent location for flying in over the low-countries and on into Germany."

Peter nodded and paused for a moment, looking pensive. Trehearn looked him expectantly.

"Out with it Peter, I can see there's something else on your mind."

"Well Sir… are you aware of what happened that led to my being here, as a flight instructor? I had a kind of nervous breakdown. It wasn't my finest hour."

"Of course I'm aware of it Peter. Well aware in fact, I was horrified to hear of Mark's death, and of how badly it affected you. But I'm also well aware of how well you've recovered. It's a credit to your strength of character, I think. I wouldn't be here now if I didn't have absolute confidence in you. Do you still have doubts about yourself?"

"As a matter-of-fact Sir, no I don't. I feel completely ready." Peter surprised even himself at just how prepared for this move he now felt. "This is the right thing for me, I know that I'm already looking forward to it."

"Excellent," replied Trehearn. "I thought that might be the case, I just couldn't see you being satisfied to sit out the rest of the war on the side-lines. I'm looking forward to having you back with me again."

Peter nodded emphatically, but he still had one more question on his mind. "On a personal level Sir, is there any possibility that there might be a position on the base for a very competent registered nurse as well?"

Trehearn chuckled. "I'll see what strings I might be able to pull, but I would say it's highly likely."

Peter smiled broadly and the two men shook hands.
"Okay!" said Peter. "Now comes the hard part!"

***

Anne sat in complete silence for many seconds after Peter told her of Trehearn's offer. It was the realisation of her deepest fear, suddenly brought to stark reality. She fought hard to bring her emotions under control before she spoke, managing to keep a veneer of calmness in both her voice and her demeanour.

"And do you want to do this?" she finally spoke.

Peter nodded. "Yes, I do. I hope you understand why."

She swallowed hard, not wanting to make eye contact with him yet. "I've been dreading this, I always worried that you might want to go back to the fighting."

Peter reached across the small table which constituted the dining room of Anne's tiny flat and took both her hands in his. He had rehearsed, many times in his mind, the words he wanted to say. Now those words were eluding him, struggling to find coherent form.

"I don't want to go back for some stupid reason, like because I enjoy the fighting. I don't. No one that I know of does but I can't sit on the side-lines anymore. I don't feel that I'm doing my part."

"Not doing your part?" Anne pulled back her hands and almost shouted at him. "I've had to nurse you back to health twice now. You've done your part, what you're doing now is important!"

"I know it's important! I do know what you've done for me," Peter's voice was almost as impassioned as Anne's. He exhaled and calmed himself before speaking again. "I know what you've done for me. I know how much this must terrify you. It frightens the hell out of me too!"

Peter reached for her hands again and spoke. This time the words came more easily to him.

"You know as well as anyone the circumstances that took me out of the fighting. You, more than anyone have helped me to heal. Thanks to you, I've now got something to live for. But if I just keep on as a flight instructor, a part of me will always wonder if I lost the nerve to ever do again what I'm training these other young pilots to do."

"Are you saying that you think of yourself as a coward?" Anne's question was brutal, but incisive.

Peter thought for a moment before replying. "I've never thought in those terms about it, but I do wonder if other people do."

"You worry that others think you're a coward?" once again, Anne went straight to the point.

"Frankly, yes I do! It is always there in the back of my mind. I've never really made any close friends at Heston. Everyone's always respectful and friendly up to a point, but no one has made the effort to include me too much if there's a shindig going on. I'm sure it's because they're unsure of me."

Anne said nothing, she realised that this was an important moment for her husband. He was clearly talking as much to himself as he was to her. Trying to understand what was driving this need he had to re-join the fray.

"I've always been aware of a distance with them. Even the mechanics! I always got on well with the 'Erks' at Redhill. Now, they say what they need to say and move on. It feels more like just a job now, than being part of a family. In 371, we felt like a family, I do miss that."

As she listened to him, she began to discern the unspoken issue that was still troubling Peter, the inner calling that was pulling him back into danger. He was no longer sure of his own self-worth.

"Will the flying be dangerous?" she was looking intently at him now; Peter sensed a change in her attitude. She was reluctantly coming to terms with the idea.

"I have no doubt it will have its moments!" he smiled, trying to make light of the idea. "But not so much for us as it will be for the main bomber force. They're the ones in the firing line, Mossies are fast, in and out. Locate the target, drop the markers and get out, they can outrun all the German fighters."

Peter hoped he sounded convincing. He had no true idea himself of what the reality might be.

"Where would you be posted to?" Anne's voice was flat. Asking questions as though she was now resigned to an outcome that she hated but felt powerless to avoid. She was just trying to fill in the gaps.

"A base called Wyton, up in Cambridgeshire, quite a large base apparently…"

Anne noticed his equivocation.

"What's wrong?" she asked with some concern.

"Nothing's wrong… It's just that… Okay! I'll say it. I asked Trehearn if there might be a position for you at the base hospital, assuming you agreed with me signing up, that is."

Anne felt an immediate, emotionally jarring shudder.

"I don't know whether to kiss you or hit you over the head with a saucepan! Are you saying that if I was to say no, you'd let this whole thing just drop? You'd stay where you are?"

It was suddenly Peter's turn to be lost for words.

"Ahhh, I guess so, I suppose," he said defensively. "I was rather hoping you wouldn't, but if you truly felt that strongly, then I would have to turn it down." Her words were not what he was expecting but he realised that had given her the latitude to consider all options.

Despite the immediate and powerful temptation to voice her stern opposition to the move, Anne intuitively understood that any sense of victory would be brief and pyrrhic at best. She realised that if Peter were to decline the offer, his Air Force career would be as good as over. It would be unlikely that he would ever be offered any opportunities for advancement again. Pilots less experienced and with fewer decorations than Peter were now Wing Commanders, whilst he remained a Flight Lieutenant. Furthermore, she wondered at the damage it might do to his still fragile self-respect. That in turn, might even have a catastrophic effect upon their marriage. As much as she would worry desperately about him, she could see no other course but to support him with the choice. Anne made up her mind.

"So, did he say for sure there was a position up there for me?" she asked wryly.

Peter brightened again. "He couldn't say for certain, but he is senior enough to pull some strings."

Anne nodded thoughtfully. "Then you'd better sign the damned form before I change my mind."

Peter could do no more than just sit and gaze at his beautiful wife, lost in the thought of how deeply in love with her he was.

Chapter 8

May 1943

"So, that's a Mosquito then?" asked Anne.

"I've been reliably informed that it is," replied Peter as he led her towards the sleek, twin-engine aircraft parked outside its hangar at RAF Wyton.

Nearly three weeks had passed since those tense moments in Anne's small flat in the village, just beyond the Redhill RAF base. They had arrived shortly before lunch and after seeing their belongings safely delivered to their new rooms in the married officer's quarters, they had decided to go for a walk around the base to get the feel of their new home.

"It certainly is a fine-looking thing," mused Anne aloud.

Once again, she was surprised at how an instrument of war, designed to undertake the cruellest and most destructive of human activities, could present itself as such a lithe and beautiful piece of machinery. She had felt a similar emotion the first time she had seen a Spitfire up close. Such grace and elegance of line and yet, its purpose was to kill. Together they walked around the aircraft, feeling the texture of the plywood panels through the layers of camouflage paint, marvelling at the resourcefulness that could conceive of using such material to build a modern weapon of war.

"When will they let you fly it?" asked Anne.

"I'll begin familiarisation flights tomorrow morning I presume," replied Peter. "Once we're settled in, it'll be straight to work, for both of us in fact."

True to his word, Trehearn had indeed secured Anne a position at the base hospital. Wyton was a much larger Station than Redhill and finding a position for a highly-regarded nurse was not difficult.

Anne nodded. "I suppose then we had best get back to our quarters and finish the unpacking."

Peter put his arm around her shoulders and hugged her as they walked.

***

Trehearn himself was accompanying Peter on his first flight.

"Do you realise, my lad," he said, "after all the years we've known each other, this is the first time I've ever sat in a cockpit with you."

Peter chuckled. "I guess we'd always been in single seaters back then. I must say, this is a remarkably nice feeling aircraft. I can't believe how light it feels, not that much heavier on the controls than a Spit."

Trehearn cautioned him. "A much higher wing loading than a Spit. Don't be too vigorous with it just yet, you need to learn its limits first. Then you'll really start to love it. Now, let's return to base, I want to see how well you can land it!"

Peter didn't disappoint, his first landing was perfect.

Trehearn laughed out loud. "I can't believe it. Your first time and you're already flying it better than pilots who've been here for over six months. I hope some of them were watching."

The following days were filled with more flying and cockpit familiarisation exercises done on the ground. Peter sat blindfolded in the pilot's seat whilst another pilot would call out the various gauges, controls and switches. Peter then had to go straight to them without delay. Most operational flying would now be at night in an unlit cockpit. His life and that of his navigator may depend on how instinctive his understanding of the cockpit layout could become.

After a week, Trehearn called Peter into this office. He knocked on the door and was promptly greeted by Trehearn's voice calling him to come in.

"Ah, Peter!" exclaimed Trehearn as he came around from behind his desk. "Peter, this is Pilot Officer Garrick Lynch."

Peter was mildly surprised. Lynch was the first black RAF officer he had ever encountered. The two of them shook hands and both turned to look at the Group Captain, who was standing by with an attitude rather like an expectant father.

"If the two of you have no objection, I should like to have Pilot Officer Lynch become your navigator Peter."

Peter turned back to Lynch and looked him over more closely. He noted the patch proclaiming 'Barbados' on his left shoulder. Lynch was examining Peter just as curiously.

"Are you any good?" asked Peter.

Lynch half smiled cautiously. "I've made it this far without too many problems. How about you?"

Peter gave him a dead-pan look. "Have you made out your will?"

All three broke into laughter. The tension was broken.

"I guess that settles it then," said Trehearn. "You two should head over to the Officers' Mess and get to know each other a bit. I'd like to see you both in the air after lunch. This should be a new experience for you Peter, having someone to do the navigation for you for once."

"At least now, if we get lost, it won't be my fault!" said Peter with a grin.

"That's assuming you can get us off the ground in the first place!" replied Lynch with a dead-pan face to match Peter's earlier effort.

"Come on you two. Out of here!" said Trehearn. "I've got work to do."

***

"So, your name is Garrick then?" asked Peter as they found a table in the Officers Mess.

"Call me Gary, please. I only ever get called Garrick when I'm in trouble with my wife!"

"A-ha," chuckled Peter. He had been immediately taken by Gary's speaking voice. He had never heard a West Indian accent before, and he was enthralled by the musical cadence in every syllable.

Peter continued, "So you're married as well. Is she over here?"

"Yes. I met her in London before the war. We were both students together at University. I was studying Meteorology and she was reading Law. We just clicked. All rather unexpected, but it's been great. How about you?"

Peter told him about how he met Anne. He didn't go into the part about his breakdown. He wasn't sure how Gary would take finding out that his new pilot had been through serious mental problems.

After they had been talking for a while, Gary leaned forward and looked Peter squarely in the face and asked, "Do you think you might have a problem serving with me?"

The question took Peter by surprise.

"What on earth do you mean?" he replied in shock.

"With me being a black man. I've had problems with some people in the past. I will not go through it again. If you're not happy, tell me now and I'll look for another pilot."

Peter sensed the significance of the moment. He had come to feel comfortable very quickly with Gary and hurried to put his mind at rest.

"I have no problem whatsoever Gary. I'll grant you; I was a bit surprised at first, but that's only because I'd never met a black officer before. If you're happy to put up with me, I'll be happy to put up with you."

Gary noticeably relaxed and leaned back in his chair.

"The last pilot they tried pairing me with was a South African. I could see from the moment he set eyes on me there was going to be a problem. The Germans are tough enough to deal with, without fighting a battle in your own cockpit as well."

Peter thought for a moment before replying. "I've heard some of the South African pilots can be a wee bit funny like that. Not all of them though, by any means. I got to meet the Sailor once…"

"Who, Malan? Sailor Malan?" interjected Gary.

"Yeah!" continued Peter. "You'd like him. Great pilot and a good man. Not at all like the chap that you had to put up with. I'd like to think that I'm a bit better than that too. Give me a nudge if I ever get out of line, right?"

Gary smiled. "I have a feeling we'll be fine."

Both of them had finished eating.

Gary looked at his watch. "Now, I believe we need to get some flight time in. No point in sitting around here."

***

Training was intense and completely different to anything Peter had ever experienced before. Their operational flying would be at night and had to be pinpoint accurate. New technologies were being developed to help crews attain levels of accuracy in blind navigation that were unimaginable only a scant few years earlier.

Their Mosquito was fitted with a transponder unit that received narrow focused radio signals from bases in England. They would ride one signal (called the Cat) until it was intersected by a second signal coming from a different location (called the Mouse). That carefully triangulated, intersecting point was where they would release their load of bombs or marker flares. The system was known as 'Oboe' and learning to fly to its exacting demands was the challenge facing Peter and Gary.

Their life quickly became long nights of flying in all conditions, listening to the sounds, like Morse code dots and dashes, coming through their headsets. They had to learn to fly along an arc, with the length of its radius being the precise distance between the 'Cat' station and the operation's intended target. The exact radius they needed to hold was indicated by a beeping tone of a specific duration. Short dots meant they were too close to the transmitting station, long dashes meant they had strayed too far on the other side. By keeping the dashes to just the right duration, they were flying along the arc perfectly.

Eventually, they would reach the exact spot where the arc would pass directly over the target. This was the point at which they would intersect the tone of the 'Mouse' signal. Here, they would release their payload. In practice, they would fly a course to the left of the target point until they picked up the 'Cat' signal and then turn right to follow it, as the track line took them along the arc. The two of them very quickly became highly proficient at the process. Up until now, they had been practicing over the open sea. Now it was time to become operational.

***

"Coming up on enemy coast Skip." Gary's voice came through the headset and Peter, once again, felt a thrill of tension pass through his body as he was about to enter a combat zone for the first time in over a year and a half.

He could feel his senses sharpening, his mind clear and alert. He suddenly realised how much he had missed it. This brief moment of reflection was over in an instant. His mind was back in focus, and he was responding to the navigation instructions coming through from Gary.

"Make Angels 25 Skip."

The instruction to climb to twenty five thousand feet. There was a heavy cloud cover down to about five thousand feet and normal operations wouldn't have been considered. Today's raid by their single aircraft was intended to put all their learning of the Oboe system into combat practice as much as it was about conducting a serious, targeted attack. The target for the raid was a small railway junction about fifty miles on the German side of the Dutch border. They were carrying eight five hundred pound bombs. No marker flares today, this was an actual bombing attack. As they gained altitude, the tone from the 'Cat' station in central England became clearer. The duration of the dots was still too short. They had yet more distance to cover before they reached to point that indicated the line of the arc.

"Steer 090 Skip," Gary's voice again.

"090? Directly east?" replied Peter. "Christ Nav, even I could come up with something more original than that!"

Gary chuckled. "I know Skip, but I didn't want to strain you too much on our first op."

The cloud ceiling cleared at around twenty two thousand feet. A clear starlit night above, excellent for flying and navigation, but also perfect for enemy night fighters. They flew on with Peter constantly checking the dark sky around them. Not quite knowing what to look for at night but looking just the same. His fighter pilot instincts had kicked back in. They arrived at their full operational altitude only a scant few minutes before the tone of the 'Cat' signal became the perfect duration. They were on the arc.

"Steer 158 degrees Skip," Gary's next course change came immediately.

Peter turned to the right and settled on the new course. Now it was up to Peter to keep them on the arc. They knew they would be about fifteen minutes flying time from the target once they intersected the arc. Now it was simply a matter of following their training and keeping an eye out for night fighters. A few flashes of exploding anti-aircraft fire began to punctuate the sky around them. The speed of the Mosquito meant that the ground gunners were seldom able to cause serious concern. The unexpected issue Peter had to deal with was how the brightness of the flashes quickly compromised his night vision. He hastily dragged his attention away from the pyrotechnics in the sky around them, and kept his concentration focused on the instruments. That, and the constant beeping tone in his headset.

"Coming up on target Skip. Open bomb bay doors."

Peter pulled back on a lever in the lower part of the centre console. They felt the sudden change in the airflow, and the wind noise level increase. Both Peter and Gary were now listening intently for the new tone of the 'Mouse' signal to interrupt the steady monotony of the 'Cat'. They didn't have to wait long. The arrival of the second higher pitched tone meant that they were now directly over to the target. Peter reached to his left and pressed the bomb release switch. Suddenly freed from four thousand pounds of weight, the Mosquito seemed to leap higher into the night sky. Peter was just about to ask Gary for their next course change when his attention was caught by a dull red glow in the distance to his left.

"I think we might have company Nav. I'm sure I just saw an exhaust glow off to port. I'm going to take us down into the clouds again."

"Right O Skip."

Peter banked steeply to the right and took the Mosquito into a sharp dive. Whether the night fighter had seen them, they couldn't know, but they soon reached the safety of the heavy cloud cover and could now dismiss its presence high above them.

"What's the course back to the target Nav? We're supposed to get some photos, aren't we?"

"Yes Skip. Give me a moment will you? That dive has mucked up my careful calculations"

After a minute, Gary had recalculated a course back to the railway junction. Peter took the aircraft down to a few hundred feet and opened the throttle fully. They rocketed over the railway twice, unable to see much in the dark but photographing as they went. Gary calculated a return course to England and Peter took them back up into the safety of the clouds one last time and set his course for home.

He allowed himself a moment to contemplate, with deep satisfaction, the raid they had just accomplished. Whilst it involved serious risk, it was an actual raid on a facility in Germany itself, it was primarily a training exercise taken to the fullest extreme.

Peter glanced over at Gary, poised over his navigation table, checking his figures and realised that he had found a partner whose qualities were the perfect foil for his own. Excellent at his job and whose company he enjoyed in their moments of down time. Most of all however, he felt quiet satisfaction at how he had performed himself. Any lingering concern over his old inner demons was finally exorcised. It didn't feel like the old days at 371, but perhaps this was better. This asked more of him and he smiled at the realisation that he was ready to give it.

***

Once back at Wyton, both of them slept well, and then met up for breakfast in the morning. Hugh Trehearn entered the Officers Mess and quickly spotted them.

Approaching the table, he said, "Do you mind both popping over to the Briefing Room once you've finished eating? We can go through the photos and discuss how it all went."

"How did we go Sir?" asked Peter keenly. "It was too dark to see much when we flew over it. I thought there would be fires and plenty of light."

"Sometimes it's like that. From what we can make out, you didn't do too badly at all. We'll talk about it more when you're in the Briefing Room."

He patted Peter on the shoulder and smiled at Gary, then left the Mess.

"Well, that didn't tell us much. I hope we didn't make a complete dog's bollocks of the whole thing," said Gary with a touch of annoyance.

"I guess we'll soon find out," replied Peter. "Don't worry too much about Trehearn, he's always loved a bit of melodrama. Hurry up and finish your egg and we'll go and see."

***

"You missed the target by about a hundred yards or so by the looks of it. We think there's a small herd of dairy cattle that you've put off their milk. So at least you've interrupted the German's food supply."

Trehearn was grinning like a Cheshire Cat.

Peter and Gary felt a wave of disappointment wash over them. They had really thought they might have done better. A hundred yards suddenly sounded like a vast distance.

Trehearn could see the disappointment in their drooping shoulders. "And now for the good news," he continued brightly. "You might not think it, but that was a quite remarkable effort."

Peter and Gary looked at each other in bemusement.

"How can that be Sir? It looks like we didn't even get close?" asked Peter.

"Think about it, you were five miles up in the air, a very dark night. Complete and extremely heavy cloud cover over the target; and it was a small target at that! You had no visual assistance and let's not forget; it was your first ever mission of this type."

Peter and Gary looked at each other, their mood beginning to lift.

"I've had far more experienced crews produce results that make yours look like a direct hit. You should be very pleased with yourselves – unless you feel bad about the cows."

They both laughed.

Trehearn indicated for them both to sit down. He pulled up a chair himself and sat, facing them.

"This is what makes 'Oboe' so important. You were one aeroplane carrying only eight bombs. Imagine if they were flares and you were marking for a full bomber raid. The level of accuracy you achieved would have been sufficient to have ensured the target would have been given a thorough pasting. This is only the beginning for you. I have no doubt you'll improve and become a real asset to the Pathfinder Force."

"Thank you Sir," said Peter. "So we're not being sent back to basic training then?"

Trehearn and Gary both chuckled.

"No Peter, not today. Now, on to another matter..." he turned to Gary. "Pilot Officer Lynch, it is with great pleasure that I can now inform you that henceforth, you are to be known as Flying Officer Lynch. Congratulations!"

He stood up and held out his hand. The last thing Gary had been expecting was a promotion. He stood up also and reached out, taking Group Captain Trehearn's hand and shaking it vigorously, breaking into an enormous grin.

"Thank you Sir! Thank you."

Peter had stood up also and took Gary's hand after Trehearn had been able to prize his own free from Gary's enthusiastic grip. Trehearn produced from his left hand trouser pocket some simple strips of embroidered fabric and handed them to Gary.

"Your new stripes Flying Officer. If you don't get them sewn on immediately, I shall have you arrested for being out of uniform!"

Gary took them gratefully and sat down again, still smiling outrageously.

Trehearn then turned to Peter. "All of which brings me to you, Squadron Leader!"

The words were like electricity to Peter. His jaw dropped open in surprise.

Trehearn had to reach down to take Peter's hand and shake it. Peter was almost numb from the shock of this, the promotion he had long thought he'd never get. Trehearn could sense the significance of the moment to Peter and grasped his right shoulder as they continued to shake hands.

"It's been a very long time coming Peter, too long really. Make no mistake though, you've earned it, and you deserve it. My very sincere congratulations to you Squadron Leader Garland."

After standing mute for several seconds, Peter finally found his voice and stammered, "Thank you so much Sir. This means a lot…"

"I'm sure it does. In fact, I know it does. Welcome home Peter."

Gary looked on with some curiosity at the intense exchange. Clearly there was some history here that he hadn't been aware of. Something personal between them perhaps…

After being advised that he and Gary that they would not be required for flight duty that night, Peter decided to book a table in the Officers' Mess so that Anne could join them. Gary, with a trace of nervousness spoke up.

"Excuse me Skip, would it be alright if my wife might be allowed to join us as well?"

Peter's eyes lit up. "God's teeth man, of course! Is she here?"

Gary shook his head. "No Skip. I thought I'd ring her in London and see if she can catch a train here this afternoon."

"Brilliant idea! Hop to it then. Anne and I would both love to meet her."

Now that the shock of his promotion was wearing off, Peter was experiencing a euphoric high and the thought of a foursome for dinner with someone who was fast becoming a close friend as well as his crewman, set the moment off to perfection.

***

Both Anne and Peter looked up expectantly as the Mess door opened. Gary had never spoken much about his wife. He had only ever told Peter that her name was Bridget and that she was now graduated in Law. The woman that entered the room on Gary's arm caught the immediate attention of every person in the Officers' Mess. Bridget Lynch was simply stunning! Tall and dark haired with an English 'peaches and cream' complexion and pale blue eyes. Gary seemed to have grown an inch taller as he entered the room beside her. Anne and Peter stood up and beckoned for Gary and Bridget to join them.

Gary made the introductions and all four became seated, Anne instantly engaging Bridget in a near barrage of good-natured questions about herself and how she and Gary had met.

Peter and Gary could do no more than smile and leave the two women to get to know each other. Anne had been starved for female companionship since she moved up to Wyton and she and Bridget seemed to find an immediate bond. Peter and Gary left them at the table and went to order drinks from the bar.

"Well! Aren't you the dark horse! No wonder you've not told anyone much about her. Every available man on the base would desert and head down to London to try and steal her away from you."

Gary chuckled at Peter's comment.

"Good luck trying," he replied with some feeling. "After everything we had to go through to get married, if she didn't love me, I would have known by now."

They carried the drinks back to the table and re-joined their wives.

Anne put her hand on Peter's arm. "Bridget was just telling me about some of the issues that they had to face before they were able to marry. I had no idea just how horrible some people can be! At least you both seem to be happy now."

"We were never unhappy," replied Gary. "From the moment we met, we've just loved being in each other's company." He took a sip of his beer.

"Fortunately, the people that matter most to us were always wonderful," Bridget spoke up brightly. "My parents had travelled a great deal before I was born and had seen enough of the world to have open minds about people. After they met Gary, they became completely supportive. Having them behind us has helped. Not everyone else was so accepting."

Peter and Anne looked at each other. How simple it had been for them.

"Yes, I can well believe it," mused Peter. "Perhaps, if there's anything good that might come out of this damn war, it's that a lot of people are coming to realise that where you come from and what you look like, matter a lot less than the qualities you bring with you. Britain has been saved by servicemen of all colours from all over the world. Let's hope they learn from that."

A brief silence settled over the table. Anne chimed in and lightened the mood.

"I believe you are now a practising solicitor, Bridget?"

"Yes indeed! In a fairly junior position at the moment, but with more experience that is likely to change. A number of the more senior male lawyers have joined up, so the partners might have to put their prejudices aside for once and start looking at us fully qualified women to fill the vacancies. I want one of those positions and I'll be up for the fight to get it if I have to!"

Gary reached across the table and squeezed her hand.

Peter and Anne both glanced at each other again and grinned. Bridget was clearly a strong and focused woman. No wonder she and Gary had made it so far. The moment was broken by the arrival of the Steward bringing a bottle of champagne and four glasses.

"Champagne! My goodness!" exclaimed Anne. "Are you sure we can afford this?"

"I'm now a Squadron Leader my darling! And Gary's a Flying Officer, so if we can't splash out on a night like this, we never will. Besides, we now have a good lawyer if we get into trouble."

The tinkle of laughter mixed with the clinking of glasses as the foursome toasted each other.

"It might not be the Ritz," said Gary, "but it's a good Officers' Mess, this one. Shall we see about ordering our meals?"

Chapter 9

October 1943

This run had been a tough one, a bombing mission to the important naval installation at Wilhelmshaven in northern Germany. The defences were well organised and vicious. The night sky had been alive with the explosions of flak shells and night fighters patrolled the periphery of the target zone, as well as the approaches to and from the target itself. The sheer speed of the Mosquito allowed Peter to get in close and drop his markers accurately, but for the following bombers, the defences took a heavy toll. Only the reconnaissance photographs, yet to be taken, would determine if the terrible cost in lives and aircraft would prove to have been worthwhile.

Peter put his hand on Gary's shoulder as they walked away from the debriefing room and started to make their way to the Mess for some breakfast, before heading off to get some sleep. They ate tiredly at the plates of greasy bacon, egg and liver which seemed to be the permanent staple of RAF breakfasts for operational crews. Neither of them noticed Group Captain Trehearn come into the Mess and look around at who was present. As soon as he spotted Peter and Gary, he turned towards them and came over to their table. Gary saw him first and began a clumsy attempt to get to his feet, despite having a mouthful of food.

"No, no, gentlemen, please stay as you are," said Trehearn hurriedly. "Would you mind if I were to join you for a while?"

"Of course not Sir, by all means," said Peter. "Are you here for some breakfast as well?"

"Not today thanks, I've already eaten," he replied. "I was actually wanting to talk with you both about a position which has become available for an experienced crew. In fact, the reason

I thought of you is due to Flying Officer Lynch's specific qualifications. You studied Meteorology at university I believe Gary?"

"Yes Sir, I did," he replied. "I started before the war and finished in 1941."

"Do you mind if I ask why you didn't join the Met Office?" enquired Trehearn. "I believe you graduated with excellent marks. I'm sure they would have been pleased to offer you a position."

"Well Sir, I wanted to serve first. I thought I could always find a professional position after the war."

Trehearn looked at Gary thoughtfully and then turned to Peter.

"You two seem to make a very good team and I would be loath to break you up, so here is what I have in mind."

Peter and Gary, despite their weariness, were suddenly alert and paying close attention.

"There's a small, specialised flight ops group within the PFF called 1409 Met Flight. They are required to fly alone, usually deep into enemy territory, and take observations of the weather over the intended targets for the coming night's raids. They fly over in the daylight, several hours ahead of the raid and supply our Operations teams here with weather information as accurate as they can make it. Sounds simple enough, don't you think?"

Peter and Gary looked at each other. Gary seemed to be almost salivating at the thought.

"Well?" asked Trehearn. "Are you interested so far?"

Peter could see that Gary was completely enthused by the idea. He himself felt suitably intrigued also.

"What do you think, Nav?" asked Peter.

Gary was trying to restrain his obvious enthusiasm but still nodded vigorously.

"Then I think we're both in Sir," said Peter, part of his mind wondering just what it might be that he was agreeing to.

"Excellent!" exclaimed Trehearn. "I had no doubt you'd jump at it. Now I know you're both fairly knackered after that last op, so go and get some sleep. Can I see you both in my office at 4 o'clock this afternoon? I shall have a great deal more information for you by then."

Trehearn slid his chair back, about to stand up, so Peter and Gary both began to do the same. Once again Trehearn stopped them.

"That's quite alright gentlemen. Please stay seated and finish your meals. I look forward to seeing you both at 4 o'clock; 'til then."

"Thank you Sir," Peter and Gary both spoke in unison.

Once Trehearn had left the Mess, they turned and looked at each other.

"This is brilliant!" exclaimed Gary animatedly. "I've heard all about the Met Flight unit and wondered whether getting into it was possible."

"Why didn't you put in for it?" asked Peter. "Trehearn is absolutely right, you'd be the perfect choice."

Gary paused for a moment before he replied. "The truth is, I did put in for it once, a few months ago. But I withdrew my application almost immediately. I didn't want to break us up as a team."

Gary looked as though he felt a powerful sense of guilt at having even considered a request to switch to a new crew. Peter felt a moment of unexpected emotion at this tacit acknowledgement by Gary of their friendship. He tried to brush it off casually.

"Yeah. I probably would have been a bit browned off if you'd shot through on me. At least now, we'll get to spend our days staring at bloody clouds and making notes about how fluffy they look. Sounds like more fun than I can imagine!"

Gary laughed. "You might just be in for a shock. There's a lot more to it than just looking at fluffy clouds. Have you ever flown inside the thunder head of a fully formed Cumulonimbus cloud?"

"Certainly not," replied Peter, affecting his stern and serious look. "I am a very sensible pilot and I avoid them like the plague."

"Well, not any more you won't!" said Gary with a grin. "You're about to find out what wonders the world of weather has in store. Make sure you buckle up good and tight!"

***

High altitude flying had always had little appeal to Peter. Freezing temperatures and bottled oxygen made the experience both unpleasant and dangerous. The specially modified Mosquitos used by the Met Flight squadron were therefore a completely unexpected revelation; they had pressurised cabins, so weight had been minimised as much as possible and they were also unarmed. These aircraft could rely only on their speed and the skills of their pilots to get them out of trouble.

On their first operation, Peter and Gary had flown at thirty thousand feet towards Berlin to create the impression that that was their destination. German air defences will have vectored intercepting fighters to wait for them over the capital. Once they had passed to the south of their true target – Hamburg, they steered north and set about their observations in detail. Gary was partly relieved of his navigational duties now. The course they were to follow had largely been prepared for them in advance by a navigation team in England. This type of mission didn't require the pin-point flying of a normal Pathfinder operation. Gary could monitor the course well enough, whilst having his attention being more focused on the completeness and accuracy of his weather observations. It was approaching the middle of November now. The night promised a full moon – a Bomber's Moon. If the weather played its part, then this night would see Hamburg tremble under the terror of a major attack. The first month of winter would often bring terrible weather to northern Germany. Many was the raid that had to be recalled due to the inability to locate the target.

Today was looking more promising though. Lots of high Cirrus, but the Cumulus at lower level was broken and not showing signs of intensifying.

"Can we go down and get a closer look at about five thousand feet Skip?" Gary's voice came through Peter's headset clearly.

"Your wish is my command Nav."

Peter was still occasionally bemused at how the authority dynamic was altered on these Met flights. The observations being taken by the navigator were the sole purpose of the mission, therefore what the navigator asked for, the pilot was expected to deliver. Peter took the Mosquito into a medium dive that lasted for nearly fifteen minutes to get the aircraft down to the altitude requested by Gary. They flew a rapid circuit of the city and nearby countryside before Gary was content with his notes.

"OK Skip. Get us up high please and we can head for home and a nice cup of tea."

Peter didn't need to be asked twice. The daylight was fading fast and the weather information they had gathered was now crucial to the night's plans for Bomber Command.

"No sign of any fighters today Skip," said Gary. "It's extraordinary how they don't seem to come after us much."

"They must think we're just photo reconnaissance types," replied Peter. "If they knew what we're really about, they'd throw everything at us."

"I reckon that one day, some bright bod is going to work out that a Mossie in the afternoon means the bombs will fall that night. Then it'll get a bit more interesting up here," said Gary thoughtfully.

"Yep, I can hardly wait!" said Peter, deep in contemplation of the prospect.

Once back on the ground, Peter's first job was to call Bomber Command with the day's observations. The first squadrons of Lancasters were already warming their engines ready to take off on the raid. The news from the Met flight was good. Tonight would see death on the ground for many residents of Hamburg, and death in the air for an unknowable number of RAF flight crew. The relentless, grinding nightmare of the allied bombing offensive would continue for yet another night.

Gary and Peter had been posted to another Station, RAF Oakington, as soon as they were confirmed in the Met Flight group. It was still in Cambridgeshire and not a long drive from Wyton, so Peter's Alvis soon became a familiar sight, driving between the two Stations. As Peter was no longer stationed at Wyton, he had had to give up his and Anne's quarters on the base. In consequence, they then rented a small cottage in the nearby town so that she could continue with her nursing duties at the Base's hospital. By now, Bridget had become a regular visitor. She and Anne had struck up a friendship to rival that of their husbands.

After the mission over Hamburg, Peter and Gary were granted a forty-eight hour pass for the weekend. They both drove across to Wyton, and Bridget caught the train up from London again.

"I heard a little rumour a few days ago."

Everyone leaned forward as Peter spoke.

"It is looking very much like our little Met Flight group is going to be relocating back to Wyton in the New Year. No more having to drive back and forth. Won't that be an improvement?"

Anne laughed delightedly. "Thank heavens! I can pack my teddy bear away again."

The four of them had been having a convivial few drinks in the tiny lounge room of the cottage. The few drinks had developed into something more raucous as the wine flowed freely.

"What do you mean? Have you been seeing another teddy bear on the side, my darling?" giggled Peter.

"If I didn't know any better Shkip, I'd swear you were as rotten as a chop!" slurred Gary.

Peter giggled even louder.

"And you are no better, my darling husband!" added Bridget, wagging a finger at Gary in mock disapproval.

"Just look at the two of you!" laughed Anne. "You are both supposed to be responsible officers in His Majesty's service." She waggled her finger also, this time taking in both Peter and Gary.

"You're behaving like school-boys who've just discovered the key to the liquor cabinet. I'm sure I would disapprove strongly if I could stand up."

She collapsed back into the lounge chair, laughing uproariously. Peter leaned forward, trying hard to look as though he was in control of himself.

"I shall have you know dearest wife; that getting completely pissed on one's days off is a long established tradition in the RAF. It's what sets us apart from the Army and the Navy."

Gary nodded vigorously. "That is absolutely right! They never get given days off at all, so they just stay pissed the whole time!"

All four of them dissolved in laughter once again.

***

Three very bleary sets of eyes greeted each other in the morning.

"I think I've just remembered why I promised myself I would never do that again," groaned Peter.

Gary looked as though he might have to leave the kitchen and rush to the bathroom at any moment. Bridget smiled wanly at her husband. She was feeling far from well herself which surprised her, as she hadn't had all that much to drink. She was very good at making a glass of wine last a long time. She knew she had got a bit tipsy, but nothing more, perhaps she was coming down with something. Anne was the last to arrive in the kitchen. She breezed in, seemingly without a care in the world.

"How do you do it?" asked Peter forlornly as he turned to Gary and Bridget. "I've seen her do this before, she must have the constitution of an ox. She can hold her own, drinking with anybody and then, coming up like roses in the morning."

Anne smiled happily as she looked at the three suffering faces before her.

"Would anyone like some breakfast? We don't have a lot, but I can make toast and porridge. Tea as well of course… anyone?"

"Maybe just some toast and tea please, darling," mumbled Peter.

Gary and Bridget just nodded in silent agreement. As Anne began to busy herself with the kettle, Bridget suddenly leapt up from her chair and hurried from the kitchen in the direction of the bathroom. Anne and Peter looked at each other in concern as Gary stood up also to follow his wife. He stood outside the door of the room as he listened to the sound of Bridget being sick into the toilet. After a couple of minutes, she emerged, having just rinsed her mouth out and drying her face.

"Are you alright my love?" asked Gary in concern.

"I think so. I don't know what came over me. I'm sure it's not the alcohol from last night. I drank the least of all of us."

They both went back into the kitchen and resumed their seats.

"Are you sure you're alright Bridget?" asked Peter. "You gave us a bit of a shock just then."

Anne looked at her quizzically. "Is everything normal with you at the moment Bridget? Have you been feeling off colour before now?"

Bridget paused for a moment before she spoke. "Well, I am a little late…"

Anne's mouth was suddenly agape. "My goodness Bridget! I think you're pregnant!"

Her words had an electric effect upon Gary. His eyebrows shot upwards and his mouth also fell open in shock.

"Dear God! Can it be? Do you think so?"

Bridget managed a wan smile. "I was trying to convince myself that I wasn't, that I couldn't be. I suspect it's starting to look as though I really am."

Gary got up from his chair, miraculously, he was now feeling completely sober. He went around to his wife, bent forward and put his arms around her as she sat on her chair. He leant his head on her left shoulder and held her tightly, seemingly for an eternity. Anne came and stood alongside Peter who, whilst still sitting, put his arm around her waist and held her tightly against him. In a time of war, amidst the horror and sorrow, there could also be moments of the purest joy.

Chapter 10

Late April 1944

Raids for the evening had been planned against the Dornier aircraft manufacturing facilities in Munich, in the south of Germany. Peter and Gary had flown in from the south, tracking across France and then continuing over Switzerland.

They were trying to take what advantage they could of the neutral airspace that existed over one of the few countries in Europe not in the grip of the conflict. Theirs was one of several Met Flight aircrafts gathering information prior to the raid. All were flying in from different directions at differing times. All intent on trying to give the planners as complete a picture of the developing weather patterns as possible.

By now, the German air defences had become alert to the dangers these lone, high flying aircraft represented. Gathering meteorological information was now nearly as dangerous as participation in the coming raid itself. Once they were tracking north-east from Switzerland, their course was straightforward enough. The flight was notable for the fine, mid-spring weather. Cloud was certainly about but scattered and broken. There was certainly no sign of it changing too much over the next twelve hours.

Gary had been occupying himself taking the meticulous notes that his professionalism demanded of him. For his part, Peter had brought them in at over thirty-two thousand feet, almost at the upper limit of the Mosquito's capability. Both of them noted with some satisfaction, the inability of the German anti-aircraft fire to get close at this height. The flak was exploding well below them, and some way behind. That left the danger of German fighters. Peter's skills at locating enemy aircraft in the vastness of the sky had become even more finely honed now that he was playing the role of the hunted. For the moment, the sky was reassuringly empty, but his instincts were pricking at him.

"How's it looking Nav?"

"It looks like it could be a hard night for Munich tonight Skip. Conditions are just about perfect."

Gary didn't share Peter's unease.

"OK. Let me know as soon as you have enough data. It shouldn't be this easy. I'm keen to get us on our way home."

"Not too long now Skip. Only another five minutes or so and we'll be right over the middle of Munich itself. Then we can scarper."

Peter nodded to himself. "Very good Nav. Keep your eyes peeled for fighters as well as the weather, just in case I miss something."

"OK Skip. Don't seem to be any about though," said Gary.

"I know," replied Peter. "That's the bit that worries me, there's usually something. I wonder if they're getting something in place to catch us on the home leg."

Gary picked up his meaning. "Would you like me to plot something further to the south?"

"It might be a good idea; I'd like to avoid the obvious flight path. I don't mind a bit of extra flying time, Bridget's not due for another couple of months."

Gary couldn't help but laugh. "I'm sure I can get us home before then. Can you imagine the strife I'd be in if I missed that?"

Peter chuckled as well. "Anne would give me the rounds of the kitchen if getting you home late was my fault."

Munich soon became visible far below them. Despite the haze and scattered cloud, the geometric lines of the city were clearly visible in the late afternoon sunlight. Gary was now content with the completeness of his notes.

"OK Skip, steer 245 degrees. Let's head back towards Switzerland shall we?"

"OK Nav. 245 degrees it is."

Peter had just completed his turn, pointing them towards the Swiss frontier to the south-west, when a tiny movement in the sky, above and far behind him caught his attention.

"We have company. Very high and behind us now. Quite a way off. We should be able to outrun it, whatever it is."

Gary looked out through the canopy. He was not as skilled as Peter at picking out other aircraft at distance, but after a few seconds he saw it too.

"I see it Skip. It doesn't look all that far off to me," a rising note of concern was becoming apparent in his voice.

Peter swivelled his head around for a second look.

"Bloody hell. It's catching up fast. I'm sure I didn't misjudge it before; the Jerries can't have anything that fast."

Peter reached for the throttle control quadrant and opened it fully. That would burn through fuel far more quickly, but that was hardly a consideration right now.

"It's still gaining on us Skip," exclaimed Gary, now sounding edgy and concerned.

Peter checked again and could see that the German fighter was closing at a near impossible speed.

"Tighten your straps and turn your oxygen on," Peter turned the knurled tap on his oxygen bottle as he spoke. Gary promptly did the same and then checked the straps securing him to his seat were firmly taut. Peter then put the Mosquito into a shallow dive to try and gain more speed. He checked the Air Speed Indicator; it was showing over four hundred and seventy miles per hour.

"It's still gaining Skip!" Gary now had a clear note of fear in his voice.

"Fuck! What the hell is it?" Peter swore in frustration.

Gary had another look through the canopy at the enemy aircraft now getting desperately close in behind them.

"It doesn't have any propellers! What the hell kind of plane doesn't have any propellers?"

Peter steepened the dive and broke to the left in the same movement. He could feel the airframe of the Mosquito protest at the immense torsional pressures that were being inflicted on it at this speed.

"Keep it together Girl," he muttered under his breath.

He was subliminally conscious of the row of large bullet holes that suddenly appeared in the starboard wing as he made his desperate manoeuvre. If he hadn't turned to the left at the moment he did, the bullets would have gone straight through the fuselage and the cockpit.

The strange aircraft shot past him on his starboard side. He had only the briefest of glimpses of the two strange pods hanging under its swept back wings as it began to dive and turn as well. Whatever it was, it was entirely new. New, and terrifyingly fast.

Peter clawed back some angle out of the dive. He didn't want to lose too much altitude too quickly; he might need it later. A quick look at the compass, directly south lay Austria, an option little better than Germany itself. They needed to fly a heading more westerly than south. Getting into neutral airspace over Switzerland was crucial.

It might mean a diplomatic incident and potential internment for the two of them, but that was better than the limited future that this frightening new German aircraft was trying to deal them. It had swung around and was now behind and above them again. As before, it was closing the distance between them at an incredible rate.

"It's easily doing well over five hundred!" Peter was as much in awe as he was cowed by the extraordinary performance of the strange plane.

He had not lost his clarity of thought however, it would be crucial in the moments ahead. He held his line, watching the

German aircraft in the rear-view mirror, mounted on the framework of the canopy above his head. His left hand gripped the throttle quadrant and his right was firmly on the control column. In the instant he saw the twinkling lights in the nose of the fighter, he pushed hard forward on the control stick and pulled back on the throttle.

In the moment that the Mosquito began a sudden dive and scrubbed off some of its speed, the shells from the guns of the fighter struck the right wing again, this time hitting the starboard engine and inner wing. The most devastating effect though, was caused by the bullets that struck the canopy. The instant the pressurised cockpit was breached, the damaged panels exploded outwards with a furious violence. The sudden loss of cabin pressure caused an instant and massive change in the inner ears of both Peter and Gary. Each of them immediately blacked out from the acute wave of uncontrollable dizziness and nausea. Peter fell forward, pushing the control column even further forward in the process, causing the Mosquito to go into a near vertical dive, out of all control. With smoke now pouring from the starboard engine and the Mosquito falling away to earth, the German pilot, content that he had made another kill to add to his tally, broke off the engagement and changed his course to return to his base.

The fog lifted from Peter's brain after nearly fifteen seconds of nothingness. Desperately blinking away the residual effects of the blackout on his disoriented mind, he struggled to make sense of what was happening around him. After another few seconds, his memory began to fill in the blanks. He had to try and regain control of his stricken aircraft. Forcing his arms forward against the effects of inertia, he grasped the control column of the stricken Mosquito. He began pulling back on the column as his feet found their way back onto the rudder bars. Gently pulling back on the column, he felt the aircraft begin to slowly recover from the dive.

A quick glance at the altimeter showed they were still at over ten thousand feet. They had been at over thirty thousand when they first spotted whatever that new plane was. The dive continued to level out still at a relatively safe height, but the controls were terribly sluggish. He looked quickly at both engines. The starboard engine was pouring smoke, and flames were licking at the plywood surface of the wing behind it. He immediately cut the power to the engine and switched off the flow of petrol. If he could regain flight control, then maybe they might still be able to get out of German airspace.

Peter gave a quick look over his right shoulder to check on Gary. He sat, slumped forward in his harness, clearly still unconscious, but hopefully, nothing worse. As the Mosquito finally settled back into level flight, Peter seized the moment to check over all the controls. The starboard engine was dead, the cockpit canopy was shattered, so this meant higher altitude flight was not possible. The flight controls felt heavy, but still functional. Another check of the altitude – they were now under eight thousand feet. A check on the compass; still heading west by south. If the aircraft could hold together and they encountered no further German fighters, then perhaps Switzerland might still be an option.

Another voice began to crackle through his headphones. Gary was regaining consciousness.

"How are you faring there, Nav?" Peter asked with concern.

"What happened?" Gary's voice betrayed his confusion and disorientation.

"That bastard shot out our canopy. We depressurised in an instant. We both blacked out for a bit," Peter surprised himself at how calm his voice was.

"I think I've got her back under control but we're not going to make it home like this," Peter spoke in measured terms.

He needed his navigator to recover his senses as quickly as possible.

"How are you feeling? Do you think you're hurt?"

Gary took a couple of seconds to reply. "I think I'm okay. I must have just blacked out for a bit. How are you?"

"Just hunky-dory. I need to you to start plotting us a course to any airfield you can find in Switzerland. They won't be happy to see us, but I'd rather be in prison there than with the Jerries."

"How do you expect me to give you a course?" Gary's response was unexpected.

"What do you mean?" queried Peter.

"All of my charts and equipment have vanished!" A note of frustrated helplessness was clear in Gary's voice,

"Christ! It must have all been sucked out when the canopy blew. At least I can get us into their airspace. Holding west-south-west should be easy enough."

No sooner had the words left Peters lips, than the Mosquito lurched viciously to the right. Both he and Gary desperately searched around them for obvious signs of trouble. It proved easy to spot. The starboard wing was beginning to delaminate.

"Oh my God!" exclaimed Gary. "The wing is falling apart."

The extreme stresses that the plywood laminations of the bullet-damaged wing surface had been subjected to were ultimately proving too much. The ply was beginning to peel back from the wings leading edge. Peter reached for the throttle lever and eased it back as far as he dared. It made little difference. The flapping panels of plywood were now causing a serious breakdown of the airflow over the right wing. Reaching Switzerland had suddenly become out of the question. Just staying alive was now the priority.

"I've got to get us down as soon as possible!" The earlier calmness in Peter's voice was now cracking also.

"We're still a fair way inside Germany. I've heard they don't like black men," Gary had voiced his greatest fear. What would the Nazis do to him if he were captured?

"I know mate, but I don't have much choice here," Peter was fighting to retain control over his stricken aeroplane.

Its flight capacity was diminishing with every second that passed. They had now descended through five thousand feet. The ground below showed neatly arrayed farm lots and meadowland. Good potential for an emergency landing, but almost certain capture and a terrifyingly uncertain future for Gary.

In the further distance though, heavily wooded mountain ranges filled the horizon. Could they make it that far? Peter still had some limited control over the wounded Mosquito, as long as he kept her on a straight course and her nose slightly up. The challenge for him was to lose as much airspeed as possible to minimise pressure on the delaminating panels, but not so much as to risk stalling. This would be hard enough to do under normal conditions, but infinitely more difficult with such a highly compromised airflow.

They passed through four thousand feet of altitude but at least, the mountains were now noticeably closer. The farm lots beneath them were becoming fewer, with more open areas of uncultivated alpine meadowland taking their place. Below three thousand feet, then shortly afterwards, two thousand. They weren't losing height as such; the ground was now coming up to meet them as they reached the steeper foot-hills of the approaching mountains. A thousand feet and they were now flying over dense stands of spruce and fir trees. They had cleared the farmlands and might now have a chance of concealment once they were down.

Once they were down…

Landing in one piece was now the issue. There were no more open fields, just rugged mountain faces and dense forests.

Peter could see that they still had just enough height to clear an approaching ridgeline, but after that, he would have no choice but to come down somewhere. What lay on the other side of that ridge was now their final hope. The Mosquito cleared the ridge with less than fifty feet of altitude to spare. Once they were over it, the land below fell away into a picturesque sub-alpine valley. Peter took in the sight of a long, narrow clearing with a small hut at the bottom end. It continued on for about a mile further up the valley, heavily forested on either side, but grassy meadowland up the middle. It was as good as he could dare hope for.

The long meadow appeared to end with what looked to be a fairly smooth expanse of granite at the far end. He needed to get down urgently before the meadowland transitioned into that granite field. The remaining meadow was fast disappearing as it passed beneath their wings. They were going to end up in the granite field after all.

"Strap yourself in good and tight mate," he said to Gary through clenched teeth.

Gary already was, but he checked the straps once again. Peter pulled the levers to lower the undercarriage, only the port wheel responded fully. The starboard mechanism could only lower the wheel about halfway.

"It'll have to do!" Peter muttered under his breath.

He continued cutting the revs on the remaining port engine and lowered the landing flaps, trying to create as much drag as possible to slow the Mosquito's approach. There was less than twenty feet of air beneath their wings. They were close enough now for Peter to see that the fast disappearing meadow below was getting rockier and more uneven as it blended into the granite field beyond.

"Hang on bloody tight mate, this is going to be rough," Peter almost shouted at Gary. "Here we go!"

The Mosquito touched down travelling at less than sixty knots. Slow for such a large aeroplane, but still terrifyingly fast over such ill-suited terrain. For the first couple of seconds Peter managed to retain some measure of control, but once the starboard wing touched the ground he became as much a helpless passenger as was Gary. The Mosquito was violently shedding parts of its structure against rocks and trees as it bounced and careened along helplessly. It took only nine seconds for the shattered aircraft to finally come to a complete halt, but it seemed an eternity for its two occupants.

Once his mind cleared from the chaotic jostling of the landing, Peter immediately shut down all the switches. There was still plenty of high octane fuel on board and the risk of fire was now intense.

"Are you okay Skip?"

The sound of Gary's voice brought Peter an immediate feeling of relief. "I think so Nav, how about you?"

There was a short pause.

"I'm not much of a beer drinker, as you know Skip, but I could sure as hell use one right now!"

Peter gave a chuckle of relief. "I take it you're alright then?"

"I do believe so," replied Gary. "Everything that needs to be attached, still seems to be attached. I think that's a good start."

"Same here. Now we need to get the hell out of here and as far away as possible, someone's bound to have seen us."

Gary nodded in agreement. "We need to grab anything useful first. Compass, rations… do you have your pistol?"

"Yep, sure do, there's also a Very pistol, it may be handy."

They both undid their harnesses and hurriedly looked around the cockpit, grabbing anything that seemed useful. They shoved them into a canvas backpack that Gary always brought along.

"That's everything I think," observed Peter. "Let's get the heck out of here."

The front of the Mosquito had come to rest against a large granite boulder, very effectively blocking the usual main point of entry to the cockpit, a small hatch, low on the starboard side. However, the destruction of the canopy gave an obvious alternative means of exit. Gary went first, climbing up and over the Perspex side window and out onto the remains of the starboard wing. From there, it was an easy drop down onto the ground. He looked around nervously, acutely aware that he was now standing on German soil for the first time in his life; the soil of a hostile country that would happily see him dead before even giving it a second thought. The pilot's seat was on the left hand side of the cockpit, so Peter climbed up onto it and from there, clambered out onto that wing.

The Mosquito had come to rest, canted over towards the right. The port wing was lifted higher due to the extended undercarriage on that side. Peter undid his parachute harness and dropped it down on the rocky ground below. Gary was making his way around the rear of the aircraft to join him. Peter lowered himself down onto his haunches, perched right at the trailing edge of the wing, close to where it meets the fuselage. Pivoting off his right hand, which held onto the wing, he pushed himself away and dropped down to the ground some eight feet below. He landed awkwardly, misjudging the sloping angle of the rocky incline. His right ankle folded beneath his weight and he collapsed heavily to the ground, grunting in pain. Gary appeared from around the tail of the Mosquito just in time to see Peter fall. He hurried to his side and knelt down beside him.

"Are you alright?"

Peter lay on his back on the rocky surface, gazing upwards and blinking rapidly with the pain in his ankle.

"I don't bloody well believe it! I manage to get us down in one piece and then I bloody well do this!"

Gary felt a momentary impulse to laugh, but the potential gravity of the situation steadied him. Peter began to lift himself up on his left elbow, trying to sit.

"Do you think it's broken?" asked Gary.

"I don't know, it might just be a bad sprain, can you help me get up please?"

Gary stood up and extended his left hand for Peter to grasp. Putting all his weight on his good leg, Peter took Gary's hand and pulled himself up to a standing position. Keeping hold of Gary's hand, he tried putting some weight on his right foot. An excruciating pain shot through his ankle, he immediately tightened his grip on Gary's hand and shifted his weight back onto the left leg.

"Well this is just bloody brilliant! It feels a damn sight worse than a sprain. Bloody hell!"

Peter's exasperation was palpable, he was furious with himself. Gary was still thinking clearly though and immediately realised he needed to take charge.

"Alright then, we need to get away from the plane as quickly as possible. If we get caught out in the open like this, we've had it."

He put down the bundle of supplies he had salvaged from the Mosquito. Then, he came around to Peter's right hand side and put his left arm around his friend's waist, trying to take the strain away from his damaged ankle. Together they began to slowly make their way towards the forest lining the edge of the granite field. With Gary's help, Peter managed to hobble nearly fifty yards into the darkening forest before the pain in his ankle forced them to pause. Peter eased himself down to sit on the trunk of a fallen tree. Gary looked back towards the Mosquito, lying just the edge of the forest.

"You wait here Skip; I have to go back and get the supplies."

Peter nodded. "Okay mate."

Gary paused when he reached the edge of the granite field. He crouched down low to keep his profile as small as possible and slowly made his way back towards the shattered aircraft. He stopped once he reached the pack containing their escape kit. Keeping low, he looked back down the valley towards the small hut they had flown over. He could make out three figures that were now standing out in the open and looking up in his direction. They were nearly a mile away and Gary could make out little detail, but he was certain that the figures appeared to be a man and two children. At least that meant they were unlikely to be soldiers.

He watched as the man turned and walked away from the children, heading back towards the cabin. Having retrieved his pack, Gary now cautiously made his way back towards the tree line and the cover it afforded. Crouching down again, he turned and looked back down the valley once more. The man was now emerging from the hut, this time carrying what could only be a rifle. Gary estimated that he and Peter had no more than fifteen minutes to get as far away from the Mosquito as possible. It would take that long before the three people reached the crash. He hurried back to where Peter was still sitting on the fallen log.

"People are coming. One of them is armed. We have to get moving."

Peter understood the gravity of the situation.

"I'm going to need your help. I can't move on my own," he said with urgent desperation.

Gary didn't hesitate. "Come on then. Can you stand up?"

Peter stood again holding all his weight on his left leg. Once again, Gary took his position on Peter's right hand side, bearing as much of his weight as he could manage. They were now travelling up the side of the heavily wooded mountain.

They had to pick their way in between trees and the fallen detritus that littered the forest floor. They were not making good time.

Gary pointed ahead, "Can you see that outcrop up there?" Indicating a rocky granite boulder field, just visible through the trees. Peter nodded, he was tiring quickly from the exertions of hopping on his left leg, despite Gary's help.

"If we can get up there, we might be able to find a spot to hide amongst the boulders. At least we won't leave any tracks." Gary was deeply aware that they had only been able to add a few hundred yards between them and the crashed aircraft. Not enough to elude any serious search.

"Come on Skip, can't stay here!"

The two of them struggled on until they reached the tumbled pile of granite chunks, the remains of an ancient rock fall.

Suddenly Peter found the going easier. Here he could use his hands and his good leg to propel himself upwards into the boulder field proper. That left Gary free to find his own way ahead. Being fully mobile, he soon pulled ahead of Peter as he moved his way across the rugged terrain. He was keeping his eyes open for a crevice in between some of the larger rocks that could provide shelter for the two of them until they felt it was safe to move again.

"I don't think you'll find much to help you up there gentlemen." A strong voice in a clear German accent stopped them both in their tracks.

Chapter 11

Gary slowly stood erect and turned to face the owner of the voice, coming up from just below them on the edge of the trees. Peter's head sagged forward, resting against the face of a boulder.

"I take it that you are the crew of that aeroplane out there?"

The speaker was a man, seemingly not that much older that Peter or Gary. He held his gun at the ready, although he was not aiming it at them for the moment. His calm demeanour caught the two airmen by surprise. He didn't seem to be as threatening as they expected he would be. Indeed, he even had a wry smile on his face. Mostly though, it was his excellent English that captured and held their attention.

"You may as well come down gentlemen. That way is very hard work and there is little reward for you as you get higher up the mountain." The German continued to look as though he was finding the encounter more amusing that threatening.

"What? So you can shoot us or hand us over to the Gestapo?" Gary called back in a soft voice. He was feeling a mixture of extreme anxiety and bullishness. "Why don't you just shoot us right here and now?"

The German laughed out loud. "This rifle is fine for shooting rabbits and pigeons, but it would take a lucky shot to kill you. No gentlemen, I don't think I'll hand you over to the Gestapo. Please come with me, it gets dark in these valleys very quickly and I can offer you a more hospitable shelter that you will find up here."

He waved his arm, indicating that they should come to him. Peter turned to look at Gary who could do no more than shrug. Then he turned and spoke to the German.

"Are you offering to help us? I don't understand."

"Of course you don't. I am German and we are all monsters, isn't that what you believe?"

There was a brief silence as Peter and Gary looked at each other again, each hoping to see some sense of decision in the other. There was nothing there in either.

"Come on please gentlemen. We do not have all evening. I assure you; you will be safe." The German waved his arm again, repeating his earlier gesture.

Once again, Peter and Gary looked to each other. Peter's face now showed resignation. He was in no condition to travel much further anyway.

"Alright then," replied Peter. "I should let you know that I think my ankle might be broken, I can't walk."

"Well then, your comrade will have to assist you, but we had certainly best get going. It will be quite dark by the time we reach our home. Please gentlemen, come on now!"

Peter eased himself down to the ground again, using his arms and his good leg. Gary had little difficulty in retracing his path back down to re-join Peter. The German approached them and held out his hand.

"Good evening gentlemen, my name is Rainer Voss."

Peter stared intently into Rainer's eyes as he reached out and shook his hand.

"My name is Peter," he replied in an even voice.

Rainer then turned and extended his hand towards Gary who also shook, despite a look of obvious suspicion and trepidation on his face.

Rainer smiled. "I have never shaken hands with a negro before. There aren't many of your kind here in the Third Reich."

"So I've been told. I believe we are just one people amongst the many who are not welcome here!" Gary spoke with an undertone of restrained tension in his voice. He was fighting hard to be civil to this unlikely captor. Rainer nodded and held eye contact with Gary but didn't reply. Changing the subject, he gestured towards the forest he had emerged from. In the gathering gloom there were two small figures standing silently.

"These are my children. We live up here in relative solitude. Now, please come gentlemen. Let's get back to my house whilst there is still some light."

Rainer and Gary took turns in supporting Peter as they picked their way back to the Mosquito and descended the valley towards the small cottage at the bottom. The two children followed in silence, both of them gazing at Gary in rapt amazement. Neither of them had ever seen anyone other than white Europeans in their young lives. Gary caught them staring at one point and smiled at them both. They instantly responded with broad smiles of their own. He began to feel some of the tension lifting.

"My name is Gary," he said aloud as they walked.

Rainer, who was now supporting Peter, turned and looked at him.

"I'm sorry?" he asked.

"Up the hill, you told me your name was Rainer. I didn't tell you mine. It's Gary."

Rainer managed a smile. "*Danke,* we can have a proper introduction soon. I meant it when I said you had nothing to fear from us, we don't live up here by choice."

Gary looked at him with renewed interest but said nothing more as they continued walking the final few hundred yards towards the small cabin at the foot of the meadow. The evening gloom had now fully shrouded the secluded valley in a darkness, relieved from totality thanks to a gentle springtime twilight. When they reached to door, Peter supported his own weight by leaning against the outside wall whilst Rainer went inside and lit a hurricane lamp and several candles. The children were next to enter and finally Gary, supporting Peter as they made their way inside. Rainer indicated an armchair that would clearly have been his own, for Peter to sit in. It was the only piece of furniture in the room that spoke of creature comforts. The remaining furnishings, limited in their quantity, were simple, wooden and rustic. Once he was seated, Rainer found a wooden crate, turned it over and set it on the floor in front of the armchair, so that Peter could elevate his injured leg and rest the ankle.

Rainer made his way over to an old wood burning stove and turned his head towards his guests. "My children and I have not yet had our evening meal. I presume that neither of you have eaten for a while either, am I right?"

"Not since this morning," Peter agreed.

"Well, I can offer you some quite passable venison stew if you would care to join us. I do tend to make it in large amounts, so that it can last us several days. Would you mind if I fed the children first? I don't have enough bowls for the five of us."

Gary finally spoke. "Please do whatever you need to, we're quite happy to wait."

Rainer and the children looked at Gary in pleasant surprise. He seemed to be feeling more comfortable in their presence. Rainer tended to the stove and got a fire going with practiced ease. He wiggled the large pot on top of the stove to ensure it was centred and gave to contents a thorough stir. Placing the lid back on, he left it to begin warming and came over to join the others.

"I should introduce you to my children." He put his arm around the shoulders of the eldest, a blonde headed young boy.

"This is Thomas, he is eight, and my strongest helper!" he said smiling.

"I'm nearly nine!" interjected the boy, also in excellent English.

"Nearly nine! I keep forgetting," laughed Rainer. He then turned to the younger child, a small girl.

"And this is my darling daughter, Marie. Marie is five and learning to read and do sums. She also likes to help me inside the house." He looked around the room and shrugged. "If I may call it a house."

Peter and Gary both smiled at her. She suddenly went very shy and snuggled closely into her father's side with a small smile. The two airmen were both immediately entranced. Peter's first instinct was to ask about the children's mother, but he caught himself a moment before he spoke. It would be a question for later, after they had eaten.

His attention instead was drawn back to his injured ankle, the pain from which was now becoming acute.

"Do you think one of you might be able to help me get this boot off? My ankle is giving me hell."

Both Rainer and Gary moved to help. Gary spoke up. "It's alright there Rainer, I'll look after it. There's an art to getting these flying boots off."

Rainer stood back and let him take over. Peter winced in pain as Gary gently worked the boot from the heel and slowly pulled it free. Next was the thick woollen sock, the removal of which caused considerably more pain than the boot itself. Once his foot was finally free, Peter felt an immediate sense of relief. The pain lessened noticeably, but what remained was still throbbing. Rainer leaned forward alongside Gary as they both examined the ankle by the limited light of the lamp. It was swollen and had turned dramatic shades of purple and black.

"Well, if it's not broken, it's certainly the worst sprain I've ever seen," said Gary. "I'm actually impressed. No one but you could have turned the simple act of getting down off a wing into a complete disaster like this!"

Peter smiled grimly. "I do seem to have a talent for damaging this leg." He looked up at Gary. "I'm sorry mate. I seem to have really buggered this up badly for us. How do you feel about going on alone?"

Rainer spoke up before Gary had a chance to respond. "Don't go rushing to any decisions just yet gentlemen. Wait until after we have eaten and then we can talk at length. I know these mountains quite well and there is much I can help you with but travelling on your own to the Swiss frontier from here is a huge undertaking. It would be foolish to try too soon."

They could both see the sense in Rainer's words. Peter exhaled and fell back into the armchair. Gary went and sat on a chair at the small table. The children sat at the table also, gazing intently at him, still fascinated by his skin colour. Rainer tended to the pot of stew which was now beginning to steam as it warmed. The smell was enticing and quickly filled the room. Soon, Thomas and Marie were hungrily tucking into their meals, still looking up at Gary in between mouthfuls. He remained at the table, enjoying the company of the children as they ate.

Rainer went over to Peter. "Would you mind if I felt your ankle? If we can try and move it gently, we might be able to work out how bad it actually is."

Peter nodded his agreement and braced himself for the pain. Rainer gently lifted the leg and slowly, carefully began to make small rotations of the foot, looking for the limits before the pain became too much for Peter to tolerate. He was also listening closely for any signs of crepitus, the sound made by the two ends of broken bones grinding against each other. He heard none. Furthermore, Peter felt less pain than he was expecting.

"You might be lucky Peter. It may simply be badly sprained after all. I'm not an expert in any way, but I do know some basic first aid. Let us hope for the best, shall we?"

He picked up Peter's flying boot and laid it on its side on the upturned wooden crate. He then set Peters leg back down, with the ball of his foot resting on the soft leather of the boot. The small act of kindness was not lost on Peter.

"Thank you Rainer. You're a far more genial host than we ever expected to encounter."

Rainer grinned. "The pleasure is mine. It's been quite a while since I've had adult company that I didn't have to worry would turn us in. We are fugitives as much as you are I fear. This little valley has been our world for over two years now. Its isolation is all that keeps us safe."

***

The children had now finished their meals. Rainer took their plates and cutlery and rinsed them in a large, galvanised metal tub, set up on a bench close to the stove. After he dried them, he then filled the bowls with generous serves of the stew and passed them to the airmen. Many hours had passed since they had last eaten and the events of the day had added to the press of their hunger. Both Peter and Gary tried to eat with some semblance of good manners, but the measure of their hunger showed in how quickly their bowls were emptied.

Gary spoke first. "That was amazing! Quite delicious! Thank you very much."

"Thank you, I can see you were both hungry," replied Rainer with a smile.

"How did you find all the ingredients for that?" asked Peter. "There were potatoes and carrots as well as the venison."

Rainer was just finishing his own bowl. "The potatoes and carrots I grow myself, the venison I hunted. There are several other ingredients that we find in the forest around here, some wild herbs and fungi. The forest has most things we need really, we're becoming rather good at finding them."

"Well, the flavour was wonderful," added Peter. "A far better meal than we had any right to expect."

He turned to Gary. "Perhaps we might be able to give the children some of our emergency rations?"

Gary had to pause for a moment as he mentally checked off the items that he knew were in the survival kits. "Ah yes! I think I know what you mean."

He got up and went his flying jacket and kit bag which he had dumped by the door. After a few moments of rummaging around he stood up, holding a bar of chocolate. The children's eyes widened in wonder as they realised what it was he had produced. They hadn't tasted chocolate in years.

"Is it alright for them to have some?" he asked Rainer.

"Please! That is most kind of you, I am no longer able to give them such treats anymore."

Gary broke the bar into several pieces. He found two that were similar in size and gave Thomas and Marie one each.

"We might keep the rest for another night, don't you think?" he asked the children. "That way, you can enjoy it for longer."

Marie scoffed her piece down quickly, but Thomas didn't want the joy to end. He nibbled away at his piece, trying to make the experience last as long as possible. Gary sat down again; the simple act of bringing such obvious joy to the children had in turn, helped lift his own spirits.

Rainer turned to him. "That was very kind of you, this has certainly been a most eventful day."

Peter spoke up. "It was the least we could do," he nodded towards Gary. "Soon enough, Gary here will be a father himself, his wife back in England is expecting their first child."

The mention of his wife suddenly clouded Gary's face. "It doesn't look like I will get to see my child now. At least not for quite a while, at best."

"My God, that's right!" exclaimed Peter. "In fact, Anne and Bridget are probably being told right about now that we've been posted missing. Christ…"

A pall of gloom descended upon them both at the thought of the horror and distress their wives would be going through at that very moment. Rainer sat quietly for a minute as the men sought to deal with what was for them, a kind of grief.

"There is no way that we can get word to them I'm afraid," he finally said. "The isolation here can be a curse as much as it is a blessing at times."

Peter looked up and nodded. "At least we are OK. They will know that there's a strong chance that we'll be alive, either on the run, or as prisoners of war. They will still have cause for hope."

"More for you than for me," said Gary morosely. "Bridget will be terrified for me if she thinks I've been captured."

"Then we shall need to make sure that doesn't happen," said Rainer in a matter of fact voice. "Let me start getting the children into bed, we can talk more shortly."

Rainer stood up and crossed over to his children who had both been sitting and reading at the table, having finished their chocolate. He quietly led them into a second room which Peter and Gary assumed was the bedroom.

While they had the room to themselves, Peter leaned over towards Gary.

"We can't allow ourselves to dwell on home at the moment mate. We know that they are safe and secure and Trehearn will make sure they are looked after by the Air Force. They'll be fine, it's up to us to make sure we get back to them in one piece."

Gary made a conscious effort to pick himself up. "You're absolutely right. Thanks Skip. At least I'm still alive to be thinking about them. It was a close run though, what the hell kind of a plane was that thing?"

"It must have had jet engines," replied Peter. "It's the only thing I can think of. I remember a few years ago, we had an experimental jet powered aircraft being tested. Made a bit of a stir at the time, but I've heard nothing about it since. Now, it looks like the Jerries have beaten us to the punch. Now we know they've got one in service. It's a hell of a development. It could possibly change everything."

Gary looked thoughtful again, "Also we've got no way of letting anyone know that it exists."

"Don't worry," said Peter with a bitter chuckle. "Everyone else will know about them soon enough. It'll probably effect the Yanks more than us, they do the daylight stuff."

"I guess so," said Gary quietly.

Peter spoke with a note of bitterness in his voice. "That was the second time I've been caught out by something new the Jerries have sprung on us. The first time was when the Focke-Wulf first appeared. I have some bad memories of that day I'll never forget and now this!"

Rainer returned to the room shortly afterwards. "I have an unusual request for you if you don't mind Gary. Marie was wondering if you would go in and say goodnight to them."

Gary cheered up immediately, "I would love to!"

He got up and went to the bedroom door. He peered around the opening into the surprisingly well decorated room that contained three beds; Marie gave a little squeal of delight.

"Can you please tell us a story?" she asked. Once again, Gary marvelled at their excellent English. He let himself into the room and sat down on the end of Marie's small, home-made bed. Two young sets of eyes were glued on him, full of expectation.

"A story is it? Well now, let me see…"

***

The children were now fast asleep. The excitement of the day had finally won out, and their small, exhausted bodies succumbed to the lure of the night. Gary and Peter sat with Rainer. He had given them each a healthy serving of a home distilled gin he had made. It tasted surprisingly good but was powerfully potent!

Looking intently at Rainer, Peter leaned forward and asked, "How is it that you all speak English so well? Perhaps a few words wouldn't have surprised me, but you are as fluent as we are."

Rainer took a sip of his drink and sat up, overly erect. He exhaled deeply and slouched forward again. "I was born in England."

Both Gary and Peter looked shocked. "You mean you're English?" asked Peter in amazement.

"Well, half English," replied Rainer. "My father was German he worked in London before the last war. He was a clock-maker, a genuine Bavarian cuckoo clock maker in fact. There were a great many of these type of clocks sold to English customers and not many people there who could service them properly. So he moved to London as a young man and opened what became a very thriving business making and servicing clocks and watches."

He paused and took a sip of the gin. "That is how he met my mother; she was a customer. They married in 1912 and I was born in 1913. The following year of course, everything changed. My father was interned for the duration of the war. He was not treated badly, but he became very disillusioned and bitter with the way England regarded him as an 'enemy alien'. He was finally released after the war and in 1920, we all returned to live in Germany. I had to learn to speak German in fact. I really only spoke English at home with my mother, while my father was interned.

"In the end, I became perfectly fluent in both languages, but my time here has seen me develop a German accent to my English. I have tried to bring up Thomas and Marie with both languages. We have days when we only speak German, and days when we only speak English."

Gary was intrigued. "So what happened that ended up with you three living alone up here?"

Rainer hesitated before he spoke again. He took another sip of his gin. "I'm sure you are both aware of the rise of the Nazi Party here. My father quickly became an enthusiastic supporter, but my mother was appalled by them. It created many terrible issues at home. If it wasn't for my mother, I would probably have fallen into line with my father's opinions and become a supporter too. But my mother saw the violence and the takeover of the newspapers and the radio. She saw how any voice that disagreed with Adolf Hitler was very soon silenced. Thanks to my mother, I was gifted the worst of all attributes in a society such as this. The ability to see clearly what was happening before our eyes."

Peter spoke. "What happened to your parents?"

"They separated in 1937, although in truth, they had been living separate lives in the same house for years before that. She moved back to London. I have not heard anything from her since just before the war began."

"So she could still be living in London? You don't know?" asked Gary.

"Yes, it's very likely, but I have no real idea. I can only hope that she is safe," replied Rainer with a deep sigh.

"Do you know where in London she lived?" asked Peter.

"The last time I heard from her, she was living in Fulham," responded Rainer.

"Well, Fulham took its share of damage during the Blitz, but most of it was left intact. If she's still there, she should be OK," added Peter.

Rainer continued, "I desperately hope so. I haven't heard from my father since 1941 either, although I have no doubt he would disown me in a moment if he knew I was still alive. I have not the slightest doubt that he would be happy to see me shot if it meant that he could be given the children to raise as young Nazis."

Both Peter and Gary looked stunned these words. Rainer's passion was deeply sad and profoundly moving.

"What happened to bring you up here?" asked Gary.

"I went to University in Stuttgart. I was studying Electrical Engineering. I met my wife Liesel there in 1933. We were both deeply opposed to the Nazis. Hitler was just coming into power then. At first, it looked to be alright, even though they never missed an opportunity to incite hatred towards anyone they saw fit. Liesel and I could see where this was going. We had decided to go along to an anti-Nazi meeting at the University one evening in 1936, shortly before Thomas was born. She wasn't feeling well and we were delayed in getting there. Well, before we arrived, the meeting was raided by the SA and there were dozens of arrests. Many close friends vanished. We never heard from them again."

Gary and Peter sat mute whilst Rainer told his story.

"Anyway, for a while we were both terribly worried that someone might have given our names to the SA or the Gestapo."

Rainer continued. "In the end, it was obvious that no one did. We carried on as we had before, now though, we kept our views to ourselves more and more. There were so few people that we felt we could trust. Thomas was born and I graduated from University and got a job as an electrical engineer with Siemens back in Munich. I did not know of it at the time, but Liesel had found a new group that called themselves *Das Edelweisspiraten*. The Edelweiss Pirates, they started out as a group of young people who had been forced into the Hitler Youth, but who hated the Nazis and how they repressed the will of people. It was 1938 by then and Liesel was pregnant with Marie. The Pirates started out just doing simple things. Teenage things, trying to be at least a bit rebellious in the eyes of the Nazis. Liesel wasn't really too involved, she just liked to be around them as they plotted things. I think it helped her keep her rebellious spirit alive."

Rainer paused for a moment as he filtered through his memories. Clearly he was getting to a part of his tale that was difficult for him. He took another sip of the gin, a large one.

"Marie was born and the war broke out several months after that. Soon after, everything began to change. The war gave Hitler the excuse to shut down anything that provided any sort of news that didn't suit what he wanted us to know. There were more and more reports going around by word of mouth that people were starting to disappear. Jews in particular, but political opponents of the Nazis were also at great risk. I simply kept working at my job, trying to keep my head down and not be noticed. At that stage, Germany was doing well and there was no pressure on myself or anyone else at Siemens to give up our jobs and enlist. But Liesel had begun to get more involved with the Pirates. They were starting to take on more active forms of protest. They would paint anti-Nazi slogans on buildings, distribute leaflets and even begin to do some simple acts of sabotage against government vehicles and buildings. Nothing too terrible really, but things the Nazi Party would not stand for. Any form of protest was crushed very quickly. Eventually, after well over a year, Liesel was found out as a sympathiser of the Edelweiss Pirates. The person who found her out was my father."

Rainer's voice broke momentarily as he said those last words. He paused again to try and recover his composure, sipping again at the gin, he continued.

"Well, my father didn't give her up straight away. Even he knew what the consequences would be. He waited until I was at home one day and came around to tell us that unless Liesel was prepared to go to the Gestapo and give them evidence against the Pirates she was in league with, he would go himself."

"How did he find out?" asked Peter.

"He visited one day while I was at work. He called around unannounced. He said he was in the area and just wanted to see his grandchildren. Liesel was at home with some young members of the Pirates. They didn't say anything to him, but they had left some pamphlets in sight. He worked out the rest. Anyway, after he gave us his ultimatum, we had to move quickly. We packed up what we could and left within a few hours. I had a car and as a valued employee of Siemens, I was able to get us well out of Munich before my father realised we were gone and went to the authorities. We knew of this place through some of our old University friends from before the war. It belonged to one of them. We knew they had been arrested a few years earlier and we hoped that this cottage might have been left undisturbed. It took us several days to find it but eventually we did. It was crude, but perfect for us. I was able to do several trips to different towns in southern Bavaria to buy goods, some tools, weapons and vegetables to plant. I never went to any place more than once. I believe my caution worked well. We have never been found. Until you arrived, that is." Rainer smiled at this observation.

"Please forgive me for asking," enquired Gary, "but what became of Liesel?"

Rainer paused for a while. He gave a deep sigh and said, "In truth, I really don't know. We came here in late 1941. She became bored very quickly, and with her boredom came the unhappiness. After we had been here about six months, I went out early one morning with my cross-bow to try and hunt for a deer. It's a cruel weapon, but it's silent. Anyway, when I returned, she was gone. The children had been fed and washed, but she had disappeared. The keys to my car were missing as well. It was too late to follow her that day and I couldn't leave Thomas and Marie on their own, so we went to where I kept the car hidden the next day. It's a walk of about five kilometres over a steep range. Of course the car was gone when we got there. I have no idea where she went, for certain. I believe she may have gone off to find any remaining members of the Pirates."

"It's extraordinary that she would have chosen to go and leave her children!" exclaimed Peter. "How could she have thought like that?"

"We lived through eight years of Hitler before then. If you were not a passionate supporter of the Nazis, it was a terrible time. It always seemed to keep getting worse. In the end, they kept us in sway through simple terror. Every day, we would wonder if this was the day they would knock at the door. I believe it all became too much for her. She needed to fight back more than she needed to be a mother. At first I blamed her terribly, but now, I think I understand things better."

For a time, all three men sat silently in the room. Rainer seemed emotionally drained and neither Peter not Gary could think of anything to say that didn't sound trite in their own minds. They each kept their own council.

After a while Rainer spoke again. "I'm sorry that I have no beds to offer you both, but there are some cushions and blankets that you may use to try and make yourselves comfortable."

He looked towards Peter. "Are you comfortable enough there? It may be better than trying to find a spot on the floor."

"I'm sure I'll be fine," he replied. "Thank you for everything you've done for us today Rainer. Tomorrow perhaps we can start looking to make some plans about what to do next."

"An excellent idea. Goodnight then gentlemen, I am exhausted I must sleep."

He went into the bedroom and emerged moments later with several blankets and pillows which he placed on the table. He nodded tiredly to the airmen and returned to the bedroom. Gary and Peter both bade him goodnight as he went off to the third bed in the room with his children. Gary picked up the blankets and handed one to Peter along with a pillow. He then took the rest and set about arranging them on the floor. He added in his flying jacket as extra padding and seemed content enough with the result.

I'm going to nip outside for a minute. Nature is calling," he said as he made his way to the door.

When he came back in he asked Peter, "How about you?"

"If you don't mind giving me a shoulder to lean on, I need to go as well," was his reply.

"Just as long as you don't ask me to help you shake off the drops!" replied Gary.

***

A light mist had settled in the valley during the night. Gary emerged from the cabin to have a look at their refuge in the early light of the new day. He was immediately awe-struck. The mist was beginning to dissipate and the sights it unveiled of the secluded valley took his breath away. The steep, mountainous sides loomed over them like protective sentinels, standing guard over the alpine meadowland that lay within their dolomite folds; the whole, a vision of spectacular scenic glory. Tiny flowers dotted the meadow as small birds and insects made their way amongst them, each playing their miniscule roles in the greater life of the valley.

Gary looked up the valley towards the Mosquito. The mist was beginning to lift, but it was still too heavy to let him see that far. Rainer appeared from the cabin as well and walked over to Gary.

"Do you like our little part of the world?"

Gary nodded as he continued to look around. "It is quite beautiful. You could be forgiven for never knowing there was a war going on."

Rainer nodded also in agreement. "I get that feeling many times. But then, there are times when we hear the sound of huge numbers of bombers going overhead. Occasionally, we might even see them, it all comes back then. I wonder where they are going and who is about to suffer."

Gary looked at him quizzically. "Have you any idea how the war is going? When was the last time that you heard any news?"

"Well, nearly two years at least," replied Rainer with a shrug. "We have no easy way of getting to any town or village since Liesel took the car. I could possibly walk, but I could never leave the children alone for that long. Also, if I was to get picked up whilst I was away, then things would be terrible for them. It is far safer to remain here in isolation. We have enough to sustain ourselves here."

Gary said nothing, he looked at Rainer for a few moments, deep in thought. Presently he changed the subject. "We need to find some wood that we can shape into a crutch to get Peter mobile again. If we're to have any hope of trying to find our way to the Swiss frontier, he will need to be able to walk."

Rainer looked at him with an unfathomable expression on his face. "We shall need to talk more about this, I don't think you fully appreciate the difficulties. But in the meantime, you are quite right, we need to fashion a crutch for him. Please, come with me!"

Rainer spent the next morning introducing them to the little self-sufficient world he had created for his children and himself. Being an engineer by training equipped him with a set of skills he had put to good use. There was a small stream that flowed not far behind the cabin. It was mostly meltwater from the snowfields above, and the freshest the airmen had ever tasted. There was a potato patch that had been planted when Rainer and Liesel had first come to the valley two years ago. That was now producing a good supply every summer. There was also a number of planted vegetables as well, but Rainer had become highly knowledgeable in the ways of finding edible plants from the forest, as well as hunting with his cross bow. The bow was silent and he was able to reuse the bolts. He was very careful to retrieve them whenever possible.

Most impressive though, was a composting toilet that Rainer had built from scratch. He had read about them at University and understood the principal. The rest was simply hard work, but it meant a level of sanitation that surprised Peter and Gary. Clearly, Rainer was a most resourceful individual.

Chapter 12

The days that followed saw Gary and Rainer make several trips up to the Mosquito. There was much in the wreck that could be salvaged for use in Rainer's small home. Thomas and Marie gleefully joined in on the expeditions. It was the most exciting thing that had happened to them in ages, and neither of them had any intention of missing out on a single minute of it.

There were tools that were secreted in compartments around the aeroplane and with them, they were able to take out the seats, the radio and first aid kit. They also retrieved Peter's and Gary's parachutes and the emergency inflatable life raft. Very important, but difficult to get out to get out due to their size and weight, were the two large twelve volt batteries which could be used to potentially bring the radio back to life.

The problem of getting all this bounty down to the cabin was solved by inflating the life raft, filling it with everything they had retrieved and then pulling it behind them. The downhill slope coupled with the smooth surface provided by the alpine grasses made this last effort surprisingly easy.

Peter had been busy coming to grips with his compromised mobility. Rainer had fashioned a very serviceable crutch for him from a fallen tree branch which he found in the forest, not far behind the cottage. His ankle was now heavily strapped with bandages from the Mosquito's first aid kit. After a couple of days he found that he was able to put some weight on the leg without too much pain. Rainer had been proven correct, it appeared the ankle wasn't broken after all, just very badly sprained. This news was immensely cheering to both he and Gary. They might be able to start planning on how to get to Switzerland sooner, rather than later.

He stumped his way outside when he heard the laughter of the children. Gary and the others were returning from their trip up to the Mosquito.

"How did you go?" called out Peter.

He hobbled out to meet them as they drew closer.

"I think we did rather well really," said Gary. "We have to go back one more time. Rainer suggested we try and camouflage the wreck as much as possible. We can lay some fallen trees over the wings and fuselage to try and break up the outline if an aircraft flies over. I think it's a pretty good idea."

"It's an excellent idea!" added Peter. "While you're up there, you should also get the aerial wire for the radio. It looks like you forgot that."

He was grinning happily, knowing that he wouldn't be the one who had to do the work, as Gary and Rainer looked at each other in resignation.

"I guess there was always bound to be something that we forgot?" said Gary in frustration. "Oh well, we were going back up again anyway."

That evening, all five were gathered around the radio as it hummed back into life. Thomas had been hugely excited to have the important job of scaling a tree to spread out the long wire that served as the aerial for the radio. Peter had reconnected the aerial to its socket on the unit and then wired it across to one of the batteries. It warmed up well, but in the confines of the valley, there was very little by way of a signal that they could receive.

There was a strong note of disappointment in Peter's voice as he stood back and looked up at the mountainside that towered over them. "I was worried that this might be the case. It looks like we're going to have to lug the bloody thing all the way to the top of one of these mountains if we're going to have any luck."

Rainer had not said much about the radio. He was harbouring a deep concern though, and finally he could stay silent no longer.

"What do you intend to do with the radio if you can get it working? Who do you expect to be able to communicate with?"

Gary and Peter looked at each other before Peter spoke. "We could try and get a message back to home. Tell them we're both alive and safe."

"How long do you think you would remain safe after you send that message?" asked Rainer sharply. "Don't you realise how likely it would be that the signal would be detected by our German military? They could trace its source right back to here very quickly. You would be endangering all of us for no good purpose!" Now that he had spoken, he was fast becoming quite agitated.

The two airmen quickly realised the strength of the point that Rainer was making.

"Bloody hell!" exclaimed Peter. "You're quite right," he looked at Gary. "We should have thought of that ourselves. Well, that puts a dampener on the whole idea."

Gary brightened. "However, the radio set can still be used just to receive. We might even be able to adapt it to tune into commercial broadcasts. We could at least find out what is happening beyond here., that would be perfectly safe."

Rainer visibly relaxed. "That would be better, far better."

Peter looked at Rainer. "Do you know of a higher spot that you don't need to be a mountain goat to climb up to?"

"I do as a matter of fact," he replied. "Up the mountain beyond your aircraft is a good spot. It's a solid climb but not too bad. There is a ridge there that dips down between two mountain peaks, so you don't have to go up so high, but it should still be high enough. There's also a small rocky cave up there, good to conceal the radio and battery in."

"Well then, that's where it sounds like the radio is going!" said Peter brightly.

Gary just looked at him, "You mean, after getting all this stuff down here from the crash, we've now got to lug it all the way back up again?"

Peter smiled with just a hint of guilt. "Sorry mate. I can't do much to help I'm afraid. Duff ankle and all that!"

Even Rainer had to laugh at the look on Gary's face.

***

Anne had been granted compassionate leave after the news of the loss of Peter and Gary's aircraft came through. She had opened the front door of their little rented cottage in response to a gentle but persistent knocking, to find a sombre faced Group Captain Trehearn standing there. He didn't need to speak; she knew as soon as she saw him what the nature of his call meant.

The days since then had been bleak and numb. Friends and colleagues from the base hospital had been with her constantly to offer such comfort as they could, but no light could fall on her soul. The knowledge that they were missing, possibly still alive rather than confirmed as being killed, somehow made things worse. It simply added worry and fear onto the grief.

The only moment of real comfort was when her father arrived from London to accompany her back on the train. The closeness of a loving parent finally allowed her some measure of ease, with the sharing of the pain. Being back in the familiarity of her old home certainly helped. After a couple of days, she found herself thinking more clearly again and being more prepared to clutch to the desperate hope that Peter may still be alive as a Prisoner of War in Germany. On the morning of her third day in London, she finally felt the strength to pick up the telephone.

"Hello?" The voice was a man's, not who Anne was expecting.

"Hello, I was hoping to be able to speak with Bridget please."

"Who may I say is calling please?" asked the voice.

"My name is Anne I am the wife of Peter Garland; he was the pilot with Gary."

"Just a moment please," came the quietly spoken response.

Within bare seconds Bridget had come on the line, her voice rushed and barely in control. "Anne? Is it you?"

Hearing her friend's voice again, clearly grasping the desperation in those few words, brought Anne immediately into tears.

"Yes Bridget," she gasped in between rasping sobs.

Bridget was now also in uncontrollable tears as well. After a minute, Anne was able to control herself enough to say, "I'm so sorry I haven't called earlier. I'm back in London now, at Daddy's house, may I come to see you please?"

"Oh yes! Please yes!" came Bridget's passioned reply. "My parents are here with me. It was my father who answered the telephone, when can you come?"

"I could come shortly if you don't mind. I'm in St John's Wood, I could catch a taxi."

"That would be wonderful, I think I need your company. Do you mind my parents being here?" asked Bridget.

"Oh no! Not at all. I would love to meet them," said Anne with conviction. "Well, I might get myself ready and call for a taxi. I have your address in Wimbledon. I'll be there as soon as I can."

"Oh Anne. I'm so looking forward to seeing you. I have just felt so lost..." Bridget's voice tailed off as she fought for control again.

"I've been the same," replied Anne somehow feeling brighter. "I shall see you shortly. Goodbye my darling."

She hung up the phone and breathed a deep sigh. The thought of seeing her friend again brought an immediate sense of great relief to her. Bridget now felt more like a sister than a friend. Their pain was shared, only Bridget could truly understand what she was experiencing because she was feeling it too. Together, they would help and support each other.

***

Another twelve days had passed. Peter could now walk without the crutch, but the ankle still felt very tender and he wasn't confident to push himself too hard, fearing that even a small slip might undo much of the still-fresh healing. Rainer had taken Gary and Thomas into the forest to go hunting for some fresh meat. A deer was what they hoped for, but there were always rabbits, hares and even squirrels to be found. Peter had stayed behind with Marie. Together they were walking around the meadow that lay beyond the cabin, gently exercising Peter's ankle.

"Do you have wolves and elephants in New Zealand?" she asked with animated curiosity. She had never heard of this strange country on the other side of the world before and without an atlas, Peter was having great difficulty in explaining to her where his home was.

"No Marie, nothing like that really… I did see an elephant at the zoo in Auckland a few years ago!" he laughingly replied. "But no wolves though."

"What do you have then?" she asked, slightly disappointed at his answer.

"Well then…" Peter had to think. He could only think of birds. There didn't seem to be much else that came to mind.

"We have quite a lot of different kinds of birds. We have one called a kiwi which is very interesting. We also have a special kind of lizard called a tuatara."

"Birds and lizards aren't very interesting!" said Marie sounding more disappointed than ever. "What kind of country doesn't have proper animals?"

"What kind of proper animals do you mean?" asked Peter. "Birds and lizards are proper animals I think."

"I mean scary ones!" said Marie with a gleam in her eye and a hint of excitement in her voice. "Do you have any scary ones?"

Peter struggled for a moment, then he remembered something. "We do have a monster animal called a Weta! They're really scary!"

Marie suddenly looked impressed, her eyes widening in excitement. "A Weta?" she replied, her German accent giving the first letter a 'v' sound. "What is a Weta?"

"I don't think I can tell you," said Peter. "I don't want to frighten you too much. Your father might never forgive me."

"Oh please!" said Marie earnestly.

"Perhaps a bit later," said Peter teasingly. "Now, I want you to think about all the different kinds of scary animals a Weta might be. Don't tell me now, think hard and tell me tomorrow. I'll let you know if you've guessed correctly."

By now, their walk had taken them a full circuit of the meadow and Peter's ankle was beginning to ache. He was pleased though; the long walk must have been the better part of two miles. His healing was progressing well.

As good as he felt about the length of the walk he had managed, he was still grateful when they arrived back at the cabin. He opened the door and Marie led them in.

Peter looked at his wristwatch. "Now Marie, I have promised your father that you would be doing at least an hour of reading and then some arithmetic. Shall we get started?"

"But I'm hungry! Can I please have something to eat first?" she begged with wide, pleading eyes.

Peter couldn't help but smile. Clearly Marie had found that this particular look got her most things she wanted. He had just discovered he was not immune either.

"Well, it is nearly lunch time, I shall heat up some stew for us both. But afterwards, it's time for study, okay?"

Marie smiled happily to herself.

Chapter 13

The murmur of approaching voices filtered through to Peter's consciousness. The others were returning, it was now late in the afternoon, and both Peter and Marie were getting concerned at how long the three had been away on their hunt. They had left just as dawn was breaking.

"How did you go?" he asked as he opened the door at their approach.

Marie ran outside and hugged her father tightly.

"We did quite well," answered Rainer whilst returning his daughters embrace. "Three hares, nice ones too there should be enough to last us for several days. Thomas got one of them"

"I didn't expect you to take quite so long. Marie has been worrying." Peter didn't mention that he had been getting concerned as well.

"We went up to the radio for a while and tried to get some news," said Gary. "We found a few broadcasts in German which Rainer said were not very informative. More like propaganda than real news. Nothing you could rely on for anything accurate."

They all made their way inside, Marie releasing her father and giving Thomas a brief hug as well. Rainer made his way over to the stove and rekindled the embers that remained from when Peter had heated lunch earlier. He began to prepare some herbal tea. He had developed his own recipe from the Elderflower and Camomile that grew in the valley.

Peter turned to Gary. "Did you manage to pick up anything from England?"

Gary nodded, but not with conviction. "There were some messages in English coming through from the BBC. Nothing that made any sense. I think they were for Resistance groups in

France and Holland mostly. All in codes from the sound of them, no actual news that I could make out."

The two of them were becoming very conscious of how cut off they were from the rest of the world. It was over three weeks since they crashed and they had heard nothing from outside their little valley since.

"They must think we're both dead!" Gary had taken a chair near the small table. He was clearly in a sombre mood.

Peter nodded solemnly. "What must Anne and Bridget be going through? I can't begin to imagine."

"How long before you might be able to walk properly again, do you think?" asked Gary.

"I had a good walk today, a couple of miles. It was sore at the end, but tolerable. Perhaps another week and I'll be right to go." Peter was finally feeling more positive about his recovery.

Rainer had been listening to them and finally felt compelled to speak up. "Have you thought at all about how you will travel? About where you will go? It is less than forty kilometres by road to the Swiss frontier from here, but that is a large lake called the *Bodensee*. It is constantly patrolled. Crossing over the wilder mountains south of here is possible, but very difficult. It will take you into Austria where there are land borders into Switzerland or Liechtenstein, but those frontiers are extremely heavily guarded. It would not be possible to get through in a car or a lorry, even if you were able to find one."

"I realise that," replied Peter. "Is it possible to get close by road and then go across open country after that?"

Rainer thought for a moment. "It may be possible, but you would need to know the area well; the places where such an opportunity might exist. Otherwise, you would just be making a wild guess and the odds would be very much against you. I would not recommend it."

Gary had been sitting quietly and listening. "Well, if we can't go through the border, can we go over it?"

Peter and Rainer looked quizzically at him.

"What did you have in mind?" asked Peter.

"You're a pilot, aren't you? Is there an airfield we could get to, where we might be able to steal a plane?" asked Gary simply. "It's the most obvious thing I can think of."

Peter looked at Rainer. "Do you know of one Rainer? It sounds like a good idea to me."

Rainer looked pensive, if there was an airfield in the area, he did not know of it.

"I am not sure. If there is one, it would be closer to a larger town or city. Somewhere like Sonthofen or Kempten, north of here. How do you propose to steal a military aircraft? They would be heavily guarded surely?"

"A military one would be, yes," replied Peter, "but a civilian airfield might be quite different. A small field with a flying club or something like that. It wouldn't get us to England, but if it only has to go a hundred miles or less, then something small would be fine."

As he spoke, Peter felt his energy levels returning. Suddenly, they had the makings of a plan. Gary began to feel equally invigorated. His earlier depression was now being consumed by the thought of taking control of their situation once again.

He looked at Rainer. "Do you have any maps of this area somewhere? What was the name of that town you mentioned? Would you have a street map of it?"

Rainer's eyebrows raised in thought. "It is called Kempten, I might actually have a map," he said, brightening. "I shall go and look."

He left the room and went into the bedroom. There was a box where he kept all the books and papers he had brought with them when they first fled from Munich. After a few minutes he returned from the bedroom. "I have a road map of southern Bavaria. I don't know how much it will be of value, but it's all

I have. I had much better maps which I kept in my car, but they disappeared when Liesel left." Rainer handed the folded map to Gary.

Peter joined them at the table as Gary opened out the map. Straight away, they could see the map was very useful indeed. Rainer pointed out the area where they currently were. The map showed little by way of towns or villages in their immediate region. Clearly, that indicated the general inaccessibility of the mountains. It was not very far however, to several towns and smaller cities. Surely there would have to be airfields somewhere nearby.

"Look for the word '*Flughafen*', it means airport," said Rainer.

"There's one!" exclaimed Gary, pointing at a spot close to a smaller town called Immenstadt, on the main road leading north to the larger regional city of Kempten.

"And another one there!" said Peter, pointing to Kempten itself. "Are they likely to be civilian do you think, or Luftwaffe?" he said, tapping the map.

"The one at Kempten would likely be the larger," Rainer looked doubtful about their chances there. "It is probably Luftwaffe; it won't be easy to get close to the aircraft."

Peter was looking at the map intently, considering the possibilities. "It may be busier and better protected, but there would also be a larger number of aircraft available. We only need one that's parked off to the side, out of the way. It's dangerous, but it may still be an option. This other one though, south of it, that looks a smaller town."

Rainer looked closely. "Immenstadt, I know that town, it may be better. I don't remember seeing any military presence there. The airfield is likely to be small, and just for civilians."

Peter now looked keen. "If it's just for light civilian aircraft, it could be perfect. Most civilian airfields would have a number of small private planes that are usually left parked in the open. It could be our best chance."

Rainer looked doubtful. "Would they not be kept locked up? Wouldn't you need a key?"

Peter smiled. "No Rainer, you don't need keys to start one. Most privately owned small aeroplanes can't be locked, they are just for recreational flying. They are not likely to ever be stolen. Getting to one is the biggest challenge. We would need to steal a car or a motorcycle to get up there."

Gary spoke up. "It can't be a motorcycle unless we can travel at night. I would be very conspicuous, don't you think?"

Peter chuckled. "A good point, I never even gave that a thought. I guess a black man on a bike would be a rather unexpected sight around here at the moment, so, a car it is."

Rainer left the table to attend to the herbal tea he was making, he returned with a cup for each of them. All three of them sat at the table, gazing over the map, each deep in thought.

Meanwhile, Thomas and Marie were outside the rear of the cabin, cleaning and preparing the hares to be cooked, unaware of the plotting and planning that was happening inside.

***

Peter's therapeutic walks had lengthened; he was now managing two full circuits of the meadow, twice a day. He knew his ankle wasn't fully healed, but it felt almost there now.

Gary looked at him as he returned from his most recent walk. A full week had passed since the genesis of the idea to steal an aeroplane had been suggested. They had eventually settled on a plan that seemed simple enough, but through necessity would need to rely on moments of audacity, coupled with pure luck. Still, neither could see a better alternative.

"How's it feeling now? You look to be moving well," he asked.

Peter looked at him and nodded. "It isn't quite a hundred percent yet, but it feels good enough for me to not be too much of a burden for everyone. I reckon we can give things a try in a day or so, what do you think?"

"Good!" replied Gary emphatically. "The sooner the better. I don't think Rainer minds having us here, but we are certainly putting a strain on his supplies."

Peter thought out loud. "It might be a good idea to get Rainer to lead us to the road, the rest will be up to us."

"Yeah, the last thing we need is to get lost in the forest before we even start. We'd look a right pair of Charlies!"

Peter thought further. "We'd better give our kit a good clean-up today. I'll look after the Webley and the Very pistol if you can make sure everything else is all good."

"Good idea," replied Gary. "How much ammunition do you have for the Webley?"

"Just the six shots already in the chambers. Hopefully we won't need to use it, it's a loud bloody thing. It'd certainly attract a bit of attention. I'm not sure about the Very pistol, but it could turn out to be useful, I think we'd be wise to bring it."

Gary nodded in agreement. "Well then, we might as well do it now then, don't you think?"

"Alright then, let's get to it!" replied Peter.

***

The quiet reverie of the late afternoon was suddenly shattered by the sound of heavy aircraft engines and machine gun fire. Rainer had been sitting with his children, giving them a lesson in geometry. Peter and Gary had finished cleaning, checking and packing their equipment several hours earlier and were now resting. Everyone leapt to their feet immediately and ran to the door.

Overhead an American B-17 bomber was trailing smoke and being harried by a German Me109 fighter. They were both only a few thousand feet above and were following the line of the valley before disappearing over the ridge at the far end, beyond the wreckage of the Mosquito. The sound of their engines carried back for many seconds after they had disappeared from view.

"Do you think he saw anything?" asked Gary.

"Do you mean the German pilot?" replied Peter.

"Yeah," returned Gary.

"We can only hope not. He would have had his mind pretty well occupied on the B-17, so most likely he didn't."

Rainer and the children stood very quietly alongside, all of them looking deeply pensive. Less than ten minutes later, they had their answer. The German fighter reappeared over the crest at the far end of the valley. It circled the wreck of the Mosquito and turned to fly down towards them, passing directly over the cabin. Once again, the small fighter circled, the pilot clearly taking in as much as possible. The track marks of Peter's walking around the meadow would be clearly visible from the air. There was also a thin wisp of smoke coming from the narrow chimney flue. There was no doubting that the pilot would be reporting his find back to his superiors. Rainer's safe haven of the last few years had finally been discovered.

The Messerschmitt gained height but remained circling the valley. Clearly the pilot was finding his bearings to give an accurate location of what he had discovered. Shortly afterwards though, he finally flew off towards the north.

As soon as he was gone, everyone emerged from inside the cabin. Peter and Gary looked briefly at each other before turning to Rainer who appeared to be in shock. For the first time since the two airmen had known him, he clearly had no idea of what to do next. Peter realised immediately that it was up to him to take charge now. He approached Rainer and with both hands, grasped him by the shoulders.

"I'm sorry Rainer, but we have a change in plans now my friend. You and the children are coming with us. You can't stay here anymore; they could be here within a few hours."

Gary stepped forward too. "Peter's absolutely right Rainer. If our plan could work with the two of us, it could work just as easily with five. Maybe even better, we have you to speak German for us."

Rainer looked at them both blankly. The change in their circumstances was so sudden and complete that he was having difficulty in processing it. He had allowed himself to believe that they could see out the war in secluded hiding, almost indefinitely. That illusion had been snuffed out in an instant.

Peter put his arm around Rainer's shoulder. "I'm sorry about this, but it's suddenly just become far too dangerous for you here. We've got to start preparing. I don't think anyone will come now. It's too late in the day for them to get near here before nightfall, but I'll bet they'll be ready to move by first thing tomorrow."

Rainer suddenly appeared to snap out of his introspection and finally grasp the changed reality they now faced. He looked around at the small cabin that been their home for nearly three years. It was now too dangerous to spend another night in. If there were soldiers coming up the path from the road, they would be trapped in the valley with nowhere else to go. They needed to get through to the road before any soldiers arrived. Rainer knew a small, hidden cave that overlooked the spot on the road from where anyone arriving to trek up to the valley would be most likely to start. They could shelter safely in it.

"We still have a little time," he said, thinking clearly again. "I should feed Thomas and Marie before we go. In fact, all of us should eat first, it might be a while before we can eat again."

This was clearly a sensible suggestion, and their evening meal was already on the stove. There was no talking as all five of them ate. Everyone was too deep in thought to want to talk. Even little Marie, the most talkative one amongst them, sat in silence as she finished her stewed rabbit.

Rainer had two proper mountaineering knapsacks which he pulled out. He filled one with clothes for the children and himself as well as a couple of blankets and gave the other, which used to be Liesel's, to Gary. He had some strips of dried venison which he packed in as well. It was the only food he had which could be easily carried with them. It wasn't much, but it would have to do.

Gary and Peter were well prepared; both of them grateful for their foresight in getting everything ready in the morning. The second knapsack allowed them to stow their escape kit securely, along with additional clothes, some tools and matches. Rainer dressed the children warmly and then hugged them closely.

"Are you ready for a big adventure?" he asked, trying not to let his own fear affect his children.

Thomas understood what was happening far more clearly than Marie. He looked with deep apprehension at his father, but for Marie, the word 'adventure' spurred her into eager anticipation.

"Where are we going Papa?" she asked with wide eyes.

"We are going to camp tonight, instead of staying here. I am worried that there might be soldiers coming to find us. We need to hide from them. I know a perfect spot, but you must promise me something."

A shadow of uncertainty flitted across her face. "What?"

"You must promise to do exactly as I, or Peter, or Gary say, as soon as we say it! Also we must all be as quiet as little church mice; can you do that for me please?"

"Yes Papa," she replied earnestly.

"Very good, my darling," he held her close and kissed the top of her head.

Looking then at Thomas, he could see fear in his young eyes. Far more so than Marie, his son had grasped the significance of the danger they were in. He tried to sound reassuring. "Don't worry my son, we have a plan already worked out. All will be well."

Thomas managed a wan smile, but his own fear still lay just behind its mask. Peter went to the front door and looked out into the fading light of the evening. There would still be usable light for another hour or so, but they needed to get going now. Gary had slung on the knapsack and Peter helped adjust the straps to make it sit better. Rainer's was already a good fit for him from previous use. Since Gary was to carry the knapsack, Peter took up Gary's small pack, along with Rainer's hunting rifle and his remaining supply of bullets. The last thing Rainer added to his load was his trusted cross bow, and the supply of bolts.

He looked at both the airmen. "I'm a good shot with this, it is very quiet. It's a better weapon than your pistol, I can assure you."

Peter and Gary couldn't help but agree, it could be a very useful addition.

They all filed outside and pulled the door closed behind them. Rainer took the lead and they set off away from the security of the little cabin that had served and protected them for so long, towards the grim uncertainty of the next twenty-four hours.

The late light had helped on the ascent out of the valley. The walk was steep in places and difficult for Peter and Marie, who each needed to stop occasionally. Gary, who had spent most of the last few weeks in the company of Rainer and Thomas had grown fitter and was better able to manage the climb despite the weight of the knapsack. Once they cleared the tree-line, their progress became easier as the gradient eased. As the last of the day's light dissolved away, they crossed over the ridge that separated their valley from the descent down towards the roadway. It was the same ridge that the Mosquito had cleared so narrowly in the dying moments of its final flight. They had all paused for a last, lingering look down into their little private world, but there was not much to see. The evening had shrouded the valley below them in near complete darkness. Turning back to the track, they began the descent into the darkness that obscured the pathway below them.

Rainer had done this walk many times, but never at night. Even though it was now getting into the third week of May, there was no appreciable twilight, only a sliver of waning moon to light the way. The gradient on this side was nowhere near as steep as on the other. Taking things as slowly as they needed, they were able to make steady progress over the next hour. The forest had completely enveloped them but Rainer's memory of the faint trail was serving them well.

Suddenly the light of a vehicle travelling along a road caught their attention. It didn't stop, it was merely a car, not a lorry full of soldiers. It did mean though, that the road was not far ahead. Rainer quietly indicated for the others to take a seat and rest. In the day, he would have had no difficulty in finding the small cave that he wanted, but it was far more challenging in the darkness.

Rainer spoke softly. "I need you all to wait here for me. The little cave is not far from here, but it might take me while to find it in the dark. I'll be able to move more quickly on my own. Don't worry, I won't be long."

He vanished into the darkness while the others sat down and waited. Nearly half an hour later, he returned. "I've found it. The ground is very rocky, so don't rush, be careful with each step."

There was no path to follow, Rainer led them over a small, smooth field of granite which soon became broken and irregular. Difficult as it was in the dark, they could be confident that they would not leave signs of their passing to be picked up by anyone coming up the path from below them. The small cave was really a natural formation hidden within a large field of stacked boulders and smaller rocks. It had been created following a significant rock-fall many millennia earlier. It had probably once given shelter to previous ancient human denizens of the forests, long before the modern nations of Europe existed. Now, it served their purpose perfectly.

Peter checked his watch in the faint light, it was not yet 10 pm. The exertions had completely exhausted the children, and Rainer made them as comfortable as he could, using the spare clothes as a mattress and the blankets he brought along for warmth. They both fell asleep almost immediately. Peter and Gary were sitting outside the cave, looking down in the direction of the road below them. Rainer joined them after the children were asleep.

"What next then, gentlemen?" he asked. "I'm afraid, this is where your expertise takes over from mine."

"Well, I guess now it's up to the Germans. We can only assume they will come, and sooner rather than later," said Peter.

"How many do you think they will send?" asked Rainer.

There was a pause before anyone spoke. It was Gary who answered. "I think no more than ten or so really, if they think that they are only looking for two crashed airmen, they won't need to send a large number of troops."

"I agree," added Peter. "They might not even come at all, but my feeling is that they will."

"How long do you think they might be?" asked Rainer.

Peter thought before he answered. "Soon, most likely I think they would want to try and stop us from doing what we have just done. They'll want to trap us in the valley, otherwise, there's no real point. We will have had time to get away."

"But with nowhere to go, that's the problem," added Gary. "They will probably think that even if we do get out of the valley, we should be easy enough to catch if we stay close to the road."

"So they'll almost certainly leave a couple behind to guard the lorry, if they come up in one," said Peter thoughtfully. "That could be our chance. If they go on up to the valley in force and leave just a few, we might be able to overpower them and take the vehicle."

Peter then looked hard at Rainer. "Are you sure you're ready for this? You may have to shoot that thing at another man in a few hours. You may have to kill someone, that's not an easy thought to deal with."

Rainer surprised them with his response. "I will be fine, I promise you. I have had to kill deer, and I hold them in much higher regard than I do these Nazi bastards. These people have cost me everything. Worry about yourselves gentlemen, I shall be fine."

Peter gave Gary a half smile. "Alright then, you two should try and get some sleep for a few hours. I'll take the first watch."

Chapter 14

Peter had quietly woken up Gary shortly after 2am. He needed some sleep, and now it was Gary's turn to continue the watch. He quickly fell into an exhausted sleep, only to be gently shaken awake, seemingly moments later. He was surprised to see vestigial daylight; it was now past 5am. Gary motioned for him to remain quiet.

"A lorry has just pulled up, down below us and over to our left," he said in a soft voice.

Peter carefully motioned forward and peered down in the direction that Gary indicated. Now that he could see, he was surprised at how close to the road they were. It couldn't be more than seventy or eighty yards away, though it was still well downhill.

As they watched, an officer and several troops began to emerge from the rear of the vehicle. Others soon joined them and presently there were a dozen troops gathered around the lorry. Peter patted Gary on the shoulder and went into the cave to wake Rainer and the children. The children were his greatest concern. Would they make any noise as they woke? Especially Marie. He gently shook Rainer's arm and he awoke immediately. Peter put his finger to his lips to indicate the need for silence.

"They have come, just where you said they would," he said quietly. "Are you able to wake up the children without them making any noise?"

Rainer nodded. "Leave that to me. This is something we've practised many times."

He carefully sat up and got onto his knees, he quietly crawled over to his children. Peter left him with them and went back out to join Gary. As he looked down on the scene below, it was clear that they were preparing to move up the steep sides of the valley very shortly. The troops were putting on packs and slinging their rifles over their shoulders. The officer had ventured the first few steps up the start of the trail before turning back to his men. The trees in between had filtered out his voice, but it was clear he had ordered them to commence the climb.

The German officer left just three troops to guard the lorry, whilst the main body went off in pursuit of who and whatever lay on the other side of the valley wall towering above them. The trail was no more than fifty yards to their left, but the forest in between was so dense that they could see nothing of the German troops as they made their way up the path.

It was a hike of at least three hours to clear the ridge above and make their way down to the cabin in the valley beyond. That meant that all they needed to do was wait at least two hours before they made their move and if they were successful, they would have at least a four hour head start on any troops that might be following. The wait would also allow the soldiers remaining with the lorry to grow complacent with boredom.

Peter and Gary were both deeply impressed at the discipline of the two children. Both of them sat quietly in the shallow cave and gave no audible hint of their presence. After an hour and a half had passed, Gary and Rainer began to prepare themselves.

It was decided that Peter, with his questionable ankle, would stay behind with the children in the cave. Gary took Peter's Webley revolver and Rainer's rifle. Rainer kept his preferred weapon, the crossbow and together the two of them quietly began to make their way back towards the track. Crouching low and taking great care over every step they took, they slowly made their way down the path towards the lorry, making sure to keep as much of the forest in between them and the German soldiers as was possible.

Once they had finally got to within fifty yards, they left the track and crept closer, using the cover of the now thinning forest to preserve their concealment. They settled on two protected spots several yards apart but now only about twenty yards away from the vehicle. Two of the guards had returned to the comfort and shelter inside the rear of the lorry. The remaining soldier sat in the passenger's seat of the cabin, closest to Gary and Rainer. He was the one who should have been most likely to see them as they manoeuvred into their positions, but he was happily occupied with a book and not paying attention.

Rainer had tensioned the crossbow before he left the cave. He now carefully placed a bolt into the firing groove and ensured the notch at the back mated with the string of the bow. He would be the one to take the first shot. The soldier in the cabin of the lorry was his to deal with. He glanced over at Gary who was, in turn, watching him intently. The other troops should be over the crest by now. Only the sound of the most raucous cacophony of gunfire should reach them. It was time to attack.

Gary nodded to Rainer, he acted quickly; too much time to think might have sapped his resolve. He aimed the crossbow at the ear of the soldier in the cabin and gently squeezed the trigger. It was almost an anti-climax. Rainer's shot was perfect. The crossbow made a soft thunk as it discharged. The bolt entered straight through the soldier's ear and into his brain. He made no sound, just slowly fell forward until his head rested against the dashboard. Gary looked closely at Rainer, he seemed alright, showing no obvious emotional reaction at what he had just done. For his part, Rainer immediately turned his back on the scene and began to re-tension the crossbow. It would soon be needed again. The two remaining soldiers in the rear of the lorry had clearly heard nothing. There was no sign of movement from them after the killing bolt had been loosed. Rainer finished reloading and returned to his former position. Now they had but to wait. They could do nothing until one or both of the other two German soldiers emerged from the rear of the lorry.

Gary had settled on Rainer's rifle over the Webley pistol as he was no marksman. At the distance he was from the lorry, he could not be certain of an accurate shot unless he used the rifle. It was only a light hunting rifle, a .22 calibre. Fine for small game but not ideal for taking down another man. It could cause a serious wound, but only a well-judged shot would be likely to kill. He knew he wasn't that good a shot and he suddenly became aware of a coldness spreading through him. He had never fired a weapon in anger, he had never even shot at a rabbit. It was Rainer or young Thomas who had been the hunters on their expeditions. He had been concerned at how having to kill another man might affect Rainer, now he was discovering that it was himself who was experiencing the emotional turmoil.

On the ground, holding a rifle, waiting for a man to appear; a man who might have a family like he did himself; a man whose company he might have enjoyed under different circumstances. A man it was up to him now to kill. It was all so much simpler in the air. So far removed from the death that he played his role in bringing to others, so many thousands of feet below. He closed his eyes and steadied his breathing, trying to relax himself as best he could. He could feel his heart racing in his chest as the tension mounted. He forced himself to breathe slowly through his nose, counting out the seconds to get into a steady rhythm and lower his stress levels. The sound of voices came from the covered rear of the lorry. Someone was calling out to the man in the front cabin. A pause as they waited for a reply. The voice called again, this time louder. Once again, there was no reply.

Gary glanced at Rainer who was looking at him. Gary had the better view of the rear of the lorry. Rainer was waiting for him to take the lead. After a few moments, the fingers of a hand appeared as the man inside grasped the upright frame of the rear covered entrance. Gary began to raise his right hand slowly, indicating to Rainer that someone was about to appear. He gripped the rifle carefully, lifting it into position whilst he moved the forefinger of his right hand onto the trigger. To his right, Rainer was also drawing a bead on the rear of the lorry.

He whispered to Gary. "Leave him for me. Don't you shoot!"

Gary turned and looked at him. Rainer motioned for him to remain still and silent. The man emerged from the rear of the lorry and jumped down to the ground. He stood upright and began to walk along the side of the vehicle, making his way to the cabin.

A gentle thunk once again. As before, Rainer's accuracy was unerring. Gary gaped in amazement as the stricken soldier collapsed against the side of the lorry, a crossbow bolt straight through his neck. He made horrific gurgling and rasping noises as he began to collapse toward the ground.

An anxious voice called out from inside the lorry and the vehicle swayed slightly as the last soldier on board hurriedly moved towards the open rear of the vehicle. His upper body appeared as he leant out and looked around the side of lorry to see what had happened to his comrade. Gary didn't hesitate. He had the shot, and he took it immediately. The bullet entered through the side of the soldiers head. It was the killing shot Gary doubted he had the capacity to deliver. The soldier pitched forward and collapsed out of the lorry onto the ground.

Gary exhaled slowly as the shock of what he had just done hit him. He had no time to dwell though, Rainer was immediately at his side urging him to move.

"Come on, we need to get them out of sight in case another car comes along."

The imperative snapped Gary back into reality and he hurried after Rainer, rapidly covering the twenty or so yards onto the roadside. They each grabbed an arm of the soldier at the rear of the lorry; he was the most visible to another vehicle that may happen to pass by. They quickly pulled him off the road and dragged him several yards into the dappled light of the forest, before going back to retrieve the soldier with the crossbow bolt through the neck.

To Gary's horror, the man was still alive and making nightmarish rasping sounds as he fought for each agonised breath.

"What do we do with him? Do we try and pull the thing out?" he asked in confused desperation.

"Help me get him up alongside the other one first," replied Rainer. "We can have a better look then."

As with the first soldier, they each took an arm and dragged him into the forest, placing him close by his dead comrade.

"We can't just leave him to die like this, he must be in agony," said Gary, almost pleading with Rainer.

For his part, Rainer was now coming down from the adrenalin rush that spurred his actions over the last few minutes. He could see that Gary was right, the man was in horrific pain and distress – Gary then remembered something.

"We have morphine syringes in our medical kit, at least that should settle him down."

He stood up and went to a clear space from where he could be sure that Peter could see him. He waved his arms to get his attention, and then made a motion similar to wrapping a bandage around his arm, hoping that Peter would realise it was the medical kit he was wanting. He caught sight of some movement up the hill in the direction of the cave, so he turned and went back to Rainer.

"I think he's got the message, we should get that last guy out of the cabin before the children come down. We don't want them seeing him there, do we?"

Rainer, who was still crouching alongside the stricken soldier, immediately stood up and the two them went down to the lorry again and retrieved the body of the third soldier, dragging it as before, up to the others. Peter was arriving just as they laid the body down near the other two.

"We need a syringe of morphine for this one," said Gary indicating the still-writhing soldier.

"My God!" gasped Peter in shock. "Rainer once said it was a cruel weapon, now I know what he meant."

Rainer now left them to go up to his children. They had stayed in the cave when Peter had come down with the medical kit. It was now time to move them and their packs down to the lorry. Every minute from here would be precious.

Peter handed the syringe to Gary who quickly prepared it and without hesitation, thrust it into the soldier's right leg and pressed the plunger. While he was doing that Peter prepared a roller bandage and began to carefully wrap it around the man's neck. Lapping in a gentle figure-eight pattern around the protruding ends of the bolt on both sides of his neck, trying to stem the blood flow and keep dirt out of the wound.

"It's not bleeding too badly you know. The bolt itself is sealing the wound but it's also blocking off most of his airway. He can still breathe, but with difficulty. If he gets help in time, he may well live." Peter spoke as much to the German as to Gary, though of course, he couldn't know if the man understood his words.

"Perhaps we should bring him with us. What do you think?" he looked up at Gary who was leaning over the two of them.

Gary nodded. "I was thinking the same thing. If we leave him here, it could be most of the day before he gets any help. At least if we leave him in the truck, he'll be found quickly enough."

"Alright then, give me a hand!" said Peter and the two of them started to lift the man carefully.

They gently placed him into the rear of the lorry and used their packs to try and position him as comfortably as they could.

After he returned with the children and realised what they had done, Rainer looked deeply troubled. "This can't be wise! What if we get stopped and they look in the back and see him? It will be our death warrant."

Peter shook his head. "Mate, if we get stopped long enough for them to look inside the back, whether he's there or not, we're dead regardless. We might as well try and do the right thing by this guy. I'd feel better if we did."

Gary spoke up. "Me too Rainer. We can't just leave him behind to die. Are you going to be okay with that?"

"You're probably right. If they stop us anyway, it's all over," Rainer sighed in resignation. "Alright then, let's get going."

The children had climbed in as well and now sat gazing at the wounded soldier in silent amazement. He was still conscious, but much more settled now as the morphine dulled both the pain and his senses. Gary sat alongside him to try and keep him steady once the lorry started moving. He had a second morphine syringe in his shirt pocket in case it was needed. Peter and Gary had collected some of the dead soldier's weapons and placed them in the back of the lorry. They were far superior to their own, although they both silently hoped they would never need to use them.

Rainer had taken the uniform jacket and forage cap from one of the dead Germans and put them on. He would be doing the driving and he needed to look the part as they travelled along. Peter lowered and secured the large canvas flap covering the rear of the lorry, then went up to the cabin.

"Should I ride up the front with you, Rainer?" asked Peter. "I think it would be best if I did."

"Then get the other jacket and cap. You must look like you belong up here," Rainer replied.

Peter went and pulled the clothes off the second dead soldier and put them on. They fitted remarkably well. He then climbed up into the passenger's side of the cab, surprised at how little blood there was spattered about, after the first German soldiers corpse had been removed. There was scarcely a drop.

The keys were still in the ignition. Rainer started the lorry and in a few moments they were moving. They were following the road to the north, in the direction of a couple of larger towns where there might also be nearby airfields. They didn't need anything large; a smaller field would be more likely to house the kind of private aeroplane that Peter had in mind.

Whilst Rainer began to get the feel of the lorry and settle into the rhythm of the drive, Peter opened the glove compartment and pulled out the contents. He was looking for a map. It didn't take long before he found what he was looking for. It wasn't in the glove compartment but was found in a side pocket of the passenger's door.

"This is perfect!" said Peter in triumph. "A military map of the region. It shows several airfields and shows the squadrons that are based there. But there are one or two that show no military presence. They must be civilian only."

They had now travelled nearly two miles from where they had stolen to lorry. The roadside was still heavily forested and there was no traffic that they had yet seen. Rainer took the opportunity to pull over to the side.

"May I have the map please?" he asked.

Peter handed it over, after a few seconds, Rainer began to understand the details. He first identified the spot where they currently were, and from there he could start to work out where to go next.

"According to this, there is definitely supposed to be a small airfield just outside of Immenstadt."

"Excellent! Are you sure you remember how to get there?" asked Peter. "Is it very far?"

"It's about thirty kilometres north of here," he replied.

Peter did some quick mental arithmetic. "About twenty miles or thereabouts. That sounds perfect, let's hope our luck holds out and there's a plane there we can steal."

"There are a couple of small villages between us and there, as well as a larger town called Sonthofen. Hopefully, we won't have to stop at any of them."

He checked the fuel gauge, there still seemed to more than half a tankful. At least diesel fuel would not be an issue. Peter checked his watch. He was amazed to realise that it was not yet 8am but so much had happened. By their reckoning, the German patrol would not be back at the roadside any time before 11am. With luck, they might all be in Switzerland by then.

Sonthofen provided their first real moment of concern. The drive up until then had been uneventful, and despite the constant tension, even pleasant. The sub-alpine countryside of southern Bavaria had left Peter in awe. Such wondrous beauty where only a few miles beyond were the larger industrial cities. Those which were having devastation wrought upon them from above, almost on a nightly basis. As the lorry found its way into the centre of the pretty town of Sonthofen, the way was partly blocked by a number of German troops milling about on the edge of the road in the town centre. Peter wound up his window, anxious to not be engaged by anyone outside the vehicle. Rainer however, showed remarkable coolness. He wound down his window and called out to some nearby soldiers in his best guttural Bavarian accent, "Hey, do you know if the road up to Kempten is clear? We need to be up there before 11 o'clock or else I'm in the guard-house."

There was a chorus of laughter from the milling troops as they waved him on saying that the road was completely fine. He gave them a grin and a wave as he began to accelerate away and back onto clear roadway once again.

After they had cleared the township, Peter relaxed again and looked at Rainer with growing respect. "You would have made a superb officer in any army you know. I've never seen anyone so cool when the pressure is on."

Rainer gave him a thin, rueful smile. "I was thinking something similar myself. So far today, I have killed one man, badly wounded another, stolen an army lorry and bluffed my way through a rabble of soldiers. Perhaps I am no better than those I despise."

He drove in silence for a minute as he considered afresh the words he had just said. "All I ever wanted was to enjoy my job with Siemens and to bring up my children with Liesel at my side. Maybe one day buy a boat. I've always wanted to learn how to sail, you know!"

Peter smiled. "No, I didn't know, you've never mentioned it before."

"It is true," continued Rainer. "It has always sounded a wonderful thing to do, but now look at me! All thanks to Hitler! That bastard! What has he done to Germany? You know, at first even I was impressed. Unemployment fell quickly and there was so much building going on. My company, Siemens, benefitted greatly from contracts with the Reich. The future could have been so bright. But that was never enough for him. There was always this ugliness behind everything and now look where it has brought us."

Peter said nothing. He was deeply immersed in the moment as Rainer continued to speak, his voice almost breaking at times.

"Look at me now! I have become a killer thanks to this man. I have had to kill because, if I didn't, they would kill me and my children. My own countrymen!" He paused for a moment, collecting his thoughts. "Do you know, when I was at school here after we moved from England, we were taught to be so proud of people like Goethe and all the others. Philosophers, scientists, musicians, writers; Germany was one of the great cultures of the world…and now look at us... now look at us…"

He sat in silence as he drove on. He was driving the lorry as though a separate consciousness was controlling the wheel. His active mind was somewhere else entirely. Peter continued staring at Rainer for many seconds after he had ceased speaking. Now he settled his own thoughts and began to concentrate on the road again. They still had an airfield to find.

***

The airfield when they found it, was indeed small, created purely for light civilian use. They had to go down a small access road to find it and when they did, they were met with immediate disappointment. They had passed through the town of Immenstadt before spotting a small sign indicating the way to the airfield. There were no aircraft of any description that were parked in the open. There was a tiny building and a couple small hangars, but the doors on them all appeared to be shut. Now they were faced with the problem of making their presence obvious to anyone who might be there. If they got out and went from hangar to hangar looking to find one left unlocked, then the attention they would draw to themselves could be conspicuously dangerous.

"Well then, what do we do now?" asked a bemused Rainer. "Shall we take the risk and look inside out a hangar?"

The lorry was stopped on the access road, just short of the airfield proper. Peter opened his door and climbed down to the ground. He went around to the tail gate, unclasped the rear cover at one corner and looked inside.

"How is everyone? How is our passenger?"

Gary replied. "We're all fine, a bit bumpy at times but no problems. Thomas and Marie have been very good."

The two children smiled, it was still a great adventure to them.

"Our German friend is still under the effects of the morphine," continued Gary. "He seems to be breathing well enough, are we at the airfield?"

"We are, but there's a wee problem. No aeroplanes out in the open. If there's anything here, then they're being kept in a couple of closed up hangars. It could be very risky going closer to look," replied Peter.

"Are there many people about?" asked Gary. "Can Rainer try and bluff his way into looking inside them? The two of you do look official enough."

"I didn't see anybody, but there are a couple of cars parked nearby. We only have the uniform jackets and caps. If we get out of the lorry, then anyone will see that we're not real soldiers. I'll get Rainer to drive past the hangar doors and see if they look more promising from closer."

"Let's give it a try then," said Gary. "We don't really have too many other alternatives, do we?"

Peter nodded. "I agree. Hopefully we won't need it, but have a rifle at the ready, just in case."

Gary patted a German rifle he held as he nursed it across his lap. "It's already done. Let's get moving, shall we?" he said with a steady coolness in his voice.

Peter grinned and let the flap fall back into place, deliberately not securing it this time.

Gary might need to move fast. Climbing back into the cab, he looked over at Rainer and said, "Let's go up and have a closer look. We can't stay sitting here forever, can we?"

He was now nursing his Webley revolver on his lap. Rainer put the lorry into gear and began to move forward again. The absence of people made them both feel easier. He drove the lorry around the rear of the three buildings and then made a left hand turn to come around in front of them, with the driver's window rolled down in case someone appeared.

The small building seemed to be the office, but it was clearly unoccupied, the door being padlocked. They slowly continued moving until they came abreast of the sliding door of the first hangar. It too was padlocked and appeared to have been unused for some time. As they approached the second hangar though, it was immediately apparent that the door was slightly open and there were lights on inside. Rainer and Peter looked at each other. Now was the time. Rainer pressed the horn button on the steering wheel. After a couple of seconds, the hangar door began to slide further back and two middle-aged men emerged from inside. Peter let out an involuntary gasp when he saw the aircraft inside. It was an English make, a De Havilland DH.83 Fox Moth. He was stunned that such an aircraft would be here. If it was working, it would be perfect.

Rainer leaned out of the cabin window and motioned the two men to approach. He was thinking fast. "Hey, we are looking for a couple of American airmen. Their parachutes were spotted not very far from here. Have you seen anything?"

The two men looked at each other and shook their heads. "No sir!" replied one of them. "You are the first people we have seen all day."

Rainer nodded. "That is good. Does that aeroplane work? They might try and steal it if it does."

The man spoke again. "It does sir, but it hasn't been flown in a while. All aviation fuel is reserved for the Luftwaffe sir."

Rainer felt his hopes sink, the plane would be useless without fuel.

"So this one has no fuel in it then?" he asked, pretending to sound pleased at the news.

"No sir, it does have some fuel, about half a tankful, but we can't get any more, so we don't use it."

"Are there just the two of you here?" asked Rainer, affecting an air of concerned authority. "Is there a telephone? We should arrange a guard in case those Americans appear."

"Yes sir, there are just the two of us. There is a telephone in the office sir, but it is locked." The man was sounding slightly nervous at the thought of desperate escaping airmen on the loose nearby.

"Do you have the key?" asked Rainer.

"No sir, I only have the key to the hangar. I come up here to work on my aeroplane from time to time. That's what we are doing today."

Rainer looked over towards the aircraft. "It looks a very good machine, what is it?"

The man brightened, he was clearly very proud of it. "It is an English machine sir, I bought it before the war. I used to run joy flights from here over the Alps. In Germany, we only made military aircraft, so I had to buy a foreign one. But it is a lovely machine sir."

Rainer turned back to Peter and spoke softly in English. "It works and it has fuel. What do you think?"

Peter whispered his reply without hesitation. "It's perfect. Let's do it!"

Rainer turned back to the two men. "We will need to secure it then. It must be protected until these airmen have been captured."

Peter opened his door, away from the sight of the two men and got down from the cabin. He went around to the rear of the lorry and looked into the dark interior. Seeing Gary, he nodded and gave him the thumbs up signal. It was time to move. He walked around then to the same side of the lorry where the two men were standing. As soon as they saw him they realised he was not a German soldier. They both began to move back towards the hangar, but Peter levelled his pistol at them and yelled out "Halt".

The two men froze in their steps and put their hands up in terrified surrender. At the same moment, Rainer open his door and jumped down to the ground. A few seconds later, Gary emerged carrying the German rifle, to join with Peter and Rainer. Both of the captives gaped in amazement to see a black man wearing a British RAF tunic.

"So, you are British?" asked the man who claimed to own the aircraft, in good English.

Peter's eyebrows raised. "You speak English then?"

The man nodded. "I speak a little, it was useful when I was buying my aircraft. I bought it in England," his English was heavily accented, but very serviceable.

"Well, I am very sorry," said Peter, feeling a twinge of guilt at the thought of what he was about to do. "But I'm afraid we are going to have to take it. Does it have enough fuel to get to Switzerland?"

The man looked aghast at the thought of losing his aeroplane. "You can't take it! It is all I have! You will leave me with nothing."

"You will still be alive!" retorted Rainer. "Which we will not be if we are caught. They will kill us all, including my two children, in the back of the lorry."

The mention of there being children in the lorry stopped the man in his tracks. "You have children with you?" he asked in surprise.

"And a badly wounded German soldier. You will need to get him to a hospital after we've gone," added Rainer.

This news completely shook the man. His colleague, who spoke no English, didn't understand the situation they were now confronted with.

Rainer turned to Gary. "Can you go over to the office building there? You will need to break in, but you must cut the telephone line."

Gary passed the rifle over to Rainer and set off straight away.

"Now please gentlemen, we must get moving. I'm very sorry but we will need to tie you up. We have no time for niceties, I'm very sorry."

Rainer and Peter led the two men back into the hangar. Fortunately, there was a plentiful supply of rope amongst all the tools and equipment. Peter kept the two men under the aim of his pistol, whilst Rainer made a quick and efficient job of tying the two of them up.

"What now?" asked Rainer, suddenly aware that as the pilot, Peter was now the most important member of their group.

Peter nodded towards the outside. "Well, I'll keep an eye on these two first, but you need to move the lorry, it's blocking the entrance."

"Of course!" replied Rainer and promptly went back to the vehicle. As he left the building, Gary returned.

"You'd best get the kids out of the back and into the plane mate," said Peter.

"What about the soldier?" asked Gary.

"Leave him where he is. Our friends here are going to have to help him once we go."

Peter now had a plan in mind about how to get medical help to the wounded man. Gary waited for Rainer to finish moving the lorry forward and then called Thomas and Marie over to the tail gate, helping them down to the ground. He led them into the hangar and Peter indicated where to sit them. The little De Havilland had a small passenger compartment right at the front. The pilot had a separate, open cockpit above and behind them.

Once the children were seated, Gary ran out to help Rainer retrieve their packs from the rear of the lorry, taking care to reposition the wounded soldier with such meagre comfort that remained. Rainer had removed the stolen uniform he was wearing and had rolled it up to help further cushion the man. Peter in turn, took off his German tunic and put on his flying jacket, helmet and goggles from the pack that Gary had brought over. He then climbed up into the open cockpit, whilst Rainer kept an eye on the two Germans. Gary stood by to help with any requests Peter might make. The cockpit was remarkably similar to the Tiger Moths Peter had flown before. His pre-flight check was swift and confident. Lastly, he pump-primed the carburettors and switched on the magneto.

He called down to Gary. "Okay mate, give the prop a hard pull clockwise for me. Get yourself out of the way immediately in case it catches."

Gary reached up and grasped the right-hand side blade of the propeller, braced himself and pulled down as hard as he could. The prop gave a full turn with the engine coughing and emitting a cloud of black smoke, then stopping. It clearly hadn't been started in some time.

Peter called out again to Gary. "Let's have another try, it might take a few goes."

It did, a few times it almost caught, but then seized again. Peter was used to engines that needed some coaxing. When he was learning basic aircraft maintenance back in New Zealand, he often had to try many times before a long dormant engine would fire up. Then finally, on the eighth attempt, it caught! It was running a little rich, but not badly so. Peter eased off the throttle to let it get up to operating temperature, hoping that once it was warm, it would become smoother. He indicated for Rainer to come over to him. He explained to him what he had in mind for the two Germans. Rainer nodded in agreement and climbed down off the wing he had needed to stand on to speak to Peter. He then went over to the two Germans, held up a sharp knife and spoke in German.

"Do you see this knife? I am going to put it at the back of the hangar on…" he looked around, "that table back there. You can use it to cut the ropes. The key to the lorry is in the ignition. The wounded soldier is still in the back. We have given him morphine but he needs urgent medical help. Can you please get him to the nearest hospital?"

The two men had become surly since they were tied up, and now they both glared at Rainer.

"Why should we want to help you? You are nothing but a traitor to Germany for helping these enemies escape!"

"You will not be helping me. You will be helping a soldier who has been wounded doing his duty. It will also make your own position look better when the Gestapo start to question you," replied Rainer in a matter-of-fact tone of voice.

At the mention of the Gestapo, the two Germans suddenly looked concerned.

"Why should they question us? We have done nothing?" said the first man again.

"They will want to make sure that you were not helping us voluntarily. If you help the soldier, it will look good for you, that is all," Rainer genuinely wanted no trouble for the two men. They quickly seemed to realise that.

"Try and keep him stable as you drive. Don't let him move around too much, he can't breathe properly. By the way, what is your name please?" he asked to the first man. "Once we get to safety, we will let the authorities know where we took the plane from and the name of its owner. With any luck, you will get it back undamaged."

The man still looked surly, but grudgingly gave Rainer his name.

"My name is Otto Brunn. This is my friend, Horst."

Rainer looked intently into the man's face for a moment. "Thank you Otto Brunn. We shall try our very best to have no harm come to your aeroplane. Thank you both. I'm so sorry…"

He left the sentence unfinished, there was too much he wanted to say. He looked back at the De Havilland, Peter was now waving to get his and Gary's attention. It was time to get aboard. Gary had finished stowing their bags in a compartment half-way down the fuselage and removing the chocks from the wheels; he now took a spot in the passenger compartment. Rainer was aboard immediately after him. As soon as Peter saw the passenger door close below him, he opened out the throttle and felt the little De Havilland begin to roll forward. The sudden increase in the air flow caused by the accelerating propeller in the enclosed space of the hangar, sent a maelstrom of dust, pieces of paper and light cloth flying around the room. Once clear of the hangar, Peter turned the nose towards the start of the runway, some two hundred yards distant, and he opened the throttle further. Back inside the hangar, as soon as the dust had settled down and they could see again, Otto and Horst made their way to the table at the rear and scrabbled for the knife that Rainer had left there. Although their hands were tied behind their backs, Otto got a good grasp on the handle of the knife and began to saw at the bonds around Horst's wrists.

Meanwhile outside, Peter had reached the start of the runway. He turned the nose of the little Fox Moth onto it and opened the throttle fully. The little aircraft slowly gathered speed. None of the urgent power of a Spitfire or Mosquito with this machine. Just a gentle gathering of momentum until the vibration of the wheels on the grass ceased; they were airborne.

***

For Rainer, Thomas and Marie it was the first time any of them had flown. Despite the danger of their circumstance, the excitement of the event still gripped them with wonder. The little cabin had a lot of windows, and the three of them gazed out on the world below in amazement as it fell away beneath them.

In the cockpit, Peter set a course heading slightly south of west. He knew they were less than seventy miles from Swiss airspace, but these were dangerous and busy skies. German fighters would patrol constantly, whilst still more would wait at the ready, in anticipation of approaching American or British bombers. The safest place was up in the clouds.

Peter could fly on instruments until he was sure he was over Switzerland. The clouds were scattered this day. He smiled, knowing that Gary would no doubt be viewing them with his meteorologist's eye. The worry though, was that there were too many patches of clear air where they would be visible to another aircraft. He had to be as alert as his well-tuned senses would allow. His airspeed was about eighty-five knots. That would mean about forty minutes of flying time. Not a lot normally, but Peter knew that in the air, there were times when even two minutes could be like a lifetime.

They emerged from within the safety of another cloud. In the distance he could make out a large body of water. He knew that this must be the Bodensee, as the Germans called it. He knew it as Lake Constance. On the other side of that lake was Switzerland. The border with Germany lay somewhere in the middle. His distraction with the lake was brief, his eyes returned to their familiar routine of constantly scanning the sky.

Bare seconds later, he caught sight of what he was dreading the most. High above and several miles north, a squadron of fighters were flying in the opposite direction to the little biplane. Peter noted their position and looked around for more. None were visible.

He looked at them closely again. Perhaps they hadn't been seen yet. That hope was dashed moments later when two of the fighters peeled away from the rest of the squadron and turned towards them. It was highly unlikely that the Luftwaffe was looking for them in particular, but they were certainly an unauthorised flight and needed to be checked out.

Peter knew he had only a few minutes before the fighters had crossed the stretch of sky separating them. He looked for the nearest cloud. Thankfully, there was a large one directly in his flightpath. He would be in it before the Germans got within firing range, that was something, but they would most likely be waiting ahead for when he emerged at the far end. His last glimpse of the earth below before entering the cloud showed just how close they were getting to the Bodensee. It lay only a few miles ahead.

Peter knew that on the southern shoreline for the first ten miles or so, was Austria. To fly directly south too soon would still see them over enemy airspace. He had to hold his nerve and keep on his current heading for a while longer. Suddenly, the cloud dissipated and they were in clear air again. It was only a brief period, another large cloud bank lay directly ahead, but in those few moments, he could see the Bodensee on his left. Safety lay so close by! A quick check of the sky and he saw one of the German fighters above and not far off to his right. It was a Focke-Wulf 190, his old nemesis. A vision of Mark's burning Spitfire flashed through his mind.

"No you don't, you bastards. Not again you don't!" he muttered to himself as he re-entered the clouds.

The German pilot saw him too in that brief moment of clear air. He swung his fighter into a left-hand turn and positioned himself to follow Peter into the cloud bank. The Focke-Wulf was much faster than the De Havilland, so the German throttled right back to try and match the speed of the slower aircraft. He made a quick assumption that the pilot of the unauthorised aircraft would continue on the same course. If so, he wouldn't be very far ahead.

The German pilot was now completely content that the biplane was doing everything to avoid being seen. Such suspicious behaviour could only mean that the flight was illegal, it needed to be dealt with. He thumbed the firing button on his control stick. Peter became aware of flickering lights around him. Machine gun tracer bullets were zipping past. He checked the mirror above his head. He could see nothing except soupy cloud. So, the German pilot could not see him either. He was firing blindly into the cloud, hoping for a lucky hit. He had nearly had it, the first shots hadn't missed by much. Peter suddenly found himself thinking like a fighter pilot again. He knew he could never outfly the Focke-Wulf in the open air, but here in the cloud, there might be a chance.

He executed a shallow dive, wanting to lose some height, but not too much. He also eased back on the throttle slightly, losing airspeed. He wanted the German to overfly him, but without seeing him in the cloud below. A hugely risky manoeuvre, but the only chance he might get, for there on his lap, he still had the Webley pistol.

Peter continued to check the mirror constantly, as well as straining his neck to see into the mass of cloud around him. Then, for just a brief moment, he saw above him a darker shape within the swirling grey of the cloud. The German was almost directly above. He had overflown Peter and was now presenting him with the most vulnerable part of his aircraft. Peter opened the throttle again to keep pace with the fighter. Suddenly he heard the ripping sound of machine guns firing and watched as empty shell casings rained down around him. The German was trying his luck, blind firing again.

Now Peter was close, very close. Even the cloud could no longer obscure the aircraft above him. He gripped the handle of the Webley tight and flicked off the safety catch. He knew that the airflow would grab at his arm as soon as he extended it beyond the cockpit so he braced himself. Taking a deep breath, he gripped the control stick in between his knees and, with both hands, held the pistol aloft, aiming at point blank range into the underside of the Focke-Wulf's engine housing. Then he started pulling the trigger as rapidly as he could. Even before he had fired the sixth and final shot, he could hear the dramatic change in the engine note of the German fighter. The Webley fired a large bullet and six of them into the engine at such close range had caused catastrophic damage.

Peter immediately brought his hands back into the cockpit and gripped the stick again. He pushed the aircraft into another shallow dive and turned away to the left. He wanted to be clear of the air space around the fighter if it suddenly began to lose control or height. In the cockpit of the Focke-Wulf, the pilot was in shock. What had just happened to his aircraft? The engine was seizing on him and he was losing hydraulics. It was becoming impossible to control his aircraft. Surely an old biplane could not have shot him down? He radioed to his wingman that he was going down and would have to bail out. The second German fighter had stayed well to the rear, in case the biplane had tried to evade them by using the clouds as cover and turning back. He was now miles behind them.

Peter dropped out of the cloud and turned hard left, heading straight towards the Swiss countryside that he could see dimly in the far distance, on the opposite side of the Bodensee. Looking back behind him, he could see a parachute emerging from below the cloud. The German had bailed out! He clenched his fist in triumph. As unorthodox as it was, it was his first 'kill' in nearly three years.

"That one is for Mark," he said quietly to himself.

He continued to turn his head from side to side, scanning the sky. He knew there was still the other German fighter in the area and the sky ahead was now worryingly free of clouds, robbing him of anywhere to hide. He kept looking back over his shoulder, as the minutes ticked by with agonising slowness; the Bodensee was now slipping past underneath them, Switzerland drawing closer by the second. Then he spotted it, the second Focke-Wulf racing towards them, though still some way behind.

He opened the throttle open as far as it would go, but that was barely a hundred knots. The Focke-Wulf could easily do three times that speed. It wouldn't be long before the German caught them. Peter looked longingly ahead, the Swiss coast seemed so close now, but still too far away. He looked back over his shoulder at the approaching German, expecting to see him closing to attack distance. The end would come soon now, he had no more tricks left to play.

Then, to his astonishment, the second Focke-Wulf banked hard and turned away. He was now flying back to check on his comrade, still descending under the parachute. Peter couldn't understand why. It would have been the easiest of kills for the German, and then it struck him; the border between Switzerland and Germany was not on Swiss soil itself, it lay up the centre of the lake, a point they were now well past. They were safely in Swiss airspace after all. They had made it!

Chapter 15

The Swiss coast of the Bodensee passed under the De Havilland's wings at last. Before Peter could even begin to relax however, his trained eye picked out two small aircraft in the distance, approaching from his right. They had been following the coastline of the Bodensee but were now turning to intercept the fugitive biplane. Peter held a straight course but kept a close watch on the two aircraft. As they drew closer, he could see that they appeared to be fighters, but of a type he didn't recognise.

The two of them crossed his flightpath to the rear of the little De Havilland. They turned to bring themselves alongside, one on either side, each one bearing a large white cross against a red background on the side of their fuselage - the Swiss Air Force.

Peter saluted each in turn, trying to indicate that he was military, but not a threat. The pilot of the fighter to his right tapped at his earphones and face mask to indicate that Peter should try and communicate with them, but he indicated back that he had no R/T to use. The Swiss pilot nodded and moved his aircraft to a leading position. It was clear that Peter had no choice but to follow him. The other fighter fell back slightly, keeping the De Havilland ahead and to his right. They were led on a new course to the south-west. It took only another few minutes of flying before the lead fighter began to lose altitude, obviously starting a descent into an airfield that Peter couldn't yet see.

Shortly after though, he began to make out the unmistakable forms of multiple runways emerging through a fine, low-level haze in the distance ahead. It didn't look like a small regional airfield, this was clearly larger and well established, like an air force base. Peter shrugged, it made complete sense that they would be vectored to one.

As they drew closer, the size of the base impressed him. The Swiss fighter led them on a circuit of the field before they descended to land. He was amazed to see what appeared to be a considerable number of American B-17 bombers among several other allied types parked at one end of the base. The first fighter pilot brought his aircraft in to land and Peter was only a few seconds behind. Close formation landings were second nature to him. He brought the De Havilland down with practiced ease. He continued to follow the Swiss fighter as it taxied towards what was clearly the main building, topped with a large, glass-sided Control Tower.

As they drew closer, he could see several armed, uniformed men appearing from inside and preparing themselves to greet this unexpected arrival. Peter finally drew up alongside them and promptly cut the engine. They were now safely on the ground in Switzerland. What would happen from here, he had no idea. As the uniformed men arranged themselves around the aeroplane, Peter picked up the Webley from his lap and dropped it down onto the ground. One of the men stepped forward and retrieved it, checking to see that it was empty of bullets.

Gary opened the front passenger door and passed out the rifle, butt end first. Another uniformed man took it off him. Then, Gary leading Rainer and the children emerged from the little Fox Moth. All of them looking apprehensive, except for little Marie, who was grinning broadly, still excited from the thrill of her first flight. She had been completely oblivious of the drama that had been going on in the sky around her as they made the dangerous passage to Switzerland. Peter climbed down from the cockpit and joined the others. Gary reached out and patted him on the shoulder. He was aware of what Peter had done and how close they had come to disaster.

"Good flying Skip," he said in a quiet voice.

Peter smiled, more in relief than in humour. "I've told you before, if I don't get you home in one piece, I'll never hear the end of it!"

One of the Swiss guards spoke in German, indicating that they all had to follow him into the nearby buildings. Several of the others had begun to look over the De Havilland and were now pulling out the stowed bags. Everything was going to be inspected. Two of the Swiss soldiers approached, indicating to the group that they should follow them into building. They were led into an unexpectedly elegantly decorated room, dominated by a large conference table and chairs.

Peter and the others were not sure whether to take a seat or wait until they were instructed. The guards themselves also seemed unsure of what to do next. After years of war, the appearance of captured allied, or even German airmen was quite routine. This time however, the inclusion of a civilian family made the situation highly unusual.

It was little Marie who broke the tension, speaking in German to her father. "Papa, I need to go to the toilet please."

Several of the guards dropped their reserve and broke into smiles. One of them knelt down to be closer to her height, extended his hand and offered to lead her to the lavatory. Another of the guards indicated that everyone else should take a seat.

A change in the mood, less tense and more welcoming, began to weave its way through the assembly gathered in the room. Along with the others, Peter sat. He began to feel the stress of the flight lift from his shoulders as the realisation that he and Gary were now safe. Detention lay ahead for the both of them, possibly until the end of hostilities, but at least they would get to see their wives again. Gary would get to meet and be a father to his child. Peter's head fell forward into his hands as involuntary tears, born from the most profound relief, welled into the corners of his eyes.

Nearly half an hour later, the door opened and five new faces entered the room. One was clearly an officer in the Swiss army, two more were civilians and the remaining two were wearing pilot's uniform, flying overalls. They were obviously the pilots of the two Swiss fighters. Peter and Gary both stood up and came to attention in recognition of their military hosts.

The Swiss pilots stepped forward with their hands outstretched, shaking Peter and Gary's hands warmly. The Swiss officer indicated with a gesture that everyone should take their seats again. What followed was partly a debriefing and partly an interrogation. The two civilians, a man and a woman, were both with the Red Cross. They took down all the personal information they could about the five escapees. As the senior military officer in the group, Peter told the story of how they had stolen the lorry and eventually, the aircraft. Realising the danger that Rainer would be in if it emerged that he, as a civilian, had killed a German soldier and seriously wounded another, Peter took the responsibility on himself for firing the crossbow. Rainer had stayed back, minding the children, Peter assured them.

The Red Cross people seemed to pay particular interest to Rainer and the children. The man did the questioning and the woman, who was clearly a skilled stenographer, took notes. It was apparent that civilians arriving by air as these three had done, was a conspicuously rare event. Their questioning of Rainer was all in German, so Peter and Gary understood very little, but they could see that Rainer was looking more and more agitated as the proceedings went on. He had put his arms around his children and was holding them as protectively as he could under the circumstances.

Finally, the questioning turned to the two British airmen. Under normal circumstances, Peter and Gary would have been compelled to provide nothing more than their most basic service details. However, being in a neutral country, despite the likelihood of internment, they felt they could furnish some additional personal information, in the hope that Anne and Bridget could be informed that they were both safe. The man from the Red Cross gave his assurance that they would get the information to England as soon as possible. Peter and Gary exchanged looks that spoke of their increasing optimism.

"Well, that should cheer the girls up a bit, at least," said Gary. "The last month or so can't have been pleasant."

He leaned forward towards the Red Cross man and asked, "Can we write to them? Is there a way we can get letters to our wives?"

The man nodded. "We have the channels to get letters to civilians in England. It is slow and not always reliable. Mail ships do get lost to submarines at times but, the chances are good. Certainly though, they will be notified of your safety. We inform the British Embassy in Berne and they will pass the information on to your government. They, in turn, will be able to inform your families."

Gary relaxed and sat back in his chair. "At least that is something. What happens to the two of us now?" he asked, looking over at Peter.

The Swiss army officer answered in cultured English. "There is a detention facility in the town of Davos in the Alps. It was a ski resort and a sanatorium before the war, but it is now used for housing detainees, such as yourselves. It holds officers only. Other ranks are interned elsewhere."

Peter gawped at what he had just heard. "A ski resort! We're going to be held in a ski resort? That doesn't sound too hard to put up with!" He grinned at Gary.

"I can assure you that regular skiing days will not be on your schedule Squadron Leader. You are being interned, not entertained!" the officer replied drily. "We will do our best to see that you are well treated and provided for, but you are here under sufferance, not as guests. So please understand that from the outset. In essence, you are both prisoners of war and you will be held according to the articles of the Geneva Convention."

These words had an immediate and sobering effect upon both Peter and Gary.

"The articles place responsibilities upon the two of you, as well as upon us. Please don't waste your time thinking of escape, there is, quite literally, nowhere for you to go. Stay in your quarters in Davos. The war cannot last forever and you will be repatriated as soon as hostilities cease. Your circumstances could be far worse gentlemen." He looked from one to the other.

"What's going to happen to Rainer and the children?" asked Peter. "Neither of us understood anything of what you were saying."

"They will be interned in a separate facility for civilians who have fled Germany. They will be safe here until after the war."

"Then how come Rainer looked so unhappy?" blurted out Gary.

Rainer spoke up, "Because they will notify any family I have of where we are. That will mean my father will be told. He may well try and claim the children, and get them sent back to Germany, to be with him! He will try and take them from me! To turn them into Nazis!"

"But what about your mother in England, couldn't she claim them equally? Wouldn't that be better?" queried Peter. "Or they stay here with you! You are their father after all, surely you should have the final choice here."

Rainer's shoulders drooped. "That is what I have said, I hope it shall be alright. Getting them to England is out of the question and I know what my father is likely to try and do. He is a Nazi party member, if he has any influence with the German government and gets them to press the authorities here, then… well, I just don't know."

Rainer's mood cast a sudden pall over the room. The two Swiss pilots were clearly sympathetic. Both of them were from the west of the country and were natural French speakers, although, like many Swiss, they also spoke good German and English. Their country's position was strictly neutral in the war, but they still had eyes and ears and they both held their own carefully contained thoughts. Unlike many Swiss, their sympathies lay more with the allied side.

One of them wrote his name and contact address on a slip of paper and handed it to Peter. "If there is anything we can do to help while you are interned here, please let me know."

He and Peter shook hands as the meeting began to break up. The two Swiss airmen left and the others stood up. The officer straightened his tunic and spoke in matter-of-fact tones.

"I am sure you must all be hungry by now, especially the children. I will have you escorted to the Officer's Mess. You will stay here tonight, and tomorrow you shall be transferred to your new accommodation."

He finished abruptly; no 'Welcome to Switzerland' or any parting words of comfort. Peter and Gary were now prisoners of war. As for Rainer and the children, they had become political internees.

After he and the Red Cross people left, two guards came forward and led them out of the room, taking them all to the Officer's Mess. It was a good, though sombre meal. The two British airmen and the dispossessed German family had become very close during their time together in the remote southern Bavarian mountains. It might now prove to be a long time before they saw each other again.

***

The last days of May were passing, soon it would be summer. The Alps though, were cold and snow was still falling.

As Peter and Gary alighted from the van that carried them and four other captured airmen on to the streets of Davos, they wasted no time in zipping up their flying jackets. It looked like a wonderland to Gary, he had never seen snow like this before. The occasional winter flurries he experienced in England, exciting at the time, now seemed tame, if not feeble, in comparison.

The four other flyers they arrived with were all American, the officers from a couple of B-17s that had crashed or been forced down in Switzerland. They had all been told that the allied officers held in Davos were overwhelmingly American. Curiously, they were also advised that there were a large number of German internees being held there as well.

"How would that go when they all get together?" Peter had asked.

"Surprisingly well," had been the reply.

Even more surprising had been the news that there was also a large Jewish population in the town. Davos had been a popular Jewish health sanatorium before the war and many Austrian Jews had subsequently fled there after the Anschluss of 1938, when Hitler annexed Austria into the greater German Reich. Jews, Germans, Americans and a smattering of RAF officers, all mixed in with the local Swiss population, some of whom ardently supported the allies, whilst others equally favoured the Nazis. For Peter and Gary, it sounded as foreboding as it did exciting.

The van had delivered them to the steps of what had clearly been a hotel of some quality.

"Is this where they're going to put us up?" asked Gary. "If news of this gets out, there'll be aircrews surrendering to the Swiss by the thousands."

Two guards who had been travelling with them in the van, now joined them and ushered the group up the stairs and through the hotel entrance into the foyer. Peter and Gary were assigned a room together several flights up and with a glorious view of the Alps behind them. The room itself was small and basic, but comfortable. Neither of them could have imagined that this would be their 'prison' once they were in Switzerland.

"I wonder if we're going to get a bill at the end of all of this?" asked Peter.

Gary chuckled. "If the Swiss had any idea of how much we got paid, they'd be taking up a collection for us as well."

"Look on the bright side mate," said Peter. "The pay may not be much, but you do get to travel."

For the first time in many weeks, both of them broke into uproarious laughter.

***

There was a knock at the door of the little cottage that Anne and Peter rented near the RAF base at Wyton. Anne had been back at work for a couple of weeks now. Boredom and constant worry were draining her too severely in London. She needed the stimulation and distraction of her work and her colleagues.

She had been home for only a few minutes after finishing her shift and wasn't expecting anyone. She opened the door to find Group Captain Trehearn standing there. As soon as she saw him she knew; Trehearn had the broadest of smiles, unable to contain the joy that even he was feeling. Anne collapsed into his arms, dissolving into tears of relief and happiness.

"I'm so sorry for losing my dignity like that Group Captain," said Anne after she managed to regain her composure several minutes later. She had invited him in and was busy getting the kettle boiling, to make a pot of tea.

"Not at all, my dear, and please call me Hugh," replied Trehearn. "The very worst part of my job is telling wives and families that they have lost a husband or a son. To be able to come bearing wonderful news for once is a rare joy that I treasure. There are times when I wish I was able to show my emotions as easily as you women can."

"That's only because you men choose to deny yourselves that release," said Anne happily. "I'm sure it's there in you somewhere."

"I'm sure you're right," continued Trehearn, "but that is a luxury for peacetime I'm afraid. In war, there is just so much sadness that if we gave in to it, and allowed our emotions full reign, we could never function."

They each took sips of their tea and began to finally relax. Trehearn then told Anne the story of where Peter and Gary were now being held and as much of the scant detail that he knew regarding how they had got there.

"I'm sure there is a lot more to it than that. They must have been on the run for weeks before they found an aeroplane. How they managed it I have no idea."

"Perhaps they will now be able to write letters and tell us more. The Red Cross can get letters through, can't they?" she asked.

"They can, but it's slow and I'm sure the letters will be censored of most of the content anyway. But hopefully, I shall get more information in the near future regardless. I promise to tell you anything I hear, as soon as it comes in."

Anne came around the table and kissed him on the cheek. "Thank you so much Hugh, I have a feeling that this news is nearly as important to you as it is to me."

Trehearn's lip involuntarily quivered, his own reserves of inner strength were being tested.

"Yes Anne, I do believe you're right, Peter and I are close. Mark was his best friend, but I fancy that they both considered me a friend as well as their leader."

He paused to regather his own composure.

"Anyway Anne," he continued, "today is Friday and I was wondering if you might care for a quick trip to London tomorrow?"

Anne was intrigued. "This is rather sudden! Whatever for?"

Trehearn hesitated briefly before he spoke. "I haven't rung Flying Officer Lynch's wife yet. I can do it immediately if you would rather, but I know that the two of you are close friends. I was wondering if you might prefer to break the good news to her in person, yourself."

Anne was delighted at the idea. "Oh, thank you Hugh I would love that!"

"Excellent!" replied Trehearn. "I thought you would, you would need to catch the train in the morning. Is it too late to arrange that?"

"Not at all, I know what time it leaves, I shall be there." Anne was now radiant at this turn of the evening's events. Trehearn couldn't help but dwell for a moment on what a fortunate man Peter was.

"Very well then Anne! I shall inform the infirmary that I have given you permission to be off the base until Monday. Now, I must be on my way, I still have work to do I'm afraid. I do trust that you enjoy the rest of the evening."

Trehearn stood up smiling as Anne came around and kissed him again on the cheek. She saw him out and went back into the kitchen.

Sitting down in the room alone, the emotions she had managed to keep in check for well over a month now finally welled to the surface and she broke down into uncontrollable tears. Several minutes later, the tears passed and she was left with a profound sense of relief and deep love, unlike anything she had ever experienced before. Her husband was safe in the care of a neutral and compassionate nation. It might take a while, but now she knew he would eventually be home safely.

The train ride down to London was a blur. She had slept well, but once awake, her thoughts were restless and disjointed. She found herself desperate to be with her friend again. Bridget would understand the depth of the emotions she was feeling, perhaps even more so, as she was now almost at the term of her pregnancy. Alighting from the train, Anne hailed a taxi. It was more expensive than a bus, but she didn't care, she wanted to get to Bridget quickly.

Once she had arrived at the house in Wimbledon, she knocked on the door only for her knocking to go unanswered. Bridget wasn't home. She had never considered this possibility in her haste and so simply sat down on the front steps of the house and began to wait.

She didn't have to wait too long. After only a few minutes, Anne looked down the street to see Bridget walking slowly up the footpath, carrying a small string bag of groceries. Anne stood up and hurried down the street to meet her.

"My goodness! Anne! What on earth are you doing here?" asked Bridget in surprise.

"They're alive! They're safe! They're in Switzerland! Both of them!" Anne blurted out in an excited torrent of words.

Bridget dropped her grocery bag on the footpath and threw her arms around Anne, dissolving into tears of utter relief as Anne herself had done the previous evening.

Chapter 16

Little more than a week had passed and Peter and Gary were settling into their new lives. They knew they were prisoners of war and in every real sense that description applied. They were required to remain within the town precinct and to abide by a list of restrictions. If they attempted to escape and were caught, the outcome was that they would be sent to another internment camp, with none of the comparative luxuries or liberties that were theirs to enjoy in Davos. There however, the sense of being incarcerated ended. They had an extraordinary amount of freedom to wander about the village and mix with other detainees, as well as local townsfolk.

Through British cooperation with the American Consulate in Berne, they were given a small, regular stipend so that they would be able to have some money for simple living expenses. Some Americans told them that they had even learned to ski during the preceding winter. Thus, they were able to meet and mingle with others in the most informal way. Several times, they even found themselves in the unexpectedly convivial company of a group German airmen. All of whom spoke excellent English and who were also being held as involuntary guests of the Swiss.

One morning, near the end of the first week of June came the news that set the entire town alight with talk.

"The invasion! It's started! It's in Normandy, wherever that is!" cried an American voice from down in the street, below Peter and Gary's room.

They both leapt out of their beds and ran to the window. As they opened it and looked out, they noticed that other windows were opening all up and down the street, excited faces peering out of each of them. Dozens of voices, mostly in American accents called down to the man in the street, asking him to repeat what he had said, or to ask for more detail. He didn't know much more than he had already called out, so Peter and Gary hurriedly dressed and went down into the breakfast room of the hotel, where there was a large radio. A crowd was already gathering around it, listening to a faint, crackly broadcast in English, from the BBC. It was true. Tens of thousands of men, as well as machines and materiel were being landed in France on the northern facing beaches of Normandy.

Jubilant faces around them cheered as the bulletin provided further information of how the events of the day had begun and what progress was being made.

After a few minutes, Peter took himself away from the radio and served himself out a bowl of a strange cereal concoction that the Swiss called Bircher Muesli. He had found himself quite enjoying the taste, and it had quickly become his breakfast preference. He sat himself at a small table away from the crowd gathered around the radio and began to eat in silence. Gary soon came over to join him.

"What's the matter Skip? You don't seem terribly excited by this. I thought you'd be as up in the air as anyone?"

Peter put down his spoon and sat back in his chair. "This is the crucial part mate. If the Germans are able to stop them and drive them back, it might be years before they try again. If this doesn't work, we could be here for a very long time indeed."

Gary looked at him intently. "You are a cheery soul at times Skip. When we get back to England, I'm going to demand a new pilot."

Peter couldn't help but chuckle at the ribbing. "I know and I really am excited, I promise! I just don't want to get my hopes up just yet. The next couple of days are going to be crucial. If they can keep advancing, then I'll start to get excited." He leant forward and picked up his spoon again. "Believe me, I want to be home just as much as you."

He returned his attention to his bowl of muesli. Gary sat in silence for a few moments, listening to the radio before he spoke again. "I wonder how our new German friends are going to react to this? It might strain the relations around here, especially between them and the Americans."

"That's a thought," replied Peter. "I'm prepared to try and keep things on a pleasant level as much as possible, but they have to want that too. Otherwise, like you said, it could get a bit tense around here."

"Those fellows we had a drink with the other day seemed alright," said Gary. "I'm more concerned about the Americans. A lot of them do seem a bit… brash. Don't you reckon? I think they're the more likely to start stirring up the whole place. That could challenge the Germans to push back a bit, we might have to be careful ourselves."

Peter nodded. "After breakfast, it might be an idea to go for a walk and see if we can find those Germans and have a chat with 'em. Let them know we want to try and keep things on good terms. It can't hurt to try, at least if things do get a bit heated, no one can blame us."

"Good idea let's do that," replied Gary as he set about preparing some breakfast for himself.

As it turned out, although there were a few instances of violent disagreement between individuals, the atmosphere in Davos generally remained comfortably constrained. Indeed, several of the Germans that had become friendly with Peter and Gary had told them quietly that they would welcome the fall of the Nazi regime in their home country.

Free of the constant mind-numbing propaganda from the Nazi controlled media in Germany, they had begun to see things more clearly. Stories of what was happening in the camps set up to hold political prisoners, dissidents and above all, Jews, were becoming too frequent for them to ignore anymore. Peter in particular, had found one of the German pilots a very amiable companion and the two had exchanged their home addresses, with a promise to stay in touch after the war was finally over.

There were now regular Red Cross deliveries with lorries arriving in Davos most weeks. Soon Peter and Gary had the luxury of new clothes to wear and most importantly, new underwear and shoes. They had been living in their uniforms and flying boots for over eight weeks and to have a change of clothes was a joy.

June turned into July and still the news from Normandy told only of desperate fighting and limited advances. The quick end to the war that everyone had hoped for, seemed now to be a forlorn dream. As the news from the Front offered little by way of cheer, another event brought unbridled delight to both Peter and Gary. They received their first letters from Anne and Bridget and Gary found out he was a father.

"It's a girl. It's a little girl."

He kept repeating the words over and over, without even realising he was speaking.

They were each lying on their beds reading their letters, deep in their own thoughts. They had both written many times since they had arrived in Davos, although according to the words from Anne and Bridget, none of them had been received before any of these letters had been posted. Due to the realities of wartime mail, they each received several letters from their wives in this one delivery.

"They are probably getting a bundle each from us about now as well," Gary had said as he eagerly opened the first of them.

Now, as they read, the sense of being so distant from the women they loved began to feel like dead-weights around their shoulders. For the first time, they both truly felt like the prisoners they were. No amount of liberty in Davos could fill the void they were each feeling in their souls. For Gary, the realisation that he was now a father was cruelly tempered by the knowledge that he might have to wait a long time still before he could ever hold his daughter.

"She's called Louise," he said softly. "Louise Norma Lynch!"

"Did the two of you pick those names out together?" asked Peter.

"We did pick out Louise together, but Bridget decided upon Norma because she was born on D-Day. The sixth of June 1944! Norma, because of Normandy. I think it's a wonderful idea."

Gary finally smiled as he thought about the names and tried to imagine how his tiny daughter might look.

"I love it!" said Peter. "She's an extraordinary woman, your wife. Despite her questionable choice in men that is."

Gary half smiled. He knew Peter was trying to cheer him up with some gentle banter. However, his desperate longing to be with his wife felt like a prison wall that could not be breached by something as banal as simple humour. Peter could see that Gary was struggling to contain his emotions. The thought crossed his mind that as the two of them had become such close friends, Gary might be uncomfortable with the simple act of asking for some privacy, fearing he might hurt Peter's feelings.

He knew what he had to do. "Look old mate," he said, "if you'd like a bit of time to yourself? I'm happy to take myself off for a bit of a walk around the town for a while."

He was used to Gary's quieter moments. He had a naturally introverted personality and was often content in his own company, but this was different. When Gary let someone in, he let them in completely. Peter knew that he and Anne were amongst the lucky few, but no one could compete with Bridget.

"Would you mind Skip? I wouldn't mind a bit of time alone right now," replied Gary.

"Not at all mate," said Peter sympathetically. "I completely understand. I might go and see if some of our trans-Atlantic friends are needing someone to share a drink with. That should give you a couple of hours of peace. See you in a while."

Giving his friend a 'thumbs up' gesture, he opened the door and left Gary alone in the room.

Gary spent the next few minutes staring blankly at the letter he was holding in his hand. Eventually, he snapped out of his reverie and went over to the small table that was one of the few pieces of furniture in the room. There was a pad of writing paper there and a fountain pen. He opened the pad out, leant forward and began to write to his wife.

***

Three more weeks had passed and the news from Normandy had finally become positive. The allies were starting to break the German lines and could now begin moving more freely in the open countryside beyond the Normandy farm lots.

Evenings spent sitting around the radio, had built a happy bond between the two RAF men and the several dozen Americans they shared the old hotel with. As the news each day told of further advances, the atmosphere around the town of Davos began to change. There was a lightening of spirits as both the internees and the townsfolk could finally anticipate an end to war in the near future.

As well as the improving war news, the summer weather had melted away all the snow from the lower slopes. The valley that surrounded them was now offering some glorious scenic walks, which helped break the monotony of internment life. This new reality had the most profound of effects upon Gary as the general air of positivity soon rubbed off on him.

"Any mail today Skip?" he asked brightly as Peter came up the stairs from the foyer below.

"Nothing today," Peter replied. "I've just heard that one of the chair lifts is going to run for a while today while they do some maintenance on it. A few of the Yanks are planning on going up the mountain on it and then walking back down. I'm keen to go along too. Are you in?"

Gary's eyebrows arched in interest. "I've never been on a chair lift. Are you sure it's safe?"

Peter looked at him in astonishment. "Mate! You've survived flying with me on how many bloody missions with the bloody Jerries lobbing flak at us; you survived being shot out of the sky by some bloody jet-powered wonder thing *and* crash landing on a field of granite bloody boulders." Peter paused for breath before continuing. "Not to mention attacking a group of armed Jerry soldiers, stealing their bloody truck *and* stealing a bloody plane. Now you're asking if a perfectly functional bloody chair lift is safe? Flamin' heck Sport!"

Gary broke into uproarious laughter. "Well, since you put it like that…"

Once they were on the chair lift, Gary began to relax and enjoy himself.

He turned to Peter and said, "You know, I thought only Australians spoke the way you did back there."

Peter looked at him and replied drily, "Who do you think they learned it from?"

***

"I'm beginning to get a bit worried that we haven't heard anything from Rainer." Peter was both puzzled and concerned. "If the Red Cross can get letters to England and back, you'd think another internment camp in Switzerland should be a doddle."

Both he and Gary had written several times to Rainer, desperate to stay in touch with him and the children. Neither of them had heard anything in reply. Nearly two months had passed and it was now mid-August. Gary didn't reply immediately; he looked up from the book he was reading as he lay on his bed and stared intently at the ceiling for a while.

"I remember what he said about being worried at what his father might do from Germany," he said after a while. "I don't know what his status is. We're military, the Geneva Convention covers us, but Rainer and the children are refugees. I'm not sure if the Convention covers them as well."

"I don't know either," said Peter. "I doubt they would be being kept in a place as nice as this, but you'd hope that it would still be okay; especially since he has the two kids with him."

"Perhaps we should have a talk to the Red Cross people when they're here tomorrow," Gary suggested. "There may be an official process we can use to find out where they are."

"Good idea," replied Peter. "Anyway," he said, looking at his watch. "It's almost time for the BBC news. Let's go down and find out if the war's over yet, shall we?"

Another invasion! The news electrified the room once again. A joint landing involving American and French forces, called 'Operation Dragoon' the bulletin said, was taking place in the south of France, along the Cote d'Azur. The Americans in the room were jubilant. Even at this early stage, the German resistance was apparently very weak and this second invasion showed every sign of being able to move north rapidly.

"Bloody hell mate! We could be home even sooner than we had hoped!" Peter was caught up in the buoyant mood in the room. His qualms immediately after the Normandy invasion were long gone; he was now as excited at the prospect of imminent liberation as any of them. Gary didn't show his feelings as readily as the others, but inside, his soul was singing.

The following day, Peter and Gary took one of the Red Cross workers aside and asked if there was a way of finding out where Rainer and the two children were; and if a letter could be sent to them. They explained as succinctly as they could, the story of how they knew the family and what they had been through together. The Red Cross man didn't speak a lot of English, but still managed to grasp just how important these people were to the British airmen. He seemed genuinely sympathetic and took down all the information that they had, promising that he would do his best. He was about to go and rejoin his fellows when he paused and turned back to the two airmen.

He looked furtive and spoke quietly as he said, "Not all camps good like this one. Some not good at all." He looked briefly at both Peter and Gary then he turned away again.

"I wonder what he meant by that?" asked Peter.

"I have no idea," responded Gary with a shrug. "So, that's that then! Now we just have to wait and see what happens."

***

They saw the same Swiss Red Cross worker several times over the next month but each time when they made eye contact with him, he could only shake his head. He had heard nothing yet. Then, in early October, they caught his attention once more as he was helping unload the lorry he had arrived in. This time he acknowledged their gaze and indicated they should join him.

"Sorry, not have good news," he said. "All have been sent back to Germany."

Peter and Gary were stunned.

"Are you sure? When did this happen?" Peter spoke so quickly and in such agitation, that he confused the Swiss.

"Please say again?" the man responded.

Peter breathed out deeply and spoke again, at a pace the man could follow. "Do you know when this happened?"

"Ah! I have written down," he said, reaching into his shirt pocket and bringing out a neatly folded piece of paper. Then, reading from his notes, he said, "First, they go to camp here in Switzerland in Hunenberg. Then, children sent to Germany to…" he struggled with the next word, finally saying it the only way he knew, in German, "*Grossvater*."

Peter look puzzled for a moment. What was 'Grossvater'?

Then it struck him. "Grandfather! Grossvater means Grandfather! The bastards! They've sent the kids back to Germany to Rainer's father, the Nazi!"

Gary forced himself to maintain his calm and looked intently at the man. "Where is our friend Rainer? Do you know?"

The Red Cross man now looked deeply distressed. "He sent to Germany also. Sent to German work camp."

Both Peter and Gary were aghast. Rainer had been sent to a Concentration Camp in Germany. He might already be dead.

"But he was safe in Switzerland?" stammered Peter. "Surely they can't do that? Switzerland is supposed to be neutral, isn't it?"

The man from the Red Cross could only shrug in helpless sympathy. He had no way of answering Peter's questions. Shoulders drooping in his own impotent agony, he turned and walked away. Gary and Peter could only stare at each other in dumb silence. Neither of them had words adequate to express the horror and rage they were both feeling.

Chapter 17

"Please understand Peter, Switzerland is an island surrounded by enemies." Albert, the proprietor of their hotel was trying to help them understand. "We have Nazi Germany and Austria to the north and the east. German occupied France to the west and fascist Italy to the south. Switzerland has to rely on German trade to survive. Sometimes, if the Nazis make a demand that is easy to fulfil, they get what they want. It helps keep the peace."

Peter was biting his tongue as he listened. What had happened was not this man's fault, but his insouciance was maddening. Gary could bear to hear no more, he turned and walked away, heading up the stairs to their room.

Peter watched him as he went, then turned back to the hotel proprietor. "So, are you telling me that nobody is really safe here? That if the Nazis demand someone, the Swiss will hand them over?"

"I only know what I have been told by the Red Cross," he replied. "I know that it does happen, I don't know if it is very common." He exhaled slowly and rubbed his temples. Speaking aloud of his own country's complicit behaviour with Nazi Germany was not an easy thing. "We were almost at war with Germany ourselves in 1940, Peter. I understand they were preparing to invade. There were quite a number of serious incidents between our Air Force and the Luftwaffe. In the end, they left us alone, but I wonder if there may have been some... agreements... some accommodations... reached between our government and Hitler. I just don't know."

Peter let these words sink in.

After a few moments of contemplative silence, he sighed. "Thanks Albert, I appreciate you telling me this. I didn't know that things had got that close to war for you. I guess we all just assume that everyone respects Switzerland's neutrality and leaves you alone. It seems it's a lot more complicated than that."

Albert nodded sadly in agreement. "Neutrality is such a simple idea. But sometimes managing simplicity is a very complicated process."

Peter sighed again in resignation and left to join Gary in their room.

***

The Americans moving north after the landings on the Mediterranean coast had succeeded in creating a section of free border to the west of Switzerland, as those adjacent regions of France were liberated. Some Americans in Davos took the opportunity to escape and try and make their way there to re-join the fight. Others hesitated to take the risk, realising that freedom was likely only a few months away at worst.

Peter and Gary were torn. Both were desperate to be back home with Anne and Bridget, but to get caught would mean a harsh internment for the remainder of the war. The lesson of what happened to Rainer ultimately proved decisive for them. They were unable to trust that they would not be handed over to the Germans, especially given their part in attacking and killing the German soldiers at the lorry. They would stay where they were.

The liberated border meant that the regular Red Cross deliveries they received were better stocked. Decent food, chocolates and cigarettes were lifting the spirits of the internees and in turn, the locals of Davos, with whom most of these items were traded, usually for alcohol. Neither Peter nor Gary smoked so their ration was always bartered away, occasionally for alcohol, but more frequently for writing material. Mail was getting through quickly now and they both wrote avidly to their wives and families.

Despite its extraordinary natural beauty, life in Davos had become mindlessly boring. News from the people they loved in the outside world kept them both sane.

***

1944 rolled into 1945.

Apart from a desperate attempt by the Germans to break the American lines in the Ardennes forest on the France-Belgium border at Christmas, the onward march of the Allied armies was inexorable, but still the Germans held out. The Soviet armies were now in Germany itself and were threatening to keep advancing until they reached her western borders.

Finally, the American and British armies broke through into Germany as well and began to advance more rapidly. There was now a secondary goal for the Western Allies. No longer was it just about defeating Nazi Germany, it was also to prevent the advancing Soviets from seizing too much of Western Europe. Otherwise, the end of one war might quickly boil over into the start of another.

The American's were now broadcasting from close to the Swiss border, so the internees were receiving constant bulletins on how the final months of the war were progressing. As good as the news was, it was still cruelly teasing. The imminent promise of getting home, tempered with the need to keep waiting.

In early March, Peter and Gary were returning from a morning walk around the village. Despite the early spring snow, they tried to get out into the open air as often as possible. The interior of the hotel had become an oppressive place during the alpine winter months and even short trips outside helped to lift their spirits. As they rounded a corner, they saw a vehicle parked outside the front of their hotel. This wasn't the usual Red Cross lorry, this one seemed to be official. It was a large

Mercedes-Benz saloon with the incongruous sight of a Union flag hanging from a short Jack-staff on the front wing. The two of them hurried their step and entered the foyer, shaking snow off their feet and trouser legs.

"Ah! Peter and Gary!" The voice of Albert, the hotel proprietor called out as soon as he saw them. "These gentlemen are from the British Embassy in Berne. They are here to speak to you both."

They both saluted and approached the group of three men. Two wore neat three-piece suits of the type favoured by civil servants, whilst the third man wore the uniform of an army Colonel.

"We apologise for being out of uniform Sir," Peter said to the Colonel. "We were not told anyone was coming."

The Colonel smiled and said, "That is quite alright Squadron Leader. We fully understand. I am Colonel Jeavons, I am on attachment to the military Charge d'Affaires at the British Embassy. These two gentlemen are civilian colleagues of mine, Mr Eric Preston and Mr Guy Thomson."

Peter and Gary shook hands with all three men.

After the brief introductions were over, the Colonel got straight down to business.

"Now gentlemen, we are here with, what I suspect you might consider to be good news."

Peter and Gary's faces grew alert with anticipation. "Are we going home?" blurted out Gary in a rush of enthusiasm.

The three visitors all smiled. "Yes Flying Officer Lynch, you are," said the Colonel.

The most extraordinary weight seemed to lift from both of their shoulders. Peter beamed the most radiant smile whilst Gary struggled to keep from shedding tears in front of the visitors.

Once they had begun to regain control over their emotions, Peter asked, "When can we go Sir? How much longer will we still be here?"

Colonel Jeavons said, "I presume you might have noticed that it is a rather large car. We can go as soon as you're packed if you have no objections."

They needed no second bidding.

Once they were underway, their new reality finally began to sink in. Packing had taken no time at all as they had so little by way of possessions. Just their few clothes and personal kit and some small souvenirs they had bought to take back to England. A quick run around the hotel to say goodbye to the American friends they had made and a final farewell to Albert, the proprietor.

"How is it that we're being released Sir?" asked Peter. "I thought we'd be there until the official end of hostilities."

"We have been negotiating with the Swiss authorities for some time now. Not just over yourselves, but on behalf of many others who have been held captive here. I can assure you that the two of you have been held in the most comfortable circumstances we have seen. We have visited a couple of other camps that have made our blood run cold."

Peter and Gary looked at each other. "We had heard that Davos was supposed to be good Sir," added Peter. "We were told that if we attempted to escape and were caught, we would be transferred to another camp that would be far less comfortable, but we weren't given any detail."

"Well," said the Colonel, "you should thank your lucky stars that you stayed put. Some of what we've seen here seems to rival what the army is uncovering in Germany right now."

The two civil servants murmured their sombre agreement at the observation.

"Anyway," he continued, "with the war so clearly reaching its conclusion and on the grounds that we guarantee that neither of you will undertake any further active part in it, the Swiss government has kindly allowed us to repatriate the both of you back to England."

"Where are we going to now Sir?" asked Gary.

"We are now on the way back to the same Swiss Air Force base at Dubendorf where you first landed here." He brightened, "Which reminds me Squadron Leader, is it true that you actually shot down a Focke-Wulf with just a pistol? I read it in your file and couldn't believe it."

Peter smiled self-consciously. "Yes Sir, it's true."

"Indeed Sir!" added Gary, "I can certainly vouch for it."

"Good Lord!" said Colonel Jeavons. "That is extraordinary."

"Well Sir, if I didn't do something, he would undoubtedly have killed us all. There was no way I could have outflown him in the open sky. Being in the cloud gave me that one chance, I guess I was lucky really."

"I believe that one makes one's own luck Squadron Leader," said the Colonel. "I suspect that what you might call luck, others would call superb flying and undoubted bravery."

"Hear, hear!" added Gary.

"Anyway gentlemen," Colonel Jeavons continued, "I hope you're looking forward to being back in the air again, because we should have you both on a flight this afternoon. Once we're at the Dubendorf airfield, you can have a meal and then you shall be flown to Geneva, where you will then be transferred to another flight. Then, along with a number of other airmen, you will be flown back to London. You should be home by this evening."

Gary was looking stunned. "Do you mean I can see my new baby today?"

"Does your wife live in London?" asked the Colonel.

"Yes Sir, she's in Wimbledon," replied Gary.

"Then in that case," said Colonel Jeavons smiling, "barring unforeseen circumstances, you shall indeed get to see your new baby this evening." He then turned to Peter. "How about yourself there Squadron Leader? What are your plans?"

"That all depends if we get there in time for a train up to Cambridgeshire, to get me back to RAF Wyton. That's where my wife will be."

"Well then, we can only hope that whoever does these things on aeroplanes, makes sure that the rubber band is wound up good and tight!" said Guy Thomson, the civil servant, with a smile.

***

Bridget was just about to put baby Louise to bed when a sharp rapping on the door interrupted her.

She looked at the clock; it was nearly 7:45 in the evening. "Who could this be?" she said in mild irritation. Carrying the baby, she made her way to the front door, opening it a small way and peered around the edge.

It took a couple of seconds to react. Her mind was frozen in the sheer weight of the moment. Then, dissolving into tears, she opened the door and fell into her husband's arms.

Gary just stood there on the doorstep, holding Bridget and the baby as though there was nothing in the world that could ever prize them apart again.

The sound of her sobs brought some of her near neighbours out onto the street to see what the matter was. When they realised it was Bridget's husband home from the war, they started to clap, almost involuntarily. Their spontaneous salute finally broke the moment, Bridget and Gary were able to stand back and look at each other again.

With calls of "Welcome home" and "Bless you both" the neighbours went back into their houses and Bridget was able to show Gary back into his. Gary was too emotional to speak. He could only look at Bridget and Louise in wonder. Bridget held out his baby to him and he finally held his little daughter for the first time. The emotion had become too great. He had kept all his longing in check for nearly a year, but now it all came rushing to the surface and he broke down into tears every bit as uncontrollable as Bridget's had been earlier.

***

Peter had managed to catch a train at King's Cross station shortly before 7pm. He found an empty compartment and took it, seeking the solitude. He laid his flying jacket and bag on the seat alongside, as he sat himself next to the window. He had now just to wait and hope he could find a taxi once he got to Wyton. The walk from the train station to their cottage was long enough to be unpleasant and he didn't relish the prospect. He reclined back in his seat, lost in thought, gazing out of the window at the deepening night, quite oblivious to the sound of another person coming into the compartment.

"Well, aren't you going to kiss your wife?" asked a familiar voice.

Peter snapped out of his reverie and leapt to his feet in a heartbeat. To his amazement, Anne was standing right in front of him. Peter put his arms out and took her by the shoulders, slowly pulling her closer until they were in a deep embrace.

After they finally broke their kiss, Peter stood back slightly and just looked at her. "Dear God, how I've missed you!"

Anne leant her head forward again and rested it against his chest. "I've been down visiting daddy and Bridget. I was two carriages behind when I saw you on the platform. I couldn't believe it was you, but at the same time I knew it was. How did you get here?" she asked.

"Well, 12 hours ago, I was still a Prisoner of War in Switzerland and now, here I am. It's been a funny old day!"

Anne smiled contentedly as she rested against him. "Now I know it's really you. Your capacity for dazzling understatement has given you away yet again, my darling."

"Oh crikey!" replied Peter.

***

The light of a new day was tinting the horizon. The two of them had not slept much that evening. Their night had been one of making love and hours spent talking. Peter had told her of everything that he and Gary had gone through from the time they were shot down up until the moment she found him on the train. He spoke of how close to Rainer and the children they had become and of his deep fears for their safety, especially Rainer's. He left nothing out.

"So, do you think Rainer is dead then?" she asked. "Are the camps really as bad as people are saying?"

Peter thought deeply. "I don't know, so much depends on which camp he was sent to. He was a strong, healthy man, so I desperately hope that he went to a labour camp. He would be worth more to them as an able bodied worker than as a corpse. He's also got a lot to live for, so perhaps that has helped keep him going..."

He paused for a moment to gather his thoughts. "As for the camps themselves, you probably know more about them than I do. But I've heard some of them are beyond description, they are so bad. The only news we got was more to do with the actual military side of things. It all came through the AFN and they only told us that we were winning the war. Not too much else."

"What's the AFN?" asked Anne.

"The Allied Forces Network," replied Peter. "I'm surprised you didn't know."

"Well, I only listen to the BBC!" said Anne primly.

Peter chuckled as he pulled her close and kissed her again.

"But as for Rainer," he said, slipping back into a more pensive mood after their embrace ended. "I can only hope. It must have been terrible for him. Just knowing that his children were back under the control of his father. That would have sapped his will, let alone whatever else they might have done to him."

"And you said his mother lives in London?" asked Anne.

Peter nodded. "Yes, I have her name and address written down in my bag. I'd like to get in touch with her as soon as possible. She deserves to know what's going on. Then I want to start trying to find out what's happened to him. I've got no idea who to talk to, but there must be someone or some agency we can go to."

His mind was starting to process the possible avenues that might be available. "There has to be somewhere to check if there's a record found of him being at one of the camps. It's probably too soon though. We've only just liberated the camps in the far west of Germany at this stage. There are new ones being discovered all the time. We probably won't get anything for certain until after they finally surrender."

"And the children!" added Anne. "We shall need to track them down. We have to find out where they are being kept, and prize them away from their grandfather."

Peter held her closely. "I knew that you would be keen to pitch in. We will need all the help we can get, I really don't know how to go about this. Who we need to talk to, who to become a nuisance to; but the fact is Gary and I are alive and home right now, thanks to Rainer and the children. We have to try and find them."

Anne revelled in the closeness of their bodies and their thoughts. "Don't worry, my darling. If they can be found, we shall find them."

***

Peter gazed back at himself from the bathroom mirror. He needed a haircut but he was washed, shaved and back in full uniform for the first time in nearly a year. The uniform hung loosely on his frame, he had little spare weight about him to begin with, but even that was all gone now. He had arrived home on a Saturday evening. It was now Monday and he had resolved to report in for duty. The battery in the Alvis had gone flat through lack of use over the last year, so Peter cadged a lift up to the base with the nurse who picked up Anne each morning. A final kiss from Anne as they dropped him off at the administration building and he walked up the steps to resume his life as a Royal Air Force officer.

The Duty Sergeant was new from the last time Peter had been here. Neither of them knew each other.

"I'm Squadron Leader Peter Garland, Sergeant. I wish to report to Group Captain Trehearn for duty. Is it possible to see him please?"

The Duty Sergeant checked the appointment book, open in front of him. "I don't have your name on the list of appointments for this morning Sir. Is the Group Captain expecting you?"

Peter smiled. "Probably not! Up until Saturday, I was a POW in Switzerland. The British Embassy managed to secure my release and get me home. Now, I'd like to report for duty please."

The Sergeant gaped at him in surprise. "I shall inform the Group Captain immediately Sir!" He stammered, getting to his feet.

Peter waited at the desk whilst the Sergeant went to inform Trehearn. He didn't have to wait long. Trehearn beat the Sergeant back to the foyer, almost running.

"Peter!" He almost shouted in delight as he emerged into the room from the corridor. "Good Lord! What a wonderful surprise!"

Dropping all protocol, the two embraced in a warm hug. "I have only just received a telegram informing me that your release was pending. I was going to go over and tell Anne the good news. I suspect that she already knows? Hmm?" he asked with a knowing smile.

"She's quite up to date in that regard, Sir," replied Peter happily. "It's good to see you again too Sir. I have a great deal to tell you about. If it's possible, might I request a formal debriefing as soon as it's convenient?"

"Of course Peter, of course! I shall get it arranged this morning. I have nothing on my schedule that can't be pushed back for a few hours."

They both became conscious of the looks they were getting from the Duty Sergeant and several others who had come into the room.

Trehearn turned to the Duty Sergeant and said, "Do you remember the talk last year of one of our pilots who shot down a Focke-Wulf with a pistol while he was flying an old biplane? Well, this is the chap!"

Everyone in the room stopped whatever they were doing and stared at Peter who suddenly blushed red with embarrassment.

"I do hope that was a true story Peter, I have made much of it since the news came through."

Peter smiled self-consciously. "Yes Sir, it's true. There's quite a bit more to tell as well."

"I'm sure there is!" replied Trehearn. "Now Peter, have you had any breakfast yet?"

"Not much Sir, just some toast and a cup of tea," said Peter.

"Well then, might I suggest you head on over to the Officer's Mess and have a decent meal and then perhaps get yourself a haircut?" Trehearn was looking at Peter's non-regulation locks with bemusement. "That should give me enough time to arrange a stenographer and a couple of chaps from Military Intelligence to join us. I'm sure they'll all be keen to listen in."

Peter stood to attention and saluted. "Thank you Sir, what time should I report back then?"

"Let's make it 11 o'clock shall we? That should be plenty of time. Now, go and reacquaint yourself with some friends. There's a few new faces around, but most of the oldies are still here."

Peter smiled warmly. "Thank you again Sir, I shall see you at 11!"

***

The debriefing went on for nearly three hours. Peter went into great detail about every aspect of their time in hiding; from being shot down, to the weeks of seclusion in the alpine valley and how they finally escaped to Switzerland.

"You were both rather fortunate with being sent to Davos," said one of the Military Intelligence officers in attendance. "We are aware of a number of camps in Switzerland that were run along very similar lines to the ones we're uncovering in Germany itself. It appears that there is no shortage of Nazi sympathisers in senior positions in the Swiss system. The very reasonable conditions you experienced in Davos are far from what most internees have been subjected to."

Peter took the opportunity to bring up the subject of the whereabouts of Rainer and the children.

"Sir, I've tried to make it clear in what I've been saying, just how much Flying Officer Lynch and I owe to this man. We owe him our very lives in fact. Is there some way that we might be able to find out where he was sent and if he is still alive?"

There was a moment of contemplative silence in the room as Peter's request was considered.

"You must understand Squadron Leader that the war is still in progress," said the officer. "There are many thousands, perhaps even millions of people who have been swept up in the camps that the Germans have created. It is likely to be several months after the conclusion of hostilities before we will be able to put together anything approaching a comprehensive list of those who've survived, let alone those who didn't."

Peter breathed out slowly, his hopes were being deflated by the realisation of the massive task yet ahead of the Allies.

"Furthermore," the officer continued, "the Russians are the ones liberating the camps in the east, not us. They are proving to be extremely reluctant when it comes to giving out information about who or what they are uncovering. At least from the point of any survivors they find who might be of military value. We suspect that they are spiriting away many that they liberate from the camps, back to Russia." He paused again and looked intently at Peter. "With the best will in the world Squadron Leader, your friend is going to need the luck of the devil and the kind hand of providence in equal measure, if he is to have any chance at all."

Chapter 18

April saw the war in Europe advancing towards what was clearly its final, desperate and bloody act. The Russians had reached Berlin itself and were fighting a savage battle from street to street, often against mere children who had been pressed into service by a desperate Nazi regime. The American and British forces were now sweeping across the country from the west, trying to secure as much German soil as they could. Not just to defeat the Nazi foe, but to keep it from falling into the hands of the Red Army, advancing inexorably from the east. The fate of post war Europe was already starting to look far from settled. Many were now talking openly of a new war against the Soviet Union being the most likely outcome following the defeat of Germany. Many senior military figures were already strongly advocating for just such a war.

Group Captain Trehearn had sent a telegram to Gary at his home in Wimbledon, welcoming him back and advising him that he wasn't required in RAF Wyton until the following Monday. This gave him a week's leave to share with Bridget and Louise. When the day came and he reported for duty, he was met by Peter and Trehearn, both of whom could scarcely conceal their delight at having him re-join them. After the first moments of reacquaintance, Trehearn ushered them both into his office.

"Well Flying Officer, there are a few matters that we need to have dealt with. Firstly, I have arranged a full debriefing for you this afternoon. Squadron Leader Garland has already had his. Based upon his report, I am delighted to advise you that you are to be awarded the Distinguished Flying Cross. This is for your actions, both in the air during operations, your skill and resourcefulness whilst in Germany, congratulations Gary!"

A medal was the last thing that Gary had been expecting and his surprise was obvious as Peter grasped his hand shacking it enthusiastically.

"Bloody well done mate, you deserve it and a damn sight more beside!" said Peter resorting to his antipodean vernacular.

After Gary had settled his emotions, Trehearn looked at him seriously and asked. "Now, the terms of your early release by the Swiss prevent you from being assigned to further service in an active air crew. So, my question to you is simple. We shall need to find some gainful work for you. There are positions available in the Met Office in Bomber Command. They are based out of London and your University qualifications, combined with your active service would make you a most natural choice. It would mean leaving the PFF, but you would be able to live at home and work in the city. Does that have any appeal Flying Officer?"

Gary could scarcely believe what he was hearing. He had to fight to keep his voice steady as he gave his answer. "That would be *very* satisfactory Sir. May I ask, would the position be only for the duration of the war, or would it extend into the future?"

Trehearn looked at him quizzically. "Are you asking if it might become a career position Flying Officer?"

"Yes Sir, I guess I am!" he replied steadily.

"Well, the RAF will, of course, go on after the war has ended and we will always be having to deal with the weather, so yes Flying Officer. If you wish to make the Royal Air Force your home, I have no doubt that a man of your quality and specialist skills would always be welcome."

Gary felt a wash of deep satisfaction pass over him. The position was the culmination of all that he had hoped for. Living in London meant that he could now be the husband and father that he longed to be, as well as being in the perfect environment to pursue the career he had chosen.

Peter was delighted for his friend, but his sense of humour compelled him to get in one last good-natured jibe. "But I've only just got this bugger trained up Sir! Don't tell me I have to do it all again?"

By now, Gary fully expected Peter's moments of irreverence and both he and Trehearn enjoyed the laugh. It was Trehearn who turned to moment back on Peter.

"Actually Squadron Leader, I feel I ought to tell you that as far as this conflict is concerned, your operational flying days are also at an end."

Peter suddenly felt completely deflated, but Trehearn continued regardless. "As with Flying Officer Lynch, you are unable to resume operational flying during this conflict, due to the terms of your early release. Which brings me to the question of your future Peter. I can now inform you, that you are being awarded a Bar to your Distinguished Flying Cross and promotion to the rank of Wing Commander, effective immediately."

It was Peter's turn to look dumbstruck, as now Gary pumped his hand in congratulations.

Smiling broadly, Trehearn continued, "You're bringing down of that FW190 with a pistol is almost the stuff of legend around here. In addition, your exemplary leadership skills and judgement make you a natural choice for higher command. You shall still have plenty of time flying, but this position is going to be more administrative. You're to be blessed with responsibility for three squadrons of unruly young men that you'll need to keep on top of. Welcome to the brave, new world of command rank, Wing Commander!"

Peter had insisted that Gary stay the night with Anne and himself and Gary had been quick to accept. After dinner, they were able to talk over the events of the day and the new futures that lay ahead for them both. All three appreciated the irony that Gary, who was the least military of them, now saw his future in the RAF after the war ended. Whilst Peter was now contemplating a future in the world of civil aviation. The thought of senior rank, coupled with a high focus on administrative duty and limited flying time, he found far from appealing. It helped him realise that the motivation that underlay all that he had achieved so far, was his simple love of flight.

For Anne though, there was now the comfort of knowing that Peter would not be resuming operational flying. The war was so nearly over and her greatest fear was that he would want one last taste of action before the end finally came. She no longer had to live with that concern. There was still the war against the Empire of Japan raging in the Pacific, but that seemed another world away and did not enter into her thinking as a possible future deployment for him. After dinner, the talk turned to Rainer and the children.

"I'll be based in London now," said Gary. "I'll be able to stay close to the Red Cross. Surely they would be getting the most up to date lists of survivors from the camps, as they get liberated."

"They would certainly be a good place to start," said Anne. "My guess though, is that the Americans would be the most likely. They're the ones finding the camps as they advance. They are moving medical teams into them at the first opportunity, so they would have to be recording the names and details of the people they are liberating. I just have no idea how to go about finding out who I can speak to, with them."

Peter sat quietly listening while they spoke. After a minute, he leant forward. "Well, the rank of Wing Commander no doubt sounds far more impressive than it really is, but I might give it a try and see how many strings it will allow me to pull. I'm sure that I'll have the ability to put out some discrete enquiries to the Americans, alongside all my other duties. It certainly can't hurt to ask."

Gary looked enthusiastic. "Well then, if I can develop some contacts with the Red Cross and you can do the same with whoever you can find on the American side, then we might just be able to turn something up. We have to give it a go, don't we?"

"Of course we do," replied Peter. "I for one, would never forgive myself if I don't, I'm certain you'd feel the same."

Gary nodded vigorously. "Absolutely I would, Rainer's a friend now, and those kids... I miss them so much."

Anne and Peter exchanged glances and reached out for each other's hands.

"Fatherhood has been the making of you, I think Gary," said Anne warmly. "I can't wait until we can come down to London and see you with Bridget and Louise."

Gary smiled contentedly. "The sooner, the better!" he said.

***

8th May 1945 – VE Day

"God bless you all. This is your victory! It is the victory of the cause of freedom in every land. In all our long history we have never seen a greater day than this."

Winston Churchill's victory day speech had been years in the anticipating. Anne had joined Peter along with many others in a crowded Officer's Mess at RAF Wyton. They were listening to the Prime Minister's broadcast, formally announcing the unconditional surrender of Germany. Whilst jubilant crowds thronged the streets of central London hoping for a glimpse of the Royal Family or were simply caught up in the profundity of the moment, the mood at Wyton was more subdued. There was still a sense of joy and triumph at having prevailed in such a climactic struggle, but it was powerfully tempered by the recollections of the many friends and comrades who had died in its attainment.

Anne sensed that Mark was with Peter at this moment. He was fighting hard to stifle a tear as he thought of the friend who would have been relishing this day; whose *joie de vivre* would have turned this sombre, contemplative gathering into a joyous party. Peter's arm was around Anne's shoulders and he squeezed her tight to him.

"Are you alright?" she asked.

He looked into her lovely face and smiled. "Yeah, I am, this is a good moment. I'm missing an old friend, but that's as it should be right now, I think."

Anne pressed her head against him. "I couldn't agree more. We've all had to put some part of our emotions to one side for a long time now. It's good that we can start to open up again." She looked around the room. "Everyone here is thinking of someone they've lost over the last six years. They all understand the price we've had to pay to be here. I thought that when this day finally came, we would all be deliriously happy. Now, I think this is better, you're right my darling, this is a good moment."

Peter brightened as they made the short drive home from the airfield. "I'm going to be giving as many of the lads as possible, a week's leave now. This is a time when they should be with their families I think. I'll see if I can wangle a few days for us as well. Be nice if we can go down to London to see your Dad, and Gary and Bridget," he finished on a note that implied there was more he wanted to say.

Anne picked up on it but didn't want to push. She knew what was on his mind and finally, she spoke.

"You're troubled because you haven't got in touch with Rainer's mother aren't you? Why don't you write her that letter? Ask if you might come down and see her? She would either reject it out of hand or hurry to get back in touch with you."

They had just arrived at their cottage. Anne turned to him and said firmly. "Let's do it now! Let's go inside and we'll do it together. We can post it tomorrow. No more putting it off!"

Peter breathed out slowly. "You're right of course. I don't know why I've struggled with the words so much, but yes, I would appreciate your help. Let's go and do it now!"

***

Finding space on a train had proved too hard. There were thousands of servicemen all wanting to get to London, so Peter and Anne had driven down instead. It had taken less than a week to get a reply from Rainer's mother. She had been overjoyed to get Peter's letter and insisted that they meet at the first opportunity, so Peter arranged leave for that weekend.

Anne had chosen to remain with Bridget, while Peter and Gary set out in the Alvis. Neither of them spoke much as they drove. Each were deep in their own thoughts as they made their way from Wimbledon along streets, many still heavily scarred from bomb damage, until they found Mablethorpe Road in Fulham. Gary was checking the house numbers as Peter drove slowly down the street. "This is the one," he said. "We're here."

Peter parked the car and as they both got out, the door to the neat two story terrace house opened. Rainer's mother had been watching for the arrival of a car and now she hurried outside to greet them.

"Thank you both so much for coming. My name is Irene Voss, won't you both please come inside?"

Both men smiled almost involuntarily. She looked so much like an attractive, middle-aged version of little Marie that they instantly began to feel at ease. Following her into the house, she led them into the lounge room and asked that they each be seated.

"I've made a cake, I'll just go and put on the kettle, I shan't be a moment!' she said, retreating to the kitchen.

Looking around the room, Gary noticed some framed photographs on the mantle. He gestured towards them, pointing them out to Peter. The two of them got up and crossed the room to have a closer look. There were several pictures of the family, with Rainer still a boy. A photograph clearly taken in happier days. The most recent one showed Rainer and the children, they were both much younger; Marie was only a baby in her father's arms. There was also a woman in the frame; both men realised it must have been Liesel. The image showed her as a slim woman, raven haired and pretty, but with an intensity in her gaze. She wasn't smiling in the picture, none of them were. The photograph seemed to capture something of the tension that was dominating their lives at the time it must have been taken, shortly before the war began.

"That came with the last letter I ever received from Rainer." Irene had quietly come back into the room.

Peter and Gary were so engrossed with the photograph, neither of them had heard her.

"He mailed it just before the war broke out. It arrived on the day Germany invaded Poland in 1939. I tried writing back, but the letter, of course was returned to me. Since then, I had heard nothing of them at all, that is until I received your letter Wing Commander."

"Please call me Peter, Mrs Voss, if anyone calls me by my rank, I worry that I might be in trouble over something."

She smiled nervously at his reply. "Please, you must call me Irene and you must be Gary, Peter told me much about you in his letter."

She held out her hand for Gary to shake and then motioned for them both to return to their seats.

"I can't tell you how much your letter meant to me, Peter. I have lived in complete ignorance of all that has happened to my family, ever since the war began. Five and a half years now of not knowing if they were dead or alive. Still not knowing in fact!"

She shuddered, her hands clutching and unclutching in an unconscious nervous action. Peter and Gary sat in silence whilst she cut the cake into slices and poured each of them a cup of tea.

Once they had been served, Irene sat in her arm-chair and looked directly at the two men. "May I ask that you tell me as much as you can remember about your time with them please? How they were, where they lived? Anything you can think of really…"

Peter and Gary looked briefly at each other and then Peter began. He talked of how they crashed and of how Rainer and the children had found them in the boulder field. Gary added much about what they did during the time when Peter was immobilised with his injured ankle. They talked about all that Rainer had built up in the valley to make their lives as comfortable as possible and of how Liesel had vanished. They spoke at length of how they ultimately escaped and how Rainer had proven his bravery and coolness. Finally, they told Irene of their flight to Switzerland and about the last news they had heard.

She was deeply shocked when she heard of how the children had been returned to Germany to be given over into her former husband's care. Also of Rainer being sent on to a labour camp, somewhere in the Reich. By the time they had finished, they had told her of everything they could remember and more than three hours had passed.

"May I ask you frankly please?" she looked intensely at the two men. "Do you believe my Rainer is dead?"

Neither answered for several seconds as they considered their own thoughts.

Gary spoke first. "No Irene, I don't think he's dead, I don't think the children are either. When we last saw him, he was fit and healthy. He had skills which they needed, he's an electrical engineer. They would have sent him to a work camp, but they wouldn't be in a rush just to kill someone if they could make good use of them first. Also, he would fight hard to get back to the children, I think he has just too much to live for, I truly believe he's still alive."

Gary's and Irene's eyes were locked upon each other's as he spoke. Tears began to well up in hers as he finished. She had been desperate for some words of hope to cling to and Gary had just given them to her. In his heart though, Peter was far less certain about Rainer's fate than Gary. He was hearing stories, coming out of Germany about the camps that filled him with horror. The conditions the inmates had been forced to endure were just unimaginable. Surviving was more than just a matter of having things to live for. Surviving might just require a miracle.

***

The afternoon was becoming the evening as Peter and Gary finally bade farewell to Irene. They had resolved to stay closely in touch and let each other know of any new information that might come to light. Gary had suggested to Irene that she go and make herself known to the Red Cross. To give them all the information she had about the last known address of her husband in Germany and that she had a legitimate interest in the welfare of these people, her next-of-kin, still there. She had been so lost from her years of grief that the thought of doing this earlier had not occurred to her.

Knowing now that were concrete steps she could take to help in the search for her son and grandchildren, her spirits lifted and she suddenly found a new determination to go on. She resolved to visit the Red Cross in central London on the following Monday morning.

***

February 1946

Bridget couldn't be at the hospital with them. She was pregnant again and suffering through first trimester morning sickness. Peter walked impatiently around the waiting room, with both Gary and Anne's father Alistair, trying to lend him moral support.

"Are you finally going to tell us what names you've chosen, now that the moment's here?" asked Alistair.

"Victor if it's a boy, Victoria if it's a girl!" Peter rattled the words out quickly, not wanting to dwell on the moment.

"Do I detect a certain rigidity of thought there, young Peter?" asked Alistair with a wry, knowing smile.

Gary sat grinning from the comfort of his chair, scarcely able to contain his mirth. Both he and Alistair knew the reason for the choice of names. Anne had told both her father and Bridget that the baby had been conceived on the night of VE Day, the year before. She just hadn't told Peter that she'd let the secret slip.

He now glowed red with embarrassment. "Look, today is the 23rd of February. I'm sure you can do the subtraction and work out what happened about nine months or so ago!"

He looked from Gary over to his father-in-law, they were both fighting hard to keep from laughing.

"You both know, don't you?! Miserable pair of buggers!" he said, throwing his hands up in the air.

Their laughter was interrupted by a door opening and a nurse coming into the room.

"Mr. Garland?" she asked, unsure of how to address Peter.

"Yes," he hurriedly replied.

She broke into a smile. "You have a beautiful baby girl! Your wife and daughter are both doing very well."

Peter just stood there beaming whilst Gary and Alistair both hurried from their chairs to come over and congratulate him.

After the celebration settled, Peter asked. "Am I allowed to go in and see them?"

"Of course you are," replied the nurse, "please follow me."

She turned to Gary and Alistair. "Would you mind waiting out here please? We won't let him stay too long, Mrs Garland is rather tired."

Alistair was a doctor himself and understood the protocol. This was a moment for the husband, the wife and the baby. He and Gary both happily resumed their chairs and began chatting to fill the time.

Anne had been returned to her bed and the new baby was neatly wrapped with just her head, shoulders and arms visible. She lay resting against Anne, who was partly propped up, semi-reclining. Peter was ushered in to join them with a look of awe on his face. They were now a family, a thought that seemed inconceivable just a couple of years earlier.

He pulled a chair close alongside the head of the bed to be close to Anne. "My goodness! Look what you've done!" He leaned over and kissed her on the forehead and then on the lips.

Anne really did look tired, but she still seemed to radiate contentment and happiness. "You had a small role to play as well, if I remember correctly."

They remained together for several minutes in silence, Peter leaning against the bed, holding his wife's hand and gazing at his new daughter. Anne was slowly drifting off into an exhausted sleep.

Peter spoke quietly. "Look darling, I'll leave you to sleep now. I'll be back in the morning, as early as they'll let me, is that alright?"

Anne nodded and smiled wearily, Peter kissed her once again. Slowly he left the room, not taking his eyes off Anne or the baby until the door closed behind him.

***

February and March both passed and with April came the first anniversaries of the milestones that marked the final days of the war. It also brought a phone call from Irene Voss to Gary.

"Oh Gary, I've had the most marvellous news! The Red Cross have sent me a letter that tells me that Rainer survived the camp. He's still alive!" Her voice was alive with excitement, her deepest hopes were being realised.

Gary was equally delighted. "That is amazing news Irene! Where is he? Do you know?"

"Not yet I'm afraid, the letter doesn't say much. Just that he was liberated from Sachsenhausen Concentration Camp by Soviet troops in late April last year. It tells me no more than that, but it means he should be alive then, doesn't it?" Her voice now trembled, a frisson of doubt taking hold.

Gary was aghast. "It's taken a year to get that information to you? I can't believe that, it is wonderful news but it's terrible to make you wait so long. Is that all it says?"

"That's all really. Just that they will send any further information to me as soon as they become aware of his current whereabouts. It's not a lot really, but the most important part is that he's still alive!" She was regaining her positivity.

"That is absolutely right! He's still alive!" Gary was thinking hard about what to do next. "Listen Irene, I'm going to get in touch with Peter and see if he can come down to London soon. All three of us should make an appointment at the Red

Cross and see what we can do to speed the process up from here. Squeaky wheels get the grease don't they? So let's squeak!"

***

Peter had little difficulty in getting three days leave at short notice. Since the end of the war, the operational requirements which kept aircrew so closely tied to their bases, had been eased dramatically.

Anne stayed up in Wyton with little Victoria, whilst Peter caught the train down to London. This time, it was Gary's turn to drive Peter. He and Bridget had bought a small Morris saloon and were enjoying the freedom it gave them, despite the petrol rationing that still hampered most car owners.

Peter was enthusing about the new jet powered aircraft that were taking their place in the RAF. "I'm sure it won't be long now before the last of the piston engine aircraft are gone, at least so far as front line aircraft are concerned. This new kite, the Gloster Meteor is a revelation! It's nearly two hundred miles per hour faster than the fastest Spitfire! An extraordinary thing to fly."

Gary sat smiling as he drove, letting Peter ramble on about flying. If he wanted him to stop, all he had to do was mention little Vicky and suddenly the tough fighter pilot instantly became a happy, gooey father.

They arrived at Irene's home in Fulham and knocked on the door. Since their first visit, Irene had become a well-established part of their lives. Gary and Bridget had invited her to visit them for afternoon tea one day, keen to see how she would react to being with a mixed race family, a rarity in a still very white England. To their delight, she was quick to accept and soon became a close friend. Even more intriguing was the unexpected relationship that seemed to be developing between her and Anne's widowed father Alistair. The two had been introduced on one of the many evenings that they all spent together, whenever Anne and Peter came down to London. Neither were rushing anything, but they clearly enjoyed each other's company.

This, however, was less a social visit and more an exploratory one. Irene had already prepared herself and was waiting, ready to join them as they then headed into the city to the head office of the Red Cross in a street simply called Moorfields. London was still an easy city to drive in. Petrol rationing was keeping unnecessary trips down to a minimum, so Gary had little difficulty in getting them to their 10 o'clock appointment just ahead of time.

They were ushered into the office of one of the many staff tasked with locating missing individuals amongst the millions of vanished or displaced people who had been swallowed up by the greatest conflict the world had ever seen. A spare, wiry man in his middle age rose to meet them, taking off his glasses as he came around his desk to greet them individually.

"How do you do, my name is Jeremy Townsend. I'm part of the investigations team, won't you please take a seat?"

He knew there would be three visitors, so he had borrowed an additional chair from a neighbouring office to accommodate everyone.

"It's very timely that you made the appointment when you did, I have just received some additional information about your son Mrs Voss. It only came in yesterday, I would have posted it out to you, if you hadn't already been coming in this morning."

He had immediately caught the attention of all three.

Jeremy looked at each of the three and smiled. "The Russians have been holding him since he was liberated from the Sachsenhausen Concentration Camp north of Berlin. It was one of the bad camps. Not that there were any good ones, but Sachsenhausen was bad. It is likely that your son was in very poor condition when he was found. The Russians didn't allow any Red Cross access to the survivors, at least, not for quite a while. We believe he was taken away from the camp and sent to some form of a rehabilitation facility well behind the Russian lines."

Jeremy paused for a moment to check his notes. "They have said that it was their intention merely to nurse him back to health before returning him to the West. Many of us think that it was more their intention to try and recruit him as a Soviet spy, based upon his already identifying as a socialist, but we can't be sure. In truth, we don't really know for certain why they've held him so long."

Irene, Gary and Peter were listening attentively as Jeremy continued. He had been saving the best piece of news for this moment.

"Whatever the case, they have at last approached the Red Cross and advised us that they are prepared to turn him over to our care within the next few days."

Irene clasped her hands in joy, Peter and Gary got up from their chairs and hugged her warmly.

After the emotion settled, Irene asked. "What news of the children? Or of Hennie - sorry - Heinrich, their grandfather? Have the Russians said anything about them?"

Jeremy shook his head slowly. "Not a word, I'm afraid, we have no news at all."

He sat back in his swivel chair and steepled his fingers. "I wish I had something to offer you there, truly I do. This is what is making our job so frustrating." He paused for a moment, gathering his thoughts. "The problem is simply the Russians. Getting any sort of information out of them is like pulling teeth. I'm not sure if you are aware of just how tense things are at the moment between the western allies and the Soviets? I hope I'm not speaking out of turn, but there are a great many who are even talking of yet another war just around the corner, between ourselves and the Soviet Union."

Irene, Gary and Peter sat in silence, staring intently at Jeremy.

"Everything is political with them, there was considerable goodwill at the war's end, but it is drying up very quickly. There are still good people on their side who understand that we are simply trying to do genuine humanitarian work only. We're not interested in the politics, we just want to help get people reunited with their loved ones. But it all takes time and goodwill, which at the moment is scarce."

He paused again, this time for a sip of water. "It's why it took so long for us to get the first piece of news to you Mrs Voss. The Russians simply would not divulge the slightest piece of information until they decided there was no political risk to them in doing so."

Peter brought the meeting back to the main point. "So, how are we to arrange picking up Rainer? Where can we meet him?"

"They will deliver him to the Red Cross in Berlin. They've done this before with other detainees they have released," said Jeremy.

"Have they given you a date yet?" continued Peter. "How much notice will we get?"

Jeremy shrugged his shoulders. "They just said 'soon' in their communique, that could mean tomorrow, or next week. Generally, once they've advised us, it happens quite quickly after that. In that respect, they have been very fair so far."

Peter turned to Irene and Gary. "I am going to arrange an aircraft, so I can fly over and collect him. Would you both like to come with me?"

"Of course!" said Gary immediately.

Irene was taking all this in, but she was, nonetheless, astounded at how quickly Peter and Gary were developing a plan.

"My goodness! You talk as though the Air Force will just let you use an aeroplane for your own pleasure any time you wish."

Peter gave her a conspiratorial smile. "Well, up to a certain point, they more or less do. I need to keep my flying hours up so, providing I don't go dropping bombs on the Hammersmith Odeon, I can take one up, pretty well anytime I fancy."

"Would I be allowed to come with you?" asked Irene. "I'm only a civilian."

"I can't see a problem," said Peter. "We have civilians fly in Air Force aircraft all the time. Do you have your passport in order?"

"I believe so, I shall check when I get home," said Irene in obvious relief.

"Even if it's not," added Peter. "You can still travel with us, but you may just have to remain within the confines of the airport in Berlin. I'm sure we can work something out."

He turned back to Jeremy. "If we leave you with our telephone numbers, can you get in touch with one of us directly you hear anything? All we need to know is where to meet him and when, we can arrange the rest from there."

Jeremy nodded his agreement. "There are some formalities that will need to be gone through first of course and don't be surprised if Military Intelligence might want to interview him as well. That would be entirely likely, especially given his socialist sympathies, and his being returned following a year in the tender care of our dear friends, the Russians. I have no doubt that they will be very keen to keep a close eye on him."

These words had an immediate, sobering impact on all of them, but especially Irene.

"My son would never become a spy for the Russians. He might believe in social equity, but he would never become a traitor."

"I guess, we will find out soon enough, I do sincerely hope that you are right Mrs Voss," replied Jeremy. He looked around the table at his three guests. "Anyway, if you can all write your telephone numbers down for me, I shall be in touch as soon as I've heard anything," he said as he slid a pad of paper and a pencil over towards them.

They each filled out their details and somewhat abruptly, the meeting was at an end.

Chapter 19

Peter had managed to secure an Airspeed Oxford to be held on standby, awaiting his call for a flight to Berlin at short notice. It was a twin engine general purpose aircraft, usually used for pilot training. This one though, had been recently converted to passenger service, with six seats and ample range to fly directly to Berlin. It was cramped and far from luxurious, but ideal for what he needed. All they were waiting on now was the call from Jeremy at the Red Cross headquarters in London.

Peter's rank now secured him the opportunity to make his own arrangements regarding impromptu flights over to the continent, secure in the knowledge that his own commander, Group Captain Trehearn would happily back him up. Peter had held an affable but detailed meeting with Trehearn to bring him up-to-date with what was happening. As long as Peter's own formal duties didn't suffer, he was content to give his subordinate the freedom he needed to arrange a flight at short notice to Berlin. Then with subsequent return, carrying civilian passengers.

The next few days passed slowly with Peter fully occupied, struggling through the relentlessly tedious administrative duties that his higher rank now demanded of him. Their meeting at the Red Cross had been on a Tuesday morning, it was now early afternoon on the following Friday and the telephone in Peter's office finally rang.

It was Gary. "I've just had a call from Jeremy at the Red Cross. He says that Rainer is being delivered to their office in Berlin today. It looks like the Russians have been true to their word."

Peter felt a thrill run through him. "That is wonderful news, have you rung Irene yet?"

Gary hesitated for a second. "I was wondering if it might be best to wait until we know for sure he is safe with the Red Cross before we call her. Just in case something goes wrong."

Peter also paused briefly whilst he considered Gary's words. "That's probably a very good idea. We don't want to go getting her hopes up, just to let them down again. When will we know for sure?"

"Jeremy said that the Red Cross in Berlin will send him a telegram as soon as he's been delivered to them. He will call me immediately after that," replied Gary.

"Excellent then!" said Peter. "It's probably too late to go over there today anyway. If it all goes to plan, we can fly over tomorrow morning. Will you be able to pick up Irene and take her with you to RAF Northolt? I can fly down and meet you there. Looks like you're back on navigation duty again mate. London to Berlin, no bombs or flares this time."

Gary chuckled but was relishing the thought of being back in the cabin with Peter again. "Do you know which airport in Berlin we can land at?"

"We have an airport in the British sector called RAF Gatow," replied Peter. "That's where we will be expected, please don't get it mixed up with one of the Soviet fields. There's a good chap."

"Am I allowed to swear at a senior officer?"

"Wait till we're off duty, then you can do it over a beer!" said Peter with a chuckle.

The next call from Gary came shortly before 4 pm. "Jeremy has just confirmed that Rainer is safely with the Red Cross in Berlin. They will look after him tonight and we can pick him up tomorrow."

"That's bloody marvellous," replied Peter. "Will we have to go to them and collect him, or can they bring him to Gatow?"

"Jeremy said that he will arrange for them to get him to Gatow, so we won't get to do much sightseeing by the sound of it," said Gary.

"Any news of the children?" added Peter.

Gary was instantly more sombre. "Nothing, not a word," he replied.

"Okay," said Peter quietly. "Well, let's hope Rainer will be able to tell us something. Anyway mate, if you can let Irene know and get her to Northolt by about 8 am, I'll be there to meet you."

***

Peter spotted Irene and Gary waiting outside the control tower building. He taxied up as closely as possible and shut the engines down. Opening the door, he attached a short metal ladder and joined them on the ground, giving Irene a warm hug.

"I just need to nip in and lodge my flight plan, I should only be ten minutes or so." He turned to Irene. "The creature comforts on this thing are pretty basic if you know what I mean. You may wish to go to the 'ladies' before we take off. There's a four hour flight ahead of us."

"Knowing all about Peter's flying" added Gary, "I would strongly recommend the idea!" Irene smiled happily and went with Peter into the building, whilst Gary stowed the food hampers that Irene had prepared on to the aircraft.

Once they were airborne, Gary looked back into the passenger compartment and saw that Irene's face was glued to the window, examining the ground below eagerly.

He clambered out of his seat and went to speak to her. "Is this the first time you've ever flown Irene?"

She looked as excited as a school-girl. "Yes it is, I've been wanting to for years, but circumstances rather got in the way."

"Well then, why don't you come up and sit in my seat next to Peter for a while. It's the best seat in the house."

Peter happily explained all the controls to Irene and pointed out the various landmarks as they flew over the Channel and the Low Countries at an altitude of ten thousand feet. Gary appeared with cups of tea from a Thermos flask and some cake that Irene had baked the evening before.

"I could get used to this," said Peter. "Usually Air Force flights aren't very well catered."

Finally, Gary had to reclaim his seat as they were now well over Germany. Irene sat at her old seat and resumed her studied gazing out of the window. Once they were over Berlin itself, the scene below shocked them all. Even after a year of clearing away the war damage, large areas of the centre of the city and surrounding suburbs were still devastated. Neither Peter nor Gary, who had only ever flown over Berlin at night, had ever had the chance to see it as they saw it now. The sight sobered them. Getting the Oxford down onto the runway at RAF Gatow was a relief.

***

Rainer was almost unrecognizable, more than a year after he had been liberated, he was still painfully thin and gaunt. His hair was unkempt and prematurely greying, his complexion was sallow and he hadn't shaved in well over a week. After a year in the care of the Soviets, it appeared they had done little to nourish and restore him.

Peter and Gary stood back as Irene hurried over and tearfully embraced him. Rainer also broke down in uncontrollable tears when he realised who it was. He had despaired of ever seeing his mother again. The depth of his emotion and his weakened physical state combined to render him mute and unable to stand for several minutes. Finally, he managed to slowly get to his feet and have a proper look at her. His eyes were glistening with tears still being shed, but the first hint of a smile was starting to appear. Then Irene, still holding him, turned her head and indicated Peter and Gary to him. They both stepped forward and joined Irene in embracing him. It was the first moment of human warmth he had experienced in over two years.

The paperwork to have him released into their care was less daunting than they had dared hope. Irene had had the forethought to bring Rainer's English birth certificate along, as well as her own passport. She gave her address in Fulham as his place of residence and in less than an hour, they were back in the freshly refuelled Oxford again, on the return flight to RAF Northolt.

Gary had left Peter alone in the cockpit and had gone back to sit with Irene and Rainer.

Rainer was finally able to speak now, even though his voice was croaky and weak. "I knew that you would be the ones who would come for me. I always believed that."

He was now back in control of his emotions and although his weak voice was being tested, he told them something of the last twenty four hours.

"After they delivered me to the Red Cross, the British Military Intelligence people spent hours with me. They seem to believe I may be a Soviet spy. After what I have seen of them, spying for the Russians is the last thing I would ever do. They are little better than the Nazis."

The bitterness in his voice, frail as it was, was unmistakable. Gary leaned forward and asked gently. "Rainer, have you any idea where Thomas and Marie are?"

Rainer's head drooped forward as he dejectedly shook it. After a minute he said. "No, I have no idea. All I know is that they were with my father and he seems to have disappeared. I know the Soviets were looking for him also. They were wanting to use the children to blackmail me into spying for them, but they couldn't find them. That was why they let me go I think, it was not worth them keeping me any longer."

Gary looked at him sitting in his seat, dejected and near broken. "We will find them Rainer, if they are still out there, we'll find them, I promise you," he said with vehemence.

Rainer looked up at him, his eyes still red and moist, "Don't make promises you can't keep, my friend. I have no idea where to even start looking."

"Well, let's get you better and stronger first," said Gary. "Then we can all start putting our heads together, the two of you know him best. Perhaps there's some memory that might give us a clue where he may have gone to ground. Try not to think too much on it now, let's get you home safely first."

***

"I'm so looking forward to having you finally meet him," Peter was driving Anne and Vicky down to London again. It had been two weeks since they had finally returned Rainer to the company of his mother.

"I know how much I have to thank him for. It will be wonderful to finally do it."

Anne was caught in a complex web of emotions at the impending meeting. She was desperately keen to meet the man who had been so instrumental in saving the lives of both Peter and Gary, yet she knew how much he had suffered at the hands of both the Nazis and the Soviets. It would be the first time she would come face to face with the results of over two years of continuous barbaric cruelty on another human. The thought of how he might look weighed on her mind. In the end, the change in him delighted Peter and relieved Anne. Two weeks in his mother's care had seen remarkable improvement in him.

"Wow, look at you mate!" exclaimed Peter on first sight.

Rainer was now clean shaven, had neatly cut hair and was wearing new clothes. Moreover, he had put on a small amount of weight and his colour was good again. He was clearly on the road to physical recovery, but his slowness in walking indicated that there was still a long path to travel. Peter gently shook Rainer's hand, unsure if a strong grip would be painful to him. He was surprised at Rainer's response; his grip came back firmly.

"Well Rainer, may I introduce my wife Anne and our little daughter Vicky." Peter moved aside as Anne stepped forward and kissed Rainer on the cheek.

"I have been waiting for this moment for such a long time. There is so much that I want to say to you, I'm just so happy to finally meet you at last." Anne was deeply relieved to see how much better he seemed, given the description that Peter had provided after they first brought him home. It was obvious that the love and care of his mother was working a near miracle.

Irene spoke up from behind her son. "Please all of you, come inside, it's much more comfortable than the doorstep!"

She led them through to the lounge room where Rainer sat in the armchair that Peter occupied on his first visit, whilst Peter himself sat alongside Anne on the sofa.

"It's good to see how much you've come along in just two weeks mate," said Peter. "You're still a bit on the thin side, but other than that, you're looking good."

Rainer smiled and pulled at his new clothes. They were noticeably loose on his spare frame. "My mother insisted on buying these for me, she says she will keep feeding me until I fit them properly. As you can see, I still have some way to go."

Peter felt a surge of emotion as he heard some humour return to Rainer's conversation.

"Your voice is sounding stronger too, are you sleeping alright?" he asked.

Rainer hesitated for a moment. "Better now, but still not well, it may take time."

"This is your baby daughter?" he asked, drawing the subject away from himself. "Her name is Victoria, isn't it?"

Anne, who was cradling Vicky in her arms, stood up and took her over to Rainer. She leant over and passed her over to him. "It is, but we just call her Vicky, it's a bit less formal that Victoria."

Rainer settled back in the armchair, closely regarding Vicky as he supported her on his lap. "I haven't held a baby since… in a long time. She is just so beautiful," he said with a breaking voice.

Anne tried to keep things light. "We think so, but I suppose all parents are very biased like that."

Rainer was intently watching Vicky who was quietly taking everything in as she, with wide eyes, gazed around the room. Holding a baby again was clearly testing the limited control he had over his still deeply scarred emotions. Anne, seeing the beginning of tears starting to form, was about to reach forward and take Vicky back, when there came a blessed knocking on the front door.

"That will be Gary and Bridget," called out Irene from the kitchen, where she was happily preparing afternoon tea.

Their arrival gave Rainer the chance to hand Vicky back to Anne and regather his composure. Whilst his attention was engaged with greeting the new arrivals, Peter whispered in Anne's ear. "He still has a way to go, doesn't he?"

Anne nodded her agreement. "The poor man, you can just see that losing his children is tearing at him."

Peter said nothing more, but new ideas were taking form in his mind.

***

"You seem very quiet tonight Peter?"

Bridget had noticed that Peter seemed unusually distracted as they chatted over dinner. Peter snapped back to reality at the sound of his name. He didn't realise that his mind had drifted away somewhere else completely.

"I'm sorry, I guess I was off with the fairies," he replied.

"Anything you'd care to share?" she added.

Peter paused for a moment to give himself time to clarify his thoughts. Then, looking from Rainer to Irene he asked, "Do either of you remember if there was any special place that you used to go to as a family? Somewhere that Heinrich might feel safe? Somewhere he could take the children and live without arousing any suspicion?"

Irene shook her head. "When we moved back to Germany in '21, we settled in Munich. It wasn't long before the economy fell to pieces and we couldn't afford to take holidays anywhere really. Hennie was able to earn extra money repairing mechanical instruments as well as clocks, so we got by better than many, but things were still quite difficult."

Then Rainer spoke up, taking the discussion on a new tangent. "My father always said it was Hitler that got Germany out of that terrible Depression. There is some truth in that, but he then just closed his eyes and his mind to all the other terrible things that he also did. For him, the Nazis seemed more like a religious movement than a political one."

Gary had been listening intently. "You never spoke very much about him when we were in the valley. You didn't even tell us his name."

Rainer nodded slowly. "You know now his name is Heinrich. I was happier not thinking of him then, but now that he has my children, I think of nothing else."

Peter leaned forward. "If he was so committed to the Nazi cause, do you know if he was actively involved with them during the war itself?"

Rainer thought for a moment. "It's possible… I don't know for sure. I had lost contact with him after he threatened to turn us over to the Gestapo. It's very possible though, he had become extremely skilled at repairing delicate instruments as well as clocks. As a Party member, they would have found him a good job, I'm sure. Why do you ask? Is it important?"

Peter leaned back in his chair and looked around the table. "I think it might be, I can't help but wonder if he might still be working for 'the cause', so to speak."

Irene's mouth opened in surprised and Rainer's attention suddenly sharpened.

"What do you mean?" he asked.

"Well," said Peter, "we know that he's not registered himself anywhere in western Germany since the war ended and neither of the children have been enrolled at any school. To all intents and purposes, he's completely vanished. I'm certain he won't be hiding in the east. He had plenty of time to get well away from the Russians as they advanced and neither he nor the children have ever been posted as having been killed."

Everyone at the table sat in silence as Peter looked around each of their faces before he continued.

"I believe he has likely become part of the underground network, helping smuggle Nazis out of Germany. I think he's gone to ground in a secure place. He may be using it as a safe haven for Nazis fugitives in transit as they get smuggled away from likely capture."

Gary exhaled slowly. "It's very possible I guess. If he's still a believer in the Nazi movement, he may well want to be involved. Where would that place be though? How do we go about finding it?"

Peter leant his left elbow on the table and began tapping with his right hand forefinger. "I'll lay London to a brick that he's up in the valley. It's the ideal spot! We all know what a perfect place it is for hiding out, it has to be there!"

There were looks of amazed agreement from around the table.

"It does make a lot of sense," said Gary. "Even if that German patrol that was looking for us burned the cabin down, all anyone else would need would be tents and supplies. The valley itself is still perfect for staying out of sight from the rest of the world."

Peter was feeling relief that his idea was gaining support. He had been dwelling on the thought for days, but he needed to talk to Rainer first. It was Rainer however, who poured cold water on the idea almost immediately.

"Except that my father has no idea that the place even exists. Even if he did, he has no idea where it is, or how to get there."

Peter felt an immediate let-down.

Rainer continued. "Do you remember, I told you once that I learned about the valley from University friends of mine, from before the war. It was a cabin that they used to go to in their holidays for hiking and hunting. I made certain that I never mentioned the place to him. I'm completely sure that he knows nothing about it; my father can't possibly be there."

From a brief flirtation with euphoria, the mood at the table returned to gloom again very quickly.

***

Anne was abruptly roused from a deep sleep as Peter suddenly sat bolt upright in bed.

"What's happened?" she asked blearily. "Is Vicky crying? I can't hear her."

"No, she's fine," said Peter. He looked at Anne as she lay next to him, her eyes now focusing as she continued to wake.

"They *are* hiding in the valley, I'm sure of it now!"

"But how?" asked Anne, trying to clear her mind from the fog of sleep and finally realising Peter's train of thought. "You heard Rainer, he is positive that he never told his father anything about it."

"Yes," said Peter. "That's right! Rainer didn't tell him, but I'll wager that Thomas and Marie did! Once they got used to accepting him as their grandfather, they would have told him everything and Thomas is old enough to remember how to get there. What's more, I think I know of a way to find out!"

Chapter 20

"So you're wanting to borrow one of His Majesty's aircraft for a personal joy-flight yet again, are you Peter?" Trehearn asked with a rare touch of terseness in his usually sanguine voice.

"Yes Sir," replied Peter steadily. "I know I've made a few flights of a more personal nature over the last few months, but if I'm right, this may be the last time I'll need to."

Trehearn rocked back in his chair and indicated for Peter to take a seat himself.

"Alright then Peter," he said with resignation, "what do I need to know here?"

Peter spent the following ten minutes outlining his thoughts about where Heinrich Voss was hiding with Rainer's children and how Peter thought it highly likely that he was involved in an underground smuggling network helping Nazi war criminals escape.

"Just so that I understand all this clearly," said Trehearn, "you have no actual evidence for any of this, it's just a hunch that you have. Is that right?"

Peter's shoulders slumped slightly. "Well, yes Sir, but it's a very solid hunch. It's one that perfectly explains the complete absence of any evidence for him or the children showing up anywhere else, either dead or alive."

Trehearn remained silent as he processed what Peter had told him.

Peter made one last point. "All it would take is a single pass over the valley in a photo-reconnaissance aircraft. One good, clean set of pictures will confirm whether I'm right, or if I'm wrong."

Trehearn remained staring intently at Peter for several more seconds, clearly thinking beyond a mere 'yes' or 'no'.

Finally, he snapped back to the moment. "Alright then Peter. As it turns out we have one of the new Vampires that's set up for photo-recon. It has all the range you would need for a flight of that length."

"Thank you very much Sir," said Peter with relief. He had never before felt as though Trehearn was on the verge of declining one of his requests. It was an uncomfortable feeling. "When might I be able to go Sir?"

Trehearn looked at his watch, it was not yet half past eight in the morning.

"I would say Peter that *we* can be in the air within an hour." Trehearn chuckled at the sight of Peter gawping at his words. "Yes my lad, I'm coming with you. The Vampire seats two and you'll need a navigator if you're going to find a target so remote."

Peter quickly recovered from his surprise. "It does make sense Sir. I hope your navigation skills aren't too rusty," he quipped.

"No rustier than your flying, my cheeky lad. Now, you head off and start getting things ready, I have to make a couple of quick telephone calls." Peter stood up, saluted and left Group Captain Trehearn's office.

The Vampire was the newest aircraft in the RAF. It had entered service only a few months earlier. The first single engine jet aircraft in the Air Force, it was scarcely larger than a Spitfire, but with its unusual design it had a cabin that comfortably held a crew of two.

"I'm going to have us tracking in from the south Peter," Trehearn was a skilled navigator himself. He had flown several Pathfinder missions in that role in his early days with the PFF.

"The weather looks perfect for once. If the valley is where you say it is, we should get some good shots with just a single pass."

"That would be ideal Sir," responded Peter. "A single straight pass at a decent height should not raise the alarms with anyone down in the valley, *if* they're there."

"Agreed!" said Trehearn. "More than one pass and they will undoubtedly start suspecting something."

Trehearn had them flying south and then veering further towards the east once they had overflown Paris. He was going to bring them over Swiss airspace once again and then Austria as they approached southern Bavaria from the south. Peter had spent time poring over charts with Trehearn, pinpointing precisely where he believed the valley would lie in the rugged, yet beautiful Alps separating southern Germany from Austria and Switzerland. As they flew over northern Switzerland, Peter looked over to his left and saw the Bodensee, known in English as Lake Constance, in the distance.

"It was on the other side of that lake that I had that encounter with the Focke-Wulf Sir," he called out to Trehearn.

The Group Captain looked intently in the direction that Peter indicated and smiled. "That will be an amazing story to tell your grandchildren one day, my lad."

Peter smiled and responded. "I love it that you call me 'my lad' Sir. You're barely four years older than I am."

"Rank has its privileges, my lad," said Trehearn with a grin.

The far eastern end of the lake gave Trehearn the chance to make a precise fix on their position. From that, he gave Peter a new heading that would see them crossing Austrian airspace before turning north on their final approach towards the valley.

Shortly after they had made the turn to the north, something about a large peak ahead of them triggered a memory with Peter.

"Your navigation is bang on Sir," he said with satisfaction. "I'm used to seeing it from the other side, but that peak ahead with the ridge dipping down to the left, that's the one that marks the end of the valley. The old Mossie should still be on the other side."

"What's our altitude?" asked Trehearn.

"Fifteen thousand feet Sir," replied Peter.

"Excellent!" said Trehearn. "That should have us seven or eight thousand feet above the floor of the valley."

The Vampire closed the distance rapidly, Trehearn had his finger on the release button for the camera system. The moment they crossed over the peak, Peter signalled for him to begin filming. Even from their height Peter could see what appeared to be several white, square shapes at the bottom of the valley, close to the cabin, they could only be tents. He flew on, holding a straight path until they were well passed the valley. Anyone down there looking at them fly over would have no cause to be concerned. The camera was filming with a strong telephoto lens. It would provide far more detail than they could see in a brief moment with the naked eye. Peter, however, couldn't help but feel now that his educated guesswork was being proven correct.

***

A female Section Officer opened the door and ushered Peter into the laboratory like room. This was where reconnaissance photographs were analysed by experts, highly experienced in the interpretation of the often grainy and indistinct images that the flight cameras took.

Group Captain Trehearn was already there, in the company of a photographic analyst. The man was middle-aged, balding and bespectacled. He was to Peter's mind, the very image of a back room intelligence analyst.

"Ah Peter!" called out Trehearn. "Come over here, my lad, I think you will find this rather fascinating."

He showed Peter towards a magnifying screen, poised over a 12" x 10" monochrome photograph. It was clearly one of the images they captured the previous day. As Peter looked through the magnifier at the image below, the Photographic Officer explained what he was seeing.

"It appears to be quite a well-established campsite. There are five tents visible, three are white and two are camouflaged. I can only presume these were all they could get, otherwise they would all be camouflaged."

Peter looked closely at the cabin. "The old cabin appears to be in ruins. A large part of the roof is missing."

"That's correct," said the analyst. "It appears to have been burnt out in the past, completely gutted in fact."

"Almost certainly by the German detachment that was sent out to find you that day, my lad," said Trehearn. "It appears Peter, that your hunch has borne fruit. As you can see, there are a number of individuals showing in this and other photographs. We've managed to confirm eleven individuals by actual count, but the size and the number of tents suggests that there could be as many as twenty people up there."

"Can you tell if any of the people in the photographs might be children or perhaps teenagers?" asked Peter.

"There's just no way to be sure I'm afraid," said the analyst. "Perhaps one day, we might have the ability to take images that will show us that level of detail but, as you can see, the grain in this picture is too coarse to tell."

"So then," asked Peter turning to Trehearn, "what happens now?"

Trehearn took off his cap and ran his fingers through his hair. "From here on Peter, it gets taken over by the authorities in Germany. They have special teams that go after fugitives such as these. This will be an operation that the RAF can have no part in, it has nothing to do with us."

Peter was far too invested in the hunt for the children to lightly stand back and play no further part. "But Sir, as good as these people in Germany might be, we have knowledge that would be of great use to them. Gary, myself and especially Rainer, know that valley in detail. I only know of one way into it, but Rainer might know others. If these Nazi types have any sense, they'll be keeping a close watch on that path. If a large group of police turns up on the main road, then they'll have a couple of hours' notice to prepare. If they're armed, it could be a real blood bath."

Trehearn's attention was caught. "So then, what are you suggesting?"

"Well, it seems to me that myself and Rainer at least should go along, if only to advise them. As I said, Rainer might know of other ways into the valley which could be extremely useful."

Trehearn could see the wisdom in what Peter was saying.

He was about to speak when Peter added. "There's one other point too Sir. I suspect it's very likely that the children believe Rainer is dead. Perhaps even his father Heinrich does too. If we can show them that's he's still alive, that may prove to be important. Especially if the police need to start negotiating with the fugitives."

Trehearn looked long and hard at his friend and subordinate. "Just you and Rainer? No Gary?"

Peter hesitated for a moment. "Well, I don't want Gary to get involved. I've already lost one good friend and I don't want to lose another. Even if we remain back from the action, there is always the chance things could get a little bit out of control. Especially if some of these guys are armed and prepared to fight it out."

Trehearn nodded. "A very sensible approach, but do you really believe for a moment that if he knows you and Rainer are involved, he will just happily sit at home and do nothing?"

***

"I can't believe that you would try and keep me out of it!" Gary exploded at Peter when he admitted that he didn't want his friend to come.

"Well, I'm sorry mate," Peter was struggling to explain himself, "but you have a family now and I thought that this might turn out to be a bit dangerous."

"I have a family?" Gary was far from mollified. "Unless I'm much mistaken, you have a family too now mate! Or do I have to call you Sir?"

Peter realised he'd put his foot in it badly. "Okay, alright! I'll admit it! I was worried about you! I've already lost a very close friend earlier in the war and I didn't want you to be around if the shit hit the fan. I just wanted to know you were safe, I'm sorry if I misjudged things."

Gary looked across at Bridget in bemusement. She in turn looked at Peter and said, "Did you say, if the shit hits the fan? What on earth does that mean?"

Peter was slightly taken aback by the sudden change in the course of the conversation. "It's something that a couple of the Americans used to say in Davos. I thought it was funny, and kind of appropriate."

Bridget looked back at Gary and the two of them burst into spontaneous laughter.

"I have to give it to you Skip," said Gary, "even when you totally stuff something up, you somehow manage to charm your way out of the shit, even after it has hit the fan!"

Peter felt an immediate sense of relief. "I guess I can assume then that you would like to be involved."

"I think you have assumed correctly, a bit of prompting, but you finally got there!" said Gary.

Peter smiled ruefully. "Well, in that case, you can come and help me break the news to Rainer and Irene. Somehow, I think he'll be even keener than you to lend a hand. Let's hope whoever's running the show in Germany doesn't say no!"

***

"Ah Peter! Wait up will you?" Trehearn was almost running across the tarmac. He was trying to catch up with Peter as he was going about a routine, early morning inspection tour of the squadrons under his command.

Peter turned towards his approaching C/O. "Good morning Sir. What's up?"

Trehearn apologised to the group of officers who were making the tour with Peter and then led him away to speak privately.

"How quickly do you think you can be on a flight to Munich? You'll need to have Rainer with you as well."

Peter looked startled. "Wow! That didn't take long. Gary wants to come too, he rather insisted."

Trehearn gave a thin smile. "Well, there's no surprise there. It works out well actually, you'll need a navigator. If you can ring him and tell him to collect Rainer and get over to Northolt, we'll get you the Oxford fuelled up and checked over. You'll need to be in Munich by 3pm today."

Peter checked his watch, it was not yet 8:30am, plenty of time, even for a slower aircraft like the Oxford.

"What happens when we get there Sir? Who will be meeting us?"

Trehearn put his arm on Peter's shoulder. "This is going to be largely an American operation, believe it or not. There will be some German civilian police involved as well, but the Yanks will provide the manpower and the equipment."

Peter's face betrayed his surprise. "Do they not trust the German authorities to do this themselves?"

Trehearn shrugged. "I suspect they don't trust them entirely yet. I suspect they think that the Germans might be hesitant to take on their fellow countrymen if any shooting starts. Anyway, that's their problem, not ours. They are, however, very keen to have you and Rainer along as guides. Your local knowledge will be invaluable."

Peter nodded in agreement. "Rainer in particular, when Gary and I talked to him about it yesterday, he told us that he does indeed know of a couple of other ways into valley. Much more difficult paths apparently, but that could be exactly what we need to get in unnoticed."

Trehearn brightened at the news. "Excellent! That should cheer up the Yanks no end! Now, you go and call Gary and start getting things organised with him, I will look after getting the Oxford prepared."

Peter saluted and began to turn away when Trehearn spoke again. "Oh, and Peter, I suggest you draw side-arms as well. Both for yourself and for Gary. Hopefully you won't need them, but best to be prepared."

"Indeed Sir," Peter gave him a cautious smile and set about his way.

***

Anne sat silently on the edge of the bed as Peter told her of the plan. He had hurried home to pack a small valise with changes of clothes and toiletries.

"So none of you will be involved in the actual arrests or anything like that?" she asked with distinct nervous trepidation in her voice.

"No, my darling, we will stay well out of the way. We are just going as guides to lead them into the valley itself. Once we're over the mountains and on the way down, we will stop and let the Americans and the Germans go off ahead and do the real work."

Anne was somewhat mollified, but still deeply concerned. She had thought that the end of the war would mean that the dangerous part of Peter's life would be behind him. His unexpected involvement in a sudden, potentially hazardous mission was leaving her with a profound sense of disquiet. Peter could easily sense her apprehension. He left the valise and sat down beside her.

"I promise you darling, neither Gary nor I have any intention of getting anywhere near the arrests. We will be hundreds of yards away from whatever action there might be. We don't even know for sure that it is a hide-out for escaping Nazis. It could be a perfectly innocent camp-site for school kids or something. We're doing all of this on my hunch and the aerial photographs."

He put his arm around her shoulder and drew her close. "This is really what the army bods call a 'reconnaissance in force'. If Rainer's father and the children aren't there, then it's back to square one for us, but I give you my word, we'll keep well away from the operation itself."

Anne could do no more than trust in Peter's experience and responsibility. She knew he had to go, but that didn't help ease her fears.

"Please swear to me that you'll stay out of harm's way and keep Gary out of it too! Please!"

Peter held her tighter. "I swear," he replied.

***

"This looks just like the aeroplane you brought me to England in," Rainer commented as he took his seat in the Oxford. Peter had flown it down once again to RAF Northolt to find Gary and Rainer awaiting him on the tarmac.

"It is the same one," replied Peter. "It's a bit of a slow old bus, but it's ideal for what we need and it was available."

Gary took up his seat close to Peter. He had packed all the navigation equipment he knew he would need and set himself up as Peter taxied to the start of the runway.

"So, what happens when we get there Skip?" asked Gary.

"Your guess is as good as mine Nav. I understand we're going to be met, but I don't know if it's by Yanks or Germans."

Gary couldn't help but smile to himself as he heard Peter call him 'nav', it was always 'mate' until they were in an aeroplane, then it invariably became 'nav' once again. He was sure even Peter didn't realise he was doing it.

Once they were airborne and settled on their flightpath, Peter could finally begin to relax and think about what lay ahead.

He turned his head and called back to Rainer. "I didn't even get to say 'hello' back there mate. Sorry about that."

Rainer chuckled. "That is quite alright, it has all been a bit of a rush, this morning."

Peter smiled and said, "A few years ago, back in 1940, it used to get a bloody sight more rushed than this. Today, I even had time to pack a bag and kiss the wife and baby goodbye."

Peter was suddenly concerned that he might have said the wrong thing, but Rainer took it in his stride. "It is my dearest hope that tomorrow, I might get to kiss my children again."

Gary also turned and looked at him, determination written clearly across his face. "God willing, Rainer…"

The Oxford touched down at the Oberwiesenfeld Army Air Base on the outskirts of Munich shortly after 3pm. They had pushed into a headwind which had made the four hour flight closer to five hours. The Base had been taken over by the Americans in April 1945 as they advanced through Germany in the closing stages of the war. It was now an Army air logistics centre.

The American controller instructed Peter to taxi over to an unmistakable large and impressive main control building. The three were immediately greeted by an immaculately dressed US Army captain as they emerged from the Oxford. Both Peter and Gary couldn't help but feel that the cut of their RAF uniforms was shabby alongside the perfectly tailored appearance of the American.

"How do you do Sir," said the captain, saluting and then extending his hand towards Peter with a rigid formality. "My name is Captain Holland. I'm here to collect you and take you over to meet Colonel Martin. He's in charge of the operation tomorrow. May I ask you to follow me Sir?"

Peter couldn't help but notice that the captain didn't try to shake hands with either Gary or Rainer. He glanced at Gary and from the look on his face, could tell that he too was well aware of the snub. Peter gave his friend an ironic smile and patted him on the shoulder as they picked up their cases and followed the captain towards a large Mercedes car that was waiting nearby.

Captain Holland gave them an outline of the operation as they drove the twenty minutes to an Army barracks in the south-west of the city.

"We have about sixty men available, plus a couple of German observers. We understand that you know of several different paths into valley Mr Voss? We'll need you to lay them out on a map for us. We want to go in from three different directions."

Rainer looked at the captain with a bemused expression. "How fit are your men captain?" he asked.

Captain Holland looked slightly insulted. "What do you mean? My men are all American troops. They are as fit and capable as any in the world!"

Rainer pressed on. "There are indeed three ways in that I know of. The easiest one is the most likely to be watched closely by whoever is in the valley. It is steep in places, but quite manageable. Of the other two, they approach from over high ridges on either side of the valley. The one to the west is a steep climb and will be testing, even for very fit men. The other, eastern approach is even worse. In places, it almost requires true alpine mountaineering skills. I went part of the way up it once, but the risk of injuring myself was too great, so I went back down. I say this, simply to make you aware of the challenge ahead. It would be a mistake to think that this will be an easy climb, even for fit men."

Captain Holland sat back in silence for the remainder of the drive.

Colonel Joshua Martin turned out to be a totally different character to Captain Holland. He exuded a warmth and affability that surprised all three.

In particular, he was impressed when he met Gary. "Well damn! You're the first Negro I've ever met in a British uniform. Good to meet you." His sharp eyes had taken in the DFC and service ribbons on Gary's tunic. He knew he was addressing a fellow soldier.

"My Unit came up through Italy, had a lot of black soldiers under my command down there. Good men, they taught me a lot."

Then he caught sight of the 'New Zealand' patch on Peter's left shoulder. "Goddamn! Another Kiwi, you guys seem to follow me around. I got to know lots of your countrymen in Italy as well. Some of the best soldiers I've ever seen, glad to have you both on board."

Peter introduced Rainer next and explained about his past and his connection to the valley.

"Well then," said Martin, "no wonder you three were so keen to be involved. Your Group Captain was pretty damn insistent that you all come along, now I get why."

He led them over to a map table and handed Rainer a red pencil.

"Can you mark out for us on the map what the best ways into the valley are? We're gonna need to be on our way in a few hours if we're to get in position before early morning."

Rainer took a few moments to understand the military topographical chart. It showed geographical elevations foremost, with roads and towns in lesser prominence. Eventually, he was able to pinpoint the places on the road that gave best access to the different routes up the mountains and over into the valley.

Rainer explained again what he had said to Captain Holland in the car. Colonel Martin was thinking deeply as he contemplated the positions Rainer had marked.

"I can see from the elevations that this eastern approach is not really viable. At least, not for a large body of men…" He suddenly stood erect and turned to Captain Holland. "Captain, will you kindly get Sergeant O'Rourke over here? I have an idea."

"Yes Sir!" said Holland as he turned briskly and left the room.

Less than five minutes later, he returned with a short, wiry man bearing sergeants chevrons on his sleeves.

"Ah, Sergeant!" exclaimed Martin. "Come over here please."

The Sergeant approached and looked down at the section of map that the Colonel was indicating.

"What do you think Tom? Do you think you could lead a small detachment up over that?"

O'Rourke looked closely at the topography. "Doesn't seem too difficult, Sir. How many men do you want?" he replied.

"Ten at the most, do you have anyone in mind to take? Only those that you think can manage a climb like that and still be fresh."

"I'm sure I can, Sir. Maybe not ten, but I can certainly think of seven or eight men who could manage it without a problem."

"Excellent work. Then get to it straight away, it's a drive of a couple of hours to get there. We will need you to be at least part of the way up the side tonight, so you can be over the ridge and into the valley first thing in the morning. Make sure the vehicle you take is left well hidden. We can't allow it to be seen, either from the road, or from the mountain above."

"Will do Sir, I'll get on it right away."

O'Rourke carefully studied the map again and wrote down the exact coordinates before he turned to leave the room. Martin called out to him before he left.

"Sergeant, your main role will be to act as a surprise attacking force in their rear if it turns out that we need one. Lead your men down into the valley in the morning but stay hidden and don't do anything until it becomes obvious that we need you. You'll be the ace up our sleeve if there's any trouble. "

After he left, Martin turned back to Peter and the others. "Sergeant O'Rourke is from Washington state. He's been climbing mountains up in the Rockies since he was a kid. He's the perfect man for this. All the men here have been fully briefed about what it is we're doing, so he knows what we might encounter."

Peter stepped up to the table. "If you don't mind my asking Colonel, I'm a bit surprised that this seems to be an all American operation. Shouldn't there be some German input into all of this as well?"

Colonel Martin thought for a moment before replying. "Well, Wing Commander, the problem is that we don't yet know who we can trust among our new German friends. Any man of the right age to join us, will have been a German soldier fighting against us only a year and or so ago. A good number of them were committed Nazis. The people we're going after now are likely to be Nazi war criminals hiding out until their turn on one of the Rat Lines comes up. I have to know that I can trust every man I have completely. It's as simple as that. There will be German observers coming along, but their job is to make sure that we behave according to the rules."

"What are Rat Lines, Sir?" asked Gary.

Martin's eyebrows arched. "Of course, you probably haven't heard the term. Rat Lines are what we are calling the underground networks that former SS and Nazi officials have set up to spirit their old comrades out of Germany, to safe countries. They seem to go mostly to Spain or Italy as far as we can tell. After that, we suspect that many are being smuggled over to Argentina or Bolivia. They have Fascist governments as well, so they're likely to be well disposed to the idea of taking in these bastards. At least, they're the rumours we've been hearing. It's incredible just how sophisticated a network they've built in such a short time."

"I can certainly believe that my father would want to be involved," said Rainer who had been listening intently. "He would have been too old to serve in the army at the beginning of the war and perhaps too afraid to serve at the end. This would be the way for him to finally lend a hand to the Nazis. It is just the sort of thing he would do."

Colonel Martin looked closely at Rainer, seeming to really notice his thin and poor condition for the first time.

"We have been told that there are likely to be children in the camp as well. More or less hostages if I've been advised correctly. Is that right?"

Rainer made a noncommittal gesture. "You are talking about my children. They likely believe that I am dead, that I died in a Concentration Camp. My father probably believes that also. They are with him, not because they believe in the Nazi cause, because I know they hate the Nazis. They are only there because their grandfather is."

Colonel Martin spoke with as much consideration as he could muster. "Well Mr Voss, it is our intention to go in and make an inspection and any arrests that might follow on, with as little trouble as possible. The war is well over now and I, for one, have seen quite enough of fire-fights to last me a lifetime.

We will be keeping an eye out for any children, I promise you that."

"Thank you Colonel." said Rainer. "I truly appreciate that."

Martin looked around the room. "Anyway, I'll have one of my men show you over to the Mess Hall. Get yourselves a decent meal and then try and get a few hours of sleep. We'll need to be on the road well before midnight if we want to be deploying before anyone in that valley knows we're there."

Chapter 21

Gary noticed that Peter was smiling, seemingly in a world of his own, despite the endless jostling of the American army lorry.

"What are you finding so funny, Skip?" he asked.

Peter snapped out of his reverie. "I'm just enjoying the irony of all of this," he responded.

"Don't you remember the reason we left the valley in such a hurry? The circumstances? Now we're in exactly the same position as those Germans that came in looking for us."

Gary considered Peter's words for a moment and chuckled. "Yeah! You're right. I never thought about it before, it's exactly the same. I hope those Nazis in the valley right now are not as prepared to meet us, as we were to meet them."

Peter looked across at his friend and nodded in agreement. "I'll never forget how you handled it, I would never have believed it if I hadn't seen it with my own eyes. You and Rainer; both of you, cool headed stuff."

Gary said nothing in reply, the recollection of killing a man was something that still deeply troubled him. It was Rainer, who had been listening as he sat next to them, who spoke.

"We did what we had to, what choice did we have?"

Peter looked at him thoughtfully, his mood growing more serious. "Exactly! No choice at all really. They were coming to capture and probably kill us, and you had to deal with them. When that moment came, you both reacted like trained professionals. That's what's worrying me now, those people up there *are* likely to be trained professionals, real killers. Depending on who we find, some of those bastards might be facing the gallows if they get captured. They're not likely to come along quietly unless we catch them completely flat-footed. I hope our American hosts here are fully aware of that, I suspect there's a fair chance this could get a bit nasty."

There were several American troops sitting close by, plus more than twenty crammed into the back of the lorry. They couldn't help but overhear the conversation one of them spoke up.

"Y'all reckon them Nazi's gonna start up a fire-fight?" he asked in a lazy southern drawl.

Peter looked over at him. "If they are who we think they are, then it's very possible. No matter what your officers say, be prepared. Keep your wits about you, all of you."

The American soldier looked around the others crammed inside the lorry. After he had spoken up, the others all had their attentions drawn to the conversation and they had all listened intently to Peter's comments. None of them spoke, but they each looked around the lorry at their comrades, and they each now wore a more circumspect look on their faces.

***

It was still dark when the two lorries passed the spot which marked the beginning of the track up to the valley that Rainer had regularly used. The darkness obscured the possible presence of any Nazi fugitive lookouts on station nearby, but Colonel Martin had no intention of taking the risk. The lorries drove on for a further three kilometres, to a point from where the next, more difficult access climb could be undertaken. There was no obvious point to start from.

Once the lorries had reached a spot where the road passed close by the outer face of the mountains that formed the western buttress of the valley, Colonel Martin in the lead vehicle ordered that they pull over. They would commence the ascent from here.

Rainer's physical rehabilitation was far from adequate enough to allow him to accompany this main body of soldiers as they made the climb. Peter and Gary, however, would go with them to act as guides to what lay below once they had crested the ridge line. Rainer was to remain with a detachment of ten soldiers who would wait for four hours and then return to the primary access path up to the valley. There, they were to secure that main pathway to prevent any fugitives from using it to try and escape.

Daylight was still more than three hours away as Colonel Martin led a column that included Peter, Gary and two German police officers who would accompany them as observers, into the stygian gloom of the forest that blanketed the lower slopes. The troops could safely use flashlights here to help find safe footings. They were far away from the prying eyes of any potential lookouts that might be on station elsewhere.

At first, the climb was easy enough as they made their way through the gentle slopes that led away from the road. It didn't take long however, before the grade began to steepen as they began the ascent itself. The first bare hints of the approaching day saw the column drawn well clear, above the tree-line. The climb had become steeper still and the rocky surface more treacherous. The slowest and most difficult part of the ascent now lay ahead.

Peter turned back to check on Gary. "How are you managing there mate? I'm just about all in."

Gary was panting heavily. "I have to say, a childhood playing on beaches in the Caribbean did not prepare me very well for this."

Peter managed a weary smile. Despite the alpine chill, there was sweat dripping from the end of his nose. He looked around at the American soldiers they were trekking alongside. They were all showing signs of fatigue as well, though not to the same extent as Peter and Gary.

"And this is supposed to be the easier climb! My leg muscles will never be the same again!" said Peter in between deep, panting breaths.

The climb continued, one foot in front of the other. A simple, repetitious process with an occasional brief pause in between each step. After over three hours of climbing, with the tree-line now well below them, Colonel Martin paused the column for a brief rest. He came over to check on Peter and Gary.

"How you fellers holdin' up? This is a damn site harder than I thought it'd be. My men and I can do a twenty mile route march in full kit at the drop of a hat, I thought this'd be easy."

Peter looked at him through weary eyes. "At least you and your men are a bloody site fitter than we are. Our version of a day's hard fighting is just sitting on our bums in a cockpit for three or four hours."

Despite his fatigue, Colonel Martin managed a hearty laugh. "Well, you can have five more minutes, after that we have to get moving. Any longer and your muscles will start to seize up."

Although the sun had not yet risen, the sky was now bright enough to have a good look at what lay ahead. The crest of the ridge seemed surprisingly close, but it was still nearly an hour of agonising climbing away. The mid-Autumn morning was cold and crisp, but at least there was no snow yet to further complicate the climb.

Eventually, Peter became conscious of the gradient easing off. For over half an hour he hadn't lifted his head, he had been looking no further ahead than the next footstep. Now he looked up and saw that the men ahead of him had all stopped and the crest of the ridge lay just beyond them. Colonel Martin indicated for Peter and Gary to join him. This was where he needed their knowledge of the valley.

"Now," he said as they crept forward and peered down into the still shaded valley below, "what would be the best direction to approach from? If you were down there, looking up in our direction, where would the blind spots be?"

Once they had oriented themselves, it was obvious that despite the exertions of the climb, the effort had brought them out in the perfect place.

Gary spoke first. "This is ideal, we're much further around than I thought we'd be. There's about… maybe about a hundred yards of bare slope below us, but after that the forest will hide us completely. From there, we can get good and close with plenty of cover."

Peter nodded in agreement. "Yep! This is as good a starting spot as we could have asked for. But we'll need to get cracking. From down in the valley, this face is very gloomy when it's in shadow. It'll give us good cover as we go down, we need to get down to the trees before the sun gets too high."

Colonel Martin grunted a response. "The sun is coming up over that ridge opposite. At least we won't cast a silhouette as we go over the crest. If you want to lead off, I'll get the men organised and we'll follow your line down."

The sight of the valley below them helped re-energise both Peter and Gary. Their legs muscles were still screaming in protest, but the descent was easier than the climb. Looking closely into the still deeply shaded valley below, they began to make out the shapes of tents and the layout of the campsite. After a few more minutes, they could even begin to discern individual people as they moved about in the gloom. Suddenly, a tiny, distant flash of light flared as a campfire was lit. Someone was about to start preparing breakfast. A later start for military men, but the solitude of the valley did not demand the discipline of regular service life.

Peter and Gary carefully picked their way down, in between boulders and the loose scree that covered the ground on the steep, exposed slopes below the crest of the ridge.

Looking back over his shoulder, Peter noted with satisfaction that the American troops under Colonel Martin were now well advanced on their descent as well. They were keeping silent and their footfalls were carefully measured, ensuring as little disturbance of the loose scree as possible.

After half an hour's careful negotiating of the tricky slope, Peter and Gary reached a point where they both felt that the intervening trees were now shielding them from the view of anyone on the valley floor. They paused to allow time for the Americans to reach their position.

Colonel Martin soon joined them and put his hands on each of their shoulders. "Well done, this is perfect. That fire they lit gave us the ideal marker to form on. Is there anything else we should know before we move forward?"

Gary spoke up. "Just be on the lookout for anyone who might have wandered off into the trees to relieve themselves. When you are getting close to the camp, you might bump into someone with their trousers down."

"Now there's a pleasant thought!" said Martin whilst handing a pair of binoculars to Peter. "You two should stay back here now, you've done your bit. You can use these to keep an eye on what's happening below. I'll start taking my men forward now."

Gary walked over to a low, flat topped boulder and sat down. Peter joined him and they both watched as the American detachment and the two German observers disappeared into the gloom of the forest. It quickly dawned on them that, as much as the forest hid them from the valley floor, they in turn were unable to see what was happening down there.

"Let's move over to the left," said Peter.

Gary immediately agreed and they began to move in a direction that would take them towards the base of the valley, closer to the old pathway that they remembered. From there, they could use the cover of the trees and still get a clearer view as the arrests were made.

The sun had now risen high enough to cast the top of the western face of the valley in its full glare. As they made the traverse to their left, their attention was caught by the glinting of something reflecting light on the crest of the eastern ridge. Sunlight reflecting off metal. As they looked more intently, they could suddenly make out the distant forms of the small team being led by Sergeant O'Rourke as they made their way over the crest and commenced their descent down the slope.

Gary had moved far enough to the left that he could now see into the camp again. "Oh God!" he exclaimed.

There was obvious animation amongst the men in the camp. They had clearly spotted the reflections too and several were pointing in the direction of O'Rourke's descending team. Peter soon reached Gary's vantage point and the two watched helplessly as several men ran into tents and quickly emerged carrying rifles, machine guns and several pairs of binoculars.

"Bloody hell!" spat out Peter. "So it's going to turn nasty after all."

They both continued to make their way further to the left. They wanted to get as close to the start of the pathway out of the valley as they could, without running the risk of being seen. They found suitable cover behind a small, but dense copse of middle growth fir trees. Through the binoculars, Peter could tell that Sergeant O'Rourke's team seemed to be aware that they had been spotted. They had ceased their descent down the slope for the moment. More of the Nazi fugitives had armed themselves and were beginning to disperse into the edges of the forest.

"I hope to hell that Colonel Martin has seen what's happening here," said Peter. "If they haven't spotted any of this, then they could be about to walk into a real trap. They'll be thinking everyone is half asleep and unarmed."

He handed the binoculars to Gary who used them to study the camp intently, paying particular attention to the tree line behind it, looking for any sign that the American troops were in position.

For his part, Colonel Martin had deployed his men skilfully. As they drew closer to the camp, he could sense immediately that something was wrong. Instead of a quiet scene where relaxed men went about preparing their breakfasts, there was intense activity. Men were carrying guns and pointing to the eastern mountain face opposite. It was obvious to him that O'Rourke's team had been spotted.

He deployed his men outwards, mostly towards the left flank, but with cover to the right as well. He looked over towards the two German police observers who had positioned themselves behind trees, close to each other and to him. Their presence underscored the realisation that this was a peace-time mission. They were there to arrest escaping Nazis, not start a war. They had now formed a line less than thirty yards behind the edge of the forest. Martin could see a number of the Nazis, all well armed, slipping into positions at the forest edge. Perhaps their focus on the detachment on the eastern cliff face would work to his advantage. These Germans all had their backs to Martin's approaching troops. His men had been given explicitly clear instructions, under no circumstances were they to open fire first. They could fire only to defend themselves.

Colonel Martin looked over towards the men deployed on either side of his position. He gave the two German observers one last look and nodded. They returned the gesture.

Exhaling deeply, he called out in a loud, clear voice, "*Hande hoch, hande hoch, bitte mein Herren*. You are under arrest. Please lay down your weapons and move out into the clearing!"

The loud voice coming from immediately behind them startled four of the Nazi fugitives into instant action. Each had been experienced Waffen SS soldiers and their trained reflexes suddenly took over. They spun around in the direction of the voice behind them and immediately began firing their machine guns.

Colonel Martin threw himself to the ground as a storm of bullets flew over him, thudding into trees or whistling off into the distance. One of the German police observers fell to the ground with an agonised groan. He had been hit in that first fusillade of bullets. The sudden explosion of action to their rear caused the Nazis out in the open field to spin around and dive to the ground. Many were now armed and brought their rifles up, preparing to open fire at the first target they saw.

The Americans now began to move forward in a line towards the clearing beyond the tree line, all the time taking care to use what cover the trees provided. They wanted to squeeze all of the Nazis out into the open. High on the slopes opposite, Sergeant O'Rourke had seen the sudden start of the fire-fight and exhorted his men back into their descent. It wasn't the way they had planned the mission, but it was clear they were needed.

Very few of the Americans had seen active service in the war. Almost all of the veteran troops had been returned to their homes and families once the conflict ended. Most of the American soldiers on station in Germany now, had come over as peace-keepers after the war was over. This gave the Nazis a decided advantage. Battle hardened, they knew how to fight almost instinctively. All too soon, their skills began to tell against their less experienced opposition, as one by one, several of the Americans fell to the ground under the impact of German bullets.

A high pitched scream of terror suddenly carried over the din of the gun fire. All shooting ceased for a moment at this new sound. A flap on one of the tents was thrown open and a blonde haired girl suddenly appeared, running as fast as she could away from the scene of the fighting. Bare seconds after she emerged, a juvenile boy also appeared, running in desperate pursuit of the girl. Both sides mercifully held their fire for a brief moment as the two cleared the combat zone. One of the inexperienced Americans, captivated by the terror of the fleeing children, stepped out from behind his tree to call out to them to find some cover. It was the last moment of his young life as a former SS marksman put a bullet straight through his chest.

Peter could hardly believe his eyes as the sight of the two children, fleeing in desperation instantly grabbed his attention. They could only be Marie and Thomas, the direction they had chosen to flee from the firing was bringing them almost directly towards Gary and himself. Peter turned towards Gary only to find that his friend was no longer there.

As soon as he recognised the children, Gary had leapt out from behind the copse of trees where he had been concealed and was running towards them as fast his exhausted legs would propel him. Peter could only watch as the distance between Gary and the children rapidly narrowed. It was obvious that they had both recognised him. As soon as Marie reached him she launched herself into his arms where he caught her and turning, began to carry her back towards cover. Thomas reached him at the same moment and Gary quickly pointed to where Peter was waiting. Thomas ran like the wind and reached Peter well before Gary who was struggling against his exhausted legs and the weight of Marie who was clinging to him in desperate relief. Peter had emerged from behind the trees and was waving frantically in encouragement when Gary suddenly twisted and pitched forward, falling hard to the ground where he lay without moving.

One of the Nazi fugitives had been following the flight of the children and seeing Gary appear, had begun firing at him. Peter gasped in horror and immediately ran out from the protection of the trees to go to him. Marie picked herself up from where she had been spilled from Gary grasp. She stood for a moment in a daze looking at Peter as he ran to her, and then back at Gary as he lay prone on the ground. Peter quickly picked her up and carried her the last few steps to join her brother behind cover before immediately returning to his stricken friend.

"Are you okay mate?" he asked anxiously as he knelt beside Gary.

"I'm hit, Skip. Can you see anything?" replied Gary in a weak voice.

Peter looked closely, seeing blood emerging from two different places. Before he could speak again, a bullet whizzed past so closely, it plucked at his tunic jacket. Without saying another word, he rolled Gary onto his side and, picking him up in a fireman's lift, hurried back to the safety of their small copse of trees. Gently setting him down and propping him with his back against a tree, Peter knelt down beside him again.

"It looks like you've been hit twice mate. Once in the left thigh and once in the lower back, off to the left side. Neither is bleeding too heavily, so they haven't hit an artery, that's a blessing."

His single-minded concern for his friend, had temporarily blinded Peter to the presence of the two children. In his haste to tend to Gary, he had almost forgotten them. Looking up, he took in their faces for the first time in over two years. They had each grown considerably, but despite their present terror, they both looked healthy and well nourished. Peter extended his arms and they both stepped forward and accepted his embrace with warmth and relief.

"Is Gary going to be alright?" asked Thomas. "You said he's been shot twice."

Peter looked back at his friend, who was looking at him as fiercely as the children. He wanted to hear Peter's words as well.

"I think he'll be fine," said Peter. "He's been hit twice, but neither looks really bad. We need to get him to a hospital as soon as we can though, but the Americans need to get this mess sorted out first. We can't do anything until then.

Peter noticed that Marie was still clinging to him tightly.

"Our Papa is dead, Opa told us," she said in a quiet voice.

Peter held her back at arm's length and looked at both her and Thomas.

He then turned to Gary. "Do you want to give them the good news?"

Despite his pain, Gary couldn't help but smile. "Your father isn't dead. He survived the Concentration Camp, he's here with us. He's just on the other side of the valley, with some more of the Americans. It's thanks to him that we're here now. He never lost faith that we'd find you."

Marie had dissolved into tears before Gary had finished speaking. She turned to her brother and the two of them clung to each other in indescribable relief. Thomas' eyes were moist with tears also.

"Why did Opa lie to us? Why did he tell us our Papa was dead?" he asked with a sudden profound bitterness.

Peter tried to be conciliatory. "I think he believed himself that your father was dead. He didn't lie to you, he just was wrong."

The continuing sound of gunfire drew their attention back to the desperate fighting still happening only a few hundred yards away. Peter turned back to the children.

"Both of you, stay here with Gary. I'm going to go around further and see if I can get a better view of what's happening."

He looked intently at Gary, "You'd best get your pistol out mate. Do you reckon you'll be up to it if you need to use it?"

Gary had a determined look on his face, "Don't you worry about me, just keep your own head down."

Peter made his way further around to the left, he was now getting close to the start of the trail that led out of the valley. He kept himself behind cover, but now had an excellent view of the fight going on in the valley before him. The experienced climber Sergeant O'Rourke had now got his team to the bottom of the eastern face in remarkably quick time. Surely the fugitive Nazis would not have expected them to be on the field so soon.

O'Rourke had organised his men and now they were now beginning to move purposefully across the meadow towards the camp. Soon they would be in position behind the Nazis as they continued to engage Colonel Martin's team, still deployed beyond the tree line.

O'Rourke was one of the few experienced combat soldiers who had remained on in Germany after the war ended. His leadership now rose to the fore. He had his small force spread out and stay low as they moved steadily towards the rear of the German line. The rate of fire from Martin's troops had kept the attention of the Nazis to their front fully occupied. From his slightly elevated position, Colonel Martin could see O'Rourke's force getting into position to the rear of the Germans. He made sure they had no time to pay attention to what was happening behind them.

O'Rourke had manoeuvred his team to within sixty yards to the rear of most of the Germans. Looking across his line to make sure every man was in position, he suddenly raised and then dropped his right arm in an order to open fire. His team all carried small sub-machine guns. Not accurate weapons, but capable of laying down a daunting field of fire when used at close range and in number.

The sudden assault from behind them caught the remaining Nazi fugitives completely by surprise. Some of them spun around to face this new threat, only to expose their backs to Martin's troops in the trees. A volley of well aimed fire dropped several of them in an instant. Within moments, the fire-fight was over. One of the Nazis stood up slowly and made a show of throwing down his weapon. Following his lead, the others began to do the same, standing erect and putting their hands behind their heads.

Cautiously at first, Colonel Martin's troops began to emerge from the trees. Some kept their weapons levelled at the now docile fugitives, whilst others set about gathering up their discarded guns. Soon, they had the captives securely herded into a group in the centre of the meadow.

Peter hurried back to Gary, Thomas and Marie. "How are you managing mate?"

Gary answered through gritted teeth. "It's starting to hurt like hell Skip. I'm not going to be able to get out of here on my own."

Peter knelt down beside Gary and put his hand on his shoulder, trying to provide what comfort he could.

"There might be a way," he said.

He turned to Thomas and Marie. "Will you both stay with Gary for a while? I need to talk to the Americans."

Thomas spoke up. "Will you find out how Opa is? He was still in the tent when we ran away."

Peter stood up and hugged the children again. "I will, hopefully, he'll be fine."

"When can we see Papa?" asked Marie in an urgent voice.

Peter smiled. "Very soon Marie, he became terribly sick in the Concentration Camp and isn't strong enough yet to make the climb here. But as soon as we can, we'll take you to him."

Peter turned from the children and started to hurry over towards Colonel Martin. Before he reached the Americans, he could see an older man being led out of one of the tents. He looked like an older, thicker set version of Rainer, it was clearly his father. Two of the American troops were leading him over to be held with the rest of the captive Nazi fugitives.

Peter quickly sought out Colonel Martin who was in conversation with Sergeant O'Rourke.

"Colonel, is everyone alright?" asked Peter.

Martin turned to him and excused himself with O'Rourke, who left to re-join his men.

"No, Wing Commander. I have one man dead and six men wounded, three of them badly. We also have four of these Nazi bastards dead and at least eight of them wounded as well.

Finally, one of the German police observers is also dead. It's been a fucking fiasco. I saw the kids run away, are they with you?"

Peter nodded. "Yes, they're fine, but Flying Officer Lynch has also been wounded. I can't say for certain how badly."

Colonel Martin shook his head, rueing the tiny piece of bad luck that had seen the operation spiral so badly out of control.

"The one thing we… I… didn't think of, the sun coming up behind O'Rourke's team. The light reflecting off pieces of their equipment and showing them up in silhouette. These bastards were warned and on edge. If we had caught them cold it would have been easy, now look at what's happened!"

Peter could only stand there mute. Martin looked over to the bottom of the valley, from where Peter had emerged.

"Can Flying Officer Lynch join us, or does he need a stretcher?"

"He'll need a stretcher Sir," said Peter. "He's been hit twice that I can see. Once in his left leg, once in his lower back."

"And we have no goddamned stretchers here. They'll have to be brought over from the trucks. What's more, there aren't enough in the trucks for all of this! I never imagined for a minute it would be a blood bath like this."

Martin was clearly shaken, their small party didn't have the necessary medical supplies or training to deal with carnage of such scale.

Peter grabbed Martin by the shoulder. "Sir, I'm certain that we can get a Dakota here. If we can get a radio up to the crest, then we can call one in. I saw several of them on the tarmac in Munich when we flew in. It's less than an hour's flight from here."

He had Colonel Martin's attention. "A Dakota? You mean a C-47? Can something that big land in here?" he asked.

"I'm sure of it," replied Peter. "I've walked over every square yard of this valley. It's a good surface right up the centre, it only gets rough towards the top. It has a noticeable down-hill slope, but that's not a problem for a good pilot. If we can get a message out, then one can be sent here urgently, with supplies and trained medics."

"All right then, let's get moving," said Martin. He called over to one of his men who had a radio transmitter in his back-pack. "Collings, I need you to get up to the top of that crest with Wing Commander Garland here and make contact with the Army Air Force base in Munich." He pointed towards the ridge at the northern end of the valley, where the main trail lay. "We're going to call in a C-47 with medical supplies to evacuate the dead and wounded."

"Yes Sir!" said the private, saluting.

"Sir," asked Peter, "may I have your map please, I don't have the coordinates written down."

"Of course, take it please," replied Martin, reaching into his blouson's inner pocket and retrieving his map.

Peter turned to Private Collings. "Come on then, young lad. I'm sure another steep climb today is just what you've been looking forward to!"

Peter's humour helped Colonel Martin manage a brief smile as he watched the two of them set off. As Peter and Private Collings reached the base of the pathway out of the valley, Peter called out in the direction of where Gary and the children were waiting. "We're going to call in an aircraft mate, I'll be back as soon as I can."

A faint voice drifted back, they had heard him.

Peter marvelled at the stamina of Private Collings. The radio was a heavy piece of equipment and he had already carried it up the daunting ascent earlier in the day. If he was feeling fatigued, he was doing an excellent job of not showing it.

"How are you managing with that radio Private?" he asked. "Would you like me to carry it for a while?"

Collings was surprised at the gesture, very few officers of his acquaintance would ever make such an offer. "It's quite alright, thank you Sir. Trouble is, if I was to put this damn thing down now, I don't think I could ever pick it up again!"

They pushed on up the slope, whilst it was nowhere near the difficulty of the earlier climb, it was still steep and taxing on legs already heavily wearied. Peter could see that they were nearing the edge of the tree line. From here, he remembered, the grade became a bit easier. The sound of footsteps approaching from behind suddenly caught his attention. Looking back down the slope, he was surprised to see Thomas hurrying up to join him.

"Thomas! Is everything alright?" he called down as the young boy drew near.

"They are okay," replied Thomas. "We lay Gary down, his back was in much pain. Marie is with him, some Americans have come over to help him."

"Why did you follow us up here?" asked Peter.

Thomas shrugged. "I just wanted to come along, is that alright?"

Peter smiled warmly. "Of course it is." He turned to indicate the soldier. "Thomas, this is Private Collings, Private Collings, this is Thomas Voss. He is the son of our friend Rainer."

"Howdy," was all that Collings was able to say. He was nearly exhausted.

Peter saw the look on his face. "Now come on laddie, give me that bloody thing. You're just about all done."

This time Collings didn't protest. "Thank you Sir, I think you're right."

He began to unclip the harness to remove the radio set. Thomas realised what was happening and he spoke up quickly. "Can I carry the radio? Please?"

Peter and Private Collings both looked at him, he seemed desperate to want to help.

"It's very heavy Thomas," said Peter "and very important, if it gets damaged, we can't call for help."

"I'll be very careful! I'm very strong!" Thomas was imploring.

Peter looked at Private Collings. "What do you think?"

"Fine by me Sir, if he's that keen…" replied Collings.

"Alright then Thomas, turn around."

Peter lifted the pack free from Collings' back and held the shoulder straps out so that Thomas could place his arms through them and take the weight. Peter helped adjust the straps to suit Thomas' smaller stature and then buckled it in place.

"How does it feel?" he asked.

"It feels good, I could carry it all day," Thomas responded proudly.

Peter and Private Collings exchanged indulgent smiles.

"Alright then," said Peter, "let's get going again."

Freed from the weight of the pack, Collings was now able to make better time. Thomas' enthusiasm saw him take the lead on the final approach to the crest, where Peter duly ordered them to stop. Collings took the radio again from Thomas and set to work powering it up and searching for the signal frequency of the American Army Air Force base in Munich. The height they were broadcasting from gave them excellent range on the set and he soon had Munich tuned in. Peter had told him in detail of what was needed and Collings was expertly relaying the request. He advised them of the number of wounded and the nature of their injuries. He confirmed that a C-47 transport aircraft, known to the British as a Dakota, would be able to land safely in the valley, if the pilot approached from the south. Once

Munich had confirmed the details and read back the summary, they advised him to hold on whilst they prepared a response.

Peter had been engrossed with Private Collings' communications with Munich. He now snapped his attention back to Thomas, who was intently gazing down the trail leading up the ridge from the other side. He turned to look down in the same direction, amazed to see Rainer; weak, but manfully struggling his way up the track towards them.

He turned back to Thomas. "It's your father laddie. You should go to him."

Thomas didn't need to be asked twice. "Papa!" he called out loudly as he began to hurry down the slope towards him.

Rainer heard the voice and looked up the slope. A wave of emotion struck, so powerful it overwhelmed him, driving him to his knees. By the time Thomas reached him he was lost in deep, wracking tears that were beyond his strength to control. For the first time in years, he was able to hold the son he never thought he would see again. The two of them clung to each other desperately, consumed in their indescribable joy.

The US Army Air Force base in Munich wasted little time in responding to Private Collings. A C-47 was being prepared and would be in the air within the hour. He reconfirmed the map reference and signed off. Rainer and Thomas had now joined Peter up on the ridge line. Rainer was clearly anxious to head down into the valley. He knew that Marie was down there, and he was desperate to get to her. He confirmed to Peter that when the Americans arrived in their lorries, they had found no one posted on sentry duty at the base of the path. The Nazis in the fugitive camp had clearly suspected nothing. The Americans were now waiting at the bottom, expecting orders to come through at any time.

Peter turned to Private Collings. "Can you radio down to them and tell them to get some men into the valley with medical supplies and stretchers urgently?"

"Sure can Sir," he replied. He re-tuned the radio and raised them immediately.

"Well done, Private," said Peter. "Will you be okay here on your own if I go back into the valley with these two?"

"I'll be fine Sir," replied Collings. "Thank you for asking."

"Well, we shall leave you to it then Private, I'm glad to have met you," said Peter.

"Same here Sir. I hope your friend's okay," replied Collings.

Peter thanked him and returned to Rainer and Thomas.

"Alright then!" he said looking from one to the other. "Are you feeling okay for the next part of the walk Rainer?"

Nothing would keep Rainer from the walk down to his daughter. "I will be quite fine, I assure you Peter, shall we be going?"

***

Marie ran, squealing in delight, to her father as soon as she saw him appear at the bottom of the path. Rainer was once again in tears of uncontrollable joy. His every wish was being fulfilled in the simple act of holding his children once again. Peter left them in privacy and went over to where Gary now lay, resting on his back.

"How are you feeling old mate? I believe some of the Yanks came over and checked you out."

Gary sounded weak and tired. "Yeah Skip, they dressed the wounds. They said the one in my side has gone clean through. Nice, neat wound, they reckon, the one in my leg still has the bullet inside. They gave me an injection of morphine, and it doesn't hurt at all now."

"So, that's why you sound so tired," said Peter. "I thought you were suffering in pain, but no! You're high on illicit drugs!"

Gary managed a weak smile before Peter continued. "Well, the good news is that there is a C-47 in the air by now that will give you and the other wounded a ride back to a hospital in Munich. It should be here any time now."

Gary nodded slowly. "That's good news, thanks Skip." He paused briefly while he looked over towards Rainer and the children. "At least something good has happened today."

Peter looked back at them too. "Indeed! It was pretty emotional, I must say. It'll be good to have them finally meet their grandmother as well."

As Peter and Gary were watching, Rainer and the children left their place at the edge of the meadow. They were making their way over towards the group of captured Nazis sitting under guard near the tents and the burnt out ruins of their old cabin. Peter realised what was happening.

He turned back to Gary. "Do you think you'll be alright on your own for a couple of minutes old mate? There's something about to happen that I would love to be a fly on the wall for."

"What's that?" asked Gary weakly.

"Rainer and the kids are going over to speak to his father," said Peter.

"Then go over please. I will need a full report on the gossip afterwards," said a now interested Gary.

Peter patted him on the shoulder and set off, staying a respectful distance behind, not attempting to catch up with Rainer. He was about twenty yards behind Rainer and the children when they reached the group of prisoners. He stopped and settled himself down on the lush grass which, despite the lateness of the season, was still heavily intermixed with delicate alpine flowers; an incongruously beautiful stage floor to play host to the carnage that occurred barely two hours earlier.

At first he was genuinely curious, but very quickly began to feel like an intruder on a deeply personal scene to which he should not be privy. Rainer and the children had walked to the edge of the circle of captives, not going beyond the boundary formed by the American guards. Heinrich, his father had no choice but to stand and come over to speak to him.

They were speaking in German, so Peter could understand nothing of the scant detail that floated through to him, but the words were obviously being spoken in anguish and anger; deeply held beliefs on the one hand, being confronted by the realised outcome of horrific personal betrayal on the other.

Peter quietly stood up again and retraced his steps back down the meadow to be with Gary. He didn't want to witness this tragedy unfold – the awful sounds of a family tearing itself apart. His task as a friend, would be to help bind the wounds afterwards, not witness them being inflicted.

***

The C-47 circled the valley twice before the pilot felt confident enough to make his landing approach. Peter's faith in the meadow as a landing strip proved to be well founded. The pilot brought the plane down with practiced precision. As soon as it drew to a halt, medical staff began exiting from its rear doorway, heading directly over to Colonel Martin, who had stepped forward and made himself obvious.

Rainer, Thomas and Marie had returned to sit with Peter and Gary. All three were deeply preoccupied with their own thoughts. For Rainer in particular, his inner-most demons had been confronted, only time would tell if they had been vanquished. For the moment however, he was finding some comfort at last by sitting in between his children and holding them closely.

Shortly afterwards, six American soldiers appeared at the bottom of the path leading from the road, each carrying a stretcher. Private Collings' radio call to them was bearing fruit. Peter stood up and beckoned one of them to come over to where

Gary still lay, unable to move. Gently, they manoeuvred him onto the stretcher. Peter and the soldier then lifted it up and carried him uphill across the meadow towards the C-47.

Peter left him in the care of the American medics and went off to find Colonel Martin. He had gone back into the forest again to make sure that all of his men were accounted for. When Peter found him, he was watching as the dead German police observer was being placed onto a stretcher. The second observer was in deep conversation with him. Peter waited until they had finished speaking before he approached.

Martin ruefully shook his head as Peter came up to him. "Just how bad is it?"

"One of my badly wounded men has just died. That's three dead with us, and the four Germans. Plus all the wounded!" he paused and exhaled deeply. He looked at Peter and shook his head. "Today has been a tough lesson for me. I should have predicted this. I thought the war was over; clearly, these people don't think it is. I'll never make the mistake of giving them that kind of latitude again."

Peter could only shrug in sympathy. "Perhaps once they are all identified, we might find some answers in their war records. Maybe, for many of them, capture might have meant the gallows."

Martin contemplated his words. "If it didn't before, it sure as hell does now!" He kicked at a small, fallen branch as if trying to release some of the frustration he was feeling.

"Anyway," he said, trying to change the subject, "all of this happened because of a hunch you had. You were absolutely right Wing Commander. Damn well done!"

"Thank you Sir," replied Peter. "I appreciate that."

He and Colonel Martin began to walk back towards the open meadow beyond the trees again.

"How is your friend, Flying Officer Lynch?" asked Martin. "Do you think he'll recover?"

Peter pointed over towards where, at that very moment, Gary was being carried on board the C-47.

"I think he'll be fine, he was lucky really. To be hit by two bullets and have neither of them do too much damage is little short of a miracle. He'll probably have a good limp for a while, but a great story to tell his kids about."

They both watched as Rainer and the children climbed aboard the C-47 immediately after Gary.

"They're the real reason we did all of this," Peter said. "When Gary and I crashed here, they cared for us and shared what little they had without a moment's hesitation. We were here long enough to get to know them well. They are fine people."

He looked around, taking in the view up the valley, to where the remains of the Mosquito still lay amongst the boulders. Even from this distance it was obvious the Germans had burnt most of it.

"Well, Wing Commander," said Colonel Martin, "I guess you can now get them back to England. I understand they have more family there. Plus, I suspect, some new friends to help them get settled."

"Thanks Colonel," said Peter. "Would you mind if I were to fly back with them in the C-47? I'd like to make sure that Flying Officer Lynch is properly taken care of."

Martin smiled and patted him on the shoulder. "I was expecting that you would. I'll be in touch once I've got all my men safely back to Munich. Then comes the fun part; writing a report explaining how all this happened. At least the other police observer has told me that we did everything by the book. He says all the blame is clearly with these fucking Nazis. That doesn't make me feel any better, but at least it's something, I guess."

Peter reached out his hand and they shook before he turned and headed over to the waiting aircraft. He paused for a while as the last of the wounded were loaded and secured on board. He looked around the valley for the last time. It suddenly felt so small. It had never seemed that way before, but now it felt almost claustrophobic, as though the dramatic escarpments on either side were closing in, telling him to leave. He was the last one to climb on board the Dakota. He had friends in his care now and it was time to start getting them home.

Epilogue

Peter's request for a twelve month leave of absence had been approved. He hung up the telephone after speaking with Group Captain Trehearn for over half an hour. Anne looked at him, one eyebrow raised quizzically.

"Well?"

"Better than we had hoped for, my darling. Twelve months on full pay, effective from the start of November," he replied.

Anne was delighted, they had been hoping for half pay at best. "Isn't that wonderful! They must have thought you were worth it."

Peter chuckled. "It's more likely that they want to keep me. Trying to give me an incentive not to resign, it's nice to be wanted."

"But I thought you were wanting to resign?" Anne was thinking back over several conversations they had had following his return from Munich, nearly five weeks earlier. "You said you were keen to look into a position with an airline!"

"I still am," he replied, slightly defensively. "Anyway, we now have plenty of time to look and think about things. You might find living in New Zealand a bit too quiet and unexciting after life in London."

"There are some forms of excitement I can well do without, thank you very much!" she replied, as much in seriousness as in fun. Anne had exploded in fury at him when he had returned from Munich, a fury driven more by desperate relief than by genuine anger.

"You told me you would both be completely safe! Out of harm's way!" she had screamed at him bitterly.

It had easily proven itself to be the biggest rift that had ever appeared between them and Anne soon felt deep remorse at her outburst. She knew that Gary had been shot because of a snap decision that he took, not as a result of anything that Peter had instigated. Still, she had not been prepared to confront the reality of her husband being placed in serious danger once again. The war had finished well over a year ago.

"Well, now that you're off the phone, can you please hurry up? We've got to be around at Irene's in half an hour."

Peter looked at his watch. "Is that the time? I had no idea we had been talking for so long."

He hurried off to their bedroom to change.

The day before, Anne had helped him choose new clothes at a tailor in London. He now looked at himself in the mirror, it felt strange wearing 'civvies' again. Almost his entire adult life had been spent in Air Force blue. It looked like a completely different person was staring back at him from the mirror.

"Give it time," he said quietly to himself. "You'll get used to it."

***

The Alvis pulled up in the street outside of Irene's home in Fulham. They were the last to arrive. They were met at the door by Marie and Rainer. Marie was desperately keen to show off the new clothes that her grandmother had bought her. "Look what Oma got me!" she rattled off excitedly. "Aren't I beautiful?"

"You certainly are!" said Peter, lifting her up and hugging her. "And doesn't your hair look lovely as well!"

He set her down and waited as Anne finished hugging Rainer. Peter shook his hand warmly afterwards as they were shown into the lounge room. It was obvious that Irene's house was very full indeed. Gary limped over to greet them, still using a walking stick, but otherwise looking his usual self.

Bridget and Anne embraced, Bridget then promptly relieved her from the task of carrying Vicky.

"How are you, my little angel?" she cheerfully cooed as she carried her over show her to her own daughter Louise, with Anne happily following close behind.

Peter looked at Gary. "How much longer do you think you'll need the stick mate?"

"I'm not that sure that I do need it anymore. I just like the way it makes me look more distinguished," he replied with a broad smile.

Peter and Rainer both laughed happily. Peter looked at Rainer and marvelled at the change in him. He was finally putting on weight, his face beginning to fill out from its gaunt, former self. He looked happy again, and very much at ease.

Anne's father Alistair appeared from the kitchen. "Do I detect the presence of my gorgeous little granddaughter?"

He happily joined Anne and Bridget picking up Vicky he returned to stand beside Irene, who had also just emerged from the kitchen with Thomas in tow. Looking at them together, it confirmed for Peter that there was a real solidity in their relationship now. They both looked happy and comfortable in each other's company. He went over to them and tapped Alistair on the elbow, motioning for him to join him into the kitchen.

"Yes, my boy? What's up?" he asked when they were in private.

"Nothing much really," said Peter quietly, "it's just that, if you ever feel you might like to make some kind of an announcement, but you're worried about how Anne might feel about it, I'd just like to tell you that she would be delighted for you. Truly, she would."

Alistair paused for a moment to process what Peter was saying. Then he reached out and embraced his son-in-law with a strong, one armed hug, Vicky still held secure in his other arm.

"Thank you Peter, I needed to hear that. How did you know?" he asked.

Peter couldn't help but smile. "It's been pretty obvious for a while now. I would be blind not to have noticed, Anne's well aware too. That's why I know she would be so happy for you both, she's already told me."

"Well in that case," said Alistair, "I'd best raise the subject with Irene at some point!"

They both chuckled and re-joined the others.

***

As before, they had pooled their ration vouchers and bought a nice leg of lamb to roast with the vegetables which, as usual, came from Irene's garden. Over dinner, Anne and Peter broke the news that they were going to travel to New Zealand. Peter hadn't seen his own family in nearly eight years. It was a long time and now that the world was at peace again, the distance between them was beginning to weigh on him. There was silence for many seconds as the news sank in.

"Will you be coming back?" asked an apprehensive Bridget. "Will we ever see you again?"

Anne rushed to reassure her. "Of course we will, Peter has a year's leave from the Air Force. That's all, it's not forever, how could we ever leave you all? And we certainly won't leave until after your baby arrives, we could never miss that."

Peter was relieved to hear her say that. He knew that Anne was keen to have him retire from the service and there was no doubt that she was viewing a return to his homeland as a likely way to ensure it would happen. Now however, it seemed that her own ties to England were too strong. So they would come back after all and then find a new path together. The return to New Zealand would thus be no more than a long, family visit. He knew his parents would understand, the world was changing. New airlines and new airliners were promising to make the world a smaller place. Perhaps, soon enough, his parents could even come and visit them in England.

He looked around the table, everyone was talking again. There was joy and laughter in almost every sentence being uttered. He locked eyes for a moment with his best friend Gary. They lifted their wine glasses in a silent toast to each other.